Before You Say I Do

BEFORE YOU SAY I Do

SHARON IBBOTSON

Choc Lit
A JOFFE BOOKS COMPANY

Choc Lit
A Joffe Books company
www.choc-lit.com

First published in Great Britain in 2024

© Sharon Ibbotson 2024

Cover art by Jarmila Takač

ISBN: 978-1781897638

*For all the fans of vampire slayers, space wizards
and gothic heroes. I see you.*

*Also, for Alexander Chiu-Smit, who helped inspire me
to write Luis. Alex, you've been a constant support,
the best ever Disney friend, my font of knowledge for all
things Latin America, as well as a Spanish and Dutch
translator when required. There's a reason you're one
of the three people in the world allowed to call me "Shazza,"
Alex, and it's because you're one of this planet's good ones.
Gracias, bedankt and thank you.*

PROLOGUE

Keflavík Airport, Reykjavík, Iceland

First the announcement came in Icelandic, then it was made again, in matter-of-fact English.

The airport was closing, and all flights were now grounded. Tom listened to the tinny announcement in disbelief, before slumping against a nearby wall. He'd seen for himself the billowing clouds pouring forth from Eyjafjallajokull, and had been following the news all day, aware that airport closure was a possibility. Still, there was a bitter sense of irony and resignation within him as he settled his belongings around him on the floor. He'd left home eighteen months ago, dejected and jaded, and after a year and a half of travelling, of seeing what the world had to offer, and remaining distinctly unimpressed with it, he was finally on his way home. To be stopped now — when he was willing to return to the family he'd left behind, even if he didn't really want to — felt like a sign.

The lights from the airport dimmed as people settled in for the night. Clothes became makeshift blankets, bags were used for pillows. Someone brought him a coffee, hot and bitter on his tongue, and Tom stretched out his long

1

legs irritably, trying to get comfortable on the hard tile floor. All around him people were annoyed and running low on patience, getting increasingly angry at the harangued airport staff. Somehow, this situation, this delay, was made out to be their fault, as though the staff themselves had pulled the lava from the ground and choked the sky.

Tom knew he'd never get to sleep, so instead he opened his bag and drew out a pack of cards. It was his oldest set, faded and worn from years of play. Once upon a time, these cards had belonged to his great-grandmother, a family heirloom of which his mother was immensely proud. If he was honest with himself, Tom had never been a fan of his family history, or the house full of knick-knacks that had been collected over generations. His childhood had been spent in a house that felt more like a museum than a home, and he'd hated the relics of the past found in every corner of every room.

He liked these cards though. French in style, the deck was prettily decorated with hand-painted images of kings, queens and knights. He thumbed through them, shuffling them absently, lost in his own thoughts.

He was laying the cards out for a game of solitaire when he sensed someone watching him. Looking up, he found a woman sitting across the terminal from him, her eyes intently watching his hands. She wasn't staring at him, not as such, but peering closely at his cards. Tom noted how she followed his hands curiously, watching as he dealt them onto the ground, her eyes steady and intent, her gaze flush with interest. Feeling a spike of annoyance, Tom abruptly stopped what he was doing, giving her a sharp glare.

He didn't like to attract attention — didn't like to be noticed. Woebegone, jaded and running from home, Tom kept his head down and voice quiet. At home he'd felt trapped and suffocated by both his parents and his brother, the weight of their lofty expectations for him heavy upon his shoulders. Running away, disappearing into the ether, had seemed like the right idea at the time. Tom Somerset had been left behind in America, while Tom Miller had been born in Europe.

He figured Marnie and Doug would be looking for him, just as he figured Corentin would be helping them. It had been eighteen months, and they must miss him, Tom reasoned. He missed them too, and often thought about them. He missed his mother's firm voice and his father's flippant playfulness, just as he missed Corentin's quirky brilliance. Still, as much as he looked forward to seeing them, he also dreaded it. Sometimes he wasn't quite sure if he was ready to face them, or the foolishness he'd left behind.

The woman was still watching his hands, even though he'd paused his game, and so he narrowed his eyes at her. Under the intense weight of his gaze, she finally looked up from the cards, and surprisingly didn't falter under the hostility in his eyes. Instead, she licked her lips, before giving him an embarrassed smile, slow and warm, her eyes bright and achingly blue.

The flip to his stomach was instantaneous, the pounding of his heart hard within his chest. She blushed again, before looking down to the battered paperback clutched in her hands. Still, the memory of her smile lingered in Tom's mind, and his fingers shook when he picked up his cards once more.

For five minutes, he glanced occasionally in her direction. The lights of the runway flickered prettily behind her, turning the ash blonde of her hair into a golden halo. He took note of her fingers, long and delicate as she flicked through her book. She was looking at him too, Tom realised, knowing by the instinctive tingle to his skin that she was stealing glances at him, just as he was at her. Finally, he could bear it no longer. He put his cards down, crossing his arms and staring firmly in her direction. When she next gazed up, meeting his eyes, she blushed instantly at having been caught looking. Before she could look away, he called out to her.

"Hey," he said, watching as she gazed at him, clearly uncertain. "Want to play a game?"

She licked her lips again, and Tom's stomach flipped once more, a surprising pull of longing rising within him.

"A game?" she asked softly, and he delighted to hear a British twang to her voice, clear and pronounced.

"A card game," he clarified. "A magic trick, if you like."

"I don't believe in magic," she replied, shifting on the unforgiving terminal floor.

"That's because you haven't seen mine," he told her, giving her an easy grin.

She hesitated, looking around her, taking note of the now nearly deserted airport, the stranded passengers sleeping on the floor. When she looked back to him, she put her book down and folded her arms across her chest, mirroring his position.

"You're a magician?"

He shrugged. "I'm many things. Right now, I'm stranded in this airport, with a long night ahead of me and nothing to do, and you look about the same."

At that she smiled. "All right." She stood and walked towards him.

Tom's heart picked up tempo, because this woman was something else. Crouched on the floor, she'd been pretty, but now, standing and moving her long legs, he could see just how beautiful she was. Sweet-faced and slim, her hair falling to her waist, she was perfection wrapped in a white sweatshirt and jeans — his mouth watered at the sight of her. Dropping his gaze, Tom took a deep breath, concentrating on the cards within his hands. Still, he couldn't help his heart from giving a treacherous leap when he felt her slip to the ground beside him, just as his skin tingled when it made the briefest of contact with hers.

"So," she began, "what do you want me to do?"

He gestured to the deck spread on the floor before them. "You just have to choose a card."

"That's it?"

He nodded. "That's it."

She regarded the cards curiously, her hand lingering over the deck. "How will I know which one to pick?"

He smiled at her, catching those bright blue eyes once more, losing himself in their summertime glory. "You'll feel it," he said softly. "I told you. It's magic. You can't explain it. When you know . . . You know."

She paused, considering his words. Her face softened, and she licked her lips again. It was a tell of hers, Tom realised. A sign of interest. A physical reaction to a moment of thought.

"Magic," she repeated, her voice almost a whisper. "But I already told you, I don't believe in magic."

There was an intensity to her eyes that made him swallow. Instinctively, he knew something was brimming under the surface here, something good and wonderful, and something he desperately wanted, even though he couldn't have put a name to it if he tried.

"Give me a chance," he replied softly. "Just give me a chance, and I'll show you magic is real."

She smiled at that before raising her hands to the cards. He watched her long, delicate fingers as they deliberated over the pack, before she chewed down on her lip, pointing to a card. She pulled it from the deck, glancing at it surreptitiously, before sliding it back to him.

"All right then," she said, in her beautiful British voice. "Do your trick, magician man."

He grinned at her, before shuffling the cards in his hands. "This one is too easy," he told her smoothly. "You chose a queen."

Her mouth gaped open, and she stared at him. "How did you . . ."

"Of course, you chose a queen," he shrugged. "Look at you. You're like a queen yourself."

She blushed but didn't meet his eyes, refusing to be won over immediately by his praise. He liked that. Liked how hard-won her blushes and smiles had been. The more he had to work for them, the more he felt rewarded by her shy smile, or that delightful tinge of pink to her cheeks.

"Which queen?" she pressed him, waiting to see if he failed.

"You picked the best one." He smiled warmly. "The queen of spades."

She gaped at him again, before sitting back, staring at him hard. "You must have cheated. There's no way you could have known which card I chose."

He shrugged at her. "It's an old party trick." He began shuffling the cards again.

"Who taught you?"

"My father." He shook his head, refusing to be drawn on that topic. "You chose a good card."

He watched as she considered his words. "You said she was the best queen? The spades?"

He nodded.

"I thought she was the unlucky queen. The worst of the deck. Surely the queen of diamonds, or hearts, would be a more fortuitous choice?"

He shook his head. "Do you know in early card decks that the queen of spades represented Pallas Athene, the Greek goddess of wisdom? She's tricky, the queen of spades. Beautiful, wise, serene . . . But tricky. There are entire games dedicated just to her. Games where people spend their time chasing her, seeking her, searching her out. The queen of hearts . . . the queen of diamonds . . . even the queen of clubs, in her way . . . They're all worth points. They're good cards to keep to hand. But the queen of spades? She's something special. Something different. She's my favourite."

He watched that amazing blush spreading over her cheeks again. Without pausing, he pulled a card from the deck, sliding it back to her. "See? Best of the deck."

He looked on, amused, as she glanced at the card in her hand, delighted by the amazement that crossed her face when she saw the queen of spades, who smiled serenely up at her. Sitting back, chewing on her lip once more, she stared at him, as though weighing up her next move.

6

CHAPTER 1: SMOKE

Eight Years Later

The ground was wet beneath her feet, the forest floor sodden with mud and fallen leaves. An earthy smell of damp was in the air, moist and rich with decay. It was a grey day, the sky the colour of slate. What little light there was struggled to break through the overhanging canopy of trees. Leaning back against an old birch tree, Ari Lightowler took a deep breath, trying to gather her thoughts.

It could be worse, she told herself, looking around with dismay at the patches of mud. On a clear day there would be dappled sunshine. Without the fine mist of rain, the over-whelming scent of moist earth would clear, leaving only the pleasant aroma of woodland trees. They could make this work, she hoped, looking around again. No, not just work. They could make this wedding *glorious*, Ari decided. The private woodland chosen as the ceremony venue was crude, but it was also natural. With a little imagination, with a little heart and hard work, this could be their best wedding yet.

Hope rapidly filled Ari's heart as she turned to her brother and business partner, Sebastian, with a smile. Sebastian, leaning against a nearby beech tree, was smoking a cigarette, blowing smoke with a huff into the damp morning air. Disappointment was written into every inch of his face, from the beautifully sculpted cheekbones, of which he was rightly proud, to the downturned lips that held his hanging cigarette.

"This isn't so bad." Ari gestured around her.

"Darling, it's a pile of shit." Sebastian took another drag.

"No, it's not. It's natural, earthy and it's—"

"It's a bog." Sebastian's eyes lingered on the mud and trees.

"It's autumnal." Ari walked into the middle of the clearing and looked around. "We can make this one of those earthy-type, bronze-and-gold October weddings." She dropped to her haunches to pick up a fallen leaf. "That can be the colour scheme, in fact. It'll be perfect."

Sebastian shrugged, blowing yet more smoke into the air.

Ari frowned at him. "You know Luis hates that," she chided. "I promised him I would look after you while we were here. Three hours after landing and you've already smoked half a pack. Do you want to die of smoke inhalation?"

Sebastian shrugged again. "Looking at this place, maybe I do — and Luis is three and half thousand miles away. He can hardly lecture me."

Ari frowned again. "Well, what about forest fires, then?"

Sebastian gestured to his mud-splattered shoes. "That's an excellent idea, darling. Let's burn the place down and force our rich 'we must have the perfect outdoor wedding for Instagram' clients to hire a venue we can actually work with, hmm?"

Ari sighed. "We can work with this. It isn't the worst venue we've faced. Remember that beach in Kent, which was great, up until the night before the wedding when Storm Ida caused all those skulls and femurs from Dead Man's Island to wash up onshore?"

Sebastian nodded, stubbing his cigarette out on the trunk of a tree.

"And remember the couple who wanted to get married in the shoe aisle of the TK Maxx where they met? Or the time

9

that couple wanted to get married in the lemur enclosure of London Zoo?"

Sebastian stared at her. "I still maintain that monkey hit me first."

Ari shook her head. "It doesn't matter. All I'm saying is that if we can work with that, we can work with this."

"Fine, fine." Sebastian shoved his hands into his pockets, coming to Ari's side. He gave Ari a nudge. "So, sister dearest, tell me. What do you have in mind?"

Ari stood, brushing her hands on her trousers. She passed Sebastian the leaf she'd retrieved from the forest floor. "Look at those colours. Quite stunning, wouldn't you say? Bronze and gold and red all wrapped into one. Like I said, we'll pitch it as an earthy wedding . . . autumnal and — wait, Americans don't call it autumn, do they?"

"No," Sebastian turned the leaf over in his hand, "fall."

Ari chewed on her lip. "So, what word do they use for 'autumnal' then?"

Sebastian sighed, crumbling the leaf in between his fingers. "Fucking fallout, probably." He pulled the pack of cigarettes from his pocket, and went to light another one as Ari glared at him.

"What?" He lit the cigarette. "A fallout is what our business is going to have if we don't get this wedding right, Ari. Might I remind you that our bride-to-be and the mother of the groom will be meeting with us in exactly one hour, ready to hear all our ideas for this piece of shit parcel of land they *absolutely must* have the ceremony on? If we don't come up with the goods ASAP, we can kiss all our plans to expand into the North American market goodbye."

"I know," Ari replied. "And I want this to work as much as you do. I've just as much at stake, you know, and . . ." Something in Sebastian's words made her pause. "What do you mean, the mother of the groom? Why not the mother of the bride?"

"Dead," Sebastian puffed at his cigarette again. "We're working with the bride and her prospective mother-in-law."

"Fuck," Ari whispered, and Sebastian gave a nod of agreement.

"Indeed." He blew out another plume of smoke. "The mother of the groom is always complicated to work with, especially if she doesn't have any daughters of her own."

"Please tell me this one has a daughter?" Ari's stomach fell as Sebastian shook his head.

"Sadly not. Groom is one of two sons."

"Double fuck," Ari whispered, and Sebastian gave her a rueful grin.

"That's the spirit," he remarked. "We have to deal with what will most likely be an antagonistic relationship between two women, all the while planning the wedding of the year on this, a shit field of dreams." He gave another depressed shake of his head. "Who in the bloody hell gets married in the woods? I mean, haven't these people ever heard of Lyme disease?"

"You tell me." Ari shrugged. "I'm the artistic director, remember? You manage the clients."

Sebastian took a long drag on his cigarette. "Miss Teen Rhode Island," he muttered, and Ari stared at him.

"What? I don't understand. Is that a cocktail or something?"

Sebastian laughed in a puff of smoke. "No, darling, it's our tree-hugging bride-to-be. Sasha Saffin."

"Sasha Saffin?" Ari furrowed her brow. "That's got to be a drink name, right?"

"Sadly not." Sebastian dangled the cigarette from his lips again, then pulled his phone out. He swiped across the screen several times, before tossing it in Ari's direction.

Ari caught it deftly, glanced down and inhaled sharply. "The bride?"

Sebastian nodded lazily. "Photogenic, isn't she?" After a final puff, he stubbed his cigarette onto the tree again.

Ari continued to stare at his phone. "That's putting it lightly," she exhaled, her voice rich with admiration.

Sasha Saffin was breathtaking — there was no other word, Ari decided, that could possibly do her justice. White-blonde of hair and violet of eye, she had the sort of glowing tanned skin that Ari — perpetually fair and pale — deeply envied in others. Sasha's face, smiling in this photograph, was shaped beautifully, just sharp enough to catch all the right camera angles, while soft enough to look womanly and young. She was without a doubt the most striking bride Ari had ever worked with

After just one look at Sasha's angelic beauty, an idea formed in Ari's mind.

"She's *aes sídhe*," Ari whispered, handing Sebastian back his phone.

He looked at her quizzically. "Now you're talking cocktail names. Care to translate?"

Ari grinned. "*Aes sídhe* — it's Gaelic."

"Still not helpful." Sebastian rolled his eyes, pulling out another cigarette and bringing it to his lips.

Ari sprang forward, yanking the cigarette from Sebastian's mouth, and snapped it in half between her fingers.

"Fuck, Ari—"

"She's *aes sídhe*," she said again. "One of the fair folk."

Sebastian looked at her blankly.

"One of the others. A good neighbour. One of the blessed."

"You mean like the Mormons?" Sebastian pulled out another cigarette. "This isn't a religious ceremony, Ari, I did ask in the client questionnaire—"

Ari groaned. "No, you muppet. Not the Mormons. *A fairy.*"

Sebastian stared at her for a moment, then rolled his eyes and lit up. "Darling, I think all this fresh forest air is getting to you. Here, have a cigarette. It'll clear your head right up."

"I don't want a cigarette."

"Well, you should, they're fucking amazing."

"*Sebastian*," Ari spoke firmly. "Listen to me. Have you ever heard about Samhain?"

Sebastian scratched his head. "I think . . . Wait, is he that bloke I slept with in the early noughties? The boy band member?"

Ari took a deep breath. "No. It isn't a person, it's an ancient Celtic festival to mark the end of the harvest. Tradition says that fairies and spirits would come out of hiding to celebrate and—Wait, what boy band member? You never told me about him."

Sebastian grinned at her. "I have a chequered romantic history. You don't know the half of it."

"Does Luis know?"

"Luis?" Sebastian rolled his eyes, but there was a fond smile playing on his lips. "He makes me tell that story *all* the time. But then, I always ask him about that soap star he shagged and—"

Ari's mouth fell open. "I have dinner with you and Luis like four times a week, and you two have never once dished the dirt on anyone famous. Instead, you're always banging on about the newest low-carb diet you're trying, while Luis is always complaining to me about that neighbour of yours who won't cut her shrub back."

"Patty." Sebastian sneered. "And her rampant bush."

Ari frowned. "I can't help but feel a little cheated here, Sebastian."

For a moment, Sebastian seemed to consider her. He inhaled on his cigarette, long and thoughtful, before blowing smoke into the air above them.

"If you want the truth, Ari, Luis and I . . . Well, we're both a little uncomfortable talking about sex with you."

Again, Ari's mouth fell open. "*Why?*"

Sebastian shrugged. "Because, point one, you're my sister and it's a little icky. And point two, well . . ." he trailed off.

"Point two?" Ari pressed.

"Well, because you don't have it, my darling."

She paused, suddenly aware of the weight from the backpack on her shoulder. Uncomfortable, she shifted it, feeling colour flood her cheeks. "I have had sex, thank you very much," she snapped.

"You have a daughter, so I figured that out for myself," Sebastian retorted. "But recently?"

Ari coloured further. "Well, I don't know how you define *recently*—"

"You're the perfect paradox, you know." Sebastian shook his head. "A wedding planner — and one of the best in the business, I might add — who surrounds herself with magic and love and all things romance, and yet has remained consistently single for . . . What has it been now? Seven years?"

Eight, Ari's head immediately supplied. *Eight years.* Instinctively, her hand reached into her jacket pocket — she traced her fingertip over the card that lay within.

"I'm not criticising you darling," Sebastian carried on. "God knows, what you do in your private time is your own business. But Luis and I . . . Well, we worry about you. Sometimes we wonder if you aren't more than a little . . . lonely."

"How can I be lonely? I have my family," Ari stuttered, and Sebastian gave her a kindly smile.

"Yes, of course you do." He blew more smoke into the air. "But if you spent any more time with Luis and I you'd be living with us, Ari."

"I'm not . . . I'm not at your house *all* the time." Even she could hear the weakness in her voice.

Sebastian raised an eyebrow at her. "We plan our meals around you. Luis calls me from Borough Market every Saturday morning while we're out on the wedding circuit, asking if you prefer Italian olives to Greek ones or Roquefort to Gorgonzola."

Ari stared at him in horror, shifting her boots in the mud awkwardly. "You don't have to plan meals around me."

"I keep telling Luis that." Sebastian rolled his eyes once more. "I keep telling him you're like a gannet with hollow legs who eats everything but the plate her food is served upon — and even that is touch and go sometimes — but does he listen to me, oh no, he's all, 'She is your sister, Sebastian, and we feed our family well in my culture,'" Sebastian sighed, dragging on his cigarette tiredly. "God, I miss him." He looked up at Ari worriedly. "Don't tell him about the cigarettes,

14

"I'm keeping this." She slipped the playing card into her bag. "Now you can't trick any other women at empty airports into playing games with you."

Tom sat back, dropping the deck of cards and taking her in once more. Blue eyes. A wide smile. Long fair hair. Something in his stomach stirred, and his heart picked up tempo once more.

"Keep it." He smiled at her softly. "I think I'm done playing games with other women. When you find your queen . . . you just know."

will you? You know what he's like — well, of course you do, you're with us all the time — he hates the smoking."

"We all hate the smoking." Ari worried her bottom lip between her teeth. "I won't come around so often when we get home, okay?" she offered quietly, and Sebastian sighed, dredging through the mud to stand by her side.

"Yes, you will, because we adore you, and we adore Reine." He pressed a soft kiss to her forehead. "Like I said, Luis and I . . . we just worry about you. We're concerned that you're going to waste your youth waiting for a man that might not—"

"Don't say it," Ari whispered, closing her eyes.

"—come back for you." Sebastian gave her shoulder a gentle squeeze.

It was like a knife running down her spine, the jolt of pain Ari felt. She rubbed her fingers over the card in her pocket once more, then took a long, cleansing breath of fresh forest air.

"He's coming back for me," she said firmly. "He promised."

"Darling, I—"

"I don't want to talk about Tom Miller right now." Ari straightened, pulling her hand out of her pocket. She tidied her hair and shifted her backpack once more. "Now, can we get back to Sasha Saffin and . . ." She paused. "Groom's name?"

"Thomas Somerset." Sebastian looked at her wearily. "Goes by Tom."

Ari paused. "Tom?"

"Another Tom," Sebastian repeated.

Ari swallowed down the lump in her throat.

"Ari—"

"I'm fine," she told him. "It's just a name. Right, okay, Tom Somerset. Let's get back to the Sasha Saffin and Tom Somerset wedding." She cleared her throat, pulled a notepad from her bag and started to jot down some notes. "I'm thinking of pitching a Samhain wedding, which, given that it's the end of September now, gives us thirteen months until the wedding day itself. Ample time to plan. I'm thinking

15

of bonfires and harvest fare and fireflies and an outdoorsy, Instagram worthy fair folk themed event. I'm thinking of Sasha in white-gold silk. I'm thinking of a candlelit walkway to this clearing in the wood. I'm thinking of a string quartet. I'm thinking . . ." Ari trailed off, seeing Sebastian's eyes resting on her oddly. "I'm thinking I have something on my face. Why are you staring at me? What are you thinking?"

"I'm thinking you're a fucking genius, darling," Sebastian replied. "I'm thinking of all the money I'm going to spend once you've pitched this idea and won us this wedding. I'm thinking that people always say you can't polish a turd, and yet, here we are in shit-central, and you've got the place shining bright, Ari."

She gave him a proud smile. "I'm good at my job. Hopefully good enough to win us this wedding."

"With this idea, it's practically in the bag." Sebastian seemed cheerier, and it pleased Ari to think that she'd helped ease his worries. Well, it was either her or the copious amounts of nicotine.

"I hope so," Ari said. "What do you know about Sasha, our bride? Anything I should be prepared for?"

Sebastian shrugged. "She's in social media, whatever that means. Was runner-up in a Miss Teen Rhode Island contest once upon a time."

"Runner-up? You mean she didn't win?" Ari was genuinely shocked. "*How?* If this girl," she pointed to the picture on Sebastian's phone, "didn't win, what the fuck did the actual winner look like?"

"So, I wondered that too," Sebastian replied. "I did a little research, and it turns out our bride Sasha didn't do so well on the interview round. A little more googling and some internet stalking, and I have the distinct impression she's more of a style-over-substance kind of woman, our bride."

"Right, well, that should work in our favour." Ari suddenly felt positive. "Style we can offer in spades. So long as the mother of the groom isn't an issue, we'll be planning this wedding in no time."

Sebastian nodded. "I have a feeling Sasha will lap up the old routine. Me, the English gentleman, ready with the compliments, while you produce a stunning visual of what her big day will entail. She should eat it up . . . just like you, with everything in my refrigerator."

"Hey," Ari huffed, but she smiled all the same. "Right, well, let's get back to the house. We have a bride to win over."

Sebastian nodded, before he frowned momentarily. "Don't you want to know anything about the groom?"

Ari looked at him in confusion. "What do you mean?"

"Well, rather interestingly, when I sent the client questionnaire over, Sasha filled in her half . . . but Tom Somerset, groom-to-be, left his section completely blank."

"So?" Ari asked, picking her way through the mud, finding her way back to the path of the ornate house where they were meeting the bride and mother of the groom for lunch.

"So," Sebastian fell into step beside her, "don't you think that's odd? Most of the time, the groom at least shows some minor interest in his wedding. But this one . . . it's like he's happy to leave everything to his fiancée and mother."

"All the better for us." Ari shrugged.

"I just find that a little odd, is all. I'd hate to think that our North American expansion plan could be scuppered by an unruly groom, and—"

"Sebastian," Ari came to a stop and put a hand on his shoulder, "don't worry about it."

"I can't help but worry about it." Sebastian shoved his hands into his pockets.

"Worry about winning over Sasha and her mother-in-law, okay? Worry about winning this pitch. Besides, in the six years we've been running Queen and Country Weddings, the groom has never been a problem." She gave him a reassuring smile. "And there's absolutely no reason for this Tom Somerset to be any different. No reason at all."

CHAPTER 2: IDES WEATHER

When Tom Somerset awoke that morning, it was with his father's face on his mind.

He wasn't sure why exactly. His father had been dead for six years now, and Tom tried not to dwell on that, or on him, too often. Douglas Somerset had been relegated to the occasional anecdotal story in Tom's world, just an odd fleeting reference, or oft-told family legend, repeated with a soft smile and a warm voice. If his father ever did unexpectedly cross his mind, Tom pushed him away quickly. It wasn't that he hadn't loved Doug — he'd idolised him, in fact — it was simply that when he thought of his father a gaping hole seemed to open within him, a wave of sorrow that threatened to pull him under, and he'd decided it was best not to drown in the tide. He clung to the safety of a shore free from Doug's memory and lingering presence, his eyes kept firmly landward, ignoring the ocean of grief behind him.

Instinctively, Tom reached for Sasha, wanting the warmth and comfort of another person, but she swatted his hand away, keeping firmly to her side of the bed.

"You tossed and turned all night," she complained irritably. "I'm going to need a bucket of eye concealer just to look presentable today."

"Sorry," Tom murmured, throwing an arm over his eyes. "I didn't sleep well."

"Mm." Sasha shrugged, swinging her long legs from their bed and walking to a nearby mirror. "You never do when you're here. You should go and see Dr Edelstein—he'll give you something to help you sleep."

"I don't want anything to help me sleep."

"Well, you should," Sasha retorted. "If you don't sleep, *I* don't sleep. Honestly, every time we visit your mother, you're exactly the same. A restless and gloomy insomniac. It drives me crazy. Your mother isn't *that* bad, Tom."

Tom watched as Sasha preened in front of the mirror, her hair a glossy mane, her skin smooth and soft.

"Sorry," he said. "I don't know what it is about this place that makes me this way."

"So, until you find out, see Dr Edelstein," Sasha retorted sharply, running a brush through her hair. "Then at least I'll get some rest whenever we're here, and not spend all night watching you toss and turn."

Tom nodded, glancing out of the window. The day was dark and gloomy, with grey skies hanging threateningly overhead. It had rained all night, and he could nearly smell the damp, earthy scent of the surrounding countryside. It was a smell he was familiar with, having grown up on this large, sprawling estate. It reminded him of his childhood, of marshmallows roasting over an open fire, of fresh-caught fish wriggling on the line, of his father, standing despondently in the woods, staring up at an ominous sky.

"This is Ides weather, Tom," Doug says mournfully, kicking at *the mud. "Bad things happen when the sky looks like this."*

Doug again. With a start, Tom sat up, telling himself to get a grip. He looked back to Sasha, who was pulling a robe over her shoulders, clearly intent on showering in the connecting bathroom. Suddenly, Tom was overwhelmed with the sensation of not wanting to be left alone.

Bad things happened when he was left alone.

19

"Come back to bed," he pleaded softly. "I'll make last night up to you. And it's Saturday . . . we don't have to be anywhere today."

Slowly, Sasha turned to look at him, disappointment in her eyes. "You're kidding, right?" Her tone rigid and stiff with disapproval. "Our wedding planners are here today, Tom. Remember? We have a lunch date with them, and your mother, just after one in the summerhouse."

Tom fell back on his pillows, exhaling hard. "Right. The wedding planners. I forgot."

"You forgot?" Sasha was clearly incredulous. "They're the reason we're here, Tom. How could you forget?"

Tom shrugged in response. It seemed easier and less likely to cause an argument than to say, *I didn't forget, I just don't really care.* Not that it mattered. Sasha was searching through her hand luggage for her toiletries, completely lost in her own world.

"Your mother is the one insisting that we get married in that wilderness out there," she carried on, without any attempt to conceal the bitterness poisoning her words, "I wanted the Plaza. Or, at the very least, the Capitale. But no. I get to have a wedding in the woods in upstate New York, shit sticks central."

"It's tradition," Tom said blankly. "My grandparents were married in those woods. My parents were married there. Now, it's my turn."

"You don't need to tell me again, I said yes, didn't I?" Sasha replied, a hint of impatience in her voice. "If it's important to you and your mom, well, I guess I can make it important to me too."

"Thanks," Tom muttered.

"You don't need to thank me for being reasonable, Tom. And at least I get to choose the wedding planners myself. If I must be married out there in the mud, we're going to do it *my* way, with style."

"The wedding planners," Tom mused, standing with a sigh and pulling a towel around his waist. "Who are they again?"

Sasha gave him another one of her disbelieving stares. "Queen and Country Weddings," she informed him tightly. "I told you about them before. They're British. Up-and-coming and *very* exclusive."

"Expensive?" Tom watched as Sasha laughed, a mean little sound that made him wince. Laughter was supposed to be happy, he thought. It wasn't supposed to sound like *that*, a mean, self-satisfied, ugly sound.

Abruptly, Tom recalled the sound of another laugh. In his mind he saw a smile, wide and cat-like, spread across two cheeks dusted with pink blusher. He saw the crinkles at the corners of two blue eyes. He heard happiness fill the air, like a warm breeze washing over you on a summer's day. The memory made his heart run faster and his stomach knot with pain — he looked down, clutching his towel in his hand.

"Criminally so," Sasha replied flippantly. "But it's all on your mother's dime, so who cares? We struck a deal, your mother and me. We get married out in the forest, without complaint, and she coughs up the cost of the wedding."

"Right," Tom nodded, but his eyes were blank. He was still caught in the past, still locked in a memory. "Right."

"Tom."

Sasha's voice was a bucket of cold water thrown over him, and Tom looked up, instantly feeling guilty. "What?"

"Are you okay?" Sasha asked, and for the first time that morning, he heard concern in her words.

"Yeah," he replied through a dry mouth, swallowing hard, and Sasha looked at him keenly.

"Are you sure?" she asked worriedly. "Look, Tom, I know I seem a little, well, *sharp* today. I don't mean to be. It's just that, I really, really, really want Queen and Country Weddings . . . I want them to plan my wedding, Tom. It means a lot to me. Just like our getting married out there means something to you."

"I know," Tom replied, before he sighed and nodded. "I get it."

Sasha stared at him for a long moment, her eyes hard, like two dark amethysts glittering in the light. Suddenly, the amethysts softened, Sasha's eyes like morning dewdrops sitting on the petal of a flower, and she smiled at him.

"I know you get it," she said sweetly, wrapping her arms around his waist. "You're going to be a good husband for me, I just know it."

Tom sighed again, dropping a kiss onto the top of Sasha's head. When she wanted to, Sasha could be very sweet. They'd been together a long time, and he knew all the colours and moods of her personality now. Sasha swung between hard and soft, waspish and pleasant, like the pendulum of a fast-running clock. Tom knew why: Sasha's work was demanding and competitive, and by default she had to be demanding and competitive too. Sometimes, and he was almost sure it was mostly unintentional, she brought home the hard-as-nails demeanour that made her a success in her field. When she wanted to though, she could be soft and warm and lovely, and they worked well together. When she wanted, Sasha's sweetness showed him exactly why he planned on marrying her.

When she wanted.

"Queen and Country are going to put my wedding on the map, you know." She wriggled out of his arms. "It will be the most talked-about event of the year, if not the decade."

"Yes," Tom agreed, even though a small voice inside him, the one he tried to keep hidden when Sasha was present, instantly spoke up. *It's meant to be our wedding, not just hers,* the voice whispered. *Why do you let her walk all over you like this?*

Wrenching himself away from an unpalatable train of thought, Tom dropped his towel, moved to the wardrobe and pulled out an old sweater and pair of jeans. He could feel Sasha's eyes watching him. When he turned, she gestured accusingly to the clothes he'd chosen for the day.

"Really?" she asked him. "Those rags?"

"I need to clear my head," Tom told her. "Maybe get up into the sky. Take my dad's old plane out."

"Tom—"

"Don't worry," he reassured her. "It'll only be for a few hours. I'll make sure I'm back and changed in time for . . . King and Queen . . . or . . ."

"Queen and Country," Sasha finished for him tightly. "Fine. But make sure you're back here and pristine by one o'clock." For a moment, she looked at him. "And make an appointment with Dr Edelstein."

He nodded as he pulled the sweater over his head. The heavens were dark, and heavy with the promise of coming rain, but he knew that above the clouds lay blue sky and bright sunshine. He longed for both. He'd fire up his dad's old plane, take a quick flight into the sun before coming back down to the dark.

"I'll see you soon." He gave Sasha a quick peck on the cheek.

She waved him away. "While you're out, don't forget to call my father back."

Tom stopped, repressing the urge to shudder. "Your father?" he asked, mouth dry. "Why?"

Myron Saffin, Sasha's father, was a force to be reckoned with. Just as ruthless and cut-throat in business as his daughter, he was sharp as a tack and just as piercing.

"He invited you to his poker night," Sasha replied. "It's a big deal, Tom. He doesn't invite just *anyone*. Make sure you go. Many of Daddy's best and most successful business associates will be there. It will be the perfect chance for you to network."

Poker. Tom inhaled sharply as a memory seized hold of him. He pictured long fingers holding a queen of spades, while bright blue eyes gazed warmly upon him. For a moment, he struggled with the wistful pang of regret that began to creep down his spine, ordering himself to pull it together. Looking down, he found his fists were clenched and arm muscles taut. He made a point of relaxing them, of stretching them out, of pushing memories back into the past, where they belonged.

Taking a deep breath, he gave Sasha a long look, and for once his voice was firm and unyielding. "I'm not going to poker night. I don't play cards."

* * *

23

He found his mother on the deck near the lake, a coffee in her hand, already dressed in her finest, her grey-brown hair artfully styled. Marnie was staring out over the water, and Tom came up behind her, giving her a quick hug and kiss and laughing when she spluttered into her coffee.

"Tom! You frightened the life out of me, sneaking up like that," she chastised him, and he grinned, leaning against a nearby wall.

"Too good an opportunity to miss. Sorry Mom."

His mother looked him up and down, taking in his old clothes with a careful eye. "You look good . . . You arrived so late last night, though. I'm sorry I couldn't wait up for you. I'm old and need my sleep these days."

"You're not old." Tom shrugged. "Had some work to finish up before the weekend, and then Sasha insisted on stopping back at the apartment to grab some extra clothes before we set off. She's in a bit of a state about these wedding planners today."

"Hmm," Marnie mused, looking annoyed. "You mean the wedding planners I had to pay to fly over from London, even before we've agreed to hire them?"

"Sasha has already hired them in her mind." Tom felt a small dart of embarrassment, and looked down. "I'm trying to make this special for her."

"They better be damned special, at the price I'm paying," Marnie retorted.

"Mom—"

"Oh, I'm going to foot the bill and not complain . . . *much*." She raised one impeccable eyebrow. "I just don't know what's wrong with Elegant Events. We've been using them for decades, Tom. Every family event and occasion, they've been there, reliable as the tide. How is it going to look when I send Frank an invitation to your wedding, which has been planned by these . . . these *Brits*?"

"It's going to look like you're inviting an old friend to my wedding," Tom replied. "I love Frank too, Mom. But Sasha . . . she's a modern girl, you know?"

"And what am I, a relic?" Marnie gave Tom a rueful smile. "Don't answer that. Well, I take it by your attire you're heading up before we all head out?"

"Quick flight, I promise."

"Make it a long one and we can cancel the wedding," Marnie quipped, before seeing Tom's stern face and giving a shrug. "All right, no more of that. Give that plane a good look over before you head up, okay? It hasn't flown since you were last here. I dread to think what state the engine is in."

Tom nodded. "I will. You know I'm careful."

Marnie sighed. "So, exactly what am I supposed to do with Sasha all morning while you're off on your jaunt?"

"Talk to her. Make nice with her. Maybe plan the wedding with her?"

Marnie frowned. "All I'm allowed to do for this wedding is sign the cheques."

"Hey," Tom gave her a gentle nudge, "we're getting married in the woods at least, like you wanted."

Marnie nodded. "Well yes, there is that. And I suppose I could mention Corentin to Sasha . . ."

Tom blanched at his older brother's name. "Corentin? Why? What does he want?"

"Well, you know how he's a man of the cloth these days . . ."

Tom held up a hand, stopping her. "I know exactly where this conversation is going, Mother. And I already told you, I can't ask Sasha to let my crazy—"

"Hey!" Marnie protested, without conviction.

"—loopy, off-the-radar brother marry us. I can't do it. I won't. She'll never agree."

"Maybe not to you, but if I throw in, say, an all-expenses paid honeymoon to a five-star destination somewhere in the world, Sasha might be more amenable."

"It worries me, Mom, that you think you can buy my fiancée's conformity like that."

"And it worries me that you persist in believing I can't."

"Mom—"

"Oh, don't worry, I'm not going to say anything," Marnie said brusquely. "But you must know that I don't like the woman and I'm never going to. I don't understand why you plan on marrying her."

"Sasha can be very sweet. Besides, you don't know her like I do."

"Small mercies," his mother retorted, and he frowned at her.

"I've been with Sasha for a long time."

"Exactly. Maybe you should try dating other women — you don't know what you're missing."

Tom felt that old pang of wistfulness start to rise, and he swallowed hard. He knew exactly what he was missing. Instinctively, he reached into his pocket, feeling for the card he always carried with him.

"I'm going up," he said shortly, watching as his mother's face fell. "I'll see you at one o'clock. Try not to bite my fiancée's head off while I'm out, hey?"

"Tom, I'm sorry," Marnie offered mournfully. "You know me. You know I can't hold back my opinions."

"Try," Tom pleaded. "For my sake, try."

Marnie nodded, looking back out over the lake. "I promise. The wedding planners are here, by the way. Credit where credit's due, they came straight here off their flight. No one's going to say they're workshy at least."

"Good." Tom nodded. He knew his mother appreciated people with a good work ethic. "They seem nice?"

Marnie shrugged. "I haven't met them yet. Apparently, they wanted to head straight out to the venue, so they could work on their *artistic vision*." Tom watched as Marnie struggled not to roll her eyes. "Anyway, they're out in the woods. I got a brief glimpse of them. They seem like clean-cut, reliable people."

"That will make Sasha happy," Tom mused, even as he reached for the card in his pocket once more.

"Hmm." Marnie was watching him sharply. Suddenly, she reached forward, plucking her hand into his pocket and pulling out the card. "What is this you keep playing with?"

Tom quickly grabbed for it, but Marnie stepped out of reach.

"It's just a playing card," he explained quickly. "It's nothing."

"You and your card tricks," Marnie shook her head in exasperation, even as she peered at the card more closely. "But this isn't 'nothing', Tom. This is the fool from Marie Leszczyńska's deck of cards. She was a queen of France, you know."

"Yeah, I know, I just—" Tom reached for the card again, but Marnie held it tight.

"Marie Leszczyńska gave this deck as a gift to an ancestor of mine, and it was passed down the family. My great-grandparents smuggled this deck out of Europe during the war. This card should be in a museum, not your pocket."

"I found the deck when I was a kid." Tom shrugged, feeling a spike of guilt. "I didn't know they were Marie Leszczyńska's until much later."

"I was going to donate them to the local museum," Marnie complained, "but I couldn't find them. I turned the attic upside down searching for them, and you had them in your pocket all along!"

"I like them."

"Tom—"

"Mom," Tom broke her off gently, "Just let me . . . Just let me keep them, okay?"

Marnie gazed at him. "Is there something you're not telling me here, Tom?"

Tom swallowed. "No," he lied.

Marnie sighed. "Look, fine. Just take care of them, okay? And don't let Sasha get a hold of them. God knows, she'd have them on Vinted in a heartbeat."

"I'll take care of them, don't worry."

Tom sighed with relief as Marnie handed the card back to him, sliding it into his pocket and feeling the comfort of its slight weight once more. "And be nice about Sasha, Mom. She's not all bad. You're just in a bad mood because of the wedding." He thought of his own dreams the night before, of Doug in his mind. "Weddings do strange things to people."

Marnie nodded again. "Maybe. Maybe not. Well, off you go. Enjoy the skies. But don't be late, or Sasha will probably kill you," she paused, "and if she doesn't I will. You know I can't be alone for long periods with that woman."

"I won't be late," Tom promised, as he turned in the direction of the old plane hangar.

"And Tom?" Marnie called out. He turned back to her. "Be careful," she warned. "The sky's so dark . . . Ides weather, your father used to say—"

"I know. I'll be careful."

"It was wet yesterday, but not dark like this." Marnie glanced up at the swirling clouds overhead with a frown. "I don't know, Tom. Your wedding planners arrive, and a storm starts brewing . . ."

"Mom." Tom gave a wry smile. "You're starting to sound like Corentin, all superstition and nonsense. Sasha's fine, and the wedding planners will be fine. You'll see."

Marnie smiled. "I'm not saying it's a *sign* or anything, but it can't be a coincidence that they arrived and then darkness followed. Maybe it's not even Sasha. Maybe it's the wedding planners themselves who're going to be the problem."

But Tom shook his head, giving his mother another fond smile. "Mom, relax." He stood taller, pushing his hands into his pockets. "The wedding planners aren't going to be a problem. I promise."

28

CHAPTER 3: THE FOOL

Ten minutes into lunch with Sasha and her prospective mother-in-law, and Ari was just about ready to admit defeat. Discomfort sat heavily in the air, weighted down by Sasha's tightly leashed fury and the groom's mother's all-too-evident disapproval. Ari sipped at the glass of white wine that had been put in front of her, trying to settle the knot of unease that was slowly growing in her stomach.

Sebastian was trying his best, Ari knew. He sat beside Sasha, elegant and poised, playing his role of English gentleman with aplomb. He was all charm and suave style and simpering compliments for the bride, who licked them up like a show pony at the trough. Sebastian knew how to play Sasha — knew to be friendly enough to win her trust, while being just distant enough to leave her wanting more. Watching Sebastian charm a bride was like watching an artist at work, Ari always thought, but today his work was spoiled, soured by a disapproving mother-in-law and an inexplicably absent groom.

"I'm sorry," Sasha apologised in her sharp American twang. "I told him to be here. He knew how important this meeting was to me. I can't believe he's late."

"Oh, darling, it's nothing," Sebastian purred with a wave of his hand. "You know, sometimes it's better if the groom *isn't* here. Quite often they just get in the way. Besides, Mum's here, isn't she?"

He gestured to the groom's mother, and Ari saw Marnie stiffen, her face like stone.

"*Mum?*" she repeated icily.

Sebastian reddened. "Well, yes. In Britain, we always refer to the mother of the bride or groom as Mum. It's a compliment, in a way."

"Well, you aren't in Britain now." Marnie's voice was as sharp as the wine in Ari's glass. "So I would appreciate it if you addressed me as Mrs Somerset."

Marnie Somerset. Something in Ari's mind stirred, the edge of a memory within grasp, and she frowned, staring at Marnie openly.

"Can I help you?" Marnie asked her, and now it was Ari's turn to blush.

"Oh, no, it's nothing—"

"You've been quiet," Marnie mused, still staring at Ari with hard, unflinching eyes. "You let him do all the talking." She glared openly at Sebastian.

"Well, he's the client manager," Ari explained.

Marnie only stared at her harder, and Ari squirmed in her seat. "He's the client manager? Fine. So, tell me, what do you do in this . . ." she gestured to the air between Ari and Sebastian ". . . outfit?"

Ari cleared her throat. "I'm the artistic director," she said weakly. "I plan the visuals of the wedding. Colour scheme, aesthetics, table settings . . ."

"Really?" Marnie asked her coolly. "And what does Sasha, the bride, plan in all of this? Does she get a say at all?"

"Oh, yes," Ari replied instantly, sitting up taller. Where her work was concerned, she was always the consummate professional. "I take all my cues from the bride. Quite often, brides know exactly what they want for their wedding, they just don't know how to make that vision a reality. That's where I step in. I take their ideas and source all the pieces, putting them together like a puzzle to make a perfect day."

"I see," Marnie said slowly, nodding. "And you've seen the woods now, I take it? What did you, as the *artistic director*, make of them?"

"Well, it's a raw setting for a wedding." Ari took another sip of wine. "But I think we have a plan that might work. Of course, I'd like to speak to Sasha and . . ." She trailed off awkwardly, suddenly unable to say the groom's name under Marnie's critical eyes. It was ridiculous, she told herself. It had been eight years.

"Tom," Marnie filled the silence icily, and Ari blushed.

"Yes, of course, *Tom*. I'd like to speak with them both and get a feel for how they see their special day."

"I want it big," Sasha piped up. "I want the best of the best. Exquisite food, a French patisserie cake, champagne and a bespoke Luis De León dress on my back."

Sebastian spluttered into his wine, and Ari shot him a look. "You want a De León dress?" he asked, wiping his mouth, and Sasha nodded.

"Of course," Sasha replied emphatically. "Luis De León is the biggest wedding dress designer of our generation. I told you — I want the best of the best. And Luis De León is the best."

Sebastian seemed to recover himself, sliding a hand across the table, taking hold of Sasha's fingers. "Yes, my darling, but Luis De León has a four-year waiting list for bespoke wedding gowns. If you're determined to have one of his dresses, we could probably alter one of his collection gowns for you, but a bespoke dress is quite impossible."

"But I want one." Sasha pouted. "I've already seen one I like, in fact, and I know you've worked with him . . . look . . ." Sasha drew out a copy of French *Vogue* from her bag.

Ari groaned internally. She knew that magazine, and knew exactly which article Sasha had read. It was a four-page spread on Luis's gowns, modelled by the newest super-model, with photographs by Stella Snow. She remembered Luis coming back from the shoot, casually mentioning to her and Sebastian that he'd mentioned their business in the magazine, at which point Sebastian had exploded.

"It's tacky to tout for business in *Vogue*, Luis," he'd shouted.

"It's *Vogue*." Luis had shrugged, completely perplexed. "The whole magazine is wall-to-wall adverts. I thought I was doing you a favour, Sebastian."

"A favour?! A fuc—" Quickly, Ari had shot Sebastian a stern look, before nodding at her daughter, Reine, who had been lying on the floor, casually colouring in. Now, the little girl was looking up at her uncles, crayons temporarily forgotten, wide-eyed and curious. Sebastian stopped, taking a deep breath. "A *fudging* favour? Look, I don't mind when you send your brides in our direction, Luis. A casual mention here and there is one thing, but a full-blown call-out in *Vogue* is quite another. We're meant to be a classy, exclusive establishment. Not a tacky, grubbing-for-business—"

"*Vogue* is classy and exclusive!" Luis had yelled. "Why do you think they wanted me?"

"Oh, let's not get too big for our britches, shall we?" Sebastian had retorted.

Luis then stepped towards Sebastian, his anger no longer explosive but smouldering. "You *like* the fact that I'm too big for my britches, Sebastian."

"That's it." Ari had stood up and gathered her things. "You're veering into PG13 territory. I'm taking Reine and going."

Both Luis and Sebastian spun to look at her, guilt flashing across their faces.

"No, honey." Luis had cleared his throat. "The two of you can't leave. I brought back apricot nectar from Paris. We're going to have *poulet aux abricots et riz sauvage* tonight."

Now, Ari watched with dismay as Sasha passed the magazine to Sebastian, whose face was pale.

"You want this dress?" He pointed to a frothy white number, and Sasha's face lit up.

"That's the one," she squealed. "Isn't it beautiful?"

Sebastian nodded slowly. "She wants a De León dress, Ari."

"Of course, I'd like to make some changes," Sasha carried on. "But that's easy enough, right?"

For a moment Sebastian was silent, and Ari could see him mentally weighing up his options in his head. Turn Sasha down, and risk losing their biggest potential client to date — as well as their move into the North American market — or call his husband and ask for a monumental favour, sealing the deal on this wedding.

"We can probably organise something," Sebastian said quietly. "I should tell you, Luis De León is actually my husband."

For a moment, both Marnie and Sasha were quiet. But it was only for a moment. Then Sasha squealed, throwing her arms around Sebastian and hugging him tightly.

"You had one of those gay weddings?" she asked excitedly.

Sebastian shrugged. "Well, we had *a* wedding."

"Well, this is just *perfect*," Sasha clapped her hands. "Now you can get me my dress. And obviously I'll want Stella Snow to take the photographs, so . . ."

At that, Ari held up a hand. "You want Stella too?"

"Well, yes, obviously. I told you—I want the best of the best."

"Stella is . . . very difficult," Ari began slowly.

But Sasha shrugged. "If you can get me my De León dress, you can get me Stella Snow."

Ari paused. She hadn't been lying — Stella Snow was difficult, in every sense of the word. But she glanced at Sebastian, who nodded slowly. Clearing her throat and breathing deeply, aware of Marnie Somerset's sharp eyes upon her, she gave Sasha a soft smile.

"She's also horrifically expensive," Ari carried on, "we know so many other photographers who are just as good, and—"

"I don't want good," Sasha cut in, her tone suddenly razor sharp. "I want the *best*. Why isn't she listening to me?" she whined to Sebastian, who tutted and gave Sasha a good-natured pat on the shoulder.

"Ari, darling, if Sasha here wants Stella, we'll get her Stella," he said. "After all, if the wedding is going to be on . . ." he glanced at his notebook surreptitiously ". . . the twenty-ninth of October next year, then—"

"This year," Sasha corrected him. "Tom and I want to get married this year."

Ari's mouth dropped open. "But that's . . . seven weeks away. We can't get Stella in seven weeks. We can't get a De León bespoke dress in seven weeks. We can't do anything in just seven weeks. Are you sure you can't push the date back?"

"Oh no," Sasha replied immediately, shaking her head. "It took years for me to get a proposal out of Tom. Now that he has, I want to seal the deal ASAP."

"Seven weeks . . ." Ari breathed deeply. "That's impossible."

Next to her, Ari heard Marnie give a satisfied sigh. "Oh dear, never mind. Well, we'll just get in our usual event planners then. I'm sure they can organise a wedding in the woods in seven weeks."

Sebastian sat bolt upright, shaking his head emphatically. "They can't get a De León dress though, can they? No. We can do it."

Ari stared at him in disbelief. "*Sebastian*. We just can't. Stella, maybe, is a possibility, if we call in the world's biggest favour . . . but Luis? He has other brides. We can't just swoop in and disrupt his timetable like that." She turned to Marnie and Sasha, shaking her head. "Sasha, I'm sorry, but getting a bespoke De León dress in seven weeks is impossible. We couldn't get one for love nor money, and trust me, Sebastian here can try both."

"But I want one," Sasha said sharply. "And I always get what I want."

Dislike for this woman, hot and intense, slid down Ari's spine. Taking another deep breath, she opened her mouth to reply, when Sebastian piped up.

"If you want one, my darling, we'll get you one."

"*Sebastian*," Ari exhaled, shocked. "You can't promise that."

"Look, if we fly Luis out here tomorrow, start the fittings right away, get the fabric ordered, it's not impossible."

Ari shook her head. "He has other responsibilities, Sebastian."

Sebastian shrugged. "He can put one of his junior designers to work on the other brides for a few days. So long as he's there for their final fittings they won't even know he didn't work on their gowns personally."

Ari stared at him through narrowed eyes, hoping against hope he would read between the lines. "No. He has *other* responsibilities, Sebastian."

Sebastian, suddenly startled, clearly understanding her, while Marnie frowned.

"I don't understand," she said. "What other responsibilities? He's a wedding dress designer."

Sebastian smiled at Marnie pleasantly. "Oh, I'm sorry, this is more of a . . . personal matter. Ari and I, well, we don't like our personal lives to impact our business. Ever. We have a good work ethic."

Marnie opened her mouth to reply, but Sasha cut in. "I want a bespoke De León dress." She sounded dangerously close to stomping her feet. "So I don't care what personal shit you two have got going on . . . I want him here, this week, for my first fitting."

At that, Ari stood. "I'm sorry. On this we're quite firm. Luis De León has other responsibilities, and if we're going to plan this wedding, there is no way we can get him here."

Sebastian also stood, abruptly pulling on Ari's arm. "One moment, darlings," he chirped to Sasha and Marnie, before leading Ari to the side.

"Are you fucking insane?" he hissed. "We can't turn this wedding down."

"We can't get Luis here," Ari insisted. "You know that. And I can't be here for seven weeks. A few days here and there, yes, but seven whole weeks? I can't be away from Reine for that long."

"Yes, I know," Sebastian said. "Fuck, I wish I could smoke right now."

"Well, you can't."

Ari watched as Sebastian took a deep breath. "Okay. Hear me out."

Ari shook her head. "No, don't say what I think you're about to."

"Ari," Sebastian said patiently. "So, Luis brings her with him."

"No," Ari's response was instant. "She has school, she has violin, she has Brownies on Thursday. You should know that, your husband is Tawny Owl."

"Honey, listen." Sebastian was using his calmest, most sincere voice, and Ari chewed on her lip, willing to hear him out if nothing else. "Forget Brownies. I know I do. Besides, school doesn't begin for what . . . six days? Luis brings her tomorrow, does the first fitting, gets the dress started, and flies back with her. Or you can. We can work a schedule out so one of us is always at home. And the wedding is late October, which is half-term. We can all be here that week with her. This can work, Ari."

Ari took a deep breath, looking at Sebastian intently. "She's my baby, Sebastian. Flying all this way . . . with school about to start . . ."

"She's seven years old," Sebastian replied calmly. "We'll give her that iPad she's been banging on about since Christmas. She'll be fine. It'll be like a holiday for her."

Ari chewed on her lip. "I don't know . . ."

"Please Ari," Sebastian whispered. "We need this wedding. We need this business."

"We don't really." Ari sighed. "But I know how much you want it."

"Look at this place." Sebastian gestured around them to the sprawling estate, the stately manor and the glass summerhouse. "This is American money at its finest, and I'd like a piece of it."

"Sebastian—"

36

"Think of Reine," Sebastian added quickly. "If you do this wedding, we'll make enough money that you can cut back your hours. We could hire more people and take fewer clients."

Ari felt a twinge of guilt. She knew she worked hard and saw her daughter too little. She recalled the look of disappointment in Reine's eyes when she'd left for the airport, recalling her downturned face and sad tears.

"All right," Ari agreed with a reluctant sigh. "Okay."

Sebastian stopped, looking down at Ari with concern. "Ari, Luis and I love that girl. She's our niece. I would never do anything that might adversely affect her, you know that."

Ari nodded. "I know."

"This can work, for all of us," Sebastian continued. "I'll put your daughter at the front of all the plans we make. I adore her. Luis and I have been like the father she doesn't have. Now come on, let's give Sasha the happy news."

At that Ari shook her head. "She has a father," she reminded Sebastian. "He's coming back for me."

Sebastian nodded, but Ari could see from the look on his face that he didn't believe her. Sometimes, when she was at her very lowest, she didn't believe herself either.

* * *

The last time Tom had been in a plane that stalled, his father had been in the cockpit. Sitting in the back of the aircraft, Tom had heard his father shouting and swearing, a litany of curses as he rebuked the plane for failing him. But Doug was nothing if not an accomplished pilot, and Tom had watched, completely unfazed, as his father started the usual stall procedure. Nose down, increase engine power, level the wings, pull up. Through wide eyes, Tom heard and felt the plane respond to his father's methodical flying, and when the plane levelled and began flying at full power once more, Doug gave him a wide smile.

"She never lets me down," he'd said to Tom with a wink, before giving his full attention to the plane again.

When they were on the ground once more, Doug had slung an arm around Tom's shoulders as they walked away from the hangar. "You can always recover from a stall," he'd explained. "Sometimes it's just one of those things. Sometimes it's just a bump in the road. But if you keep your head, you can always get back to where you need to be. Remember that, okay?"

Over the years, Tom had been through many stalls. He'd experienced more bumps in the road than he cared to remember. The biggest bump of them all — his runaway years, Marnie sneeringly described them — he tried not to recall at all. His father's death was another bump, just another stall.

He recovered from them all. Nose down, full throttle, level wings, pull up, fly once more. Every stall in life was always the same. Doug had been right . . . all Tom had to do was keep his head, and all would be fine.

The only time he hadn't kept his head was when he'd been presented with a blue pair of eyes and pink lips curved in a smile, a smile that was only for him. Tom had lost his head and his heart in a big way, and he'd never really recovered. Nose down, full throttle, level wings, pull up and fly . . . For the first time in his life, it hadn't worked. Some stalls, it seemed, you couldn't recover from.

He didn't know why, but when Doug's plane stalled that morning, with Tom flying solo in the cockpit, he thought of Ari. As the blue sky dipped away, and the plane glided into the dark clouds, dangerously out of control without an engine, her face crossed his mind.

The ground loomed before him, getting closer and closer with every passing second, and all Tom saw was Ari. He steered the plane as best he could, knowing he would crash with her face in his mind.

* * *

"If I'm your queen of spades, what does that make you?" she asks him one night, her head turned in his direction. She's naked, just a

38

sheet draped over her legs, lying on her front, her hair falling over her shoulders like a Botticelli angel. He sweeps it away, pressing a kiss to her shoulder blades, sighing warm against her skin. "The king?" she suggests with a smile.

But he shakes his head. "Not the king."

"The knight then," Ari suggests, "protecting the queen in her castle."

He shakes his head once more. "Nope. Not the knight either."

"The ace?" She laughs. "Or . . . I don't know . . . the seven? The eight? Tell me."

He grins back at her, pulling her into his arms and rolling on top of her. He presses his lips to hers, marvelling once more at the feel of her in his arms. She's soft and warm and lovely and his, and each and every one of these facts is like a small miracle to him.

"The joker, the fool," he tells her, and she laughs.

"You do yourself a disservice. You aren't a fool."

"But I am, where my queen is concerned." He lays his head on her shoulder, breathing in the smell of her. "Always the fool, now and forever and always."

"I don't want you to be a fool for me," Ari whispers softly, and he sighs.

"But I am. And I always will be, Ari."

* * *

When he realised his father's plane wasn't just stalling but was in full engine failure, Tom prepared for impact. Nose up, level the wings. The ground was close, and he was hurtling towards it at speed. From his pocket he pulled out the playing card and glanced at it quickly.

The fool. Faded, old and creased in places, as well as worn where he'd stroked it thoughtfully over the years, but still undeniably obvious. Even now, at the very worst of times, it made him smile.

And so, with a card clutched in his hand and Ari's face in his mind, Tom braced for impact, still the fool, now and forevermore.

CHAPTER 4: TEA SET

On Marnie's wedding day to Doug Somerset, her mother-in-law gave her a tea set. Julie Somerset, blonde and brash with a proverbial heart of gold, had clearly put thought and time into her choice of gift, presenting it to her new daughter-in-law with a proud smile and flush on her over-blushed cheeks.

"It's a pretty pattern, isn't it?" Julie enthused, holding one of the delicate teacups up to the light. "Could be an antique."

The white china was painted with a gold, pink and blue flower motif, gaudy and old-fashioned, which made Marnie cringe. Eight cups and eight saucers, all identical.

"A set," Julie added, with a knowing wink at the slight curve to Marnie's belly, "to pass on as an heirloom, one of these days."

To say Marnie hated the tea set was an understatement. She actively *despised* it. Marnie had been through a tumultuous few years, a time when her rebellious teenage phase morphed into an experimental college phase, which then morphed into a business-first adult mindset. Her idealistic optimism gave way to a hard-hearted ruthlessness, a determination to take the inheritance of her family and improve upon it. As such, Marnie worked, and she worked hard. She grafted and grifted and Doug . . . Well, he was supposed to be the antithesis of all that. He was meant to be an attempt to reclaim her carefree youth, as well as an inappropriate boyfriend her father hated, which perversely made Marnie want him more. Doug was a race-car driver, literally the hottest new thing on the circuit, and Marnie's father's company had sponsored him. When she first met him, he'd been leaning on the hood of his car, the sun on his face, watching her move by her father's side closely.

Marnie had been smitten, but still practical. Doug Somerset was never meant to be a long-term thing. He was meant to be an itch to scratch before she moved on to more suitable pastures. So to find herself both pregnant by him and then married to him caused Marnie's world to spin on its axis. What she had planned as merely a whirlwind romance had turned into a perpetual storm of a marriage, and Julie's tea set — that tacky, over-decorated, cheap pile of plates — represented everything Marnie hated about what her life had become.

It wasn't that Marnie was unhappy, because she was pragmatic and practical and always made the best of any situation. She knew that with Doug she had made her bed and she'd decided to sleep in it, and even if life with him wasn't all feather pillows and satin sheets, it was still good quality cotton, and she was content enough. As for Corentin and Tom . . . Well, her boys were the highlight of Marnie's marriage, and both she and Doug knew it. She found it hard to look into her children's big brown eyes and regret any of the decisions and choices that had led her to them.

Julie's tea set sat in a glass cabinet in the least used of Marnie's three dining rooms, hidden in a corner and mostly ignored. During her worst arguments with Doug, Marnie had been tempted to shatter the cups and saucers one by one, hurling them against a wall and watching that hideous pattern of replica Victorian flowers turn into a whole new kind of mosaic. Still, she'd always resisted the temptation, knowing deep down that the guilt she'd feel from destroying Julie's well-meaning gift would far outweigh any satisfaction she'd gain. Besides, Marnie told herself, one day — *one day* — those cups and saucers could be passed on to her own daughter-in-law. It was only fitting, Marnie thought. Julie had wanted them to be an heirloom, and what better legacy for her son's wife than this china, a gift for the shotgun marriage that culminated in his arrival. Marnie was practical, but not above a little petty irony.

"Can you clean this set up?" she asked Mrs Hollis, her housekeeper, pointing to the set in their glass cabinet prison. "I'd like tea served in them after lunch today."

Mrs Hollis glanced at her in surprise. "But you never use this tea set. Dollar store trash, you've always called it."

Marnie nodded. "That's true. I want to give the set to Sasha though." She swallowed down a mouthful of bile. "Tom seems determined to marry her — heaven knows why — and I promised him I would try my best with her. Giving her this tea set feels like a good place to start."

"With the dollar store trash?" Mrs Hollis asked sceptically, and Marnie nodded.

"Yes. Don't give me that look, Doris. I have my reasons."

Mrs Hollis continued giving her 'that' look anyway. "So, tea and coffee, served with this tea set, at two o'clock? An hour after lunch?"

Marnie nodded. "Yes. Once the wedding planners are out of the way I'll tell Sasha about my gift. She's out for all she can get, that girl, so I'm sure she'll be delighted."

Mrs Hollis frowned at her. "Perhaps comments like those aren't the best way to win your future daughter-in-law's heart?"

Marnie only shrugged. "I could care less about Sasha. No, I'm doing this for Tom." She held her head high. "For Tom, and for the children he'll one day have. I'm no fool. I know Sasha's type. As soon as she has Tom's child in her arms, she'll make me pay through the nose for access to them. And I'll pay for it too. I know it, and so does she."

It was the truth. Marnie was widowed, somewhat retired and mostly bored, and had begun to realise all too late the

Marnie had learned the hard way that family came first, and she intended to put hers at the forefront forever more.

Though, not being an idiot, Marnie kept these thoughts to herself. Sasha was vapid enough and stupid enough not to see beyond Marnie's tight smiles and vaguely hidden insults, and as they sat, discussing wedding plans with the people from Queen and Country Weddings, she threw out several. Sasha missed every single one of them, only having eyes and ears for the blond-haired wedding planner who fawned sickeningly over the bride. But the blue-eyed woman next to him, quiet and thoughtful, glanced at Marnie surreptitiously several times. Ari Lightowler was smart, Marnie realised, watching the woman sip at her wine. In just ten minutes, Marnie was fairly sure Ari had figured out exactly what the situation was here and Marnie, who appreciated people who were honest and without pretence, warmed to her instantly.

For a few moments, Marnie watched the wedding planner pick at a small salad, trying to find fault with her, but found she couldn't. No. There was something genuine about her, something true and down to earth, and Marnie tried and failed to dislike her. Ari's brother, on the other hand, she already detested. Sebastian Lightowler was putting on an act, Marnie knew, and simpering for Sasha's approval in a way that Marnie found she just couldn't respect.

Marnie took a deep breath. Queen and Country would plan this wedding, of that there was now no doubt. Sasha wanted them, and what Sasha wanted, she invariably got. That didn't mean Marnie had to make it easy for the two wedding planners though, who were probably twitching with excitement at the commission this wedding would earn them. Still, while it was easy enough to dismiss Sebastian, it wasn't so easy to dismiss his sister, who answered all of Marnie's questions thoughtfully, with a clear voice and pleasant smile.

No. The more she talked, the more Marnie liked Ari Lightowler. *Tom would like her too,* a small voice piped up in Marnie's mind, which made her sit up with surprise. *It's the truth*, she realised, *Tom would like this woman*. In fact, Marnie suspected he would like her very much.

"Good news!" came the hair-raising, sing-song voice of Sebastian. "We've had a chat, a little rethink, and we've decided we can do anything you want us to, darling."

Marnie watched as he sank into the chair beside Sasha, who clasped her hands together in excitement.

"If you want Luis De León," he continued, "we'll get him for you. If you want Stella Snow, well, you've come to the right people."

It made Marnie want to be sick, the way Sasha embraced him, as if he was an old friend and not someone who had already spent — mentally anyway — at least half a million dollars of Marnie's money.

"And you can do everything in *seven weeks*?" Marnie asked, emphasising once again the tight time frame.

"Oh, absolutely!" he gushed, still holding Sasha's grasping hands. "Of course, it won't be easy, or cheap." He winked at her. "But we can do everything our little poppet has her heart set on."

Marnie nodded, reaching over to take a large swig of her own drink. She looked at Ari, who seemed slightly worried, a small crease in her forehead as she stared at her food.

"What was the issue?" Marnie asked her. "What did you need to talk about?"

"Oh . . ." Ari blushed. "It was nothing. Sebastian and I have sorted it."

"It took you a good ten minutes to work through that 'nothing'," Marnie remarked. "Are you sure?"

Sebastian, who must have a bloodhound's nose for smelling trouble, looked up. "It was just a little issue about childcare. We worked it out though."

Marnie looked from Ari to Sebastian and back again in confusion. "You mean . . . The two of you have a child? I'm sorry — I thought you were brother and sister."

At that, Sebastian burst into laughter, and a small smile even graced Ari's face.

"We are," she explained gently. "I have a daughter. She's seven. Luis watches her whenever Sebastian and I are out on the wedding circuit. He's a good uncle. He'll bring her over with him when he comes to do Sasha's dress fitting."

"*You* have a seven-year-old?" Marnie asked in disbelief, taking in Ari's young features and slim frame. "I don't mean to pry, but you can't have been very old when you became a mother."

"Twenty-one," Ari admitted.

Twenty-one, thought Marnie with dismay. *Too young to be a mother.*

"Are you married? Or divorced? Or . . ."

Or. At that question, Marnie saw what she thought was a hint of pain cross over Ari's pretty features.

"No," Ari said softly. "No. My daughter — her name is Reine — anyway, her father is . . . not on the scene. At least, not at the moment."

There was something poignant in the girl's words. So poignant, sad even, that Marnie opened her mouth to speak before thinking better of it. She didn't want to pry into what was clearly a point of pain.

Sasha, however, wasn't quite so tactful. "What does that mean, 'not at the moment'?" she asked.

Marnie nearly groaned.

"Oh, trust me, this is a can of worms you two don't need to open," Sebastian intoned playfully. "Let's talk more about your wedding. So, then, Sasha. How are you feeling about a veil? Is it a yay or a nay?"

Marnie eyed Sebastian sharply. Beneath his flippant tone, she was certain she could detect a kind of concern. Suddenly, she was convinced he was trying to move the conversation away from Ari and back to Sasha — not out of deference to the bride, but out of concern for his sister.

Which, of course, made a vulture like Sasha only curious to know more.

"No, I want to know about Ari's baby daddy." Sasha smiled, tapping Sebastian's fingers sharply, and Marnie

— sharp-eyed — saw Sebastian stiffen. So, he hated her too, she thought.

"Well, we only have seven weeks, darling," he wheedled her. "We should really—"

But Ari suddenly cleared her throat, patting Sebastian's shoulder gently. "It's okay. I don't mind talking about him."

"Ari, are you sure?"

But Sasha hushed him. "Let her talk."

Ari gave a small shrug. "Honestly, Sasha, there really isn't much to tell. I fell in love during my gap year."

"Gap year?" Sasha frowned.

"A break between studying and work," Ari explained. "I finished a foundation course in art and design, and then went off to do a European tour. I fell in love, and we had six months together. And then his father got sick, and he had to leave and . . ." Ari trailed off, and Marnie could see her trying to talk over what must be a lump in her throat. "Anyway, he had to go, but he promised one day he would come back for me, and then I found out about Reine and . . ." She trailed off again, falling silent at the table.

"But didn't you try to find him? Once you knew about the baby?" Sasha asked.

Ari nodded. "Yes. But there was just no trace of him. Not anywhere. All I had was a phone number, which only ever led to a dial tone. It was like he just . . . disappeared."

"He promised to come back, but left you with a fake phone number?" Sasha raised a disbelieving eyebrow. "That's not a man who's coming back. That's a man who got what he wanted and took off, honey."

"Sasha," hissed Marnie under her breath.

But Ari, rather than looking bothered by Sasha's cutting words, simply smiled. "He left me with something else." There was a note of pride in her voice. "He left me with something he treasured."

"A diamond? An emerald?" Sasha asked excitedly.

"No . . . A playing card."

Sasha rapidly seemed to deflate, clearly losing interest in the conversation, but at Ari's words, Marnie sat up.

"What do you mean, he left you with a playing card?"

"The queen of spades," Ari said warmly, a smile on her lips as she spoke. "And not just any playing card, but one that came from a deck that once belonged to a queen of France."

A shiver ran down Marnie's spine, almost like premonition, or maybe superstition. She inexplicably thought of Corentin, of where he was and what he was doing, feeling a sudden, intense need to speak with him.

"A queen of France?" Sasha queried, furrowing her brow. "How did he get a playing card that belonged to a queen of France?"

"I don't know," Ari said. "I don't know how he got the card, but—"

"Tea, ma'am," a voice interrupted, and Marnie, taking deep, steadying breaths, watched as Mrs Hollis came towards them, laden down by a tray stacked with Julie's hideous tea set. Marnie's fingers remained clenched as the housekeeper set the tray down, ladling out cups and pouring out tea all the while making innocuous remarks about the dark weather. Abruptly, she seemed to notice the empty chair and remaining cup on her tray.

Mrs Hollis looked to Marnie questioningly. "Tom's not here?"

Sasha pouted. "No," she snapped. "He's fucking late."

Marnie unclenched her fingers, only to find them shaking slightly. She picked up her tea, taking a small sip, trying to mask the uncertainty in her hand.

"Get used to it," she told Sasha. "You know what these pilots are like. Doug was the same. Once they get in the air, they lose track of time."

"Well, I'll be sorting that out first, no mistake about it," Sasha said tetchily, drinking her own tea. "He promised he would be here, and I'm going to be his wife. I should *always* come first."

48

"Tom will be here, don't worry," Marnie reassured her, before turning back to Ari. "Did you know the groom was named Tom? Have you met him yet?"

"I did know his name, but we haven't met him yet. To be honest, after this tea we might head over to our hotel and freshen up. We need to call Luis too, get him over here—"

"With your daughter," Marnie said bluntly. "You said he'll be bringing your daughter."

"Um, yes," Ari said. "I'm sorry, it's not very professional, I know, but—"

"Your daughter's father," Marnie interrupted. She felt on the precipice of something big, of something huge, and she needed to *know*. "What was his name?"

Ari stared at her, her eyes wide and uncomprehending. "I don't see why that matters."

"I have contacts," Marnie lied on the spot. "They might be able to find him, you know. He was British like you, yes?"

Ari cleared her throat. "Actually, no. He was American."

There it was again, that slight rush to Marnie's head and stomach. As the adrenaline running through her blood made her feel queasy, she picked up her tea, bringing the motif of pink flowers to her lips and taking a sip.

"American." Marnie repeated.

"Yes." Ari gave a small smile. "American."

"What was his name?" Marnie demanded, clenching her cup in her hand.

"Tom," Ari said simply.

"Another Tom?" Marnie gave what even to her sounded like a hollow and entirely fake laugh. "I have a Tom. The groom. The groom's name is Tom," she chattered on, full of nervous energy. "Looks like they're everywhere."

"Maybe." Ari smiled back. "This one was called Tom Miller."

The cup in Marnie's hand shattered, pink and blue flowers raining onto the tablecloth, tea spilling in every direction.

things she'd missed as a working wife and mother. She adored her sons, but being time-poor and work-rich while they were growing up meant expensive nannies, schools and tutors had been substituted in place of herself.

She'd missed Corentin and Tom's first steps. Missed their first words. She hadn't been there for their first days of school or the nights of their high school proms. It was only when Corentin rebelled his way into a religious calling and Tom disappeared that Marnie realised — with a large stab of pain — just how much she missed them.

When Tom returned at last, weary, sad, jaded and quiet, Marnie worked hard to regain his trust and love. She knew her child — knew something had happened to him in the years he'd been gone. The boy who'd clambered to race cars and pilot planes like his daddy suddenly worked in finance. The boy who'd been all passion and feeling suddenly wanted to settle with Sasha. But, mostly, the boy who'd been all smiles and joy suddenly seemed lifeless and tired, as though a heaviness weighed him down. Marnie would give anything to fix him, to help him find that joy again. But all her efforts seemed only to push him further from her, and at last she gave up.

Tom would carry on working a job he hated. He would marry Sasha. He would live life as a disappointed man. These thoughts made Marnie feel sick, but she consoled herself with one small, tiny ray of hope. That Tom might father children, and give both her and him a second chance at a family life.

Marnie *itched* for a grandchild. A small boy or girl she could pour all her time and effort into. A child who would reap the rewards of her industrious youth. In one respect, she was thankful for Tom's choice in Sasha. Sasha was a heartless, money-grabbing woman, no doubt about it, but she was also a woman who could be easily bribed. Always one to pre-pare ahead, Marnie had already hired the services of a New York lawyer famed for child custody battles. A.A. Andrews, attorney at law, was ready to take down Sasha if needed, so that Marnie and Tom could retain full access to his children.

"Marnie!" Sasha jumped up, brushing spots of tea from her immaculate white dress, while Marnie sat there, her hands empty and shaking.

Ari reached over and took Marnie's hand. "Good God, are you all right? You look like you've seen a ghost."

For a moment, Marnie stared into Ari's kind, soft eyes.

Tom Miller. Eight years ago. They had six months, and Ari . . . Ari had a baby.

"I'm fine," Marnie replied, a strange kind of calm running through her. "Although I should probably go and clean up."

She watched as Ari and Sebastian exchanged looks.

"Well, we should probably head to the hotel," Sebastian said slowly. "As for contracts—"

"No hotel," Marnie announced. "You'll need access to the bride and wedding venue. You can stay here."

"Oh no, we couldn't ask you to—"

"I'll have rooms made up for you. And for Luis De León," Marnie said firmly. Then her voice softened. "And for your daughter, Miss Lightowler."

"Oh, you don't have to do that," Ari said gently. "She's very exuberant and—"

"A big old place like this could do with a young child about it," Marnie interrupted. "I'll have the rooms made up immediately, and as for contracts, I'll sign one now."

Sebastian stared at her. "We could run through it with you first if you like."

"That won't be necessary." Marnie dusted the remains of one of Julie's teacups from her fingers. "I'll sign them all and transfer you your deposit. In fact, do you have the contract with you? I can sign it right now."

Wordlessly, Sebastian pulled a pile of paperwork from his bag.

"This is the standard contract," he explained, "obviously I'll send you an item-by-item breakdown of the expenses and—"

"Excellent," Marnie replied mindlessly, pulling out a pen and signing the contract in all the places Sebastian pointed out.

50

Sasha looked delighted, turning to Sebastian and pulling him into a hug once more. But Marnie only had eyes for Ari.

"Your daughter," she started slowly. "You said her name was Reine?"

Ari blushed. She was very pretty, Marnie realised. She could see why he'd been taken with her.

"Reine means queen, in French," Ari explained. "Like my playing card. I wanted Tom to have a say in her name, even when he wasn't there."

Marnie felt a rush of warmth run through her. "You must have really loved him."

"Yes," Ari replied. "He was everything to me."

Something inside of Marnie warmed further. *She still loves him*, she realised. *She's never stopped loving him.*

"Well, I am most assuredly looking forward to working with you, Miss Lightowler, and—"

But Marnie didn't get a chance to finish her words. Sasha's phone was ringing. When she answered it, she went pale, clutching Sebastian.

"Marnie," Sasha called. "It's Tom."

"What about Tom?" Marnie asked.

"He's in the hospital," Sasha replied, "His plane crashed."

Marnie fell back into her chair with a slump. "Is he . . . Is he . . ."

"No," Sasha answered. "Only injured. But we need to get to him. Now."

* * *

When Tom opened his eyes, his mother loomed over him like an agitated spectre.

"I need to talk to you," she said sharply.

He moaned. "I've literally just woken up after crashing Dad's plane. Can we talk later? My head hurts. Go and get a doctor."

"The doctor already spoke to me, you're fine. A bit beat up maybe, and they're going to keep you in overnight in case you have a concussion, but otherwise you're in pretty good shape for a man who just fell out of the sky."

"How's the plane?" Tom asked.

"Salvageable," Marnie replied. "Just."

"Great." Tom closed his eyes again. "Can I have some pain relief now?"

"Later," Marnie snapped. "I want to talk to you."

"Yeah, you said that. What about?"

Marnie took a deep breath. When Tom opened his eyes, she was pacing about his tiny hospital room.

"Mom," he complained. "You're making me nervous."

When Marnie turned back, her eyes were black. "Growing up in our family, you learn not to ask questions," she began, and Tom groaned. *Great*, he thought. *Another 'in our family' chat.*

"Mom, not now, okay? I'm—"

"My mother died of cancer and my father couldn't cope. I accepted that. I was shunted from family member to family member while he got himself together, from good old Uncle Corentin who farmed *worms* to good old Uncle Tom who played chess in his dressing gown. I never asked any questions, I just did as I was told."

"Uncle Tom was cool, you said as much yourself, that's why you named me for him and—"

"I'm not finished," Marnie said. "I didn't ask any questions when I suddenly went back to living with my father, and my father didn't ask any questions when I married your father. All this silent acceptance . . . it carried on and on. I didn't ask any questions when your father ran off with his floozies. I didn't ask any questions when your brother decided to become a *Druid* and celebrate solstices at ancient stone circles." She paused, almost dramatically. "Tom, I didn't ask any questions when you came back after an absence of years."

Tom blanched. "Mom," he whispered.

But Marnie shook her head. "Today I'm going to ask you questions, Tom," she said firmly, "and you are going to answer them."

He swallowed, his mouth dry.

"And I want to know, first and foremost, about the woman you met back when you were calling yourself Tom Miller."

CHAPTER 5: MAGIC

When Tom was around nine or ten years old, he broke his mother's antique vase. He'd been playing a game he wasn't meant to, in a room from which he was forbidden, and when the football made contact with the blue and white china, causing it to topple before it came crashing to the ground with an almighty smash, Tom felt sick. That vase had come from Europe, a priceless heirloom from France. When Tom's great-grandfather had fled the continent during the ravages of World War Two, he'd taken a small trove of treasures with him, this vase included. It made Tom's stomach churn and skin pale to think that the priceless antique had survived a perilous journey across France, with an army not two steps behind it, a dangerous transatlantic crossing and then eighty years sat in this draughty room, before being felled by the clumsy antics of a bored child.

Guilty and scared, Tom had run from the room in a panic, then hid in his bedroom for the rest of the day. When he was called down to dinner, sick to his stomach, his small heart beating fast within his chest, his mother stared at him. Her eyes were dark and posture bone rigid, and Tom had to look away from the unflinching accusation in her eyes. *She knew*, he realised. *She knew about the vase.*

Sick with nerves, he waited for the yelling to begin. He waited for the recriminations, the punishment, the verbal dressing down his guilty heart told him he deserved. He waited to be sent to bed without supper. He waited for his mother to speak, to say something, anything, and end the miserable guilt he'd carried from the moment the vase had hit the ground.

But Marnie remained silent, picking at her food, the only sounds in the echoing dining room that of her fork scraping across her plate, and Corentin's inane chattering. Tom, his appetite destroyed, picked at his food, conscious of his mother's eyes upon him, watching closely, waiting — Tom instinctively knew — for him to crack.

It took four days before he did. Four awful days and four uncomfortable nights before Tom, wracked with guilt and fear and misery, went to his mother's office and confessed all, crying on her shoulder.

Marnie, surprisingly, was gentle with him. She wiped the tears from his cheeks and the hair from his damp forehead.

"Thank you for being honest with me," she said softly. "That's all I ask for, Tom . . . honesty."

Sitting in his hospital bed now, his mother glaring down at him, Tom was reminded of that moment. His mother stood rigidly, her arms crossed tightly over her chest, one foot tapping restlessly on the clinical linoleum of the hospital floor.

"I want to know, first and foremost, about the woman you met back when you were calling yourself Tom Miller."

Tom swallowed hard, watching his mother with nervous trepidation.

"There was no woman," he lied with a shrug, trying his luck.

"Stop," Marnie interjected, her tone so full of vinegar it was caustic. "That was a lie."

"There was never any woman," Tom said again, indignant at his mother's presumption that he was lying, even though he was.

"You really expect me to believe you went years without female company?"

"Well, there might have been one or two nights where . . ." Tom began, before shaking his head. "Mom, I do not want to have this conversation with you. My sex life is my own business."

"Absolutely," Marnie agreed. "But I'm not asking you about your sex life. I want to know about the *relationship* you had with a woman back when you were Tom Miller — when you stupidly went off the grid for years, draining your trust fund to nothing."

Tom flushed a dull red. "Yeah, well, I did a lot of stupid things back then."

Nodding, Marnie slid into the plastic bucket seat next to Tom's hospital bed. It was the fluid movement of a snake ready to strike. Nervous, Tom leaned away from her.

"So," Marnie began calmly. "Was Ari one of the stupid things you did back then?"

Instantly, Tom's hands felt clammy, and his stomach dropped. His heart began to beat faster, as it always did whenever he heard Ari's name, and his mouth ran dry of moisture. He stared at his mother, his mouth hanging open, stunned into momentary silence.

"Where did . . . Where did you hear about Ari?" Tom finally croaked, and he watched as his mother sat back in her chair, snapping open her bag and pulling out — of all the fucking things — her knitting.

"Never you mind about that," she said shortly, her needles clacking together. Knitting was a hobby Marnie had taken up in her retirement, something to keep her hands and mind busy, and although she was terrible at it — sending Tom and Sasha crooked tea cosies and sweaters so ugly and itchy that Tom became convinced they were meant as instruments of torture — she seemed to enjoy it immensely. "I told you, I'm asking the questions today."

"But . . . But Mom—"

"No lies," Marnie reminded him. "Tell me about Ari."

"I . . . Ari was just . . . She was just . . ."

"Just what? A one-night stand? A quick fling?"

"No," Tom snapped sharply, a flare of protectiveness running through him. "Don't talk about her like that."

Marnie looked up from her knitting, a sudden interest filling her eyes. "She was more to you than that?"

Tom swallowed uncomfortably. "Yeah. She was more to me than that."

"Care to clarify? If she wasn't a fling, what was she to you?"

"Everything," Tom replied honestly, his fists clenching. "She was everything to me."

Marnie's face suddenly softened, and she nodded. "So, there was a woman then."

Tom sighed. "There was a woman."

"Ari," Marnie said softly. "Her name was Ari."

"Ari Lightowler," Tom informed her, his tongue slipping over the syllables, relief flooding through him at finally saying out loud the name that had tortured him internally for years. "She was from London, although I suspect you already knew that." He gave his mother an inquisitive glance.

Marnie shrugged. "It isn't about what I know, it's about what I don't know. So, this Ari . . . How did you meet her?"

"At an airport," Tom said softly, looking down. "Keflavík, in Iceland."

"I forgot you went to Iceland." Marnie dropped her knitting for a moment to stare at him. "Why did you go there again?"

"Why not go there?" Tom shrugged. "It doesn't even matter why I was there."

"And Ari?"

Tom clutched the bedsheet in his hand. "She was travelling. She'd just finished a course in art and design. It was meant to be her round-the-world adventure before she settled down to work. She wanted to be an artist. She was going to paint landscapes. When she held a brush in her hand and stood before an easel, something inside of her . . . She just lit

56

up. It was like looking at a candle flickering in the dark, like watching a . . ." Tom trailed off, suddenly embarrassed. He caught his mother's eye, and realised she was looking at him oddly, her eyes soft and almost woebegone.

"An artist?" she asked him, and he nodded, looking down again.

"Yeah. I hope it happened for her." He cleared his throat around a sudden lump that had risen. "I hope she still found time for it, even with—" Abruptly, Tom stopped, shaking his head as a painful memory reared forth.

"Even with what?" Marnie asked sharply, but Tom only shook his head once more.

"No. It doesn't matter."

Marnie gave him a look that showed she didn't believe him. However, she picked up her knitting again, the needles clacking lightly as she spoke.

"So, you met at an airport?"

"Yeah. Volcanic activity meant all the flights leaving Iceland were grounded. I was on my way back to the States, she was headed to Norway. She was sitting on the ground by a window, her bag next to her, and I was playing cards nearby."

"You were playing with Marie Leszczyńska's cards?" Marnie asked in disbelief. "In an airport?"

Tom nodded. "Yeah. I just . . . She was so pretty, and her eyes were so blue, and when she smiled at me—" Tom stopped, giving a rueful sigh. "The first time she smiled at me, I was gone for her. That was it. I was a lost cause. We played cards for a while — kept each other company. I showed her a magic trick."

Tom closed his eyes, suddenly feeling suffocated by the memory of that night, and the pang of regret that followed and threatened to consume him. Next to him, he could hear Marnie's knitting needles still moving, just as he could hear the bleeps of nearby hospital monitors, both noises grating on his fractured nerves. He missed Ari so much sometimes that he could hardly breathe.

When he opened his eyes again, Marnie was rolling her eyes. "Magic tricks and card games," she huffed. "You're your father's son, all right. Those were the sort of lines your father used on me, back in the day." She scowled. "And on a dozen other women too, I bet."

"Let's leave Dad out of this," Tom said painfully.

Marnie shrugged. "Fine. So, you played some magic tricks on this poor girl and caught her attention. What happened next?"

Tom sighed. "We spent the night in the terminal, just talking. At around five, maybe six in the morning, I bought her breakfast. Croissants and coffee," he reminisced with a smile. "Jam on the pastry and sugar in the drink . . . Ari liked everything to be as sweet as she was."

The knitting needles paused once more, and Tom looked up, catching his mother's eyes.

"You really loved her, didn't you?" Marnie asked, and Tom nodded, a catch in his throat.

"Yeah," he muttered. "I really did."

"Do you still love her?"

Momentarily, Tom's mind went blank as he blocked a painful memory from rising. He gripped the bedsheets, the bones of his fingers showing white under his skin as his hands clenched into fists.

"I'm marrying Sasha," he said simply.

"That wasn't an answer to my question, Tom."

"It's the only answer I'm prepared to give right now," Tom retorted. "Look, I don't even see what business this is of yours. Why are you even asking me about Ari? Why now? What's going on?"

Marnie eyed him sharply. "There's nothing going on. There are just massive gaps in your life story that I'm trying to fill. I told you, I'm tired of lies and unanswered questions."

"Mom—"

"You had breakfast," Marnie interjected, dismissing Tom's attempt to lead the conversation. "Then what?"

Tom swallowed hard, a flush of red rising to his cheeks.

Marnie paused, appraising him sharply. "Then what?" she asked again. "What happened next?"

* * *

By three in the afternoon, they're both exhausted. They've been together all night and day, laughing and chatting, but caffeine and adrenaline can only do so much, and now they're both tired. Tom feels dirty, sweat pooling under his shirt, while his feet ache within his shoes. Ari looks tired, dark circles developing under her eyes, and Tom can sense she's close to tears when the airport announces that all flights are suspended for at least another twenty-four hours, and that baggage claim is likewise closed.

"I'm just so tired," she tells him, resting her head on his shoulder, making his body warm with content happiness. "I just want to sleep. Clean clothes, and a sleep."

They queue for two hours to speak with a harassed airport official, who sighs when he opens a laptop and begins to type frantically.

"I'm sorry, we have very few hotel rooms left," he apologises. "I can get you a room, but it's basic, and you'll have to share."

Ari shakes her head instantly. "We literally just met," she protests. "We can't share a room, we can't——"

"She can have the room," Tom announces. "I can sleep on the airport floor. It's not a problem."

The man nods, and Ari turns, looking up at Tom keenly. "I can't ask you to do that."

"Yes, you can," Tom replies, before he turns back to the official. "Book her the room."

He escorts Ari to her hotel room, pausing awkwardly once she's turned the key in the lock. "Well, Ari, it was nice to have met you."

She nods back, chewing on her lip. "You too, Tom."

It was better this way, he tells himself. He's not meant to be falling in love. It's best not to get close to anyone. Best not to reveal too much. Best to keep evidence of his existence so small it was almost like he didn't exist at all.

Tom Miller is a fallacy. Tom Miller isn't real. But this moment with Ari is, and Tom wants to make it count.

Before he can think twice, he leans down, pressing his lips to Ari's and marvelling at their softness.

"Goodbye," he whispers against her skin, and he feels a soft sigh issue from her mouth.

"Tom," she whispers. "Don't go yet. Stay with me a little while longer."

And she pulls on his hand, drawing him into her room.

* * *

Marnie's face is like stone. "You slept with her? After what . . . twelve hours of knowing her?"

Tom felt indignation pulse through him. "It wasn't like that."

"Well, what was it like? Because, I have to say, this whole story sounds seedy. A young girl trapped in an airport, seduced by a trickster with a fake name. I knew when you were playing your role as Tom Miller that you did some shitty things, but this . . ."

Tom sat up taller in his hospital bed. "It wasn't like that, I told you. What Ari and I had was special. And that night was special. That night was the moment that changed my life. That night was the—" He stopped, taking a moment to catch his breath. "That night was the best of my life."

* * *

She lets him use her shower, and the water on his skin is like a balm to his soul. Both excitement and trepidation run through him concurrently, because he feels like he is walking on the precipice of something incredible. And that feeling both excites and terrifies him, because he's tired of drifting. Tom knows that Ari can change his life. He's known her a little under a day, and already he's doubting his previous life decisions.

For her, he's ready to live. For her, he's ready to change.

And that makes him want to both jump for joy and shake with fear.

He dries off with a towel, and is considering putting his filthy clothes back on when he hears a tremulous knock on the bathroom

60

door. He opens it, and Ari is there, a hotel robe wrapped around her. Delicate ankles and smooth calves peek out from under the faded terry cloth, and she plays with the sash nervously.

All the blood in Tom's body rushes south at the knowledge that under this robe she's naked, and he jerks his eyes to the floor, taking deep breaths.

"Um, I thought we could give our clothes a quick rinse in the bath," Ari explains awkwardly. "And then hang them to dry on the shower curtain. It means we won't have to, um, that is—"

"No, it's a good idea," Tom replies, keeping his eyes firmly on the floor. "I'll, uh, wash mine first. Then, when they're dry, I can get out of your hair and let you sleep."

He feels a shaking finger run across his jawline, and he tingles at Ari's touch. She pushes his chin up so that he's forced to look her in the eye, and she smiles at him softly.

"You don't have to rush," she tells him. "I kind of like having you in my hair, magician man."

They scrub at their clothes with cheap hotel soap, and when they're wrung out and hanging on the shower rail, Tom sits nervously on the edge of the bed.

"What now? More magic tricks?" He's trying to joke, but Ari's face is thoughtful, and she licks her lips once more.

"Ari?" he asks nervously, and she shakes her head.

"I'm just contemplating something," she replies.

"Oh, okay, well—"

But Ari's mind is made up. In one fluid movement, she pulls the robe from her body, and moves towards him, straddling him firmly. Instantly, Tom clutches at her, his heart pounding wildly, relishing the feel of her naked skin under his fingertips. She runs her hands into his hair, looking down at him.

"You showed me a trick earlier," she tells him. "Maybe it's my turn to show you a trick or two."

"I don't think this is a trick, Ari," Tom whispers, moaning gently when Ari takes his hands and places them across her breasts.

"No?" she asks, kissing the pulse point in his neck, making him writhe beneath her. "What is it then?"

Tom snakes one hand into her hair, pulling her lips towards his.
"Magic," he whispers, before silencing them both with a kiss.

* * *

Marnie had apparently been rendered silent, and Tom shifted uncomfortably in his bed.

"It wasn't seedy, like you think," he said, his voice almost hoarse. "It wasn't planned, or . . . I don't know, a *seduction*. We were just two kids who fell in love."

"Are you still in love with her?"

"I told you, I'm marrying Sasha," Tom snapped. "Now can we talk about something else? I've told you about Ari. Let's talk about another topic. The wedding planners, I know I missed them. Were they okay or not?"

Marnie gave an ugly laugh, shaking her head at Tom incredulously. "Trust me," she muttered. "You don't want to talk about the wedding planners."

"Fine," Tom retorted sharply. "You know what? You're right. I don't want to talk about the wedding planners. Sasha can have whatever she wants — whatever makes her happy. I don't give a shit. I don't care."

"Because you don't really care about Sasha," Marnie added blandly, and Tom felt a jolt of anger run through him.

"Don't do that. Don't put words in my mouth."

"Why not?" Marnie shrugged. "As today has proven, you never tell me anything. I might as well fill in the blanks for myself."

"I told you about Ari," Tom said again. "There isn't anything else to add."

Marnie stared at him. "Except that somehow you lost her."

Once again, Tom's hands clenched. "Yeah. I did. But that's my business. You asked about Ari. I told you all you need to know. Why we ended things—"

"You mean why you left her," Marnie interjected, and Tom's eyes snapped at once to hers.

"How did you know I left?" he asked, his voice full of suspicion.

"I told you, it isn't about what I know," Marnie stared at him for a long moment. "Did you try and go back for her? Ever?"

Tom took a deep breath, an old painful memory rising to the surface, threatening to overwhelm him. "I don't want to talk about this," he whispered, his voice broken. "Mom, please, let's talk about something else—"

But Marnie was unrelenting. "Did you ever try and go back for her?"

Tom nodded bleakly. "Yeah. I did. Two years after I left her in Germany. I tracked her down. Searched every Lightowler listing I could find in South-East England. Know where I found her? She was in London, in this — this fucking upmarket apartment in a good part of the city. She was doing well for herself," he sneered. "She'd gone up in the world since me."

"You sound bitter," Marnie remarked, her words cutting.

"I was bitter."

"Are you still bitter?" Marnie asked sharply.

"Of course not," Tom retorted. "I have Sasha, don't I? And Ari has her baby and her perfect—"

At his words, Marnie was on her feet, her knitting falling to the floor with a loud clatter. She was pale, each breath a snarl, her fists as clenched as Tom's. She was livid, Tom realised.

"Do you mean to tell me that you knew about the baby?"

"Yeah," Tom muttered. "I knew about the baby."

For a moment, Marnie stared down at him. There was real anger in her eyes. Tom felt a sliver of unease run through him.

"Mom—"

Marnie shook her head. "I don't think I can be around you right now. I don't think I can even look at you."

She picked up her bag and turned on her heel. Tom sat up, staring at her retreating form.

"Mom!" he shouted. "What the actual fuck? Why do you care about Ari and her baby?"

As soon as he'd spoken the words out loud, a thought came to him, so horrifying and unbelievable he felt panic rise in his blood.

"Mom!" he yelled louder. "You've got it all wrong! The baby isn't mine!"

Marnie was gone though, the sound of her heels disappearing into the noise of the hospital. Tom sat back in his bed, thoroughly confused and more than a little worried. Why was his mother talking about Ari? Where had she heard of her?

He closed his eyes, taking deep breaths, clearing his mind of all thought. Thinking of Ari was painful. Thinking of Ari's baby, on the hip of an attractive man who could only have been the father — *Ari's husband*, Tom reminded himself painfully — was worse.

He needed to get the hell out of this hospital and get back to his mother's house, he decided. He needed to get back to Sasha and the scraps of a life that were left to him.

As he stood, calling for a nurse, he stepped onto the sharp needle of his mother's knitting. In her hurry to leave, she'd abandoned it. Frowning, Tom picked up the skein and needles, a small section of something bright in his hand.

This was no ugly sweater or crooked tea cosy, Tom realised. No, this was pink and soft and small and the perfect size for a child.

Whose child?

Tom swallowed hard.

He needed to get home. He needed to get home right away.

CHAPTER 6: CHOICE

If anything, Marnie's temper got worse on her journey home. As she drove through the winding roads, the sky pitch-black and the trees ominously hanging over the road, she gripped her steering wheel with hands like iron, negotiating turns and banks at a pace that even Doug — who considered speed limits a suggestion and not a hard and fast rule — would have considered reckless.

But Marnie didn't care. She was tired and angry and generally pissed off, so much so that when a deer darted in front of her car, causing her to slam on the brakes and lose velocity, she wound down her window to shout profanities as it disappeared into the inky darkness of the forest.

Her disappointment in her son was staggering. So staggering that she felt it all the way from her mind to stomach, both of which turned and went into overdrive. Tom had gotten a girl pregnant and abandoned her. He'd met his daughter — *my grandchild*, Marnie thought indignantly — and walked away from her. Marnie's fury was as hot as the blood pumping around her body, and she took a deep breath as she started her car's engine once more, speeding again until the lights of the house appeared on the horizon before her.

She parked her car on the drive for her chauffeur to deal with in the morning, then slumped back in the driver's seat, abruptly feeling exhausted. The burst of angry energy that had sustained her drive home dissipated into the evening air. Her mind considered a new and awful realisation, a sliver of doubt in herself suddenly arising: *Part of this is my fault.*

It suddenly occurred to Marnie that if Tom was the kind of man who would abandon a pregnant lover, the kind of man who would walk away from a child of his flesh, well, then she was the mother who'd raised that kind of man. She knew she hadn't been the best of mothers. She knew she'd worked too much during Tom's childhood, knew that her distance from his beloved father had hurt him, knew that her dedication to her business and the protégés who had swarmed around her, like drones to a queen bee, had made him feel second best. But she always thought, beyond everything, that she'd instilled in him the values she'd cherished. Those of honesty, hard work and accountability.

With Ari and his daughter, Tom had abandoned all three.

Marnie walked into her house, slipping her heels off in the hallway and taking a small measure of relief from the feel of the cool, marble floor. She considered the sweeping staircase before her, knowing she should probably go upstairs, shower and jump into bed, but the thought did not appeal. What she really wanted, right then, was a hard drink and a cigarette, although she knew there were no smokes in the house. Doug, for all his hard-drinking and hard-living ways, had been surprisingly firm on nicotine.

"Not in my fucking house," he'd growled at her, and Marnie, young and in love and wanting to please her new lover, had watched as he'd snapped every last cigarette she owned in half.

It was a rule that had stuck over the years, and even now, when Doug was long gone, every member of her staff still followed the same routine. If ever Marnie was tempted to smoke and bought cigarettes, they were duly destroyed. Mrs Hollis was particularly good at it, taking an almost sadistic glee in flushing her tobacco stores away. Right then, desperate for a hit of nicotine, Marnie hated her. She hated them all.

She turned right, walking into the library with its French doors left open to the evening air. *That's odd*, Marnie thought. The doors were always closed in the evening when the household went to bed. They were never left open, not even on the hottest of summer nights.

She was about to call for Mrs Hollis, about to make a scene, when she smelt it — smoke, rich and heady, like the peatiest of open fires, drifting through the air. *Cigarettes.* Marnie's heart sang, drawn to the scent like a sailor to a siren in the open sea. She turned, following its direction.

She stopped when she saw a man sitting in an old armchair, facing the open doors. His legs were crossed languidly, and he was dressed in a robe and slippers. It was the wedding planner, Marnie realised. Sebastian. The one who fawned over Sasha and planned to bleed her coffers of money. Ari's brother. The one who had spent more time with her granddaughter than she ever had, and more than likely ever would. A flash of anger passed through her, and she was ready to have it out with him, to berate him for his presumption in smoking in her nicotine-free establishment. The fucking nerve of him, she thought viciously.

Fists clenched, red-cheeked, she stormed to his side, mentally working out what to say. He glanced up at her, taking another long drag on his cigarette, seemingly unperturbed by her obvious anger.

"Smoke?" he asked, offering up his pack of cigarettes, and after one small moment of hesitation, Marnie nodded tightly.

"Thank you," she replied, leaning down to slide one out, allowing Sebastian to light it up.

She slid into the armchair next to his, drawing long and hard on the cigarette and feeling her body sag with relief at the sweet hit of tobacco. She felt Sebastian's eyes on her, and she looked towards him.

"What?" she snapped.

"You look as though you've had a right shit of a day, is all," he replied easily, his face placid.

Marnie took another drag. "My son fell out of the sky earlier today, in case you'd forgotten."

Sebastian nodded, taking another drag himself, his face so utterly unconcerned and emotionless that it suddenly occurred to Marnie that he had probably forgotten, or — much more likely — simply didn't care. They'd signed the contracts. At this point, Marnie paid up whether the wedding went ahead or not.

"How is our groom?" he asked. "No horrible scarring, I hope?"

"Why? Worried it will ruin the wedding photos?"

"God no. Stella Snow is a fucking genius and could make Quasimodo look like Brad Pitt if she wanted to. But it is a bit of an inconvenience to be constantly pausing a wedding to apply cold compresses to stitches, or to mop up the occasional spurt of blood."

Marnie raised an eyebrow. "That happen often in your weddings?"

"Ari and I planned this one wedding where the groom got shit-faced at his stag party and tried to climb Nelson's Column at Trafalgar Square. As the police were pulling him off the poor bastard smacked his face onto one of the lion's asses, cracking his cheekbone and losing two teeth." Sebastian gave a satisfied grin. "It was hilarious. He had to spend the entirety of his wedding looking left."

"Was that his good side?" Marnie asked wryly, and Sebastian laughed.

"Darling, when you've busted your cheekbone and lost two teeth, you don't have a *good side*, trust me."

Marnie considered him as she sucked down another lungful of nicotine. "You really enjoy what you do, don't you?"

"Well, I like people," Sebastian replied easily.

"More specifically?"

He shrugged. "Well, I like their money. I like that they pay me for my opinions. I like that women trust me when they're at their most vulnerable."

Marnie thought instantly of Sasha. She would never describe her particular breed of bride as *vulnerable*, not in a million years. Her face must have given her thoughts away, because she saw Sebastian looking at her with a knowing sort of interest.

"Sasha is—"

"My soon-to-be daughter-in-law," Marnie cut in sharply, her voice a warning. "And I promised Tom I would be kind."

"Well, yes," Sebastian replied, before he leaned in closer to her. "But he's not *here*, darling. Bitch away, if you like. My ears are open, but my mouth is sealed."

Marnie flicked the ash from her cigarette into the tray Sebastian had beside him, and then looked twice at the cut crystal glass.

"That," she pointed, ignoring his comments about Sasha, "came from France, you know."

"France," Sebastian mused thoughtfully. "I love France."

"Yes, I do too. My name's actually Marine, you know. But at my first school they wrote my name down wrong, and Marnie has stuck ever since."

"My name is Greek. So is Ari's. She's actually Ariadne, though we never call her that."

"Greek?" Marnie asked.

"Yes. Our mother was an actress. Or at least, she wanted to be. Sebastian and Ariadne come from *The Two Gentlemen of Verona*."

"My boys are Corentin and Thomas." Marnie paused, then gave Sebastian a look. "You talk about your mother in the past tense. She's dead?"

Sebastian shrugged. "To me and Ari she is."

His tone of voice showed that he would say nothing more on that subject, and so Marnie sat back, enjoying the quiet for a moment as the nicotine began to sing in her bloodstream.

Without asking, Marnie reached for another cigarette, lighting one up and drawing on it slowly. She gave Sebastian a long, level look, weighing up in her mind whether she liked this man or not.

"Why do you call everyone 'darling'?" she asked him finally. "What is that?"

"An endearment." Sebastian stubbed out his own cigarette before also lighting another. "Women appreciate it."

"You think that's what women want in life? Endearments?"

"My brides certainly do. Well, I suppose they might want something else too. But it's nothing I'm equipped to give them."

Marnie made a small noise of disgust. "If you're talking about sex—"

Sebastian laughed. "Darling, no, absolutely not. You ask a bride what she wants, and she'll lie to you. She'll give the usual spiel . . . love, world peace, designer heels, a happy marriage. But," he leaned closer to Marnie, so close she could see the perfect white pearls of his teeth, "if you ask her what she *really* wants, she'll be honest with you. Trust me. I've planned weddings for a hundred brides, and they've all wanted the same thing, and sex has never come into it."

"So, you're saying none of your brides wanted sex?" Marnie asked disbelievingly.

"Nope," Sebastian replied easily. "They were all brides. They were all in relationships. They were all *having* sex, darling. They didn't want more of what they already had. No. What they wanted was something *better* than sex."

"Better than sex?" Marnie raised an eyebrow. "All right. I'm hooked. Tell me, what did they want that was better than sex?"

"Prestige," Sebastian replied, his voice barely above a whisper. "To win."

"Win what?" Marnie asked in confusion.

"The wedding game. They want to win the wedding game."

"What in the actual fuck is that?" Marnie dragged again on her cigarette. "I mean, *the wedding game*. I've never heard anything like it."

"That's because you've never played it," Sebastian explained. "So, let's take your soon-to-be daughter-in-law Sasha, yes? The one we're absolutely not going to bitch about." He winked at Marnie. "She wants a De León dress — which are the most exclusive designer wedding dresses money can buy — and Stella Snow to photograph her in it. Why do you think Sasha wants those things, darling?"

"Because they're expensive," Marnie shot back. "Just like you."

"No." Sebastian shook his head. "No. The expense is part of the exclusivity. If it wasn't expensive, it wouldn't be exclusive. No, Sasha doesn't want these things because they're expensive. And Sasha doesn't want these things because they're the best, because they're not—"

"Aren't you married to Luis De León?" Marnie asked. "Should you be saying things like that?"

"My Luis is sexy and talented . . . But he's also a hack who got lucky. He knows it, and so do I."

"Still, that's somewhat harsh."

"I make it up to him." Sebastian paused. "And I *am* talking about sex this time, just in case you hadn't—"

"Good, well, that's fine," Marnie interjected quickly. "It's your marriage. I don't need the details." She cleared her throat. "So, let me understand you. You think Sasha wants what is perceived to be the best because it will help her win this wedding game?"

"Yes," Sebastian nodded. "That's exactly it. She wants to spend the rest of her life looking back on her prized wedding pictures and her designer wedding gown, knowing that she had the best wedding of all time. The prestige from just one day . . . a bride can feed off it forever."

Marnie stared at him. His words sat like lead in her stomach, leaving her feeling vaguely queasy and unsettled.

"But a wedding should be what the couple make of it," she offered weakly. "It should be about love. Not about having the best wedding ever. There's no such thing as the best wedding ever."

"My entire career hangs on the opposite being true. By the way, while we're talking about the best wedding ever, I have this for you."

Marnie watched as from within his robe Sebastian pulled a sheet of paper. He handed it to Marnie wordlessly, inhaling on his cigarette and blowing a thick plume of smoke into the night air.

"What is this?"

"I called Stella this evening while you were at the hospital," he replied. "This is a list of her terms and conditions. Basically, she won't take the job until you promise to supply everything in this contract."

With a feeling of trepidation, Marnie began to read. "She retains the exclusive right to sell the photographs as she sees fit. She will retain copyright over all images, though the bride and groom may distribute them to their close friends and family as they see fit. A room must be provided to store sensitive photography equipment, which must be kept at a minimum temperature of twelve degrees Celsius and a maximum temperature of sixteen degrees Celsius. The gauge to measure the temperature of said room must be in Celsius as the photographer is not a New World peasant . . ." Marnie looked at Sebastian, scowling. "There are twenty-eight terms and conditions on this list, you know."

"I do know," Sebastian replied. "I've worked with Stella before. She's a delight. A real fucking delight."

Marnie carried on reading, until she came to clause twenty-three. She cleared her throat. "If the wedding dress is designed by Luis De León and or the wedding is planned by Queen and Country Weddings, the bridal party must provide the photographer with two boxes of Leibniz dark chocolate butter biscuits, kept at the same temperature standards as the photography equipment." She stared at Sebastian in disbelief. "This is insane."

"Yes, that's an odd one, but it's always in her contract for any wedding where Luis and I are involved," Sebastian replied.

"Why does she want chocolate . . ." Marnie frowned, scanning back over the contract ". . . chocolate butter biscuits when you're involved with the wedding?"

"Fucked if I know."

"But haven't you asked her? I mean, this is a crazy requirement. I don't even know if I can get . . ." Marnie frowned again, scanning the document once more ". . . Leibniz dark chocolate butter biscuits."

"If you want Stella, you'll find the biscuits," Sebastian warned.

"Aren't you the wedding planner?"

Sebastian shrugged. "I'm better with people than the actual planning side of things. That's Ari's department."

Ari. At the woman's name, Marnie felt that earlier dart of anger returning. "I need another cigarette," she muttered.

Sebastian grinned at her as he handed over his pack. "I have to say, darling, it's so refreshing to smoke with a woman who treats her body like a chimney, as I do mine."

"Do you call Ari 'darling'?" Marnie asked suddenly, staring at him intently.

"Yes," Sebastian replied. "Although in her case I say it truthfully. She *is* a darling."

"What about Reine?" Saying her granddaughter's name caused a sudden lump in her throat. "Do you call her darling too?"

"No," Sebastian replied. "I call her sunshine, and that's the truth. She is my sunshine. She's my girl."

"But she's not your girl. She's just your niece. She's some . . . some other man's girl."

Sebastian sat back in his armchair, considering Marnie carefully for a moment. "You sound like Ari. She tells herself that lie too."

"What lie? Reine does have a father."

"Actually," Sebastian said, his earlier easiness withdrawn, "she has two in fact. Me and my husband."

"You aren't her father. Luis isn't her father," Marnie argued, feeling a strong sense of loyalty to her son that

73

overrode her current anger with him. "Her father is my — I mean, this other man."

"Tom Miller," Sebastian mused, lighting another cigarette and drawing on it, long and pensive. "A fictional name for a fictional character, wouldn't you say?"

"You think Ari is lying?"

"No. I told you — Ari is a darling. I think Ari was lied *to*. I think this Tom Miller chap took my sister for a fool and left her high, dry and pregnant. Ari tells herself he's coming back for her . . . she actually believes she hasn't been abandoned. But she has. He left her, and he's not coming back. Not ever."

"What if he does?" Marnie asked quietly.

"Unlikely." Sebastian shrugged. "But if he does, and he wants Reine, he'll have a fucking fight on his hands."

Abruptly, thankfulness crossed Marnie's mind as she remembered that she'd already hired the services of a lawyer in New York who specialised in child custody battles. Andrew A. Andrews was the best in the business. She'd thought she'd be fighting Sasha, of course, but still. She was ready.

"Do you know what I remember the most when I think about Tom Miller?" Sebastian suddenly asked, and Marnie shook her head. "I remember when Ari was four months pregnant, poor as a church mouse and working as a cleaner. She was living in this filthy flat share in Brixton. She had nothing. Absolutely nothing. Luis and I tried to help, but she was determined to do it all herself. If Tom Miller couldn't help her, no man was allowed to help her. Even me, her own brother."

Momentarily, Marnie felt a flare of guilt, and another, much stronger flare of anger for Tom.

"One day," Sebastian carried on, "Luis stays late at work on a dress, and she was crying her eyes out. She'd been for a scan, you see, and found out she was having a girl. What should have been a magical moment in her life was nothing but sadness to her, because this bloke, this *Tom*, had missed it."

"Maybe he had his reasons for not—"

"No," Sebastian snapped. "There's not a single reason in the world good enough to miss something like that. There's not a single reason in the world for leaving a girl like Ari in the position that he did."

"You think so?" Marnie asked miserably.

"I wouldn't let her leave after that night. Luis brought home dinner, determined to fatten her up—he's a feeder, my Luis. He's never had much success with me, because I like to keep my lines neat and clean, but with Ari, he found a willing victim. My God, if you ever saw that woman eat, you'd—"

"You wouldn't let her leave?" Marnie interrupted.

"Well, we'd been planning on getting a cat, but in Ari we found the next best thing."

Marnie paused. "I'm sorry, did you just say you were planning on getting a cat, but instead decided to take on a whole person?"

"Two," Sebastian clarified cheerily. "She was pregnant."

Marnie stared at him — Sebastian shrugged.

"Well," he conceded, "I suppose it sounds bad when I say it like *that*, but Ari's my sister. She's something special. We held a mock baby shower on that first night. Luis designed an all-pink menu. Smoked salmon blinis followed by rare pink steak and then an unbaked strawberry cheesecake. Of course, she couldn't actually *eat* any of the fucking stuff because of the baby, but still, she appreciated the effort. Luis has made it his life's mission to feed her ever since."

"So, how did she end up going from a cleaner to your business partner?" Marnie asked curiously, making mental notes for her lawyer.

"Because, you might not believe it, but under her miserable exterior and sordid life story, Ari's quite the artist. She can take someone's words and make them into a visual work of art. The brides love her. They can say, 'oh, I quite fancy being married on a beach at sunset with candles flickering in the distance' and Ari makes it happen. We were the perfect partners, in a way. Once she did her first wedding with me,

75

she was hooked, and so Queen and Country Weddings was born. In Ari, I got a business partner, and from Ari, Luis got a guaranteed ticket into BarbieCon. Best thing for both of us."

Marnie paused again, eyeing Sebastian warily. "I'm sorry," she said slowly. "What do you mean, Luis got a guaranteed ticket to BarbieCon?"

"Oh," Sebastian shrugged, "my husband collects Barbie dolls. He has around two thousand."

Marnie's eyes widened.

"Yeah," he agreed, "it's odd, but the heart wants what it wants, and his heart wants eleven and a half inches of hard vinyl."

"Don't we all," Marnie remarked sardonically, taking a long puff on her cigarette. "So, how does Ari provide his 'guaranteed ticket' to BarbieCon?"

"Through Reine," Sebastian explained. "You see, at certain parts of the expo, there are sections reserved for parents with children. Luis was never allowed in before, but with Reine . . ."

"So, let me get all this straight. You were going to get a cat, but you took on Ari, and you did so because she was good with visuals, and because she had a daughter that your husband could use to buy Barbie dolls?"

Sebastian stopped, seeming to consider Marnie's words. "Well, when you say it like that, it sounds bad. But she's also my sister, and we're happy, the four of us. Things are good. And at the next BarbieCon in Japan, we're going to take Reine to Tokyo Disney. It'll be grand."

Marnie stubbed out her cigarette, standing wearily. "Unless Reine's father comes back."

"He won't."

"You don't know that." Marnie suddenly felt exhausted, her earlier anger having mellowed out, both from the nicotine and a methodical plan coming to mind. "You know, one day my Tom might—"

"Your Tom?" Sebastian asked sharply. "Your son? What's he got to do with this?"

Marnie paused for a beat too long, and she saw Sebastian's eyes narrow. "Nothing," she said breezily, trying to recover. "I was just thinking about him in the hospital. I should call him. Sasha said she was going in to sit with him, but she . . ." Marnie stopped. "I'm tired. I got mixed up."

Sebastian's eyes, bright and blue, rested on Marnie warningly. "It will be very interesting to meet your son," he said. "I didn't know he was a pilot until today. It wasn't in the fact file Sasha compiled for us."

"He's not a pilot. Not professionally. It's just a hobby. It was my husband's hobby too. I call it the family curse," Marnie explained hurriedly.

Sebastian eyed her. Marnie watched as he lit another cigarette, sitting back in his chair and taking a long drag on it. "Ari doesn't talk much about Tom Miller, you know. But one thing she does talk about is the day she knew she loved him. It's a sweet story, you should ask to hear it. They were on an airplane. Turns out Tom Miller was a pilot too." Sebastian paused, exhaling smoke like a dragon in its lair. "Just like your son," he added. "Just like your son."

"Isn't that a coincidence," Marnie remarked.

"Yes. Isn't it. How old is Tom?" Sebastian asked. "Did he ever spend time in Europe? Did he ever—"

"I'm going to bed," Marnie announced. "You want to know about my son, check your damned fact file."

"I'll do that," Sebastian replied evenly. "Right after I've called my husband."

Marnie paused. "He's on his way? With . . . with Reine?"

Sebastian nodded slowly. "They'll be here tomorrow."

"Good," Marnie replied, before she could think twice. She watched as another look crossed Sebastian's face.

"What was your name before you got married?" he asked, and she blinked in surprise.

"What?"

"What was your maiden name? You said your given name was French. What about your maiden name?"

Marnie paused. "I don't see why that matters."

"Humour me."

She stared at him. "It was Millet," she admitted reluctantly.

Sebastian's eyes didn't leave hers. He took another draw on his cigarette, exhaling into the cold night air. "You know, I'm starting to wonder if Luis bringing Reine here is such a good idea."

"Why?" asked Marnie sharply.

There was a long pause. Sebastian was now as unwilling to give anything away as she was, Marnie realised.

"Oh, you know," he finally replied. "Children and weddings and all that. They can get in the way."

"I'm sure it will be fine," Marnie said lightly. "I'll have her room made up, ready for her in the morning."

"You don't need to do that," Sebastian said, his face thoughtful. "You don't need to, but I think you want to. And now I'm sitting here trying to work out why that might be."

Marnie licked her lips. "Thanks for the cigarettes."

He threw the rest of the pack at her. "Finish them. Luis hates smoking. He says they're bad for me, and bad for Reine to be around."

Marnie let the packet drop to the floor. "No, thanks. Your husband is right. They're bad for Reine."

* * *

When she wakes in the morning, Tom's arms are still tight around her waist. She peels his hands from her body, and he mumbles in his sleep. She takes a shower before pulling on her now dry clothes, and when she returns to the room, he's sitting up in bed, looking at her with soft eyes.

"Why Norway?" he asks. "Why are you headed there?"

She blushes. "Oh, I want to go to the National Gallery. That's what I'm doing with this year . . . visiting all the great art museums of the world."

"London didn't have enough for you?" he asks wryly, and she grins.

"London doesn't have The Scream.*" She sits on the edge of the bed, suddenly nervous around him. "Um, it's in Oslo. That's where I'm going."*

A soft hand rests on her shoulder and she turns, meeting his eyes.

78

"Ari," he says gently. "Don't be frightened of me, okay?"

She blushes again, looking away from the chocolate depths of his eyes. "It's just that, uh, I've never, um, done this kind of thing before."

"The sex?" Tom asks, clearly confused.

"Well, no, I mean, I have done that, but not . . . not like this . . ." she stammers.

"Like what?"

"You know. A one-night stand."

She hears a sigh issue from his lips, just as she feels his thumb trace her cheek. He tilts her chin up, so she's forced to look him in the eye once more.

"You think this is a one-night stand?" he asks her, and she nods.

"Well, what else could it be?" she queries him. "I'm going to Oslo, and you're going to . . ." She pauses. "Where are you going?"

"New York. That's where I'm from. Well, this house upstate, it's—" He stops, and clears his throat. "New York. That's where I'm going."

"Well, the airways are clear now," Ari replies, more than a little sadly. "I just got a message from the airline. My flight leaves at 2 p.m."

"Mine leaves at four," Tom says, and she thinks — or does she hope? — that the same sadness she feels also tinges his voice.

"We have the morning," she says softly. "If you want, we have the morning."

"I want," he replies instantly. "I want very much."

She blushes again. "More card games?"

"No," he answers. "More magic."

He pulls her back into his arms and kisses her softly. His eyes are soft, and his breath is warm and his lips are firm, and she could melt, right then and there, from all three of them.

"How am I going to say goodbye to you?" he whispers, and she isn't sure if he's asking the question of her, or of himself. "How do I do that, Ari?"

"I don't know," she whispers back, allowing herself to run a finger along his bottom lip. "But we don't have a choice. It's just something we have to do."

"There's always a choice," he says, just before he kisses her once more. "And with you, I want to make the right one."

* * *

They say goodbye in the departures lounge. As Ari boards the plane, she tries to stop the tears that have treacherously gathered in her eyes. She bites her lip, pushing her hand luggage into the overhead containers and trying to see reason.

It was just a one-night stand.

He was only ever going to be a fling.

He would just be a story she told.

It was never meant to be.

She sits in her seat, staring out of the window miserably, looking at the airport terminal and wondering where Tom is, where he's sitting and what he's doing.

Wondering if he's already missing her the way she's missing him.

It's then that a voice sounds from above her, and she turns.

It's Tom, and he's sliding into the seat beside her.

"What?" she whispers. "How are you here?"

He smiles at her, before claiming her cheeks with his hands and kissing her passionately.

"Ari," he says. "I told you. There's always a choice. And you know something? I just made the right one."

CHAPTER 7: THE ENDS OF THE EARTH

It shouldn't be possible to fall in love this quickly. It shouldn't be possible to feel so strongly, so movingly, about anyone this quickly at all. Love isn't like that. Love isn't lust, which can hit you like a tonne of bricks. Nor is love like anticipation or excitement, both emotions that crash over you in waves, building upon one another in your bloodstream like a tidal pool of pleasure. Love is more than that. Love is slow-building, slow-moving. Love isn't an ocean wave, but a gentle stream, a river that carries you away gradually. No, Ari thinks, staring at Tom while he sleeps. It can't be possible to fall in love so quickly. It just can't.

So, why then does she feel it? Why then does her stomach twist in knots in his presence? Why does her heart pound quicker, her blood run hotter? Why does the mere sight of him fill her with gladness? With happiness? With excitement and so many other emotions that she feels full to the brim with them? Why is that?

They're lying in a hotel room in Oslo, the sheets knotted around them. Tom's hands are in Ari's hair, her head cradled lovingly against his chest. Absently, she runs her fingertips along his skin, tracing a pattern into his hip. He stirs against her, and she smiles, inhaling the smell of him in the warmth of their bed. It's heady, his smell. Almost intoxicating. She could live off his smell, she thinks. Give up food and drink forever in exchange for a lifetime of this aroma.

She frowns at that, shaking her head. Five days with Tom and she's become nonsensical, her mind turning to butter around him. Rational thoughts are all but gone, replaced by ridiculous ideas of love and romance. It's infuriating. It's demeaning. But it's also wonderful.

She hadn't come to Europe to look for love. No, that hadn't been on the plan at all. This was her year to be wild and free. Her year to travel and have adventures. Her year to explore, to paint, to follow in the paths of great artists. Her pencils were packed, her paints securely fastened into her luggage. This was her year, a gift of time she'd given to herself. One day, soon enough, she would settle down to work. A meaningless role in graphic art, or marketing, or maybe web design. Something moderately well-paid and secure, in a generic London office. Grey work in a grey city, she'd always wryly thought. Ari, who'd had independence thrust on her from a young age, was realistic about the future. And grey was fine. It was safe and non-threatening, after all. Grey offered security — after a lifetime of stark black and white, of bleak prospects and even bleaker day-to-day living, security was all Ari could ask for.

It was all she wanted, really.

But not yet. Not just yet. First, she would have this year. She would give herself this one year, so that in the years of grey ahead, she would have the memory of something colourful to cling to. Something bright, something vivid. To prepare for the years to come.

Falling in love like this, so quickly and so completely, had not been part of that plan at all. She wasn't ready to settle down just yet. Wasn't ready to give herself so utterly to anyone or anything. Every morning she woke, her mind made up, her resolve strengthened by sleep, to turn to Tom and tell him to go.

"We had fun," she would say, more flippantly than she felt, "but it's time to go our separate ways."

And then Tom would open his eyes, those damnably brown eyes flecked with amber and gold, before smiling that lazy smile of his, and Ari's resolve would falter. By the time he ran a finger down her cheek and pulled her in for a kiss, her resolve was all but gone.

"Tomorrow," she'd think. "I'll tell him tomorrow."

From Oslo they go north, travelling across the country to Kristiansund. It's a coastal town, a palate of greys, whites and ocean blues, and Tom sits by Ari's side while she tries to capture the colours. He's silent for the most part, and occasionally she looks back to him, only to find him staring out to the ocean, seemingly lost in thought. Towards the end of the day, when the sky starts to streak pink and purple with the coming night, her curiosity gets the better of her.

"What are you thinking of?" she asks, absently adding colour to her canvas, and he startles at her words. His face instantly sharpens, and there is a hint of a scowl to his mouth, as though unhappy at being caught in a moment of self-reflection.

"Oh," he says with a shrug, "I was just thinking about where we are. How far from everything it feels."

"Too far?" she queries, and he shakes his head.

"Not far enough."

She pauses at that, chewing on her lip. A question suddenly rears up, one that has been on her lips from the moment he first boarded her plane to Oslo.

She clears her throat. "Tom," her voice is gentle, "are you running away from something?"

He stares back at her, and his eyes are intent, searching her face as though looking for something.

"Yes," he replies slowly, and her stomach drops.

"Is that . . . is that why you're here with me? Am I just something for you to latch onto? Something to help you escape?"

"No." This time, his reply is instant. "No. I'm here with you because, from the moment I saw you, something felt different."

"Bad different?" she asks warily.

"Good different," he says, a smile creeping across his cheeks. "Wonderful different."

She nods at that, although she doesn't understand, not really. She has so many questions about Tom. There's still so much she doesn't know about him. She looks back to her painting, to the myriad of greys and pastel sunset tones, and suddenly can't make sense of it. The colours blur together in a confusing mix of oils and acrylics, and she frowns.

"Ari," Tom suddenly says, but she keeps her head down. "Ari, look at me." He's more insistent this time, and she takes a glance in his direction. He's gazing at her steadily, his face full of concern. "Ari, you have to understand something."

"What?" she whispers. "What do I have to understand?"

He sighs. "Life isn't simple, Ari. It isn't easy. There isn't a map to follow, or one road to take. There's hundreds. Thousands even. And sometimes you can take the wrong one."

"Did you take the wrong one?" she asks.

A frown briefly crosses his lips. "Yeah." She's taken aback by the bitter tone to his words. "Yeah, I took the wrong one. A dozen wrong ones. The wrong career. The wrong girl. The wrong decision. I took them all."

A dart of pain runs through her, and her skin must pale, because in an instant Tom is beside her, wrapping her into his arms. "You aren't the wrong girl," he whispers passionately into her ear. "You'll never be the wrong girl."

"But you said . . ."

"I know what I said. But that wrong girl . . . she isn't you. You aren't the wrong road for me, Ari, you're the right one. The only one."

She nods, Tom's heartbeat a steady thump on her cheek. He tilts her chin up, so she's forced to look him in the eye, and he smiles down at her. "Ari," he says softly, his voice as gentle as the sea breeze on her face. "Sometimes you have to get lost to find your way."

"What if I want to be lost though?" she asks, trying not to melt too much into his gaze, his arms or heart. "What if I want to try different roads?"

She sees him swallow, sees a shadow of doubt flicker over his face. "Then you should try them," he says, and she can see the effort it takes him to speak those words. "You should live your life, exactly the way you want."

He moves away from her, disentangling her from his arms. Is that it? she wonders. Is that the end for them? It was what she wanted, what she planned, and yet, now that she's standing away from him — away from him and his smell and his eyes and the heartbeat that sounded so steadily against her — she feels bereft. She feels lost. Her heart is broken, she realises. He's broken the heart she hadn't even realised she'd given him.

"Tom," she says, and when he looks at her, the ocean breeze rippling through his hair, she feels a knot of want in her stomach. "Take the wrong roads with me," she pleads. "Stay with me."

She's in his arms again in a moment, and his lips are hard against her own. He kisses her lips, her cheeks, her neck . . . every scrap of flesh that is available to him, he puts his mouth to passionately.

84

"Yes," he agrees. "I'll follow you to the ends of the earth, Ari. Anywhere you want to go."

"The end of the earth sounds good," she smiles into his kisses. "And it isn't far from here." She cups his face in her hands.

"So, let's go," he says. "As soon as your painting is dry, let's get out of here. To the end of the earth and then back again."

Ari looks at her painting. It's a mess of colour, with jagged yellows and pinks cutting into the grey of the town and blue of the ocean. It's nothing like how she intended it to be, nothing like how she saw it in her mind. Just like Tom, she realises.

He's just as unexpected. Just as unplanned.

"Don't worry about the painting," she shrugs. "It's no good. Let's just get out of here."

But Tom shakes his head. "No," he says firmly. "The painting is wonderful. Let's wait for it to dry."

"No, it's really not worth it, it's really—"

"Ari," he says again, patience in his voice. "The painting is good."

Her body sings at his praise, and she smiles up into his eyes. "Then it's yours. You can have it."

He seems momentarily taken aback, and there is a hint of wonder to his face. How long has it been since someone gifted him something? she wonders. But by the expression on his face, she suspects she knows the answer. A long time.

"Are you sure?" he asks tremulously. "I don't want to presume—"

"Tom," she interrupts him gently. "It's yours."

He nods, shoving his hands into his pockets and swallowing heavily. "Does it have a name? It'll be hanging in a gallery one day, you know. Right next to all the other great artists."

She gives a small laugh at that. The idea that one of her works, small and inconsequential, would ever hang in a gallery, next to one of the greats, is ludicrous.

"No name," she says. "It doesn't need one."

"It does." Tom frowns. "I'll think of one."

Two days later, they travel to a small, local airport, where he ushers her into a small plane he's hired.

"You can fly?" she asks dubiously, watching him settle comfortably into the pilot's seat.

"Yeah." He shrugs. "It's the family talent."

"What do you mean?" she asks. "Are your family pilots or—"

"Let me check your restraints," he interrupts, reaching over to pull the straps across her chest. "There are heavy clouds today . . . It could get bumpy during take-off."

She nods, and when Tom is satisfied that she's safely buckled into her seat, he manoeuvres the small plane along the runway and then into the sky. Without meaning to, Ari holds her breath as they rise, and it's only when they break through the low-hanging clouds and begin to soar through the blue skies above that she allows herself to relax. Behind the controls, Tom is confident and relaxed, keen to share something he clearly loves with her, a wide grin on his face, and she stares at him in amazement. He's beautiful, she realises. He's wonderful and beautiful and everything she has ever wanted in life.

When they begin their descent into Tromsø, she continues to stare, and Tom grins at her.

"What are you looking at? What can you see?" he teases.

"Roads," she answers truthfully. "So many roads."

"And do any of them look good to you?" he asks with a smile. Something about him in that moment makes her catch her breath. He's a puzzle, she realises. But he's a puzzle she wants to work out.

"Yes," she admits with a swallow. "One does."

He nods — understanding passes through them. Their eyes lock momentarily, and it feels like homecoming. She watches as Tom tears his eyes from her to turn back to the controls, but Ari continues to watch him, relishing in the knowledge that, at last, she's found her way.

It shouldn't be possible to fall in love so quickly, *Ari* thinks. *But somehow, she already has.*

* * *

An insistent tapping woke Ari from her sleep. Turning over on the soft mattress, buried under a layer of thick blankets, she tried to push the noise from her mind. Although exhausted, she'd stayed awake as long as she could the night before, trying to beat the inevitable jetlag, finally falling into bed a little after midnight. Now, after what felt like the blink of an eye, she was awake again, although her body and mind were tired, weighed down by the long day before. Glancing at her phone briefly, she took in the time with disbelief.

"No," she muttered into her pillow. "It's six fifty-three in the morning. Go away, Sebastian. I need more sleep."

The tapping continued, however, and Ari gave a long, resigned sigh.

"Fine, fine, fine," she complained. "I'll wake up. But this had better be worth it—"

She sat up, turning towards the doorway and instantly turning pale. Because standing in the doorway, immaculately made up, her jet-black hair slicked back from her pale face, while one of her heeled feet tapped irritably on the floor, stood Stella Snow.

"Stella," Ari spluttered, jumping out of bed and snatching up her robe. "Stella, how nice to see you, how nice to—" She stopped, looking at Stella keenly. "Um . . . What are you doing here? At . . ." she checked the time once more ". . . six fifty-four in the morning?"

"The little blond-haired man called me," Stella said smoothly, one heel still tapping. "Some sort of . . ." she gave a dismissive wave of her hand, ". . . wedding photography emergency, apparently. I checked my calendar. I had a fifteen-minute window of time available, so here I am."

"A fifteen-minute window at six fifty-four in the morning?" Ari queried. "That's very, um, precise."

"The little blond-haired man assured me this wedding would be worth my while. So, I made an effort."

"At six fifty-four in the morning?" Ari asked again.

"I was in New York on a shoot for *Vogue* yesterday," Stella explained blandly. "That finished at 2 a.m., at which point I read the little blond-haired man's message. My next shoot doesn't begin until 11 a.m., so my assistant and I jumped in the car and made our way here."

"Wow, that's really, um, good of you to come so quickly. The bride will appreciate it. Obviously, so do Sebastian and I, and I really hope that—"

"I haven't agreed to do the wedding yet, Ms Lightowler," Stella reminded her. "You have ten minutes to convince me it's a good idea."

"Oh." Ari frowned. "But I thought you had a fifteen-minute window of time?"

"I did," Stella said shortly. "But you've wasted five minutes of that in making me explain *why* I had a fifteen-minute window of time. You're down to ten."

Ari nodded, mute with terror of this woman. Where the fuck was Sebastian? He was always best at dealing with Stella. There was a reason he was the client manager, while she did the behind-the-scenes work.

"Okay, well, let me just—wait, I'll get Sebastian, he can at least show the venue and—"

"There's no need. I've been here before," Stella cut in, and Ari stared at her.

"You've been here before?"

"Yes," Stella replied idly, her face still rigidly unmoving. "I photographed Marnie Somerset for *Esquire* . . . When was it? Four? Five years ago? We took a few shots here, and a few in Paris."

Paris. The word hit Ari with a jolt, and she bit her lip, hoping the physical pain would stop the emotions from cutting through her.

Stella, however, was as sharp as her nails. "What is it?" she asked. "You look distressed, and your pain is exquisite. I wish I had my camera with me to capture it."

"Oh . . . I . . . it's just, I went to Paris once. I went with someone I cared for. I, um . . ."

Abruptly, Stella looked bored. "I have no time for tawdry stories of love affairs, Ms Lightowler. I'm here to photograph a wedding."

"Isn't a wedding, um, a love story?"

For a moment, Stella stared at her in wonder. "The very idea." She laughed, and the sound was odd, coming from her unmoving lips.

Ari licked her lips, standing taller and trying to regain control of this situation. "Okay, so you've seen the venue . . . It's early, so the bride won't be up yet — there was a bit of a hiccup with the groom yesterday, she had to see him in hospital and . . ." She trailed away as Stella began to wave her hand in a 'hurry up' gesture. "So, um, I guess I'll get Sebastian to get your copy of the contract so you can run over it and—" She stopped, staring at Stella anew. "Stella, it's *seven in the morning*. Who let you into the house?"

"Why, I let myself in," Stella answered slowly, as though Ari were some kind of idiot. "My assistant and I arrived, and the gate was open, so we pulled up the drive. And then the decorators were downstairs setting up their ladders, so we just walked inside."

"Decorators?" Ari asked. "Marnie has decorators in?"

"Mm, so it seems. Something about a room for a little girl and—" Stella stopped, suddenly peering at Ari curiously. "Where's your small?"

"My small?" Ari asked in confusion, before her mind caught up. "Oh, you mean . . . Do you mean Reine?"

"Obviously," Stella said, disdain dripping from the word. "Your small. Where is she?"

"Luis has her," Ari explained. "He's flying over with her now."

"And she'll be staying here? With you?"

"Well yes, I have this room and Marnie's put aside the room next to mine for Reine. Just until the wedding, of course."

Stella stared at Ari, her crystal blue eyes sharp even in the soft morning light. "Guest quarters for staff? That's not the Marnie Somerset I remember. When I last saw her, the house was strictly for family only."

"Oh." Ari exhaled. "Well, she seemed very friendly yesterday. Very keen on having Reine here too. I was touched."

"Hmm." Stella looked around Ari's room, taking in the soft bed, the plush carpets and the ornate furnishings. "Hmm," she murmured again.

89

"Stella, we only have about five minutes left. Let me go and get Sebastian, and a large coffee, and he can run over the wedding details briefly with you. The wedding is in seven weeks, so it will be a tight job, but I know Marnie will pay you well for it and—"

"And my biscuits?" Stella cut in. "You know the rules. When I work on one of your weddings, or a De León wedding, I get two boxes of dark chocolate Leibniz."

"Yes, I know all about your biscuits, and we will sort it out, don't worry." Ari did her best to sound confident. "Please let me go and get Sebastian. He'll be in his room and—" She stopped, staring at Stella once more. "Um, why did you come into this room? After letting yourself in?"

"Because the decorators were headed here, and I was curious."

"Right." Ari thought for a moment. "Because the decorators are coming in to . . . to paint a room for Reine . . . and . . ."

Stella leaned forward, a rare and sudden spark of interest on her face. "Odd when you say it like that, isn't it?"

It was odd. Marnie hardly knew her, or Reine, and yet had given them two of the best rooms in her home. It was admittedly a large home, and Ari knew she had the space to spare, but still. Something about the situation suddenly sat ill upon her, and she frowned.

"Let me get Sebastian," she said. "Wait here and I'll come back—"

"I left my assistant in the gallery downstairs," Stella cut in. "I shall wait there. Tell your brother he has three minutes."

"The gallery downstairs, absolutely, we'll meet you there," Ari replied, trying not to feel too overwhelmed. Of course, in a house of this size, with all its trappings and riches, there would be a gallery. Of course there would.

Once Stella had disappeared, Ari sprang into action. She hastily tied her robe around her and ran into the hall, passing the room next to her own, in which men with ladders and pots of paint were hanging protective sheets over the carpet. She ran into Sebastian's room, opening his door without knocking and dashing to his bed.

"*Sebastian*," she hissed. "Wake up. Right now."

"But I don't want pancakes this morning, Luis," he murmured sleepily. "Feed them to Ari."

"*Sebastian*," Ari hissed again, prodding him this time. "*Wake up.*"

"All right, all right," he muttered, rolling over. "I'll have one pancake but only if you add the syrup I like."

Ari stood taller, crossing her arms over chest. "Sebastian," she said loudly. "Stella Snow is downstairs, and you have three minutes left before she walks out the door and costs you this dream wedding and all associated business."

Sebastian sat bolt upright in bed, his eyes snapping to Ari. "What time is it?" he asked, before shaking his head. "Never mind. No time for the time. Stella is here. Fuck, where is my suit?"

"Just put on your robe," Ari replied sharply. "You haven't got time for your suit. You have three minutes."

"Get downstairs," Sebastian ordered her. "No, wait, I need to talk to you—"

"Talk to me after Stella has gone. We need her to sign up for this wedding or the whole thing will be off. I'm going to go sit with Stella and her assistant in the gallery downstairs. Be down in one minute with the contract or—"

"Which assistant?" Sebastian interrupted, looking aghast. "Not Brandon?"

"He's Stella's assistant, of course he's here. And if you let your history with him become an issue—"

"What history? We don't have history."

Ari stared at him. "Didn't you and Luis have a threesome with him?"

Sebastian shrugged. "Brandon and Luis had some chemistry — I let them work it out. That's how you keep a successful marriage."

"Through threesomes?" Ari asked, raising an eyebrow.

"Don't sound so dismissive. It worked, didn't it? I won, didn't I?"

"It was a threesome. There isn't meant to be a 'winner' in a threesome."

"No? Then how come I won? Look, we don't have time for this. Get downstairs, delay Stella any way you can. I'll be right behind you."

Shaking her head, Ari quickly ran from Sebastian's room towards the stairs. She passed the room next to her own again, and this time she stopped, her mouth falling open when she saw the men applying a thin layer of pink paint to a wall. *Pink for a little girl,* she thought. Marnie was redecorating an entire room just for Reine. Stella was right, Ari realised. This was odd.

Shaking herself, she ran down through the house, searching the ground floor until she came across a room that could only be the gallery. It was long and well-lit by the morning sun, a parquet floor shining cleanly beneath her feet, while on the walls were hung dozens of paintings. This was what money could buy, Ari reminded herself, trying not to gape at the pictures on the wall. One glance told her that many of these paintings were priceless masterpieces, and she reasoned that Marnie's family had probably brought them over from Europe. Her passion for art suddenly flared, and she longed to take a long stroll through this room, absorbing the great art on the wall.

Business first, she reminded herself, tearing her eyes from the walls and walking towards Stella and Brandon, who waited by a window.

"Ari." Brandon grinned, swooping her into his arms, and Ari hugged him back. She liked Brandon. He was good-natured and warm-hearted, open and affable, the exact opposite of his formidable employer. How Stella had ended up with an assistant like Brandon, Ari could never work out. "Where's Reine?"

"On her way," Ari replied warmly. "It's good to see you, Brandon. Sebastian's coming."

Brandon blinked. "Yeah, of course he is, he—"

"—has exactly sixty seconds," Stella cut in icily. "I do have other plans today, Ms Lightowler."

"He'll be here, I promise," Ari said.

"Nice digs," Brandon said, gesturing around them. "It'll photograph well on the wedding day. Haven't done a wedding for ages. It'll be nice to fit one in."

"Well, the house is lovely, but the wedding itself will be in a field outside. A forest, actually—"

Ari stopped, her eyes suddenly caught by a flash of orange in the corner. Her arms dropped to her side. She froze, her mouth running dry and her heart picking up tempo.

"*What?*" Ari whispered, taking a tentative step towards the corner.

"You okay, Ari?" she heard Brandon ask her, but she waved her hand to quiet him.

Stella followed her, her sharp eyes watching Ari's until they settled on a painting in the darkest corner of the room.

A dark blue sea. A dark grey town. Whites and blues mixed with a sunset sky above. For a moment, Ari felt faint.

"That's a good painting," she heard Brandon say. "Atmospheric."

A good painting, Ari thought, staring at something she never thought she would see again. She stared at it silently, until she felt Brandon's hand on her shoulder. She watched as he ran a finger along the frame, tracing the name of the painting in a brass plaque underneath.

"*The Ends of the Earth*," he muttered. "Cool name."

Ari nodded, still frozen silent.

"No artist though," she heard Stella remark. "I wonder who painted it?"

Ari cleared her throat, searching for her voice. "I did," she answered finally, her words small. "It was me."

Next to her, she felt Brandon and Stella glance at each other.

"I don't understand," Ari said. "It was . . . it was a gift. He would never sell . . . he would never . . ."

"Brandon," Stella's voice was clear, cutting through Ari's anguished babbling. "Clear our schedule for the day and find me a camera."

"Are you sure? It's a packed calendar."

"I'm very sure," Stella replied. "I have this wonderful feeling that things here are about to get *very* interesting."

CHAPTER 8: GOLD FLECKS

There's no night in Tromsø. This close to the Arctic, there's just pure, unrelenting sunshine, from midnight to noon and back again, with light seeping in from every corner. And yet, despite the midnight sun, Tom sleeps. He sleeps and he sleeps and he sleeps, Ari held tight in his arms, her body a pleasant warm weight against his own. He can't remember the last time he slept so well, or for so long. He can't remember the last time he felt so light or free. He can't remember ever being happier, or more content.

Because he is happy, he realises with a feeling akin to shock. He is happy. He is content. He, Tom Somerset, has found happiness at last. That restless hunger and almost violent need for something, anything, away from the stifling home of his youth and the family name that weighed him down has finally gone. At last — at long, long last — he is free.

He transfers all his money from the bank accounts his trust fund set up for him into an old one from his teenage years, which he suspects Marnie has probably forgotten about. He closes the others quickly and sits back with a sigh. It's the first easy breath he's taken in years.

He and Ari go hiking in the nearby hills. They drink coffee in the town cafes. They go whale watching and paragliding. They spend hours in their hotel room, learning the secrets of each other's bodies. Tom loves every minute of these endless days and nights. He engraves them into his heart, brands them onto his soul and vows to remember them forever.

He sits for hours while Ari paints, and every canvas she discards, with a frown or a sigh, he secretly saves and posts to his New York home. What to Ari's eyes seems imperfect, with colours or a texture unlike how she envisioned in her head, to him seems wonderful. He knows little about art, knows little about the creative process or artistic temperament, but he recognises beauty. After all, he's with Ari, isn't he? She's the most beautiful thing he's ever seen, and to his mind her work is an extension of her. In the curves of her brushstrokes, he finds hints of her smile. She captures the colours of the ocean, but he sees only the blue of her eyes. In the rolling landscapes he recognises her soul. He can't bear to see any of her work discarded, and so he saves them all.

They travel from Norway into Sweden before rolling into Finland. From there, they debate their next move. He wants to go west, towards Denmark, while Ari wants to go south, towards the Baltic states.

"It's the Baltic," he says, by way of an explanation for his reluctance. "Isn't it cold there?"

"Says the man who just spent time in the Arctic." She laughs. "I'd like to go to Riga, actually. There's a special exhibition on there. About the eggs."

"Eggs?" Tom raises his eyebrow.

"The Fabergé ones," Ari explains, and then, at his continuing silence, looks aghast. "Oh, Tom . . . tell me you've heard of them?"

"The only eggs I know are the ones I have sunny-side-up in the morning," he answers wryly, and Ari stares at him.

"How can you not know about the Fabergé eggs? That's impossible."

"I told you . . . art was never my thing. You want to talk about cars and planes? Great. But art?" Tom sighs. "Well, I'm just not your man."

Ari rests her head on her hands, looking at him with those wide blue eyes that turn his insides to butter. "Tom," she says firmly, "you're my man regardless of whether or not you like art. You know that, right?"

He stares at her, his mouth suddenly dry. "Really?"

"Yes, of course," she replies earnestly. "Besides, I kind of like that you don't know about art. It means I get to teach you. Show you."

He smiles at her. "And you want to start with eggs?"

"Not just any eggs," Ari insists. "Fabergé ones."

He grins at her, reaching for his coffee and taking a long sip. "Okay, so what's so special about these Fabricate . . . Farber—"

"Fabergé," Ari corrects him with a grin. "They're surprise eggs. An outer layer with a surprise hidden within. They were made by Fabergé for the Tsars of Russia, who gifted them to their wives and mothers for Easter. They're beautiful. Works of art, all of them. Made with diamonds and rubies and gold and silver. Each one tells a story. Each one is an adventure."

Tom has to stop momentarily to take a breath, because when Ari talks about art, she glows with a happiness and passion that's so vibrant it's almost infectious. He reaches forward to brush his fingers down the pink blush to her cheek, and sighs.

"What is it?" Ari asks, looking at Tom with worry. "I'm talking too much, aren't I? People are always telling me I talk too much, especially about art, and . . ."

"No, no, Ari," Tom reassures her. "No, I was just thinking about you and me."

"About you and me?"

"Yeah. About how lucky I am."

She blushes again, and this time the pink to her cheek is deeper, though just as adorable. "You think it was luck that brought us together?"

"No," Tom explains. "Not luck . . . Fate."

"Fate?" Ari frowns. "You think it was fate?"

Tom nods, putting his coffee cup down and reaching for Ari's hands. "Do you know how long it takes for a volcano to form, or how long it takes for them to erupt?"

She shakes her head. "No."

"Hundreds of thousands of years," Tom muses. "Hundreds of thousands of years for the earth to create the funnel, and hundreds of thousands of years for it to fill with magma. And that's just to create the volcano . . . It then takes another ten thousand years for the pressure inside to cause it to erupt. Can you imagine that? You and me, Ari, we were half a million years in the making. Half a million years waiting to be in the same place at the same time, forced together through an act of nature."

Ari looks at him with soft eyes. "So, if we were brought together by fate, why are you lucky?"

"Because someone or something up there, or out there or wherever, thought I was worthy enough of you to send millions of tonnes of ash into the sky at the exact right moment to bring us together."

Ari squeezes his hand with her own. "I didn't know you were so sentimental."

"Neither did I," Tom replies wryly. "I guess you bring it out in me."

A slow smile creeps across her face. "With lines like that, you're lucky we're in a public place. If we were alone, I'd be all over you."

"Feel free to be all over me later," Tom grins, and Ari laughs back. The sound is like music to his ears. "Fuck it," Tom decides. "Let's go to Riga."

"Really?"

"Yes. I want to see these eggs of yours. Take another adventure with you."

"An egg is always an adventure," Ari replies immediately, her tone suddenly parrot-like. "It may be different each time."

"Right." Tom grins, and Ari swats at his hands.

"It was a quote, Tom. Oscar Wilde."

"I'm never going to remember that."

Ari gives him a shrug so cheeky and playful he suddenly wishes they were alone. "Maybe one day you will."

He can't help himself. He bends forward to kiss her, pressing his lips to hers for a long moment, relishing once again in the shape of them against his own. "An egg is always an adventure," he whispers.

"An egg is always an adventure," Ari whispers back. "Let's go and have some more of our own."

* * *

Sasha was distraught when she turned up at Tom's bedside, her face tear-stained and red.

"Your mother is such a *bitch*," she said viciously, plonking herself into the bucket-chair by his bed and crossing her arms. "I'm your fucking fiancée, but she got first visitation rights?"

"Well, once we're married—"

98

"I mean,. I'm going to be your *wife*," Sasha spat. "Does that mean nothing to her? For fuck's sake, I'm your *bride*."

"Yes, I know, but she's my mom."

"So?" Sasha asked. "You live with me, don't you? Honestly, the whole system is ridiculous. And she was here for *ages*. I mean, what were the two of you talking about? You never talk to your mom for that long."

Ari's name and face briefly crossed Tom's mind. Closing his eyes, he settled back on his pillows and took a deep breath.

"Nothing," he lied. "We didn't really talk about anything. She was just making sure I was okay. I am okay, by the way," he added, suddenly realising Sasha hadn't even asked. "They're keeping me in overnight, just as a precaution."

He saw her give him a quick, sharp glance. "Well of course you're okay," she said, matter-of-factly. "I have to say, I'm incredibly relieved you don't have any visible wounds or scars, Tom. That would have fucked up our wedding pictures completely."

He stared at her, a little shocked, and she blinked.

"And of course," she added, her voice sweeter, "I'm so glad you're okay. I was so worried about you. When they called and said the plane had crashed, my stomach just dropped. But you're okay, and you don't have any scars."

"No," Tom murmured quietly. "No scars."

Sasha gave a satisfied nod. "Good. Oh, and that's it, by the way. No more flying for you—"

Tom smiled at Sasha's concern for him even as he opened his mouth to protest.

"—until after the wedding. You can crash all the planes you want once Stella Snow has finished taking our photos, but until that moment, you keep your feet on the ground."

The smile dropped from Tom's face. "Fine," he agreed with a sigh. "Look, Sasha, I need to get out of this hospital. My mom has . . . Well, she's made a mistake and I need to rectify it and—"

"We got Stella Snow, did I tell you?" Sasha carried on, as though Tom hadn't even spoken. "Our new wedding planners

99

— you'll love one of them, by the way, he's divine, I'm sure we're going to be the best of friends—anyway, they pulled the rabbit out of the hat and not only managed to snag a Luis De León dress for me but a Stella Snow wedding shoot too. The wedding planners are miracle workers. I'm so lucky."

"You mean *we're* so lucky," Tom corrected her tiredly, and Sasha gave a shrug.

"Well, obviously. We found each other, didn't we?" she asked, sweet once more. "Fated to be together."

Tom paused, wondering why Sasha's words, still hanging in the air like her cloying perfume, suddenly sounded so ominous and vaguely threatening. He was probably tired, he decided. The crash and his mother's visit were catching up with him, and his mind was done for the day.

"I think I need to sleep," he announced, abruptly exhausted. "I was going to come home, talk to my mom . . . but I think I need to sleep first."

"Oh." Sasha looked slightly annoyed. "But I drove all this way."

"Come and get me tomorrow morning," he suggested, pulling a blanket over his legs. "I just need to sleep. I'd be no good to you tonight anyway, and—"

"I can't come and get you tomorrow," Sasha replied irritably. "Luis De León is arriving tomorrow, and I need to go over wedding ideas with . . . oh, what was her name, Ari something or other—"

"What did you say?" Tom snapped, sitting upright in his bed and staring at Sasha with dark eyes. "Who are you talking about? Who is Ari?"

Sasha looked at him sharply. "You are tired," she decided. "Ari is the wedding planner, silly."

Tom's heart pounded hard in his chest, his hands felt damp and sweaty. "Ari . . ." he said, in utter disbelief. "Ari who?"

"I don't know," Sasha shook her head, an odd look in her eyes. "She's from Queen and Country Weddings. Although now that I'm thinking about it, Ari might not even

100

be her name. It might have been Carrie. Or maybe Sally. I don't know, I didn't pay much attention to her. She didn't say anything of importance."

Tom sat back, suddenly feeling like a fool.

"Yeah," he muttered. "I shouldn't have . . . it doesn't matter."

But Sasha was still looking at him oddly, sharp curiosity in her face. "You jumped at the name Ari. Who was she?" she asked, her voice syrup sweet. "An old girlfriend?"

Tom, sensing danger in her words, set his face into carefully bland lines. "No," he shook his head. "She was just someone I, uh, worked with. Once upon a time. Besides, she's married now. Happily married."

"Oh," Sasha looked bored again. "Well, this Ari, or Carrie or whatever . . . She wasn't married. She's never been married."

Tom felt, once again, that sharp stab of disappointment. *When will it end?* he asked himself. *When will I forget?* But he shrugged to Sasha, trying his best to look nonchalant.

"Right," he said. "I guess it can't be her then. Look, Sasha, I really am tired—"

"Fine, fine." Sasha stood, stretching up on two elegantly heeled legs. "Look, I can't come and get you tomorrow. I'll get your mom to come and pick you up—"

"She won't come," Tom said bluntly.

"Right." Sasha nodded, without even asking Tom why. "Okay, so, rent a car then. Charge it to your mom though. I don't want to pay for it."

"I'll pay for it," Tom said, repressing a hot bolt of anger at Sasha. He needed to sleep before he said something he regretted. "It's not like we can't afford it, Sasha. And Mom is already paying for the wedding."

Sasha must have sensed his frustration, because her face abruptly softened, and she leaned towards him. "Look, I don't really care how you get back, just get back safely, okay?" She kissed him softly. "I don't like being away from you. It's an exciting time for us. We should be together."

101

Tom kissed her back. "It is an exciting time," he agreed, though his words sounded strangely flat.

"It really is. I can't wait for you to meet the wedding planners." Sasha straightened up. "And Luis De León is flying in . . . It's so wonderful, he's probably on his way right now, they said he was going to get the first flight he could." She gave Tom a broad, genuine smile. "I can't wait to meet him and start talking about my dream dress."

Tom couldn't help himself, returning Sasha's smile, enjoying her obvious display of excitement. She was so blunt and to-the-point normally, hardly ever allowing herself to show her true feelings. It was probably why they got along so well, Tom thought, with a rise of bitterness that took him by surprise.

"Don't worry about me," he told her honestly. "I'll get back somehow. You just make sure you enjoy yourself tomorrow with this wedding dress person—"

"Designer," Sasha corrected him, picking up her bag.

"Right, designer," Tom smiled at her. "It's our wedding, Sasha. I want you to be happy. It should be exciting. It should be an adventure."

Adventure. It was a word he associated with Ari, one that brought to his mind memories of sweet summer kisses and European cities and the smell of paint on slender fingertips. It was a word that made him both smile and sigh, a word that filled him with wistful longing and regret for times gone by. It was a word that he loved, but one that had been missing from his life for far too long.

Life with Sasha wasn't an adventure, he suddenly realised. Life with Sasha was one long road of hard tarmac with no turn-offs. He swallowed, uncomfortable. He didn't know where his mind was at today. Clearly the crash, and then his talk with his mother, had taken it out of him, or why else would he be like this?

"I need to sleep," he said again. "It's late."

"Well, you can blame your mother for that," Sasha shrugged. "I'll see you tomorrow, yeah? Try to be a little . . .

Well, *better* than you are right now. You need to meet the wedding planners and Luis De León tomorrow, and I want you to make a good impression."

"Right," he answered. "A good impression."

Sasha stopped at the flat tone to his voice, and she gave him a worried glance. "You are excited too, aren't you Tom?" she asked. "Look, I know I've been a nightmare recently. I know I've been preoccupied and distracted and probably not as nice to you as I can be. It's just that this is my wedding and—"

"Hey," Tom cut in softly, mollified by her conciliatory tone. "It's okay. I get it."

"Do you?" Sasha's voice was small.

"Yes," he said firmly. "It's a wedding, and you're a bride, and you're entitled to be a little bit extra before it all." He saw Sasha's face relax. "I'll try to be on my best behaviour tomorrow, okay?"

She nodded. "Great." Now her tone was bright and breezy, the tense moment between them almost forgotten. "Try and be back at your mom's place for lunch, okay? By all accounts Luis De León is a bit of a foodie, so I've asked the chef to prepare a quail egg salad."

Tom grimaced.

"You and eggs," Sasha rolled her eyes. "I'll never understand why you don't like them."

"It's not that I don't like them, it's just that I choose not to eat them."

"Well, you'll just have to put up with them tomorrow. I want Luis De León to see how cultured we are. We need to serve an adventurous dish."

"Like eggs?" Tom asked wryly.

"Exactly," Sasha answered, clearly missing the sarcasm in his voice. He watched as she applied a thick layer of lipstick.

"Well," he added, "I guess an egg is always an adventure — it may be different each time."

He'd spoken the words without even thinking, and the moment they left his lips he sat back, stunned. Ari's face, her satin skin dusted pink and her beautiful smile immediately crossed his mind. Longing, painful and hot, struck him hard.

He missed her so much.

Next to him, Sasha rolled her eyes. "You and eggs," she said again. "Get some sleep and I'll see you tomorrow."

* * *

After a restless night, Tom discharged himself as early as he could from the hospital, before the sun had even begun to rise. He gathered his things and took an Uber to the nearest Avis. He rented a small car for the rest of the week, figuring it was probably a good idea to have two vehicles. He knew that if Sasha's dress design session didn't go well, she would refuse to leave until it did. For Tom, that was an unpalatable thought. He didn't want to linger at his mother's house, didn't want to have time to wallow in the past when he could bury himself in work and the grime of the city.

With a sigh, he started on the long road to his mother's place, watching as the small town near where she lived turned into long and winding country roads. About twenty minutes from home, a car ahead stood stationary on the road, hazards flashing, and Tom slowed. A man waved him down, a cell phone clutched in his hand, but Tom carried on past him. Sasha would kill him if he was late for the wedding planners, would kill him if he missed playing the happy groom for the wedding designer, and he couldn't afford to invoke any more of her ire. He felt a momentary flash of guilt, because under normal circumstances he would stop and assist, but right now he was tired and feeling more than a little blue, and he didn't want another fight with Sasha to pull him down further.

Tom glanced in the rearview mirror and abruptly swore, pulling his car to a sudden stop. Behind the stationary vehicle, sitting on the grass verge with her head resting on her knees, was a little girl. She was small and tired-looking, and Tom swore again before he opened his door, stepping out onto the grass.

A lone traveller he was happy to ignore, but not a kid. Tom knew that in this part of the world they might be by the side of that road for hours waiting for roadside services, and, at heart, he was a good guy. He didn't like to see children suffer.

He plastered a fake smile on his face and headed to the man he'd passed earlier. "Can I help at all?" he asked.

"Oh, thank God," the man replied, grinning at him. "I thought you were gonna drive right past us, to be honest."

"No, not me," Tom lied, feeling more than a little ashamed. "What's up?"

"The car stopped, and my phone doesn't work here," the man explained. "Any chance I can use yours to call the rental office?"

"It's a rental?" Tom asked.

"Yeah, we just got into town," the man said, scratching his head tiredly. "It's been a long journey, and we're exhausted. Do you mind if I use your phone? I can pay you for the call and . . ."

"No, that won't be necessary. Here." He handed over his cell.

The man grinned again, and something about his smile, something about his face and the handsome curves to his cheek, made Tom stop.

"Have we met before?" Tom asked slowly, but the man shook his head.

"No, I don't think so."

"Oh," Tom said, rubbing his eyes. "It's just . . . you look familiar to me. I don't know where to place you though."

The man gave him another smile. "Well, I am kind of, well, famous, in my field."

"Oh. That must be it."

He must be an actor, Tom decided. A man that handsome, that ruggedly well-built, with a megawatt smile like he had, was made for the screen. He'd probably seen him on one of those terrible Netflix shows Sasha liked to watch.

Tom watched as the man punched in a number and held the phone to his ear. When he started to speak, giving details about his journey and the problem with the car, Tom remembered the little girl behind the vehicle and turned to her.

Surprisingly, she was looking up at him, and something about her eyes, about the curve of her face, made him pause again.

"Hey," he said.

"Hello," she replied, in a soft voice, a voice that was childlike and silky and British, of all things.

"You're English," Tom remarked, thoroughly confused. Because the man she was with, a man who Tom could now hear speaking rapidly in Spanish, had all the markings of an American accent.

"Yes," she replied, still staring up at him with those eyes. They were unnervingly familiar to him, so big and wide, the brown of her irises flecked with gold. Her hair hung in honey-coloured waves around her face, and faint freckles dotted her nose. Tom's stomach felt tight, his skin inexplicably hot, and he stared at her.

"Are you all right?" the girl asked him suddenly. "You look pale."

"I was, uh, in an accident yesterday."

"Oh."

"I crashed a plane," Tom added, even though there was no need to say anything further.

"Did it break?"

"What?"

"The plane," she clarified, giving him a wary look.

"Uh, no, well . . . nothing I can't fix. I'm good with planes," he told her, and she crossed her arms over her legs.

"I thought you just said you crashed one?" she queried, and Tom's stomach flipped again. Something about her face, about the way she spoke, was familiar to him, in the same way her father had been. Was she an actress too? he wondered. A child one? With a famous father, that sounded right.

Relieved without knowing why, he nodded sagely. "The weather was against me yesterday. I flew into a storm."

106

She nodded. "We flew in this morning. There were no storms though."

"You flew in?" Tom asked her.

"From London," she explained, before peering at him. "Have you been?"

"To London? No. Not for a long time, anyway." He swallowed, staring at her eyes once more, wondering where he'd seen them previously. "That's a big journey for a girl like you."

"Yes," she said, and there was a hint of ruefulness to her voice that made Tom sit up. "I'm really hungry now. I haven't eaten since the plane. We were supposed to get breakfast but then the car stopped working."

"I'm sorry," Tom replied.

"Do you have anything to eat?" she asked him curiously. "I like chocolate biscuits."

"I don't have anything. I was on my way home when I saw your dad's car and—"

"He's not my dad," the girl interjected. "He's my uncle."

Ah, thought Tom. That explained the difference, not only in their accents but also their looks.

"Right," he said. "Well, I don't have any food, I'm sorry."

The girl sighed, shifting her head and trailing her hand over the grass. "I guess I'll just have to be hungry then."

There it was again, that odd flash of recognition running through him. Tom stopped, staring at the girl before him. She was achingly familiar, and not just her eyes, and the shape of her face, but the way she spoke too. The way she turned her head and moved her hands and wrinkled her nose.

"Hey," Tom said, shifting his feet. "About ten miles down this road there's a diner. They serve the best waffles in the state. Get your uncle to take you there as soon as the car is fixed, okay?"

"Waffles?"

"They're really good," Tom continued. "You can have them with strawberries, or caramel, or cinnamon, or chocolate. Any way you choose."

She seemed to think about that. "I'm not supposed to have too much sugar. Mummy says it rots your teeth. I'm supposed to eat healthy things only."

"Like spinach?"

"Or broccoli, or cabbage, or boiled eggs." The girl wrinkled her nose again. "But I don't like any of them."

"I hate eggs as well," Tom replied. "They're horrible."

The girl nodded. "Mummy says they're an adventure, that each one might be different, but I don't think *adventure* is supposed to taste like old socks or—"

"What did you say?" Tom's heart suddenly pounded hard in his chest. He stared at the girl again, at the gold flecks in her eyes, and his chest grew tight.

But the girl abruptly seemed cowed by his burst of energy. "I'm not supposed to talk to strangers," she said primly, standing and walking away from him.

"You said an egg is an adventure, right?" he asked her, and he couldn't keep the edge from his voice. "What's your mom's name? Where is she?"

"*Tío,*" the girl said, moving towards the man from earlier. "*Tío, este hombre me está asustando.*"

Spanish, Tom thought hurriedly. She was speaking in Spanish. The man looked up from Tom's phone sharply, quickly taking the girl's hand and pulling her to him.

"*Qué te pasa,* Sunshine? *Te está molestando?*"

"*Sí. Está preguntando por mamá. Aprendimos sobre el peligro de los extraños en la escuela. Es un extraño y percibo el peligro.*"

The man shot Tom a filthy look. "Look, I'm glad you're helping us out, but you're scaring my girl here. Keep your distance, hey?"

"I just want to know about her mom, okay? Look, the two of you . . ." Tom shook his head. "You both seem really familiar to me. If I could just know about her mom, then I . . ."

"Then what? I told you, I'm a little bit famous. You've seen me in a magazine or something."

"Yeah, fine," Tom snapped. "But I recognise your niece too. Something about her eyes and face and the way she talks and—"

108

Tom stopped, as realisation dawned on him. His mouth gaped open, and his heart seemed to stop within his chest.

"Oh my God," he breathed out. "Oh my God."

The girl was looking up at him from the safe confines of her uncle's arms, and Tom stared back at her. Suddenly, he knew exactly where he'd seen her eyes before — those brown eyes flecked with gold.

It had been in every mirror he'd ever looked at.

They were his eyes, he suddenly realised. This girl had his eyes.

CHAPTER 9: SPERM JACKPOT

She tries not to let it bother her that she knows so little about him. Tries not to let it show how worried she is that he shares so little of himself with her. Tries not to fret that after weeks and weeks of travelling, living and sleeping with this man, he's still nothing more than a closed book to her.

It's not that she feels unloved. With Tom, she feels anything but that. His love for her is written into the touch of his hand, into the press of his kisses and into the sheer, unadulterated adoration that seems to seize his eyes whenever he follows her with his gaze. He looks at her with a fierce possessiveness that makes her feel wanted and whole — when she walks into the room, he lights up with a glow that makes her feel happy and proud.

At first, that pride surprises her. Because why should she feel proud for merely invoking a feeling of happiness in a man? It's so simple a feeling, happiness. So easy and universal. So primitive that she shouldn't see it written in the face of her lover and then feel a rise of pride that she — she, Ari — made it happen. When she sees Tom light up with happiness, her pride feels both unearned and yet deserved. Unearned because he should be happy, with or without her presence, Ari thinks. And yet . . . and yet, she also relishes in the knowledge that she's brought him a moment of joy. Deep down, Ari suspects that Tom has not been a happy man, that joy has been hard-won by him, and that happiness has eluded his life.

She suspects but doesn't know.

Because he never talks about himself, beyond the day-to-day conversations of their lives. They talk about the world, and their travels, and the food they eat and the sex they have and the politics of the day and so many other mundanely amazing things that Ari's head struggles to remember it all. She talks about herself, only a little at first, until she grows in confidence and opens up a little more. In the absence of any stories from him, she tells him all of her own, starting from the first memories of her life to the day they met. She tells him about finding her love for art aged seven in a London gallery, staring at Van Gogh's **Sunflowers.** *She tells him about the day her cat was hit by a car and Ari watched it die in the street, the feline's eyes panicked and frantic as it gasped for breath, before they finally turned glassy, all life having ebbed from its broken body. She even tells Tom about her parents, about their xenophobia and homophobia and how they'd reacted when her older brother came out.*

"They kicked him out," she whispered. "He was seventeen. I was six. He visited me as often as he could, but my parents were relentlessly intolerant. When he asked me to be bridesmaid at his wedding, my parents wouldn't allow it. I snuck out of the house to be there, and when I got back, they'd changed the locks. All my things were by the side of the road."

"That's awful," Tom replied, aghast, suddenly thankful for Marnie. He was fairly certain his mom would love him no matter what.

"They'd had enough of me, I guess," she said sadly, looking up to find Tom's eyes ablaze with anger on her behalf. His fists were clenched, and his frown was deep, and she leaned over to kiss his knuckles, to bring him out of his fury and back to her.

"It's okay," she whispered. "I don't need them. I don't miss them. I only feel sorry for them, now."

"No child should be treated like that," he returned fiercely, and it suddenly crossed Ari's mind that perhaps — just perhaps — Tom might have had a life story a little like her own.

"Were your parents like mine—" she began, before Tom abruptly stood.

"The museum will be open now." He pulled her up and threw a handful of notes on the table for the server.

111

He's good at deflection, Ari learns. So good that often she didn't realise he'd deflected a question until she replayed the conversation hours later in her head. He's good at evasion and deflection and silence. He's good at all the things that make her worry and wonder, while she tosses and turns in his arms at night.

"Who are you?" she whispers to him, staring at his slack and peaceful face, beautiful even in sleep. "Who are you, Tom? Where are you from? Who are your people, beyond me?"

She desperately wanted to know. These questions played on her mind, plaguing her so that she slept badly and ate poorly. Who was this man she'd taken into her life and bed and heart? All she really knew about him was that he was an American, a pilot and a magician. A magician, Ari mused. Wasn't magician just another word for trickster? This thought made her stop and pause. It worried her to think that she loved a man who only offered her his shell. It worried her that she loved him without really knowing him. Would she still love him if he shared everything else too? Would she still take him into her heart? Or would she turn from him? Or even hate him?

Together they travel across the Baltic states, before crossing the water from Lithuania to Denmark. Tom keeps his passport in his backpack, bringing it out only when they cross borders, before furtively stashing it away once more.

"Why don't you want me to see it?" Ari asks him curiously, and he gives her a strange shrug.

"I, well, it's just a——" He pauses. "A bad photo," he finishes, a little lamely. She nods, accepting the answer, though she keeps her eyes firmly locked on the sea. She's not a fool, and she heard the odd lilt to his voice when he spoke. A lilt that made her question the truth of his words.

Still, she says nothing, choosing to bury herself again in his arms and in the happiness she knows they share when together. Maybe Tom isn't the trickster, she thinks to herself bitterly. Maybe she is, though her only victim is herself. A simple wave of a magic wand, the turn of the right card and she can and will fool herself into believing anything Tom tells her. It's the trick of the century — the blink-and-you'll-miss-it lie in the dark. And she falls for it every time, because she loves him, and she knows he loves her too. He loves her, and tricks or not, she knows he would never deliberately hurt her.

Ari has so little experience of love in her life. So little experience of happiness. And so she tries to console herself, even when she hears Tom deflect, evade or lie in his silence. They are happy. They are in love. Their happiness and love cannot be deflected or evaded or silenced, even if Tom and the man he is can be.

It has to be enough for her.

She's starting to learn that, with Tom, there won't be anything else.

Denmark is a pleasant country, clean and floral and populated by generally cheerful and open-minded people. Ari and Tom spend two weeks there, soaking in the Northern European charm. One night Tom takes Ari to a tiny restaurant in Copenhagen, so small it hardly fits four tables, where they drink wine by candlelight and eat frikadelle and oysters. Afterwards, he takes her back to their hotel and strips her of her clothing, piece by piece, running his hands over her skin with disbelief at each new patch of skin that's revealed to him.

"You are so beautiful," he whispers against her, his lips brushing over her body so that she erupts into thousands of goosebumps. "You are so perfect. I can't believe you let me touch you like this. I can't believe you let me anywhere near you."

Later, when she's lying naked in his arms, content and sated, she can brush her worries aside. In those moments, she knows she'll take Tom any way she can have him. Even if it's just like this, nothing more than a string of romantic moments with a man she hardly knows.

A man she hardly knows but loves more than she can say.

Once they've exhausted Copenhagen, once she's painted and discarded another three canvases and restocked her supplies, the old, inevitable question again rears its head: where next?

"Switzerland," Ari says eagerly one afternoon. "We can go through the Netherlands, Belgium and Germany into Switzerland."

"More eggs?" Tom asks with an easy, playful grin, and she returns his smile.

"No. But the art . . . Oh, Tom, you've never seen such art. The architecture in Switzerland alone is worth a visit. We could even visit the Alps and see snow."

"And the chocolate?" he asks.

"Why? You like it?"

He shrugs. *"It depends on what's being served with it."* He gives her a long, hot gaze that brings colour to her cheeks. *"You'd look good in chocolate,"* he says lightly, though his words are heavy with promise. *"I'd lick every last drop from you."*

She bites on her lip. *"Yes,"* she agrees slowly. *"Let's go to Switzerland. For the chocolate."*

He nods, and she settles into his arms, letting him trace patterns on her arm.

"Maybe we could pop over the border from Switzerland into France," she suggests. *"We could go to Rouen, see the Musée des Beaux Arts de Rouen—"* She stops, noticing that Tom has stiffened behind her, his arm rock still, the veins in his hands showing.

"What?" she asks worriedly. *"Is something the matter?"*

"No, it's nothing, it's just . . ." Tom pauses, a strange look settling on his face. *"My mother's family comes from France."*

"Oh," Ari says, her heart suddenly racing at the knowledge that he just shared something with her. Something of him, of his past. Ari pauses. Tom has a mother. A mother with a French background. In the absence of any other real information, it feels like a staggering intimacy. *"You, um, never talk about your family."*

He shrugs then, as if it's no matter, and perhaps it isn't. Not to him.

"My cards . . . the queen of spades . . . that deck is from Rouen," Tom admits, and Ari nods, soaking the information in.

"I didn't know," she replies. *"I should give the queen of spades back to you . . . I should . . ."*

"No," Tom says suddenly, his voice firm. *"That card belongs to you now."*

"But it belonged to your family . . ."

"Yes, it did. But I gave it to you. I want you to have it." He pauses. *"I like that you have it."*

"Have you ever been to Rouen?" she asks curiously, and he shakes his head.

"No. My mother never saw the point. She doesn't look back, my mom. Just like my brother."

"You have a brother?" Ari asks curiously, and Tom nods, but his eyes have gone dark.

"Yeah. But he's . . . a little odd."

"Odd? Odd how?"

"Just odd," Tom replies, before he stands abruptly. "Let's go out for dinner. Have a final meal in Copenhagen before we head for Holland."

"But is your brother, like, I don't know . . . mentally incapacitated? Or is he—"

"Ari," Tom says, "let's go out for dinner. I'm hungry." He pulls her to him roughly. "And after dinner," he adds languidly, "I'd like to eat some chocolate."

"But just tell me if—"

He silences her with a kiss, his mouth hot, hard and insistent against her own.

Ari's not a fool. She knows what this is. It's deflection, evasion and silence, wrapped in the sweetest package. And Ari tries to pretend at this moment that it doesn't bother her, that this doesn't worry her.

But it does. Because she wants to love more than a shell.

She wants to love the whole man . . . whoever this stranger might be.

* * *

She stared at the painting and felt strangely dead inside. Empty of everything, all emotion having fled at the simple sight of a Norwegian sunset caught in blended shades of acrylic. She could recall, with perfect clarity, the cool northern breeze on her face and the clean smell of the fjords in her nose. She could still feel Tom beside her, his voice warm as he said, with confidence and pure conviction, *"Ari, the painting is good."*

She gave this painting to him. She gifted it to him, this canvas, a little piece of her heart and soul. She *gave* it to him, and yet here it now sat, forgotten and alone, in a cold and dark corner of this gallery.

He abandoned it, Ari realised. Abandoned this painting, just like he did her.

"He sold it," she whispered, her voice little more than a shadow. "He sold it."

Behind her, she heard a voice clearing. A hand on her back, calm and reassuring. Sebastian. She felt him step forwards, a manicured hand resting on her shoulder.

"Ari, love," he said kindly. "I don't think he did."

She turned to him, anguish in her eyes. "What do you mean?"

For a moment, Sebastian chewed on his lip. It was, she knew, a sign of his uncertainty, because she did it too. In fact, it must have been an old family trait, because Ari had a vague memory of their mother doing the same. Sebastian was a great believer in appearances, a man for perfection and order. With Sebastian, there was never a hair out of place, or a word spoken unnecessarily. His suits were always pressed, and his shoes always shone. His nails were perpetually clean and his eyes bright. If she had to put money on it, Ari would have bet that — underneath his designer vests and underwear — Sebastian's body was as smooth and hairless as a sphynx cat, or maybe a baby seal. He did moisturise, after all.

"So, it's a good news day and a bad news day." Sebastian finally spoke, his voice brightening.

Ari stared at him incomprehensibly. "What?"

He paused. "Well, there's good news and there's bad news and—"

"Sebastian," Ari interrupted. "I heard you. I just don't have the foggiest what you're talking about."

"Okay, right." Sebastian nodded, brushing an invisible piece of lint from his shoulder. "Just hear me out for a moment, will you?"

Ari gave him a wary look. "You only say things like that when you're about to say something I don't like."

"Oh no," Sebastian said, straightening. "It's fine. Like I said, it's bad news *and* good news."

Ari gave a tired sigh. "Okay. So, tell me the bad news first."

Sebastian nodded. "We're in this gorgeous house. The wedding is in the bag. The mother of the groom has already paid the first part of what is going to be a most *sizeable* bill,

116

and the bride is ecstatic with me, her soon-to-be-designed dress and the photographer we've managed to get onboard."

Ari watched as Sebastian winked at Stella behind her back.

"I asked for the bad news first," she snapped, trying to bring him back to the bloody point.

"Well, that's the thing," Sebastian carried on slowly. "All this is the bad news, because the sour pickle in the sweet jar here, my darling, is that you appear to not only have slept with the groom, but also to have borne the fruit of his loins."

Ari's mouth dropped open. "Are you . . . what do you . . . I mean . . ." she stammered, searching for thought, reason and clarity. "I . . . you said there was good news too."

"Oh, there is. Darling," there was an uncharacteristic squeak to his voice, which made Ari take a step back, "the groom is fucking *loaded*, my love. Have you seen this place? Do you know just how much money you've shagged your way into? My God, the retrospective child support alone will be worth millions. Oh, my darling," Sebastian ran a proud, tender hand down Ari's cool cheek, "you couldn't have picked a better man to be humped and dumped by. You really did hit the sperm jackpot with this one. Brava, my lovely."

Behind her, Ari heard the click of a camera.

"Brandon," she heard Stella intone bluntly, "take a note of the time and the name of the corresponding photograph. *Sperm Jackpot.*"

Horrified, Ari shook her head. "Can you all just . . . just *stop* for a moment." She took a deep breath, trying to stay calm, searching for the logic in this nightmare. "Sebastian, you don't know what you're talking about," she said slowly. "I've never even met this . . . this *Tom Somerset*. I've never met him before in my life."

"Well, maybe you did," Sebastian shrugged. "Back when he went by the name *Tom Miller*."

Ari's heart thudded in her chest, a vague feeling of nausea swept over her. "That's . . . that's quite a leap to make,

117

Sebastian. You don't know anything about the groom . . . this . . . this Tom Somerset. You don't know anything about him at all. And," an icy snap creeped into her voice, "you don't know anything about Tom Miller."

She watched as Sebastian gave a long sigh, a look of pity in his eyes as he gazed at her. "Ari, my darling, neither do you."

It was like poison being thrown over her skin — Ari recoiled from her brother.

"Ari," Sebastian carried on calmly, "listen to me and listen to me carefully. We've been here just a few days, and yet the mother of the groom has developed an unhealthy interest in you and particularly in your child. So much so that she's just redecorated an entire bedroom to accommodate her. Doesn't that strike you as odd? I had a discussion with her last night, and she all but told me that her son Tom Somerset is Reine's father."

Ari froze. "She said that?"

"Well, not in those exact words, but—"

"So, she didn't say it," Ari interrupted him. Relief poured through her as she clung to a final thread of hope. "Of course she didn't. It isn't true. Tom would never do that to me. Do this to me."

Sebastian chewed on his lip again, regarding her with a new hint of annoyance. "You knew Tom Miller for what, all of a few months? And in the eight years since you last met, you've heard diddly squat from him. You told me and Luis that you gave him your name, your number, your life story . . . He's had ample opportunity to find you, like he promised he would. Ari, it's time you accepted the fact that he's broken that promise. That—"

"Sebastian," Ari cut in, her voice breaking, along with her heart.

"No, Ari, you listen to me," Sebastian said sternly. "He's broken that promise, which means one of two things. That he has something to hide, or he's dead. Regarding Tom Somerset, if you speak for any length of time with his mother, you find out quickly that he sure as hell has a shady past and something to hide."

"Maybe not. Maybe . . . maybe my Tom did die," Ari whispered, saying out loud a fear that had long settled in her heart. "I would never have known."

"No, he's not dead. He's Tom Somerset, who — despite falling out of the fucking sky yesterday — is emphatically not dead yet."

"Yet?" Ari asked.

"Yet," Sebastian said firmly. "Because if I find out Tom Somerset really did masquerade as a man named Tom Miller, seduce you, impregnate you and abandon you, I'm probably going to kill him."

At that, a brief smile crossed Ari's face. "Sebastian—"

"Oh, after we change his will in Reine's favour, darling," Sebastian said smoothly. "Trust me," he gestured to the hall around him, "we're going to want a piece of this."

Ari paused, considering his words. "Okay. So, say our groom is . . . is . . ." she struggled over the lump in her throat ". . . Tom Miller. There's no way to prove it, no way to know. Not without coming face to face with him, and I don't want that . . . I don't want to meet him again like this. As his *wedding planner.*"

"Hmm." Sebastian seemed to ponder this point for a moment. "Okay. So, let's do some digging. Do a little spy work. His mother has already started doing a little digging of her own, I'm convinced of it."

Ari felt a tug of worry. "Because of Reine . . . she wants to know because of Reine."

Sebastian nodded. "Because of Reine."

Ari exhaled deeply. "Reine can't come here — quick, call Luis. Tell him to stop the car. Tell him to check into a nearby hotel."

"I've already tried," Sebastian replied mournfully. "But his phone is out of reception, or service, or battery or something. I got a garbled message from him that he was having car trouble before the call cut out. Honestly, this is what happens when you buy a shitty Android, even though working to a joint iCalendar would make so much more sense for both of us."

"Sebastian, focus," Ari snapped. "Car trouble? So, they're probably stopped on a road somewhere? Right. I'm going to go and find them."

"Ari—"

"Sebastian, there is only one road that leads to this massive house, and Luis and Reine are bound to be on it. I'm going to find them. I have to find them. I can't let Reine walk into this . . . this situation."

"Ari—"

"She's my *daughter*, Sebastian," Ari said. "My daughter. I have to protect her."

Slowly, Sebastian nodded. "All right, fine. Take the car. Drive carefully. But first, something to eat and a drop of coffee."

Ari stared at him. "Breakfast? Really? Now?"

Sebastian stared right back at her. "Yes, really, now. Look, we're jetlagged, we're tired, we've been up for less than half an hour and it's already been a busy day. We've arranged a wedding photographer, looked at some nice art, found the ex-lover who fathered your child and then went missing for eight years . . . you need fuel, Ari. It would be irresponsible of me to let you drive on an empty stomach." He paused. "And irresponsible of me to keep giving advice without caffeine."

Ari frowned, but she heard some sense in her brother's words all the same. "Fine," she agreed. "But as soon as I've eaten, I'm out the door."

"Okay. And while you're gone, I'll—"

"You're going to find out if this Tom Somerset is really my Tom Miller," Ari told him firmly.

"Right," Sebastian said. "I'm going to stay here and find out if Tom Somerset is Tom Miller. Um . . . how?"

"However you can," Ari replied.

"However I can," Sebastian repeated, parrot-like. "Ari," he suddenly turned to her, one hand on her arm. "What if he is?"

A sharp stab of something that resembled pain, longing, betrayal and anticipation ran through Ari.

"I don't know," she replied honestly. "I just don't know."

"Don't worry about it for now. Worry about Reine. I'll do the dirty work here. I'm good at dirty work."

"You're the cleanest man I know," Ari said flatly.

"The cleaner I am, the dirtier I can become," Sebastian offered with a mock salute. "I'll think of some way to catch him, don't you fret."

Ari nodded, turning back to the painting in the corner. "Ask him about this," she said softly. "Ask him how this painting ended up here."

"I would, but I think I already know the answer to that."

Ari looked at Sebastian quizzically, and he sighed.

"Ari, you told Luis and I that Tom always said your work would hang next to the greats, and just *look* at this gallery. Look at it. Holbein, Picasso, Dali . . . and you. Tom Miller might have broken one promise to you, Ari, but he kept this one. You are hanging next to the greats. *He* hung you next to the greats."

Ari closed her eyes, remembering once again the softness of Tom's face as he gazed at her. She remembered the feel of a brush in her hand as she caught the pink and orange glow of a sunset. She remembered Tom's pride in her work, his fierce belief that she would be an artist, and a great one at that. She remembered those golden flecks in his brown eyes, which shone even more brightly when settled in her direction.

When she opened her eyes again though, all she could see was Reine, and the golden flecks in *her* brown eyes. The eyes she'd inherited from her father.

Ari swallowed hard. She had to go and get her daughter. She had to find her.

CHAPTER 10: FERTILE SPECIMEN

Tom's mind was working overtime — every muscle in his body was tight and on edge. Nausea had settled in his stomach, causing waves of sick nervousness to wash over him, a sheen of sweat sticking to his skin.

An egg is always an adventure, he thought worriedly, hearing the words over and over and over in his mind, once again recalling the image of a girl with honey-coloured hair and his own brown eyes staring up at him.

It can't be, he told himself, taking a corner a little too fast and hardly feeling the angry spin to the rental car's wheels. *It just can't.*

He'd known Ari had had a baby. He'd seen the child for himself, held tight in her father's arms — *Ari's husband's arms,* Tom reminded himself bitterly — a pink rabbit in her hand, her face tucked under her father's chin. She'd been small and delicate, and Tom had stared at her, wondering how baby-soft skin could cut him so deep. The man who held her had looked at him oddly, and Tom had quickly noted the wedding ring he wore, and the litany of pictures on the wall behind him. He was in every one of them. His presence told him, loud and clear, that Ari had moved on, and quickly too. Clearly Ari hadn't missed him like he'd ached for her.

She probably hadn't loved him at all — had no doubt relegated him from lover to the beginning of some tawdry story starting with, *"Did I ever tell you about this one guy in Europe . . ."*

She promised to wait for him, but she'd broken that promise. It was a fact that still caused torrents of pain to cut through Tom, a bitter pill he'd swallowed over and over, the worst kind of medicine for his tortured soul. Ari had married, had a baby and moved on. Tom, after grieving her loss, decided to do the same. He couldn't have the woman he wanted, but he could still have a good life, maybe. A shadow of what it could have been, perhaps, but still worthy, still his. It was what his father had wanted, after all. What his father had asked of him on his deathbed. *Live your life for you, Tom. Don't ever live it for anyone else.*

Tom was so lost in thought that, as he turned into the gates of his mother's house, he nearly smashed into a car flying fast in the other direction. He slammed on his brakes, turning to swear and glare at the offending vehicle. But it was already sweeping down the drive and into the trees, and Tom exhaled tightly, shaking his head.

"Learn to drive," he growled, turning back to the wheel.

He needed to speak to his mother. Uneasily, Tom recalled their conversation from the previous day, when Marnie had asked about Ari, then stormed out when he'd casually mentioned knowing about Ari's baby. *She thought the baby was mine,* Tom realised. *She thought it was mine, and that I abandoned her.*

That thought made Tom's stomach turn, because if there was one thing he swore he'd never do, it was to abandon his own child. He'd heard Ari's stories of her own miserable parents. Tom might have done some shitty things in his day, but not *that.* When he became a father, it would be for keeps.

Once again, Tom's mind dragged forth the image of the baby in Ari's husband's arms. She'd been a sweet little thing, and for a moment Tom's heart leapt in his chest at the thought of having fathered her, of *being* a father to her. What must that be like? What would it be like to come home to a house where Ari was his wife and their child snuggled into his shoulder, her baby arms around his neck and her pink rabbit in her hands?

It was a useless dream though. She was another man's child, and her mother was another man's wife. Tom had to accept it.

Taking a deep breath, Tom stared at the wheel of the car, still tightly gripped in his hands. He would speak with Marnie and clear the air with her. Tell her the truth — that yes, Ari had had a baby, but no, it wasn't his. And as for the girl on the side of the road earlier . . . Tom shook his head at his own stupidity. How many children had brown eyes? Millions upon millions of them. That this little girl had eyes like his own didn't mean anything, not when seventy percent of the world shared them too. It was still that damned lingering strand of hope within him. Tom scowled. He'd had Ari on his mind, and when he'd met that little girl he'd put two and two together and made six. So what if she'd quoted Wilde? Big deal. Every British child did that, right? And even if they didn't, there was no way that he'd fathered a child with Ari. It was impossible.

He was just a perpetual fool, Tom realised. A perpetual fool who needed some calm and quiet after the stresses of the last twenty-four hours. Thank God, at least here at his mother's house he could — well, not quite *rest*, that wasn't the word. He could never really rest here. Still, it was quieter than the city, and given that Sasha would be busy with her dress designer and the wedding planners, he would have lots of time to sit and switch off his fevered mind. His mother's house was so out of the way, so lost in the countryside, so peaceful and—

A loud noise to his left interrupted Tom's thoughts, and he looked up, blinking in confusion at the sight before him. A large yellow excavator was slowly passing him, beeps sounding, a man in a hard hat carefully edging towards the house.

124

Tom stared at it, then stared some more. *An excavator?* he thought, rubbing his eyes. *What the fuck is an excavator doing here?*

He stepped out of the rental car, looking around and doing another double take. Because his mother's house, normally so pristine and out of the way and peaceful, was absolutely *heaving*. There must have been a dozen cars and at least twenty people, most of them men, most of them wearing yellow jackets and carrying ladders, buckets of paint or pouring over design plans. They all looked busy and purposeful, and Tom dazedly approached the nearest person, gesturing around him.

"What's going on?" he asked, just as a drill sounded in the distance, the noise cutting into the air and drowning out Tom's words.

"What?" the worker shouted back, and Tom stepped closer, raising his own voice.

"What's going on? With all this?" he shouted, and the worker nodded.

"Oh, we're building the playground," he yelled, and Tom stared at him.

Playground?

Mercifully, the drilling abruptly stopped, and Tom took a deep breath. "Sorry," he offered a tired smile, "for a minute there I thought you said you were building a playground."

"That is what I said," the worker replied cheerfully. "It's a rush job though. Are you one of the designers?"

"Designers?"

"For the playground."

Tom's face must have remained blank, because the helmeted man suddenly smiled. "Oh, sorry, you must be one of the decorators. Well, your lot are all inside, working on the bedroom."

"Bedroom? What bedroom?"

"I don't know. I'm not a decorator. I'm building a playground today. Although playground doesn't feel like the right word, given that the owner wants a small-scale stone castle in the middle."

125

A small-scale stone castle? Tom swallowed hard. *Why the fuck is Mom building a playground?*

Shaking his head, he walked away from the worker, picking his way through equipment scattered over the gravel drive. He headed to the entry of the house, walking in and by habit wiping his feet on the mat by the door.

"Mom!" he shouted. "Mom! Where are you? I need to speak with you! Mom! I'm home, I'm here, and I'm—"

A sudden flash of light snapped in front of Tom's face, and he blinked at the onslaught, clutching his head in his hands.

"And I'm *blind*," he snarled, rubbing at his eyes, wondering whether his retinas had detached or simply seared themselves to the back of his skull. Peeling his fingers from his forehead, he blinked as his vision slowly returned, the image of a person, tall and intimidating, taking shape before him.

"Hello Jawline," a razor-sharp voice intoned, and Tom stiffened. He knew that voice. Knew it all too well, having spent six hours in its owner's presence while being shifted from position to position so she could 'capture the best light'.

"Hello," he said formally, his face instantly falling into a scowl. "How nice to see you again. I didn't think I would, to be honest, after the last shoot we did together."

"Ah, yes, the *Forbes* shoot," the woman replied drily.

"Yes," Tom said tightly, "the one where you said the light 'just didn't favour me'. That was a pleasant day."

"It was, wasn't it?" The woman nodded, either not hearing the sarcasm in Tom's voice or choosing to ignore it. "You would think with a face like yours you'd photograph beautifully. Your mother has cheekbones to die for, after all. But no." She looked at him without really looking at him, her icy eyes trailing critically over his face. "You're all angles I can't make work—a jigsaw with too many jagged edges. There's no softness in you. Of all the limited disappointments in my career, your face has been the greatest."

"Thank you," Tom said again. "So, dare I ask why you're even here?"

She gave him a sideways glance, her lips unnervingly still as she spoke. "Why, I'm your wedding photographer. Your fiancée specifically requested me."

Tom felt every muscle in his body grow tense. *Stella Snow*, he thought miserably, hardly believing her words. *She* was going to be their wedding photographer? How had this been allowed to happen? Tom couldn't stand the woman — hated being around her with the fire of a thousand blazing suns. Surely Sasha knew that? But even as he asked himself the question, the answer settled in his mind.

Sasha didn't know about his issue with Stella, and why would she? Tom had never mentioned it, and yesterday, when Sasha had brought Stella up, he'd been so wrapped up in his own troubles he hadn't paid her the slightest bit of attention. Under normal circumstances, he would never have agreed to this. But because of his own ridiculousness, because of his own distraction, he'd blindly walked into allowing Stella back into his life. Scowling at his own ineptitude, he drew in a shaky breath.

"How nice," he said through gritted teeth. "I'm sure my mother will be thrilled."

"Less so when she gets my bill, I should imagine," Stella remarked coolly. "Speaking of which, you still owe me a box of chocolate biscuits."

"Chocolate biscuits?" Tom asked, puzzled, wondering why everyone seemed to be speaking in nothing but fucking riddles this weekend. "You mean a cookie? Why would I owe you a box of cookies?"

Stella stared at him with an even expression. "Whenever I photograph a Queen and Country wedding, I need the biscuits. The small invariably pops up, and she—"

Abruptly, Stella stopped speaking, staring at Tom with an even more intense expression. She stepped closer to him, peering into his eyes closely.

"Do you have a problem?" Tom asked quietly, unnerved by the clear blue eyes Stella had pointed like daggers on his own. "Do you—"

"How interesting," Stella remarked, though Tom instinctively knew she wasn't talking to him. "How very interesting."

"I don't know what you're—"

Another blinding flash snapped in Tom's face, and he recoiled, swearing loudly.

"Will you stop doing that?" he seethed. "You're going to blind me."

"Don't be such a baby." Stella shook her head dismissively. "Look, see?"

She held up her camera for him to glance at, and he found himself staring at an image of himself, caught by her lens. His eyes were wide, brown and glassy, his mouth caught in a round shape of surprise, his jaw unclenched and lax. He looked, Tom thought miserably, absolutely ridiculous.

"I'm going to call this one *Unknowing*," Stella said, her voice rich with self-approval. "And then later, after everything, I'm going to take another one and call that one *Knowing*. It will be a wonderful series, and you, my gormless boy, will be the star. The camera might hate you, but by God, the people will love you." She peered at him critically once more. "You know, I may just find that softness in you yet."

Tom stared at her. "You know half the time I have no idea what you're talking about."

Stella, however, didn't seem to hear him. "Isn't that nice," she replied absently, before shouting "Brandon!" and walking towards the gallery, her heels clicking on the polished marble floor.

Tom watched her go with a feeling of trepidation.

"Mom!" he shouted again. "Where are you?"

* * *

Tom found his mother in the study, the French doors thrown out to the garden, smoking cigarettes in his father's old armchair. Beside her, lying languidly on the chaise lounge, was a blond-haired man in a pressed suit, also smoking calmly. They were oddly silent and, after the fracas of the drive and

128

hallway, both oddly calm. They stared out into the garden with looks of absolute boredom on their faces, inhaling in tandem and blowing wispy plumes of grey smoke into the air.

"Mom! You're smoking again! What is going on today?" Tom snapped, and both his mother and the blond-haired man swivelled their heads towards him, looking at him with detached interest.

"Why, hello darling," his mother replied calmly, taking a final drag of her cigarette before stubbing it out in the nearby crystal-cut ashtray. "You're home from the hospital."

"Yeah," Tom muttered. "No thanks to you."

"You have Sasha, don't you?" his mother returned instantly. "I assumed she would take care of you."

Tom frowned, not wanting to drag Sasha into this. "I have Sasha," he said, "but you're my *parent*. Aren't you supposed to take care of me?"

At that, Marnie sat forward, a knowing look on her face. "Oh, you want to have *this* conversation?" she asked, her tone caustic, letting him know in no uncertain terms that he was going to regret ever having spoken. "Please, Tom, why don't you tell me exactly how a parent should care for their child? You're clearly the expert, after all."

"I know what you're thinking," Tom replied, "and you're wrong, you have it all wrong, you don't know—"

"I know enough," Marnie snapped back. "And I know a damn sight more about being a parent than you do, so I'll thank you to close your mouth on the subject."

Silence fell, heavy and oppressive. Tom kept his breathing calm, taking deep inhalations and releasing them slowly. He looked from his mother to the man beside her, who was sitting up now, staring at Tom with an air of concentration, holding his cigarette to his mouth between two manicured fingers. Distinctly uncomfortable with the man's intense gaze, Tom looked back to his mother.

"Mom," he said calmly, "maybe we can discuss this somewhere else. In private. I just need to tell you . . . the thing you were thinking yesterday, well, you were thinking wrong and—"

"I know exactly what to think," Marnie cut in, standing up and coming to stand by Tom's side. She smelled of cigarettes and her floral perfume, and she placed a hand gently on Tom's cheek. "And we will work this out. We're a family, after all. And no matter how lowly I think of you right now—"

"Mom," Tom pleaded, but she held up a hand to silence him.

"—no matter how lowly I think of you," she carried on. "I still love you dearly. Now, go and clean up. We're having a special brunch today. I've asked Chef to throw together some smoked salmon and poached eggs, followed up by a tarte Tatin."

"Brunch?" Tom exploded. "Brunch? Why are you so calm? You want to sit and eat fish and apple pie—"

"*Tarte Tatin*," the blond-haired man suddenly interrupted, stubbing out his own cigarette and standing. "Not apple pie. Please. Let's show a little class, hmm?"

Tom stared at him. "I don't even know *who you are*."

The blond-haired man nodded. "And I bet you don't know who Caroline and Stéphanie Tatin are either, but they just turned over in their graves at you calling their signature pastry an *apple pie*."

"Right." Tom looked at his mother desperately. "Mom, please. Please let's talk. It's like this house has hit the twilight zone. You're building a castle and playground outside—you have decorators upstairs and there are random British people dotted around like this is the Royal Shakespeare company. Please talk to me."

Marnie sighed, giving Tom a small pat on the shoulder. "Oh, you mustn't fret, Tom. Everything will work out. Besides, I've invited the one person who can make everything right for us."

Warily, Tom eyed the blond-haired man next to them, who shook his head, a wry smile on his face.

"Not me, chap."

Tom looked back to his mother, finally taking in the calm, eerily still expression on her face. She looked like she'd spent three days at the local spa, and there was a lightness to her being she hadn't possessed the day before.

Tom felt a knot of worry begin to build in his stomach. There was only one person in the world who could ever make his mother look like *this*. Only one person who could calm her and reason with her when she felt like the world was against her.

"Oh no," he breathed out. "Just no. Please don't tell me you called . . ."

"Your brother," his mother supplied cheerily. "I spoke with him this morning and he's hopping on the first flight he can."

"Oh no," Tom shook his head, "no, no, no, no, no. Mom, how could you? He's crazy."

"*Tom*," his mother admonished, shaking her head, "don't speak that way about your brother. He's a man of the cloth, after all."

"He's a Druid," Tom deadpanned. "The only cloth involved is made of hemp." He rubbed his temples, which were suddenly aching. "I can't believe you did this."

Marnie suddenly turned to him, looking at him evenly. "There are lots of things that have recently come to my attention that I can't believe, Tom. Now, go and clean up. Get that hospital smell off you. Oh, and get Sasha too. She'll want to join us for brunch, I'm sure."

Suddenly, the blond-haired man spoke again. "I don't know about that," he said. "She'll be fitted for a dress once Luis gets here. She might not want to bloat out with food beforehand."

"Whether or not she eats is up to her," Marnie replied calmly, "but in my house, at meal times, we eat at the table as a family."

"Good for you," the blond-haired man replied.

Tom gaped at them. "Do you two *know* each other?"

Both his mother and the blond-haired man looked up at him.

131

"Why darling, how rude of me," Marnie said. "This is Sebastian, one of your wedding planners. Of course, you missed him yesterday because of your little mishap."

Sebastian. Something that felt a little like unease ran through Tom, the hint of a memory pushing up, and he paused.

"Little mishap," he repeated slowly. "You mean, when the plane I was flying crashed out of the sky."

"Don't dramatize it, Tom," his mother replied with a sigh. "Gliding a light plane into a field is hardly '*crashing out of the sky*'."

"It's so lovely to meet you." Sebastian stood, extending a smooth hand towards him. Tom took it, shaking it liberally.

"My, my," Sebastian said, "that's a strong arm you have there, isn't it? You must be a healthy, fertile type. Are you?"

Tom stared at him. Did this man honestly just ask him if he was healthy and fertile? "I'm, um, sorry?"

Sebastian gave a small laugh. "No, goodness me, how rude I am today."

"It's fine," Tom replied, relaxing slightly. "I just—"

"I'm talking through a mouthful of coffee. Do forgive me. I asked, are you the healthy and fertile type?"

Tom waited for the punchline, because this man could not be *serious*. "I'm going to go and get Sasha," he said by way of reply.

"You've got about an hour before brunch, darling," his mother said. "The salmon has been freshly smoked."

"Salmon, what a lovely choice," Sebastian said smoothly. "Very good for the prostate, is salmon. Just in case you have any trouble in that area, Tom. Do you? Have trouble in that area?"

"I'm going to take a shower and get Sasha," Tom said again. He turned to his mother. "And then we're going to talk."

* * *

At brunch, Sasha threw her arms around Sebastian like they were the best of friends, before taking her seat next to Tom and helping herself to a large glass of water.

132

"No food for me today," she said easily. "I want to be skinny for my first fitting with Luis De León."

"You're already a rake, darling," Sebastian gushed. "But have some wine, if nothing else. It's your wedding dress, which is worth celebrating."

"I will, but not too much, I don't want to get woozy," Sasha replied, and Tom watched as Sebastian filled her glass.

"A little champagne now and then is good for the body and soul, I always say," Sebastian replied, before his eyes drifted from Sasha to Tom. "Unless you have some form of erectile dysfunction?"

"No," Tom answered shortly. "And I will take a glass. A large one."

"Large, just like you," Sebastian remarked. "How did a man like you come from a tiny thing like your mother?"

Marnie smiled. "Well, his father was a tall man."

"Ah, that would explain it."

Tom sat back, watching Sebastian cut his fish into small pieces on his plate.

"So," Tom cleared his throat. "You're the wedding planner?"

"One of them," Sebastian replied easily. "Ari's gone to pick up Luis for Sasha's dress fitting. He had some car trouble on the way here."

Hearing Ari's name spoken so casually over salmon and champagne made Tom's heart freeze in his chest, and he gripped the table edge between tense fingers. *Sasha is right there*, he told himself. *Keep it together. You can't fall apart every time you hear her name.*

"Ari?" he asked through a mouth that had gone paper dry. "That's, um, an interesting name."

"Yes," Sebastian answered slowly, and Tom could feel himself being watched carefully. "You don't hear it often, do you?"

"No. I guess not."

"She'll be here at any moment with Luis. Like I said, he had car trouble. Something about the rear differential. Well,

I guess having trouble with your rear would stop you in your tracks." Sebastian shrugged, putting another mouthful of fish in his mouth. "Do you have trouble with your rear, Tom? Does it stop you in your *tracks*?"

"Sebastian." Sasha laughed, hitting him playfully on the arm. "Don't tease Tom."

"I would never." Sebastian smiled back, playfully tapping Sasha back. "I just like to make sure my brides are getting the full package before their wedding day."

"You don't need to worry about my *package*," Tom replied drily, sucking back another mouthful of wine. "My package is just fine."

"I'm sure it is," Sebastian replied instantly. "Like I said, you look to be a perfectly healthy and fertile specimen."

"You're a strange man." Tom watched the wedding planner cut up another piece of fish.

"Tom!" Sasha muttered under her breath, but Tom ignored her.

"And you're planning our wedding?"

"Well, yes," Sebastian popped salmon in his mouth, "with Ari."

"Ari," Tom said, the syllables coming out as more of an exhale than a word. It felt so good to speak her name again, after all these years.

"Ari is charming," Marnie announced.

"Isn't she just?" Sebastian nodded enthusiastically. "Well, she'll be here once she's fixed Luis's car. A dab hand with a wrench is our Ari. Of course, I would have preferred a sister who could dress hair, but you take what you're given, I suppose."

Sister. Once again, Tom felt his heart pause within his chest. *Sebastian. My Ari had a brother named Sebastian.* Shaking slightly, Tom forced himself to take a deep breath, forced himself to cut up a piece of fish and put it between his lips, the moist flakes like rubber. It had to be a coincidence, he told himself. It couldn't be her.

"A mechanic?" he asked, fishing for information. "How did a mechanic end up a wedding planner?"

"No, not a mechanic as such, she's actually an artist, our Ari. She just happens to be an artist with an interest—"

"In engines," Tom finished numbly, his stomach dropping. *Oh my God, it was her. Ari. It was Ari.*

His fork fell back to his plate with a clatter, and when he looked up again he found Sebastian's eyes resting on him intently.

"I drove past a stopped car on the way here," he said, his voice strained. "A man. He had a little girl with him."

"Yes," Sebastian nodded, and now the silence in the room was thick. "That was probably them. Luis is travelling with Reine."

"Who's Reine?" Tom asked, although he knew. *He knew.* He'd known since he first saw her.

"Ari's daughter."

Tom inhaled sharply. He turned to his mother, who was staring at him with wide, understanding eyes.

"You didn't know," she whispered. "You didn't know, did you?"

Beside him, Tom felt Sasha stiffen. "Know what?" she snapped. "Tom, what didn't you know?"

* * *

Their car breaks down outside of Rouen, and Ari surprises him by cracking open the bonnet and peering inside.

"Where did you learn about cars?" he asks with interest, and she gives him a grin.

"Paid my way through art school with a side job at a mechanic's," she tells him. "Paint brushes and a wrench . . . I'm good with my hands."

Tom grins back at her. "Don't I know it."

She throws a towel at him. "You can be cute later." She turns back to the car, peering into the open hood. "Although it might be much later. This doesn't look good."

"What is it?" Tom asks, peering over her shoulder to take a look himself. He's no mechanic, but he's messed around with enough

of his father's old cars to know his way around an engine. "What do you think?"

"I think we'll need a new part." Ari sighs, sitting up and looking around her. The sun has just set and it's getting dark, an azure sky settling in above them. "What are we going to do?"

"There was a small town about half a mile back," Tom remarks. "Let's head there, find somewhere to stay for the night. In the morning we'll try and get a mechanic out to look at the car."

"I can fix the car," Ari says proudly, standing taller. "We just need the part."

"Okay," Tom agrees. "We'll find a mechanic to get the part from then."

She nods, before putting down her wrench and coming to stand beside him. Tom wraps his arms around her small frame, feeling that pulsing light of happiness run through him at her nearness. She nuzzles into him, and he presses his lips to her hair, inhaling that smell of hers that he loves.

"Just another egg to crack, right?" he says softly. "Another adventure for us."

"Yes," she agrees, looking up and catching his eyes. "Another adventure."

"Come on," Tom says, "we passed a hotel in that town. Let's go and check in. There's nothing we can do here now."

Ari nods but makes no attempt to extricate herself from his arms. "I like you," she tells him, a smile on her lips. "I like being with you."

"I like being with you too," Tom replies, kissing her gently. Her mouth is soft and sweet, and he sighs against her lips. "Come on, let's get to the hotel."

"What was it called?" Ari asks, and Tom thinks back to the sign he'd glanced at as they'd driven through the town, dark letters against a wooden board.

"The Hotel La Reine," he says. "The Hotel La Reine."

CHAPTER 11: HACER LA VISTA GORDA

When Ari saw Luis and Reine come into view, sitting on the side of the road beside their broken-down vehicle, she felt a deep torrent of relief. Her body relaxed, her heart beat slower, and some of her uncertainty, some of that terrible jitteriness, dissipated on seeing her daughter whole and well.

It was one of the things no one had told her about motherhood, this odd dislike of being parted from her child. It was something she'd been unable to prepare for, no matter how many books she read or parenting vlogs she watched. No one had ever told her that, once her baby was in her arms, she would spend the rest of her life feeling incomplete when she was away from her. It was as though there was an invisible string between herself and Reine, and whenever — through necessity or choice — Ari had to be away from her, that string pulled on her heart, making her feel nervous, woebegone and incomplete.

She still remembered, with startling clarity, the first time she'd ever been away from Reine. Her daughter had been six weeks old and just starting to give Ari gummy, heart-melting smiles, when Luis and Sebastian had walked into her flat, dressed head-to-toe in running gear, sweatbands on their foreheads and a nappy bag strapped to their backs.

* * *

"Right," Sebastian intones, taking in the sight of Ari on the sofa with Reine in her arms, a bottle of Lucozade by her side and Homes Under the Hammer *playing on repeat on the television. "It's time."*

"Time for what?" Ari asks, protesting when Luis reaches down and scoops Reine from her arms.

"Time for you to get up, shower and get out of this flat," Luis answers, cradling Reine and grinning at the baby. "Tío Luis and Uncle Sebastian have found a Mum's Bums and Tums running group at the park, we've invested in a top-of-the-line baby jogger and are ready to take this one for the day in a cardio-friendly fashion."

"No," Ari replies instantly, reaching for Reine. "No, you can't. I'm not ready yet. Besides," she adds, "she breastfeeds. What about when she gets hungry?"

Luis pats his backpack. "I have three bottles of defrosted breast milk ready to go."

Ari stares at him blankly. "Please tell me it's mine, and that you didn't buy it on the internet."

Sebastian gives a huff. "Of course it's yours. We popped in last night when you were passed out next to Reine's cot and took it from the freezer."

"Oddly, that doesn't reassure me." Ari rubs her hands over her face. "Guys, I'm just not ready yet."

"You'll never be ready, Ari," Luis says softly, dropping to the sofa beside her. He lays Reine against his shoulder, rubbing her back, and gives Ari a smile. "Parents aren't meant to do this alone, you know. It takes a village to raise a child. We're your village, Ari. We're here. We want to help."

"That's sweet, but I don't need help. I'm taking care of her, aren't I?"

Luis and Sebastian make no reply, but Ari sees them exchange a glance. Suddenly, she's very aware of her unkempt state, her unwashed hair and of the dishes and mugs sitting in piles on the floor. For a moment silence rings out between them, broken only by the muted sounds of a BBC home renovation programme playing on a loop.

"You're doing an admirable job of raising your child," Sebastian finally says.

"Yeah, Ari. I mean, look at this kid." Luis indicates to Reine's baby soft skin, her downy hair and the clean onesie she wears. "She's

138

perfect. You're doing a great job with her . . . but you're putting yourself second, and, well . . ."

"What he means is that you look rough, love," Sebastian breaks in. "And there's a bit of an odd smell to you. Like sour milk."

"Sebbie!" Luis snaps, but Ari sits up, brushing awkwardly at her pyjamas.

"It's not my fault," she says miserably. "Reine keeps being sick all over me."

"So, let us help you," Luis wheedles. "Let us take the baby. She can be sick on us for a few hours."

At that, Sebastian pulls a face, but Ari sees Luis give him another sharp look.

"Go and shower," Luis suggests. "Clean up a little. Or take a walk. Whatever you need."

Ari nods, watching as Luis bundles Reine into a pink blanket and then the shiny new city jogger by the door.

"You'll take care of her?" she asks, already feeling regret for agreeing to let her go.

"A jog around the park, espresso for lunch and then a look-see around Kensington? She'll be fine," Luis reassures her.

Once Reine is gone, Ari takes a shower, looking at herself in the mirror for a long time. Sebastian is right, she has to acknowledge. She does look rough. Her hair is lank and unwashed, her skin pale with large bags under her eyes. Her breasts ache with milk, and there are blue veins visible under her engorged skin.

"You wouldn't even recognise me if you saw me now," she whispers, thinking again of Tom.

She's always thinking of Tom. These days, every minute of every day, she has a living, breathing and crying reminder of him. Beneath Reine's dark and baby-fine lashes are a pair of eyes that exactly match her father's, and Ari feels an ache when she looks at her daughter. Their daughter, she reminds herself.

He's missing so much.

Ari busies herself around her flat after her shower, tidying up and washing her and Reine's clothing and bedding. She indulges in an afternoon nap, but when she wakes at three, to find her flat still empty

139

and Reine still away, an ache in her stomach begins to grow. By the time she hears a key turn in her lock at four, she's nearly frantic.

"Thank God," she exclaims, immediately unbuckling Reine from her buggy and holding her close. "Where have you been?" She turns to Luis and Sebastian, who look clean and calm, sifting through the multiple carrier bags attached onto the back of the buggy. "Did you go to Harrods?"

"We wanted afternoon tea," Sebastian replies calmly. "And then I picked up a few bits for supper in the food hall while Luis took the baby to look at the Barbies."

"She's six weeks old." Ari turns instantly to Luis. "She can only just focus on my face. She's still considered legally blind. She doesn't need to look at Barbies."

"Who said it was for her?" Luis replies jovially, pulling a shiny box from one of his bags and stroking it happily. "I picked up a 1992 Radiant in Red Barbie from the special collection. She's one for the shelf, I think."

"Right," Ari says tightly, although Luis leans forwards, stroking Reine's head.

"You look better, Ari."

"And the smell is gone," Sebastian adds cheerfully, walking into the small kitchen and flicking on the kettle.

"I showered," she replies. "Thank you." Her voice grows softer. "I appreciate what you're both doing for me." She looks around at the flat. "Everything."

Luis smiles at her. "You're welcome. And don't worry about leaving little Miss Reine with us. So long as we aren't working—"

"Or at Pilates!" Sebastian shouts from the kitchen.

"—or at Pilates," Luis carries on. "We're here for you. Get your-self booked into the salon for next Saturday. We'll take Reine again. Mum's Bums and Tums was quite good fun."

"Agreed, although my bum and tum are already in excellent shape." Sebastian comes back into the living room, holding out two cups of tea. He collapses onto the sofa, stretching out his long legs. "So, same time next week?"

Ari hesitates. It's brief, but Luis has sharp eyes, and he peers at Ari carefully.

"What is it?" he asks.

"It's nothing, well, not nothing . . ."

"Yes?" Sebastian presses her, sipping from his tea. He hands the other cup to Luis wordlessly.

"It's just . . . I'm so grateful for everything you're both doing for me . . . taking me in, giving me a job—"

"You're my sister," Sebastian protests. "I haven't forgotten that you chose me over our parents, either. And to be fair, you're amazing at your work. Don't sell yourself short. You're earning your keep."

Ari nods. "Yes, but you gave me a place to live too, until I sorted myself out. And you were there when Reine was coming and—" She pauses, taking a deep breath. "I just . . . don't want you both getting attached."

"Attached?" Luis asks. "To our niece?"

"Yes," she says awkwardly. "Tom is coming for me, you see, and I might have to leave and . . . Well, I don't want either of you to get hurt."

"Tom." Sebastian's voice is blank. "Of course. He's coming for you. We keep forgetting."

Ari swallows, shifting Reine in her arms. "Yes, Tom. He promised he would find me."

Again, there's silence. Ari shifts Reine once again, hoping the baby would start to cry, or gurgle, or do something — anything — to end this quiet.

A look of something like compassion crosses Luis's face. "Of course he's coming, Ari. But you don't have to worry about us. Let us help you, just until he arrives. And then he can take over, and we'll carry on being the best uncles in the world."

* * *

But he never did come, and Luis did get attached.

Now, he was sitting by the broken-down car with Reine next to him. When Ari pulled up beside them, cutting the engine and stepping onto the verge, she heard Luis's voice speaking to her daughter clearly.

"*Mira, princesa, tu mamá está aquí,*" he was saying, but Ari had already scooped Reine into her arms.

"Hello, Mummy," Reine said as Ari held her tight. "I'm hungry."

Ari laughed. "You always are." She kissed Reine's dark honey hair as she placed her down. "Are you okay?"

"Yes. Just hungry."

Ari turned to Luis, who hugged her warmly. "Are you okay?" he asked, but she shook her head.

"No. No, not really."

A look of concern crossed Luis's handsome face, and he frowned. "What's up?"

Ari chewed on her lip. She looked down at her daughter, running a hand down her cheek.

"There are some biscuits in my bag in the car," she told her. "Go and find them and have a few, okay?"

Reine nodded, eagerly moving towards the car, and once she was at a distance Ari turned back to Luis.

"It's Tom." She watched as Luis's forehead creased.

"Tom?" he asked. "What about him?"

Ari chewed on her lip again.

"Ari?" Luis reached for her hand. "What about Tom?"

"It's just . . . I think I've found him."

Luis blanched, his face falling. He looked behind Ari to the car, where Reine was happily munching on her snack.

"Seriously? You found him?"

Ari nodded mutely.

Luis took a deep breath. "He was supposed to find you though."

"Yes," Ari agreed. "Yes, he was."

"But you found him instead?"

"Yes."

Luis stood for a moment, regarding Ari with concern. "There's something else, isn't there?"

Ari nodded, bitterness flooding through her. "Yes, there's something else."

"What is it?"

"He's getting married," Ari said miserably, before taking a deep breath, "and I'm the one planning his wedding."

* * *

They found a diner fifteen minutes away, where Luis and Reine ordered a late brunch.

"The man said there are waffles here," Reine announced, "and they serve all kinds of sauces too. Chocolate, syrup . . ." Her little face frowned. "There was something else too, but I can't remember."

"What man?" Ari asked, but Luis gave a dismissive shrug.

"Some guy stopped to help us earlier. Let me use his phone to call Sebastian. Turned out to be a creep though, and took off in a hurry," Luis rolled his eyes. "I think he was, how do you say it in English?" He turned to Reine. "*Se le zafó el tornillo?*"

Reine grinned. "He went nuts, Tío."

Luis grinned back. "Yeah. Crazy. Like he'd seen a ghost or something."

Ari sighed. "Okay, well, at least you're both all right. And you can have the waffles another time, Reine. Something sensible today, all right my lovely?"

Reine frowned, but Ari remained firm.

Her daughter would be healthy, loved and strong. Her child would have the best. Though, at this diner, the best turned out to be an omelette with a few vegetables on the side, which Reine picked at unhappily.

"*Haz feliz a tu mamá y cómetelo, mi sol,*" Luis cajoled her, before looking at Ari. "And you should eat too."

But Ari shook her head. Her stomach protested at the thought of food. Sebastian had thrust a single piece of toast at her earlier, and watched like a hawk as she swallowed every last crumb, each mouthful heavy and dry. Ari couldn't bear the thought of having to eat anything else. Instead, she drank a black coffee, the liquid sitting greasily inside her queasy belly.

Tom had always drunk his coffee black, Ari remembered suddenly. Tom who wasn't Tom Miller at all, but a different Tom. Tom Somerset.

She tried the name out in her head, trying to equate her memories of Tom — with his brown hair and brown eyes and plush lips — with what she knew of this Tom Somerset. But she couldn't do it. All she knew of Tom Somerset was that he was a pilot who crashed his plane and was engaged to his — how had Sasha described it? — ah yes, *childhood sweetheart*. Ari cringed. If Sasha had been his childhood sweetheart, then what did that make her? Ari swallowed hard. She knew what it made her. It made her the other woman. True, it was inadvertent and unintentional, but still, that's what she was.

Her eyes drifted to Reine. She took in her daughter, beautiful and intelligent and healthy, and realised that being Tom's other woman made her daughter his lovechild. *His bastard*, Ari thought with a knot of pain. She wondered if that was what Sasha would call her. She wondered if that was what Marnie would think of her. She wondered if Tom would use that word. Wondered if he would berate the existence of his daughter to placate his fiancée. Wondered if he would dismiss and denounce her to save his relationship with Sasha.

With a clatter, Ari's cup dropped to the table, spilling black coffee in all directions.

"God damn it," Ari cried, the words coming through a throat that was thick with unshed tears.

Luis eyed Ari sharply before turning to Reine.

"Reine, *cariño, ve a sentarte en esa mesa en la esquina y mira tu iPad mientras tu mamá y yo limpiamos este desastre. No tomará un minuto y estaremos aquí todo el tiempo.*"

Reine looked at Ari, who was dabbing at her eyes with a cheap paper napkin. "Mummy, are you okay?"

"I'm fine, lovely girl. Just fine." Ari shook her head, dabbing again at her tears. "I spilled my coffee is all."

"Reine, *sigue,*" Luis said. "*Te volveré a llamar en un momento.*"

He blew the child a kiss as she picked up her iPad and headed for the corner, turning back to Ari and looking at her keenly.

"I spilled my coffee, Luis," she whispered helplessly, and he gave her an understanding smile.

"We can get you a new coffee, honey."

"Yes. Yes, we can." Ari cleared her throat and sat up taller. "I need to get it together," she told Luis in a low voice. "For Reine's sake."

"Reine's fine," Luis replied. "She's jetlagged and tired, but fine. It's you I'm worried about."

"I'm okay."

Luis gestured to the table stained with coffee. "The furniture and I would beg to disagree."

Ari gave a small smile. "Maybe I'm not fine. Maybe I'm not okay at all."

Luis nodded, reaching over the table to take Ari's hand.

"The coffee on your shirt—" she began to protest, but Luis shook his head.

"I can buy new shirts. In fact, I can design and make my own shirts, if I really wanted to. The shirt isn't important. You and Reine are my priority right now."

Ari nodded, squeezing Luis's hand. "He lied to me, Luis," she said, her voice small. "He *lied* to me."

"Yeah. Of course he did. He's an asshole." Luis shrugged. "The fact that it's taken seven years for you to figure that out is somewhat surprising though. You're a smart girl, Ari."

"Not where he's concerned, I'm not. Where he's concerned, I'm the world's biggest fool."

"Incorrect." Luis sat back, sipping from his own drink. He kept a tight hold of Ari's hand, rubbing his thumb on her palm. "He's the world's biggest fool, firstly for lying to you, and also for ever letting you go."

"He used to say he was a fool for me." Ari half-smiled, half-cried. "He had this playing card. The fool. He carried it everywhere."

"Oh, Ari."

"He told me he had a family emergency," Ari said softly. "That's what he told me. A family emergency. His father was sick. He had to leave me in . . . where was it? Germany? He wouldn't give me an address. Just a phone number that led to nowhere. He kissed me, told me to get on with my life, and said that he would find me again."

"Oh, honey," Luis said with a sigh. "He really did a number on you, didn't he?"

"I loved him. I really did. And I so wanted to believe him. I so wanted to believe that he wouldn't do what he did to me, or to Reine." She swallowed hard. "But he did."

"Does he know about Reine?" Luis asked, glancing at the little girl over Ari's shoulder.

"By now? I should imagine so. His mother is—" Ari paused. "Something else."

"Okay," Luis replied, nodding. He looked as though he was thinking, tapping the fingers of his free hand in a puddle of black coffee. "Okay, so they know."

"It's pathetic, really," Ari mumbled, shaking her head. "I so wanted to be the one to tell him about her. When I was pregnant, I used to imagine him finding me. I would let him stroke my belly and would imagine his eyes lighting up at the thought of a family." She gave a bitter laugh. "He always inferred that he didn't have one, like me. But not only does he have a family, and a *fiancée*," momentarily, she let the word hang unhappily in the air, "but it turns out they own half of fucking Connecticut too."

Luis stared at her. "What do you mean?"

"Tom?" Ari gave a huff. "His name isn't Miller at all. He's some guy named Tom Somerset. He flies planes and his mother is—"

"*Marnie Somerset*," Luis finished for her, his mouth dropping open. "She's old money, Ari. One of her relatives was a first-class passenger on the Titanic. The family knew the Rockefellers. Her mother's family were practically French royalty at one point. Holy shit, Ari."

"You've heard of them too?" Ari shook her head again at her own unworldliness. "Sebastian informs me that I've hit the sperm jackpot," she added wryly.

Luis looked once again at Reine. "You gave birth to Marnie Somerset's grandchild?" He gave a long exhale. "That's unbelievable."

Ari nodded. "Sebastian told me." She gave another bitter laugh, reaching into her jacket pocket and pulling out a faded playing card. It was creased and lacklustre — finger-worn from where she had rubbed at it. Sighing, she passed it to Luis. "Tom gave me this. A treasure from France."

"The queen of spades," Luis muttered, turning the card over in his hand. "I've seen this in your hands more times than I count."

"I like to hold it sometimes," Ari admitted. "When everything becomes too much, or I'm missing him, or wanting him, or needing to remind myself that he was real, that we were real," she clenched her hand, "when I wanted to think that Reine came from a place of love, and not from some shitty place of abandonment."

Luis looked stung. "She isn't from a shitty place of abandonment. I love her. Sebastian loves her. You love her."

"Yes, I know. But he was supposed to find me. He was supposed to come for me. He told me we were forever."

"Reine has only ever known love," Luis said softly. "She doesn't need her asshole father."

Ari looked at him sadly. "I know. But I loved him, and I believed him when he said he loved me too. I believed him when he said we were forever. And I believed him when he said he would come for me. But it was all lies."

"Ari, honey—"

"Lies," she said again, plucking the queen of spades from Luis's hand. "Lies that I believed, and all paid for with a cheap magician's playing card."

Before she could think twice, Ari viciously tore the queen in two, the rosebud lips on the regal face turning into an eternal scream as the card ripped in half. She crumpled the pieces in her hand before tossing them onto the table. Momentarily, regret rippled through her. She'd had that card for so long. Had loved it for so many years.

"Ari," Luis exhaled. "Oh, Ari."

But Ari shook her head, sitting taller and straightening her shirt. "He never loved me, he lied to me and he used

147

me. That's the truth. A truth I think I've known for a long time," she paused, looking at Luis sadly, "I just didn't want to believe it. But it doesn't matter now. It doesn't matter at all."

"What are you going to do?" Luis asked her. He glanced once again at Reine. "I mean, if this Tom Somerset guy really *is* Tom Miller, and you never know, he might not be—"

"He is," Ari replied. "I feel it."

"Okay, so, say he is, and say he knows he's Reine's . . ." Luis trailed off. "Well, if he *knows* about her, is he really just going to sit back and do nothing?"

"I don't care about him," Ari lied, "or what he wants. Reine is mine."

Relief fluttered across Luis's face, and once again Ari was forced to acknowledge the bond he had with her child. Luis had always been fiercely protective of Reine, loving her intensely. From the moment she'd been born, he'd looked out for her, helped to raise her and taken on a far greater role in her life than Ari had ever intended. Whenever she and Sebastian were out on the wedding circuit — a frequent occurrence — Luis stepped in to care for Reine. He'd designed wedding gowns with her by his side, he'd taken her to fashion weeks across the world, first in baby carriers, then strollers, and finally with the child walking beside him and holding tight to his hand.

"She's my little sunshine, and my protégée," he'd once said in an interview, and Ari had felt a knot of worry at their closeness. *What if Tom comes?* she would ask herself. *What if he comes to take them away and she has to leave Luis and Sebastian behind?*

Not that it mattered now. Not now that Tom Miller's — *no, Tom Somerset, his name is Tom Somerset,* Ari reminded herself — true colours had been revealed.

"He's marrying Sasha," Ari said, suddenly feeling overwhelmed and tired. "*Miss Teen Rhode Island,*" she added bitterly. "He won't want a child hanging over that. He won't want me around."

"So, what will you do?" Luis asked again.

Ari chewed on her lip.

"Nothing," she decided. "Carry on as normal. I'm going to bet that Tom . . . Tom won't want anything getting in the way of his nuptials with Sasha. He won't want Sasha finding out about his past infidelity. So, I'm going to return to that house and act as though everything is completely fine. I'll plan his fucking wedding," she added viciously, "and I'll do an amazing fucking job of it too."

Luis glanced at her in surprise. "Are you sure you're okay?"

"Yes, I'm fine. I just need to get this job done so we can get the hell out of here," Ari replied. "And then I can get on with the rest of my life. One that I won't spend waiting for someone who's not coming. One that I won't spend wondering about him."

Luis nodded. "Right. So, I'll get there and design the dress? Is that still part of the plan?"

"Sasha wants a De León dress."

"Yeah, I know she wants," Luis replied, "but I'm asking you, honey. And if you say right now that you don't want me donning that woman in tulle and satin, I'll get on the first flight back to London."

Ari smiled at him. "You're a good friend."

"Truth be told, I don't want Reine around this guy or his family," Luis admitted.

"Neither do I. But I have a feeling if we turn up now without Reine, Tom's mother . . . I mean, Reine's grandmother . . . will be all over it. Sebastian had a bad feeling about a conversation he had with her yesterday. I don't think she'll rest until she's seen Reine for herself."

Luis nodded. "So, your creepy lying asshole ex was raised by an overbearing and obsessive mother? Wow, he just gets better and better. When we get back and you start dating again, remind me to vet all your boyfriends."

Ari shook her head. "I'm not dating again. I'm done with that."

"Ari—"

"No, Luis," she said, her voice serious. "I'm done with it. I can't go through all this again."

"Not all men are lying assholes, you know."

"Maybe not. Just the ones I fall in love with, hey?"

"He must have been honest with you about something," Luis suggested. "I mean, six months of solid lies must have been exhausting for him, and all just to what? Keep having sex with you? I mean, I'm sure you're a great lay, Ari, but there must have been more to it than that."

"I really don't care."

"I think you do," Luis said gently, "but I'm not going to press you on it."

Ari sat back, turning once again to look at Reine. "What should I tell her?"

Luis took a deep breath. "Nothing. She's going to meet some guy called Tom Somerset. Someone who'll be desperately trying to cover his tracks, so his fiancée doesn't find out that he cheated on her years ago. She doesn't need to know anything."

Ari nodded. "I need to get into my work head," she said, slumping slightly into the plastic covered fabric of the booth. "Even while going through a crisis, I'm still mentally ticking off my to-do list. De León dress, woodland wedding, Stella photographs—"

"Stella?" Luis asked. "Holy shit, this is a Stella wedding too? Did you get her biscuits?"

"Not yet," Ari replied, worrying her lip between her teeth. "It's on my to-do list."

"I'll order them in. Don't worry about it."

Ari nodded, but she didn't feel any better. Her stomach still hurt, and she felt jittery again, full of nerves.

"Ready to head back?" Luis asked gently. "Ready to . . . uh, *hacer la vista gorda?*"

He was looking at her intently, and Ari felt a tremor of fear run through her. *She was going to see Tom again. She was going to see him. She was going to introduce him to their child.*

"No," she whispered. "I'll never be ready for that."

"I'll be there," Luis promised. "Now, come on. Let's get the bill, get Reine and get back. I've got a bride to design a dress for."

Before they hopped in the car, Ari turned to squeeze Reine's hand lightly, checking once again that her child was well and healthy. When she turned back, she noticed Luis squinting at something.

"What is it?"

"Look at this sign," Luis said, gesturing to a photograph stuck on the wall outside of the diner. "It says, *In loving memory of Douglas Somerset, who loved this diner and all the pie within it.*"

Ari stared at the photograph. It was of a man, grey-haired but handsome, sitting in the diner, a mouthful of pie on a spoon before his cheeky smile.

"Somerset," Luis mused. "Do you think he was a relative?"

"Yes," Ari whispered. Something about the shape of the man's face was familiar, striking her oddly. She turned to Reine, taking in her daughter's chin as if for the first time.

They were the same.

"Yes," she said again. "I think so."

Luis read the sign again. "He died just before Reine was born. You said he said his father was sick, right? That's why he had to leave you in Germany?"

* * *

"My father is sick," Ari hears Tom say, and he sounds dejected, defeated and terrified all at once. "My father is sick, and I have to go to him."

She nods, because what else can she do? What else can she say?

"Of course," she whispers. "Of course, you have to go."

"Today," Tom carries on, rubbing his eyes tiredly. "I need to leave today."

"Yes."

The heartbeat running through her body must echo through her voice, because Tom suddenly turns to her, gathering her fiercely in his arms.

"I'm coming back for you," he tells her, his voice half-growl, half-promise. "I'm not letting go of you."

151

"We never . . . we never said this was forever," she utters, trying to be reasonable, trying not to feel bereft, trying not to feel abandoned all over again.

"I asked you to marry me," Tom disagrees, pulling Ari even closer. "I meant it. We are forever, Ari. I'm coming back for you. I promise. I love you, Ari. And I'm coming back. I'm coming back for you. Magic, remember? That's what we are. That's what we'll always be."

* * *

"Yes," the simple word a struggle as memory threatened to overwhelm Ari, "that was what he told me."

"Well," Luis shrugged. "Looks like Tom didn't lie about one thing, then. Hmm. Maybe there are other things he didn't lie about too?"

"Keep your voice down," Ari hissed, looking at Reine. "And I told you, I don't care now. I don't care what he did or is going to do anymore."

"Okay," Luis said, his face thoughtful. "But I need to warn you . . . I get the feeling this isn't going to go the way you think it is. I get the feeling there might be more to all this than you know."

"Maybe," Ari replied, her voice harsh. "But I don't care enough to find out. Come on," she added, "get in the car. You've got a bride to dress, and I have an ex-lover to ignore."

"Ari—"

"Luis," she said again, and now her voice was firm. "I don't care about him anymore. And after this week . . . I never want to see him again."

CHAPTER 12: MEET YOU

The call comes on their first morning in Rouen.

Ari is asleep, the morning sun drifting in through the window and lighting her fair skin. Her hair glows like honey in the sunshine, and Tom smiles at the sight, running a hand lightly through her tresses. Her smell is heady, a mix of sex and the fresh linen of their sheets, and Tom resists the urge to kiss her, knowing that once he starts, he won't be able to stop.

One kiss with Ari will never be enough, Tom knows. He loves her. Adores her.

He wants to be with her forever, he realises. He wants to be with her, live with her, love her and have children with her. He wants to grow old with her.

He wants to marry her, he decides. He wants to marry this woman and keep her forever.

The thought quickly overwhelms him and he licks his lips, running a hand over the naked skin of Ari's shoulder. He wants to marry her. He can't be without her. He needs her forever.

Which is a problem. A big one.

Taking a deep breath, he leaves Ari asleep in their bed, stepping into his clothes and heading for the door. He needs to breathe in fresh air — needs to feel the morning sun on his skin. Needs to think and solve the problem that has been hanging over his shoulders since the first

153

time he saw Ari in that airport and decided — against all his better judgement — to pursue her.

He blinks in the morning sunshine, shuffling further into his jacket to keep out the cool morning air. Near their hotel is a river, and he heads towards it on impulse. Before today, neither he nor his mother had ever stepped foot in Rouen.

"Why would I want to go there?" Marnie had asked, genuinely perplexed. "I've no interest in seeing the ghosts of the past."

Rouen should have been strange to Tom, but it wasn't. For although Marnie had no interest in visiting the town, she still talked about it. The stories she'd been told by her grandparents lived in her heart, and she told Tom about the winding city paths with their cobbled streets, about the imposing gothic churches, and about the cathedral, painted by Claude Monet, no less. Her stories meant that it was no trouble for him to find his way from the Hotel La Reine to the city market, where he sits at a table under an awning, drinking black coffee and casting his eyes over the town that — if not for war and politics — might have been his home.

Not that he wants it, he reminds himself. He's like Marnie in that respect — happy to let the past die and move on from it. He's only here in Rouen because Ari wanted to visit, and he's hoping they can move on again soon. Once the car is repaired, he plans on whisking Ari out of this city and over the border into Germany. He'll take her to Freiburg, where they can drink beer under the shadow of the Münster and eat noodles in small taverns. Ari can paint landscapes up in the cool shade of the Black Forest, while he sits by her side, happy just to be near her in quiet repose.

If the timing and mood is right, he might even tell her the truth, he decides. He could finally confess to her that he wasn't the man he claims to be — that he wasn't really Tom Miller — blackhearted wretch and lost soul, as well as a damned liar — but actually Tom Somerset, still a wretch, still lost, but now and forever a fool for her. He could tell her about the oppressive years of his upbringing, about the heavy weight of family name and heritage upon his shoulders, and about how he finally cracked and rejected it all. He could tell her about his wilderness years travelling the world, living under a pseudonym and searching for his place in it. He could tell her how the boy who once wanted nothing more than to be a pilot like his father turned into the worst kind of trust-fund nepo baby, spending money he hadn't earned, hiding from the world. He could tell her about the day when he'd seen her by that airport window, lonely and serene, and how he'd been so drawn to her he'd decided, then and there, to claw back a shred of happiness for himself. He'd buried Tom Somerset so deep within himself he thought he'd lost him forever, but Ari had drawn him back up towards the light. Ari had brought him back to himself, he knows. He owes her so much. He owes her everything.

Would Ari still want him though, if he confesses all? Tom worries, staring into the black depths of his coffee. He's a fool, but also a realist. He knows that in telling Ari all he might lose her forever. But he also knows that he can't keep her on a lie — that one day she will discover the truth about him and who he really is.

The thought of losing Ari is terrifying, and he runs a hand over his face, rueing the day he'd ever left home and taken on the mantle of Tom Miller.

Abruptly, his phone buzzes in his jacket pocket, and Tom frowns before pulling it out. It was a phone he'd picked up in Norway with a number he'd only ever given to Ari. He only uses it for the internet, photos and maps, and no one should be calling him, especially not at this time in the morning, while he sits in the Rouen marketplace.

"Hello," he says into the receiver, expecting to hear the crackle of a machine as it begins a sales pitch, or the tinny voice of an agent as they follow a marketing script.

But no.

"Tom," a voice says, and he stiffens instantly, automatically recognising the fluid voice on the other end of the line.

Corentin.

"How did you get this number?" he automatically returns, and hears a sigh.

"I've had people looking for you," Corentin replies. "Even for the smallest of movements. Quite the traveller these days, aren't you? I had an alert for this number from a hotel in . . ." for a moment, Tom hears his brother rustling papers ". . . ah yes, in Switzerland. The number was used at reception as a contact for a traveller named Tom Miller, but paid for from an account registered to a Tom Somerset. It was easy to follow you after that."

"You don't need to look for me, I'm not hurting anyone."

"Aren't you?" his brother replies, infuriatingly calm as always. "The hotel said you were travelling with a woman."

"There's no woman," Tom says in a panic.

"Okay," he hears his brother muse. "So, you're alone?"

"Alone," he lies once more. "I'm alone."

"Right. So, where are you now?"

Tom closes his eyes. "You don't want to know."

"I really do, Tom. I really do."

"Rouen."

For a moment, a stunned silence comes over the line.

Eventually Corentin clears his throat. "Well now, that is a surprise. Rouen. Mom will be thrilled—"

"Don't tell her," Tom pleads. "She doesn't need to know. She doesn't need to know anything."

An uneasy quiet follows. "Tom, with all due respect, that's unfair. You broke Mom's heart, leaving the way you did. We've had nothing on you for a long time. It was only when you got to Iceland that I picked up a trail."

"How do you know I've been to Iceland?" Tom demands.

"I told you," Corentin replies patiently. "I've had people searching for you."

"You're a Druid," Tom snarls. "Not a fucking detective."

"Watch your language," Corentin says, still calm. "Like I said, you broke Mom's heart leaving like you did. She entrusted me with . . . Well, not finding you, not exactly. She always said you would only be found when you wanted to be. But she did ask me to keep an ear out for you, which I have done. For about a year there was nothing, and then, nearly six months ago, Tom Somerset suddenly appeared on the radar again. An old bank account of yours was reactivated, and a significant sum of money was transferred into it days later. I've been seeing digital receipts from your travels ever since. Norway, Finland, Sweden, Belgium, Italy, France . . . Like I said, quite the traveller these days, aren't you?"

"I'm on my European tour," Tom replies through gritted teeth. "Taking some time to myself."

"I'm happy for you — and don't get me wrong, Tom, I really am happy for you. Hearing your voice again is the best thing to happen in *years. Awen — blessings be upon her — answered my calls to bring you home."*

"Don't, please don't," Tom begs, "I don't need another lesson in goddess paganism today."

"It wasn't a lesson, merely a commentary, and you sound so lost—"

"I'm not lost. I told you, I'm in Rouen," Tom snaps.

"—and so alone that you could do with the goddess lighting your way," Corentin carries on, as though Tom hasn't even spoken. "Well, we all find our path in our own time, I suppose," Corentin sounds almost cheerful, "but Tom, I have to ask you now to cut your European tour short and come home."

"No."

"Tom—"

"No," Tom snaps again. "I'm not coming home. There's no need for me to come home."

"There's nothing to keep you in Europe either," Corentin says, and Tom swears he can hear his brother shrugging. "Unless there's something you aren't telling me?"

Tom says nothing and feels Corentin — damn his intuition — sense something in the void.

"The woman," Corentin says gently, "is she really not with you anymore, or . . ."

"She's gone," Tom replies. "I'm alone. She was nobody. Just some woman."

Nobody, but not to him, he thinks. Ari's everything to him — the whole world, wrapped up in a wonderful package.

But Corentin and the others can't find out about her. Not yet. He needs to clear the air with her himself first. Tom knows his mother. He understands all too well that if his mother ever got wind of a potential daughter-in-law, she'd be on the first plane to Rouen, ghosts of the past be damned. God knew she had the air miles to use.

"Okay," Corentin says. "Time to come home then."

"No, I'm busy, I'm travelling, I'm—"

"Tom."

"I said no, okay? Just fucking listen to me for once, I'm not coming home. There is nothing on this earth that could get me to leave

here and step foot near that miserable pile in New York my mother calls a home—"

"Tom, Dad's dying."

At these three simple words, issued so cleanly from Corentin's plain-speaking mouth, all the air seems to be sucked from Tom's lungs. He gasps, frantically clawing oxygen back into his body, his fingers gripping his phone with a bruising hold.

"What?" he whispers, and he can hear Corentin sighing.

"It's Dad, Tom. He's dying."

"But he . . . he can't be. He's always been so . . . so . . . full of life," Tom argues.

It isn't a lie. Doug Somerset, rogue and pilot, daredevil and gambler, is a man so fervently full of zest and life it seems to drip from every pore of his body. He's spirited and joyous, charming and kind, with a streak of honour within him that puts most others to shame. He's the sort of man who helps ladies across roads, who stops to open doors for others, who compliments everyone he ever seems to meet. He'd taught Tom to pilot planes and drive cars, and always encouraged him to fly a little faster and take the road unseen.

"You can get this bird up to Vh at least," Doug would drawl from the co-pilot seat of his Cessna, patting Tom on the back in the pilot's chair.

"That's a risk," Tom would reply, but he'd apply thrust all the same. "Why are you such a daredevil?"

"Hey, don't knock it. Being a daredevil got me into this plane and married to your mother," Doug would wink in response, "now get this bird up to Vh and let's soar, hey kid?"

Douglas Somerset. Dying. Tom takes another desperate breath, struggling with the thought.

"Tom?" he hears Corentin ask kindly. "Are you okay?"

"Fine," Tom gasps out. "I'm fine."

"You need to come home, Tom. You need to—"

"I have to go," Tom says abruptly. He pulls the phone away from his ear and disconnects the call, cutting off Corentin and his protests.

His father can't be dying, he tells himself. His brother is wrong. He's just trying to get him home. It's just another attempt to get Tom back in the family fold — another attempt to control the direction of his life.

When he goes back to the Hotel La Reine, Ari is still sleeping. Tom curls up in the bed beside her, pulling her naked and intoxicating warmth towards him. He allows himself to run a hand over her skin, dipping his fingers between her thighs and stroking her silky and wet heat. She wakes with a moan upon her lips, a moan that turns into a smile when she opens her eyes and sees him next to her.

"You need to stop," she says softly, even as she opens her legs wider to Tom's searching hands. "We ran out of condoms last night — we don't have any protection—"

But Tom is already covering her mouth with his own, silencing her wise words. He wants to bury himself and his troubles within her, wants to feel her gorgeous and slippery warmth clenched around him. He kisses her again, trailing his mouth down to her breasts, and now Ari is out of words, and so is he.

Afterwards, he sees Ari counting days on her fingers, and feels a dart of worry. They'd had slip-ups before, had given in to lust at times they shouldn't, and it had always been okay. Still, he feels nervous until he sees Ari smile.

"We should be okay," she tells him. "It's the wrong time for anything to have — well, it was the wrong time."

"I'll get condoms as soon as I can," he promises. "I'm sorry, I shouldn't have—"

But Ari silences him with a kiss. "It's fine," she says again. "I'm as much at fault. But next time we need to be more careful, okay?"

He nods, but it's all in vain, because there isn't a next time.

The second call comes just after they arrive in Germany, and this time it's his father.

"Tom, please," his father begs, and Tom looks over at Ari.

"I need to go," he tells her. "My father is sick. I need to leave."

* * *

"What didn't you know?" Sasha said again, and Tom could hear his heart hammering in his chest. He opened his mouth to speak, before closing it again rapidly. He felt sweat beginning to form on both his neck and brow, and he licked his lips, clenching and unclenching his hands at the table.

"What didn't you know?" Now there was a danger-ous tone to Sasha's voice, and he looked over at his mother desperately.

But Marnie, for once, was silent. She was staring at Tom in shock, horror and something that looked a little like hap-piness. She was pleased, Tom realised. She was happy at this unexpected turn of events.

"He didn't know that Ari was bringing her daughter," a quick and cheerful voice suddenly broke in, and both Tom and Marnie turned to Sebastian, who was all at once by Sasha's side and refilling her wine glass merrily. "And I know what everyone is thinking, it isn't professional to bring a child into our work. But I can assure you both, Sasha and *Tom* . . ." the knowing tone to Sebastian's voice made Tom snap to attention, and he saw Sebastian shoot him a look ". . . we will be nothing but professional where your special day is concerned. Your happiness is our priority. In fact, I might just call Ari now and tell her to check into a hotel with Reine. Luis can come here, and—"

"No."

Tom looked up at the sharp tone his mother was using. Marnie was sitting at the table, her shoulders tense and eyes dark, staring at Sebastian dangerously.

"No?" Sebastian asked. "With all due respect, Mrs Somerset, you of all people can see that Ari bringing Reine here would be *entirely inappropriate*."

"Because of the wedding," Sasha piped up. "This is my day and, honestly, I don't want some brat running around and getting all of the attention."

At the word 'brat' Sebastian seemed to tense. Tom watched as he bit his lip, clearly swallowing down a response. "As you say, darling," he finally purred, and Tom heard the lie on his lips.

He hates her, Tom realised. *He hates Sasha.*

He looked over to his mother, who was also staring at Sasha with venom. *And my mom hates her too. Everyone hates her but me, and even I sometimes . . .*

Tom swallowed as an uncomfortable thought struck him. He didn't hate Sasha. But nor did he love her, he realised.

"Right," Sebastian said, ushering Sasha up. "Let's go and get you ready for Luis. He'll want to measure you right away, darling. I know you look dazzling and rake-thin in that trouser suit, but let's go upstairs and slip you into something a little easier for an initial dress consultation."

"Yes, you're right," Sasha replied, staring at herself critically in a mirror. "I have this summer dress that would be perfect. Bring Stella up too. I want every frame of this moment captured by her camera." She gave Tom and Marnie a dazzling white smile. "I'm going to have a hardback book produced of the wedding photographs, did I tell you?"

"You have a publisher interested in your photos?" Marnie asked tightly, but Sasha gave a flippant laugh.

"No, of course not, I'll self-publish — at your expense, naturally, given that you're paying for the wedding. It should sell like hot cakes though. Me, a one-time model, marrying Tom Somerset of the Somerset family, in a De León dress with Stella photographs. I mean, who *wouldn't* want to see those pictures?"

Marnie rolled her eyes, but Sebastian had already laced his arm through Sasha's and sped her from the room. "Stella!" Tom heard him calling out. "The bride would like you upstairs!"

With a relieved slump, Tom collapsed back into his chair. All at once, Marnie was upon him.

"*You have a child*," she said fervently. "You have a little girl."

A child. A little girl. Tom felt himself grow pale.

"Yeah," he said weakly. "Yeah, I do."

"Reine," Marnie said, and now her voice was warm. "Reine. My granddaughter."

Tom could hear the pleasure in her words, and he turned to her worriedly. "Mom," he pleaded, "don't get too excited, or carried away—"

"Why ever not?" Marnie cut him off. "I have a *granddaughter*, Tom. I'm going to celebrate that fact and love her. A little girl, Tom. A little girl."

161

She clasped her hands together, closing her eyes, and Tom sighed. His mother was picturing ballet lessons and tap class, horse riding and pink dresses. His mother was picturing a little girl with his eyes sitting primly at their table, with Marnie beside her, brushing out the fine strands of her hair.

She's already carried away with this, a voice in his head warned him. *She's already redecorated a bedroom and is building a playground, and she hasn't even met the kid yet.*

"Mom," he said slowly, trying to be gentle, "you must know that Ari might not want us in . . . in the girl's life."

Marnie frowned at him. "Not *the girl*. Reine. She has a name. A beautiful one. It's French . . . It means *queen*." For a moment, she paused. "Queen and Country Weddings," she finally said, "that must be where her name came from."

"No," Tom corrected her softly. "Her name is from a hotel. The Hotel La Reine. In Rouen."

Marnie's eyes snapped towards his own. "Reine was conceived in Rouen?"

"Yes," Tom confessed.

For a moment, Marnie looked stunned. "My, my, my . . . how the world does turn," she finally whispered, then shook herself together. "But of course, Ari will want us in Reine's life. We have money and influence. We can give that girl everything and more."

"It's not that simple," Tom argued, and heard Marnie give an annoyed grunt.

"Why aren't you more excited by this news?" she asked him crossly. "You have a daughter, Tom. A daughter. There's a whole person out there with your genes, and you're sitting here like a dull-witted idiot, hardly able to say her name."

Tom shook his head. Where Reine was concerned, he was without words. "I need time," he replied. "I just need time to process this—"

"You want time?" Marnie snapped. "In about ten minutes, your ex-lover — sorry, your *wedding planner* — is arriving with the daughter you sired upon her eight years ago. You want time? You have ten minutes."

"I don't — I can't . . ."

"Tom, you need to get yourself together. I don't know what happened between you and this Ari all those years ago, why you broke up and why you never knew about the child, but—"

"We didn't break up," Tom whispered. "We never broke up."

"She's here to plan your wedding to another woman," Marnie replied waspishly. "I would hardly call that still together."

"No, I didn't mean—" Tom stopped, taking a deep breath. "I mean, we were together, and I had to come back because of Dad, and I meant to go back for her and just . . ."

Marnie stiffened. "You *ghosted* her?"

"No, not exactly, and — and how do you even know that phrase?"

"I read the internet," Marnie replied.

"What, all of it?"

Marnie held her head up high. "The bits that count. And don't change the subject. Did you ghost this woman, Tom?"

"In a way," Tom replied, "but I didn't mean to."

"Well, so long as you didn't mean to, that makes it okay," Marnie huffed, sarcasm dripping from her lips.

"Mom—"

"Why did you ghost her?"

Tom took a deep breath, shame suddenly filling him. "Because I lied to her," Tom said, looking down. "I lied to her about everything."

For a moment, Tom could feel his mother's eyes boring into the back of his neck. Finally, she sat beside him, drilling her fingertips against the tabletop.

"Define everything."

"She never knew who I really was. She thought I was Tom Miller—"

"Well, you *called* yourself Tom Miller, back then," Marnie interrupted. "It was just a name, *my* name in fact.

163

You know my family were the Millets. What does any of it matter though? It was still you, no matter what you were calling yourself."

Tom shook his head. "No. It was more than that. Deep down, I knew it wasn't real. Deep down, I was always Tom Somerset. But I never told her. I never told her at all. She knew nothing about you. Nothing about all this," he gestured around them. "Nothing about Dad. Nothing about Corentin. I didn't tell her that I went to Cornell, that I was meant to take over the Somerset empire until I absconded to Europe. I didn't tell Ari anything about the real me."

"Okay. So, what did you tell her?"

"I may have implied," Tom cleared his throat, "that I was like her . . . in that, um, well . . ."

"Tom," his mother uttered warningly.

"Her parents basically kicked her out when she was sixteen. I, um, gave her the impression that I was likewise, uh . . ."

Beside him, Tom saw his mother grow pale.

"You implied that I . . . that I *kicked you out*?" Marnie asked, aghast. "Tom, tell me you weren't so callous . . . so damned *mean* as that."

Tom felt another torrent of shame flood through him. "I just . . . I just loved her so much," he replied pitifully. "I wanted her to love me too."

Marnie shook her head at him. "Oh, Tom," she said with a sigh. "That's not how love works. You know that."

"I know. And it didn't work. She moved on. Even with my—" Tom swallowed down another painful lump in his throat "—baby in her arms, she moved on. She didn't wait for me."

"What are you talking about?" Marnie asked, confusion written into the lines of her face.

"Ari got married," Tom said bitterly, "when I went to London for her . . . when I finally got my act together and went back for her . . . she was married to this guy."

"No, that's not right—"

164

"Mom, I saw him with my own *fucking* eyes. I found her address in London — I went to her apartment. This guy answered the door, a baby in his arms. He was wearing a ring. He didn't look like a babysitter, and there were pictures of him on the wall with the baby and with Ari and—" Tom broke off, struggling for breath. "Anyway, I didn't hang around to speak with her. She'd moved on, and I knew I needed to as well."

"But the baby—"

"If I'd thought for a minute the baby was mine . . . if I'd known . . ."

"What?" Marnie snapped. "What would you have done?"

"Stayed," Tom whispered. "Stayed, whether she was married or not. But the baby was still a baby. Little enough to need carried around still. She was small and I did the maths in my head and realised that she couldn't possibly be mine."

"But she is yours," Marnie replied, drumming her fingers on the tabletop again. "And why you didn't stay until you ascertained for certain her parentage, I'll never for the life of me understand."

"I told you, she was little, still being carried around, she didn't look like an eighteen-month-old—"

"Because she was still being carried?" Marnie asked, rolling her eyes. "For fucks sake, Tom, your father and I carried you around until you were nearly six, and you were a big kid. You should have demanded to see Ari and asked her for yourself—"

"What, in front of her husband?"

"He wasn't her husband, you idiot," Marnie seethed. "He was her brother-in-law. He's married to her brother Sebastian and helps Ari out with childcare when she's working. You fucking idiot, Tom." Marnie shook her head. "You've wasted so many years, and all because you lied and then ran away when your pride was hurt."

"My pride? You mean my heart, Mom. My heart broke when I saw that man and the baby," Tom whispered, hardly able to look up. "I thought that she was married . . . She broke my heart."

"Except that she didn't," Marnie snapped back. "You're the one who did the heart-breaking here, Tom."

Tom nodded slowly. "Yeah," he agreed sadly, "yeah, I did."

"So, what are you going to do?" Marnie asked quietly. "You can't run from this now, Tom. You have a child. Responsibilities. And Ari, you need to consider her too. You owe her the truth, if nothing else."

"You saw her?" Tom asked, looking into his mother's eyes. "You met her?"

Marnie nodded. "Yes, I did."

"And?"

Marnie's face softened. "She's a lovely woman. I can see why you fell in love with her." She paused. "Can I ask something? Do you still love her?"

Beneath the table, Tom clenched his hands. He could feel his fingernails digging into his soft palms, could feel the hard lines of his knuckles under the pads of his thumbs. He chewed on his lip, contemplating his mother's words. It would be so easy to lie. So easy to shrug and mutter something about time passing and feelings fading. So easy to wipe Ari from his life and take the easy path, the path that led to Sasha, and life going on much as it had for the past six years.

But he'd lied enough. To Ari, to his family and to himself. He looked his mother directly in the eyes.

"I'll always love her," he confessed. "I'm never not going to love her, Mom. She's my other half."

Marnie reached over, taking one of his hands in her own. She nodded. "Okay, okay," she said, and Tom could hear the cogs of her mind working. "So, what will you do?"

He shook his head. "I don't know. I don't even know where to begin with this. I have a *daughter*," he said, and the enormity of the words hit him hard. "I have a daughter, Mom."

"Yes, you do," Marnie nodded. "And acknowledging that and acknowledging her seems like a good first step to take right now."

"I saw her, you know, on the road headed here," Tom confessed. "She talks and walks like Ari . . . But she has my eyes."

"I can't wait to meet her," Marnie said softly. "I can't wait to see her for myself."

"She's going to be so overwhelmed by all this." Tom squeezed his mother's hand. "So overwhelmed by us, and this house, and—"

"Tom!" A screeching sound echoed through the dining hall, and both Tom and Marnie looked up into Sasha's giddy face. "Oh my God, Tom, he's here!"

Tom felt his stomach sink even as his heart began to beat quicker. "Who?" he asked, though he knew.

"Luis De León, my dress designer," Sasha squealed. She grabbed Tom by the arm and hauled him up, and for a woman who was a quarter of his size, the strength in her grasp was truly frightening. Clearly all the hot yoga was paying off.

"He's with Ari," Sebastian added calmly, although Tom could see a nervous twitch to his eye. "And Reine."

"We can deal with the kid later," Sasha shook her head, holding her nails up to the light and inspecting them closely. "Come on, Tom, come and greet him. He's flown all the way from London to design my dress — we have to be nice to him."

She began pulling him across the room, Marnie following behind, and only stopped dead when they reached the entry hall. She flung her arm around Tom's waist, and he could feel the excitement through the bones of her thin body.

"Mr De León!" she exclaimed. "You're so very welcome here!"

Tom looked up, all blood draining from his face. A man was pulling his coat from his shoulders, ruggedly handsome and oh-so-familiar to him.

The man from the road.

The man from Ari's apartment, Tom realised with horror. The man he'd thought was her husband.

But he couldn't look at him for long. Because behind the man, standing still and staring at him with a look of heartbreak and longing all over her face, was Ari. His Ari. *His* Ari.

He met her gaze and held it, hoping and hoping against hope itself to transfer just a little of the love and yearning he held for her from his soul to her own.

There's still magic between us, he tried to tell her. *It's you and me. It's always going to be you and me.*

But whatever magic still lay between them dissipated when Sasha spoke, turning to dust before his eyes.

"Mr De León, you have no idea how glad we are that you could make time for our simple little garden wedding."

At the words 'we' and 'our' all the softness in Ari's eyes fled, and now she gazed at him with hard eyes. Eyes that were full of recrimination and anger. Tom felt pain strike him hard as he saw himself through her eyes. A wastrel of a man, cold and calculating and with another woman's arms around his waist. He'd thought he'd sunk low during his years as Tom Miller, but he realised now, with startling clarity, just how much deeper the mire beneath him was.

"I'm glad to meet you," De León replied smoothly, in that caramel voice of his. "It's always lovely to meet a bride."

"This is my fiancé, Tom," Sasha carried on, stroking his arm possessively, but to him De León only nodded, his eyes narrowing.

"Okay," De León said, the caramel tone replaced with a voice full of hard toffee. "So, this is him."

Silence fell, broken only by the occasional click of a camera. Stella, damn her, was collecting every image — a hoarder of raw human emotion and ultra-polite bullshit.

Tom looked pleadingly back to Ari, but her face was still hard and worryingly blank of any emotion but hate.

"Ari," he finally broke, his voice slamming into the void between them. "Ari, I—"

"Mr Somerset," she cut in, her voice like brittle glass. "How nice to finally meet you."

CHAPTER 13: TOKENS

Tom's been gone for five weeks, and the number he left Ari with is useless, endlessly ringing out whenever she calls it. At night she lies in her hostel bed, her phone clutched in her hand, hoping against hope that he'll answer, or call her, or send her a text. An email even. At this point, she'd even take a post-it note sent by a carrier pigeon. Something, anything really, to let her know that he was real, and they were real and that he is coming back, one day, just as he promised. But as time drags on and the silence on the other end of the line remains stark and unending, Ari is forced to come to terms with the truth: that Tom is gone, and all he has left her with is a faded playing card and a phone number that leads to nowhere.

Well, not the only things he left her with.

The second line appears in a depressing hostel room in Amsterdam, and Ari cries into her pillow until the cheap polyester fabric is sodden with tears. She's travelled half-heartedly since Tom left, her backpack heavy but heart even heavier, until the exhausting sickness she first put down to food poisoning made her stop. She buys the test before checking into her hostel, splurging on a private room so that she can vomit and cry in peace. For two days, she stares at the box with wary eyes until, after another bout of horrific puking, she bites the bullet and opens it up.

She can't be pregnant, she tells herself. She just can't be. She's twenty years old. She has her whole life ahead of her. She's friendless and mostly without family. She's poor and ill-equipped to deal with a whole other person. She can't have a baby. For a moment, Ari closes her eyes, praying for the first time in her life to any and all the gods that she can think of.

Please don't let me be pregnant.

Please don't let me be pregnant.

When she opens her eyes, the second line stares back at her. Ari sinks to the floor in a ball, before crawling onto her borrowed bed, tears flowing down her face.

Later that night, when she's all cried out and the moon shines in through her window, lighting the tear-tracks on her pale and woebegone face, Ari picks up her phone.

As usual, the call goes nowhere. This time however, she lets it ring through to the voicemail, and when the beep sounds, she lets out a shaky breath.

"You need to come back for me," she whispers into the receiver. "Please come back for me. Please. Please come back. Please don't leave me alone like this. Please."

* * *

She considers having an abortion and moving on with her life. It's one of the options the kindly NHS doctor she sees in London gives her, and Ari chews on her lip while considering her words.

"It's up to you," the doctor says, not unkindly. "It's your choice. And you don't have to decide now. Support networks are in place. I can put you in touch with the right people."

"And if I have the baby?"

The doctor nods, looking unsurprised. "That's also your choice. I can put you in touch with support groups for that too."

"Support groups?" Ari asks. "You mean, for pregnant women?"

The doctor clears her throat. "For pregnant teenagers."

Ari stares at her. "I'm twenty years old. I'll soon be twenty-one. An adult."

"Don't take it the wrong way, Ari. I refer all pregnant under twenty-ones to that support group. Pregnancy is hard. Babies are hard. And you told me yourself, you don't have parents. And the father of your baby—"

170

"Is coming for me," Ari says firmly, sitting up.

The doctor gives her a small but disbelieving smile, reaching over to take her hand. "Take the leaflets for all the different options, and the support group numbers too. You aren't alone in this, Ari. You really aren't."

Ari nods before leaving her office. She stumbles out of the clinic, blinking in the bright sunshine of Grafton Street, before she walks in no particular direction, holding her stomach.

Holding where her baby grows.

London's an odd city, Ari thinks to herself as she blindly walks through Tavistock Square. A mix of wealth, privilege and utter poverty. A mix of old architecture, mellowed by the sun, with newer buildings, their steel and glass exteriors glinting down at her. Not that their age matters. New or old, they all seem to bear down upon her — grand, intimidating and judgemental.

She finds herself outside of the Foundling Museum, sitting on the cool stone steps, wrapping her cardigan around her arms and staring at the ground.

A baby. She's having a baby. Tom's baby.

It's so odd and utterly ridiculous that she wants to laugh. Her laughter comes out as silent tears though, tears that streak down her cheeks, leaving damp and salty patches on the thin fabric of her shirt.

Next to her, a woman clears her throat before offering her a tissue.

"Been to the museum, have you, love?"

"Yes," Ari replies, accepting the tissue gratefully and wiping her nose. It's easier to lie than to tell the truth. Easier to believe a lie than hear the truth too, she reflects sadly.

"It's a hard place to visit," the lady says with a sigh. "Very sad. Well, you cry it out. I did when I first came."

"Thank you," Ari whispers back. The lady stares at her.

"Was it the tokens? Is that what made you cry?"

"The tokens?" Ari asks stupidly, her mind blank. The lady gives her a sharp look, before her eyes drift over Ari's arms, still tightly wrapped around her stomach, and her face softens.

"The tokens left by the mothers when they brought in their babies. The women who were too poverty-stricken to care for their own children, or the women who were forced by their families to be rid of an unwanted

171

child. That's what they did here at the Foundling, love, they took in unwanted babies. Twenty-five thousand of them, in fact. The mothers . . . well, most of them hoped to come back for their children, when times or circumstances were better. So, they left tokens with their infants. Scraps of cloth. Treasured rings or bracelets. Small snippets of paper. Thimbles or dried flowers or anything else of worth they owned. Most of the tokens were worthless, but to those women . . . they were the most important things they owned. And they left them with their babies."

Ari looks up. "How many of them came back? For their babies?"

The woman sighs. "Out of twenty-five thousand? One hundred and fifty-two."

Ari's mouth drops open. She feels a wave of sadness wash over her, and she shifts on the cold stone steps of the museum.

"How far along are you?" the woman asks her, and Ari wipes at her eyes.

"Eight weeks," she swallows nervously. "How did you know?"

"Just a hunch I had."

"I'm twenty years old," Ari carries on. "I have no money. A hundred years ago, my baby would have ended up here too."

"Perhaps," the woman says. "But it's not a hundred years ago, love."

Absently, Ari pulls the queen of spades playing card from her pocket. She keeps it with her at all times and likes to run her thumb over it when worried, or sad, or missing Tom. As a result, it's fraying at the edges from overuse.

She's always missing Tom.

"The father of the baby gave me this," she tells the woman, holding the queen of spades up to the light. "A token. A hundred years ago, I would have left it with the baby here. The most important thing I own."

"You're a melancholy thing, aren't you?" the lady remarks, giving Ari a gentle smile. "I told you, it isn't a hundred years ago now. We have social services these days, love. Social housing and medical care. You and your baby will be fine. Start claiming the right benefits. Right away."

"Even with benefits, I'll need a job," Ari says, her voice dull. "Babies are expensive. And who in their right mind will hire a pregnant twenty-year-old? Nobody, that's who, and—"

At that, the lady leans forward. "Are you really all alone?"

Ari shakes her head. "I have an older brother."

The woman thinks for a moment. "Have you told him about the baby yet?"

"No."

The woman smiles. "Tell him about it."

Ari opens her mouth to speak, before closing it quickly.

Sebastian isn't an idiot. When she'd arrived home from her gap year four months early, looking thin, pale and weary, he'd immediately sat her in his living room, handed her a cup of tea, and told her to tell him everything.

"Start with his name," Sebastian ordered her, "and go from there."

She hadn't told him everything though. Hadn't told him about the baby. Telling him would have made it too real.

"I don't know," she says to the woman now. "I don't know what I want to do. If my boyfriend was here . . ."

The woman gives her a kind smile. "I know. But he isn't here, love. So, it's up to you."

* * *

It's Luis who finds Ari a job as a night cleaner at one of his wedding studios.

"With your art background, you're overqualified for the role," he tells her regretfully. "But it's quiet and will keep you going until a plum role in art or design comes your way. You're still sending your CV out, right?"

Luis and Sebastian still think of her as a kid looking for her big break in life, she realises, and she doesn't have the heart to tell them that she's all but given up on her dreams of a career in art. Mentally she's boxed them up and stored them away, with a label attached that reads 'Never going to happen now'. Dreams, Ari thinks bitterly, are for idealistic young people. Dreaming isn't for those who'll soon have another mouth to feed.

"I don't mind at all," Ari tells Luis, running a finger along the pristine white bags along one of the walls. "I've given up on art anyway, I think."

She's not telling lies. Ari really doesn't mind the studio at all, and she hasn't had an urge to paint since Tom left. Surprisingly, she finds cleaning numbingly therapeutic. She likes losing herself in the wiping away of dirt and dust and invisible regrets. She likes the immaculate studio, with its plush white carpets, oak flooring and the rows upon rows of white fabrics, kept in a cool workroom at the back. At 9 p.m., when all the sewists and fitters and consultants leave, Ari finds a strange sort of calm in the studio, armed with her dusters and scrubbing brushes and vacuum cleaners. She doesn't think of Tom while cleaning. It's only when she stops, when she has time to think and grieve and feel sorry for herself, that she ever thinks of him. The longing for him is so strong it's almost painful, and she has to breathe deep in those moments. Breathe deep and push him from her mind. She hasn't got the luxury of missing him, she reminds herself. She has a baby to support soon. A child to consider.

She takes another job at a temp agency, because she's desperate and pregnant and will do anything to keep food in her belly, a roof over her head and Tom from her mind. She finds herself working an endless circuit of desks as an office receptionist, answering phones and taking mail, glad at least to be sitting and off her feet, finding a cold sort of comfort in the utterly dull and entirely repetitive work sent to her. The other receptionists notice her growing belly with wide smiles, enthusiastically asking her about her baby and the father and Ari always smiles back but says little.

"Is it a girl or boy?" asks Ehlii, one of the other temp workers, but Ari only shrugs.

She doesn't like to talk about the baby. She doesn't like to think about the baby. Thinking about the baby means thinking about Tom, and that only leads to sadness and longing and the feel of a playing card against her fingers, as she worries the queen of spades against her skin. She's detached from her pregnancy and detached from her baby and avoiding her brother, and sometimes, late at night in her miserable bedsit, she pushes down on the growing bump of her belly and wonder how she got here, and what the hell she's doing with her life.

It's easier not to think about the baby, really. Easier to keep the baby from her mind.

She goes to her twenty-week scan alone. The radiographer looks tired, taking measurements and making notes, and when he turns to *her and asks her boredly if she wants to know the gender, Ari looks just as bored back, shrugging her shoulders.*

"Sure," she says, "why not?"

"A girl," he says, pointing to an image on the screen of which Ari can make little sense. "You're having a daughter."

She takes the single scan image she's given for free on the NHS straight to her night job, without looking at it as she changes buses, and it's only when she's getting out her cleaning supplies, taking care to avoid the sealed bags of satin and silk wedding dresses, that an overwhelming earthquake of raw and unadulterated emotion trembles through her. She drops the cleaning supplies, taking a deep and rasping breath.

They're having a girl. A **girl.** *A daughter. Tom is having a daughter and he'll never know.*

Abruptly, Ari hates the wedding dresses, sitting on their pretty white hangers in their alabaster white bags. She hates them with the burning passion of a thousand hot suns, seeing in them a future that she and her daughter will never have.

Tom isn't coming back, *Ari thinks bleakly, doubt creeping through her. He's never coming back for her. If he really loved her, he wouldn't have left her, not for anything. If he really wanted her, he would have left her with a number, an address . . . anything other than just a wretched playing card, tired and old.*

A token isn't a future, Ari realises. A token is just an empty promise.

He offered to marry her, but he never meant it, Ari tells herself, tears once again falling from her eyes. She'll never wear one of these pretty dresses to marry Tom. She'll never stand by him in a church, vowing to stay with him forever. Ari's sadness, acute and miserable, stretches forth into the future too, as she realises with a stab of pain that their daughter, if she ever marries one day, will never have her father by her side.

She's truly alone in this. Placing a hand on her belly, Ari cries again. It's not just her now. It's them. Them, and they're truly alone. Alone, as she's always been, and as she always will be.

She doesn't feel the arm that sneaks around her shoulders, holding her as she sobs. She doesn't register the male presence, making sooth-ing and sympathetic noises in her ear. It's only when her cries subside, transforming from sobs into soft hiccups, that she startles to find Luis beside her. She jumps up, hurriedly wiping at her eyes, taking a few steps back and adjusting her uniform, hoping it covers her bump.

"Ari," *Luis says, his eyes sweeping over her.*

Ari goes pale, dismay causing her stomach to sink. "I'm so sorry," *she whispers,* "I'm really sorry."

"You should probably be sitting down," *Luis remarks, taking in the rounded bump of her belly.* "Right?"

She nods sadly. "Right. I am sorry," *she says again, her head down, and she can feel her brother-in-law's eyes upon her.*

"No need to be sorry," *he replies jovially.* "Have you seen this place since you started? Spotless. I love it. And you're having a baby. That's wonderful news."

At that, Ari looks up, giving Luis a small smile.

"That's better." *Luis smiles back.* "I'm going to call Sebastian. We should go out for dinner. Celebrate. Oh, and maybe have a little talk too."

"I didn't mean to cry," *Ari begins to explain, but Luis holds up his hands good-naturedly.*

"Crying women in a wedding dress studio is kind of par for the course," *he tells her.* "My brides cry, their mothers cry, their sisters and aunts cry, grandmothers cry . . . and I guess whoever gets my bill cries too. Come on. Let's go out and have that talk. I'll call Sebastian, get him to meet us at the restaurant."

Luis takes her to a nearby Mexican place, where he scowls at the menu. Salvadoran, he takes his Latin American food seriously.

"My mama would cry if she saw what they put in their tamales here." *Luis shakes his head, before waving the server over.* "But their cocktails are amazing," *he adds with a wink.* "Two Macuás with extra rum and a virgin piña colada."

They make small talk until Sebastian arrives, and when her brother walks into the restaurant Ari throws herself into his arms and cries. For about five minutes he just holds her, and tells her, again and again, how everything will be okay.

Eventually, when she's all cried out, Sebastian takes a seat and stares at her. "How far along are you?"

"I just had my twenty-week scan."

"That's exciting. Know what you're having?" Luis asks, sipping at his Macuá, even while Sebastian frowns.

"Twenty weeks?" Sebastian asks. "And you've only just told us?"

Wordlessly, Ari pulls her scan picture from her pocket, and hands it to the two of them.

Sebastian looks at it blankly. "I don't know what I'm looking at here."

"It's a girl."

Luis grins at her. "That's amazing, congratulations," he says, and even Sebastian smiles.

At that, Ari's lip wobbles, and she takes a deep breath, which is not lost upon them. She tries to regain her composure, chewing on her lip, before straightening up and tucking the scan picture back into her coat.

"Sorry," she whispers again.

Luis looks at her curiously. "Have you eaten this evening, Ari?"

She gives him an odd look. "What?"

"You're really thin for a woman twenty weeks pregnant. No wonder we had no idea. Are you eating well? Getting enough vitamins?"

She shrugs. A look crosses Luis and Sebastian's faces, and Sebastian grabs the menu.

"Ooh, tamales," he says, but Luis makes a face.

"No," Luis says. "No food from here. Let's take her home. I'll feed her."

Later, with food in her belly and a warm cup of tea pressed into her hands, they ask about the baby's father once more. Ari feels better about the world — nothing feels as bleak as it did earlier. The cloak of sadness that has covered her since Tom's departure feels lighter, and she smiles easily, stroking the curve of her bump and telling Luis and Sebastian all about Tom and their six-month romance.

"Tom's father is sick, but he's coming back for me," she finishes, pulling out the queen of spades playing card and showing it to them proudly. It's a token of Tom's love, she reminds herself. How could she have ever doubted him?

"But what if he . . ." Luis begins, but Ari cuts him off.

"He's coming back for me. Coming back for us. He promised."

* * *

Tom's hand was cool in her own, and Ari shook it with a feeling of utter and complete detachment. There was a loaded silence in the room, and it suddenly occurred to Ari how ridiculous this all must seem.

Tom was here and she was here and their daughter stood behind them, and everyone in the room seemed to know it except for Tom's blushing bride-to-be, who smiled sweetly all the while. Abruptly, Ari dropped her hand, brushing it against her thigh.

"I'm Ari," she offered, although how she spoke through a dry and brittle throat was a mystery to her. "Ari Lightowler."

"Ari," Tom said softly, and he gazed at her with eyes that seemed full of . . . not wonder, not quite awe, but something else.

Regret, her mind immediately offered. *He's looking at you with regret.*

Regret that he ever met her, probably. Regret that she was here today, to ruin his bride's special moment. Standing taller, Ari cleared her throat. She would be the height of professionalism, the wedding planner of the century. She would be so professional, in fact, that he would never look at her and see the Ari he'd known in Europe. Tom might regret having romanced her, once upon a time, but he would never regret hiring her, she decided viciously.

"This is Mr De León," Ari carried on, "he's here to design your *bride's* gown," she emphasised the word bride, letting it hang in the air for a moment.

She was a professional, but still, she wanted to see him squirm a little. She'd given birth to his child and had earned a moment of pettiness.

His child. Reaching out, Ari took Reine's hand, gently pulling her daughter to her side. Reine cuddled into Ari's waist, and Ari ran a hand over her daughter's soft hair.

"This is Reine," Ari said calmly, though her heart was hammering inside her chest. "My daughter. I'm so sorry I had to bring her with me," she caught Tom's eyes and held them bitterly. "I'm a single mother. I had childcare issues."

"No, that's . . . um . . . that's fine," Tom stammered, and he dropped Ari's gaze. Ari watched as his eyes darted suddenly over Reine, and she found herself holding her breath.

Please love her, her heart inexplicably begged. *Please love her as I do.*

But Tom said nothing, staring at Reine dumbly. His face was still and impassive, devoid of any emotion, and he made no move to talk to their child. Behind her, Ari felt both Sebastian and Luis take a possessive step forwards. They were ready, Ari realised, to pounce into action at any moment.

Not that they needed to. Pushing her son out of the way with a look of pure exasperation on her face, Marnie Somerset dropped to her knees next to Reine, brushing a stray hair gently from the girl's eyes.

"My, my, my," Marnie exhaled. "Oh my."

In Marnie's voice and face Ari found the emotion she'd been desperately searching for in Tom. Her daughter's grandmother stared at Reine with the awe and wonder Ari had hoped for, and Ari saw the older woman's face soften as she smiled at the small girl.

"I'm Marnie," she said gently, "and you must be a very tired little lamb."

"Yes," Reine admitted, still clinging to Ari's hips.

"She's had a hell of a long day," Luis admitted, stepping forward to run his hand over Reine's head, affection in his voice. *"Quieres dormir un poco ahora, mi sol? Necesito trabajar, pero el tío puede llevarte arriba a tu habitación."*

"Quiero que mami venga conmigo," Reine replied, and Ari blanched. Her Spanish was awkward — nowhere near the fluency of her daughter, who'd spent her life speaking with her Salvadoran uncle — but still, she recognised *I want my mummy* when she heard it.

Instantly, she felt like a terrible mother. Reine hadn't seen Ari in days, had travelled over four thousand miles in the last twenty-four hours, and was probably jet lagged, tired and hungry. It was only natural for her to want her mother.

179

"Baby, I have to work—" Ari started to reply, before Marnie held up her hand.

"*Tu madre puede llevarte arriba de inmediato,*" she began, in fluent Spanish. "*Te he preparado una habitación. Y cuando te despiertes, quizás tú y yo podamos jugar juntas. Si tu madre y tus tíos están de acuerdo con eso?*"

Luis looked at Marnie quizzically, and the older woman shrugged.

"I did languages at Harvard. It was good for the business. I take it Reine is fluent in Spanish too?"

Luis nodded and a glint of satisfaction passed through Marnie's eyes. At that, Sebastian stepped forwards.

"She's also learning French," he said proudly. "She's our clever cookie. Although she's only taking French because of that ridiculous school Ari makes her attend."

"Ridiculous school?" Marnie asked.

"Reine goes to a *state school,*" Sebastian said, barely repressing a shudder. "She should be at St Paul's Girl School, learning a useful language. Like Latin."

"Latin is not a useful language," Luis scoffed, and Ari saw Sebastian turn to him.

"I beg your pardon, but I learned Latin at St Paul's."

"And how often do you use it?"

"Often enough."

"Fine, fine, fine," Luis shrugged. "Next time we take Reine on a city break to *ancient Rome,* I'll remember to get you to order the table wine."

"With that attitude, you won't be getting any wine at all on our next city break. *Or anything else you normally partake of at night,* you uncouth swine—"

"Excuse me?" A tight, irritated voice rang out, and Ari turned to Sasha, who looked annoyed to high hell. Her lips were pressed together tightly, and the hand that wasn't clasped within Tom's was held against her hip. "Um, this is my wedding, and my initial dress fitting? Let Ari take her brat upstairs and—"

"Don't call her that," Tom abruptly interrupted. Though his voice was soft, there was a hard note to it that made everyone take notice.

"Tom," Sasha whined, "she shouldn't even *be* here. She's ruining my moment—"

"She isn't ruining anything," Tom replied, though once again, his eyes had locked with Ari's. They were soft and imploring, and Ari's breath caught in her throat.

It had been years, but his eyes still made her stomach jump and heart race.

"No, she's not," Marnie agreed. "Right, Ari honey, you take Reine upstairs. I've had the decorators open the windows to air the smell of paint out. But if it's still too strong, let her sleep in your room. Reine's the priority here—"

"Reine is not the priority here," Sasha cut in, indignation all over her face. "*I'm* the priority. I'm the fucking bride here."

"Don't use that kind of language in front of my—" Marnie paused, collecting herself. "In front of Reine. She's a child. Ari will take her upstairs, and you can take Mr De León upstairs for your initial dress fitting."

"Sasha has big ideas for her dress," Ari said softly, although her eyes never left Tom's. "Once I've settled Reine, I'll come through to help with the fitting."

"You'll do no such thing," Marnie intoned. "You'll take a moment of your own. We'll all have dinner together tonight. We can talk about—"

"—about *the wedding*," Sebastian slid in, warning in his voice. "We can all talk about *the wedding* then, can't we?"

"Yes." Marnie nodded, her tone indicating she understood exactly what Sebastian was saying. "We can all talk about *the wedding* then. I think I have a few questions about *the wedding* of my own."

"Darling, we all have questions we want answered about *the wedding*," Sebastian agreed. "I've been thinking about *the wedding* for years."

"Right, so then, that's a plan," Marnie nodded. "Ari, my love, you get this little sweetheart of yours up to bed to get some sleep. Sasha," Marnie's eyes narrowed, "you take Mr De León to the morning parlour to take your measurements. And Tom—" abruptly, Marnie turned to her son, though Ari noticed he didn't take his eyes from hers, they were still staring at each other, still drinking one another in "—Tom, you come with me and Sebastian here. We can start talking about the, uh, the—"

"*The wedding*," filled in Sebastian smoothly. "Although in Latin that would be *nuptia*. Or *proditio*," he added, his eyes narrowing at Tom. "Depending on how you look at it."

With a silent nod, Ari tore her eyes from Tom's, taking Reine's little hand within her own. It worried her how little he was looking at Reine. It worried her how little interest he was taking in their child. He'd been staring at her, imploring her to be silent, she realised. He didn't want his dirty little secret reaching Sasha's ears. Didn't want to spoil his precious bride's happy day. Ari felt her heart harden against him. She would keep his secret, she knew.

But she wouldn't make it easy for him.

"Sasha, remember to take off all your jewellery but your engagement ring," Ari said coolly, keeping Reine's hand in hers while turning to the bride.

"Why?" Sasha asked.

"In art, we'd call it a blank canvas," Ari explained. "Luis will design your gown to complement you and your engagement ring. Your token of Mr Somerset's *love*." She restrained the anger in her voice. "Any other jewellery might spoil the effect."

"Oh, that's a good tip," Sasha smiled, blooming under everyone's attention once more. "And my engagement ring is beautiful, isn't it?"

She held out her hand, letting the light catch the massive diamond ring on her finger.

"It's lovely," Ari agreed, her voice catching on a lump in her throat.

He'd given Sasha this ring. A token of his love.

"Diamonds are the most valuable of all gems," Sasha intoned, smiling at her ring. "Thank God Marnie wouldn't let Tom give me the Somerset family ring. That hideous, sapphire thing—"

"What?" Marnie straightened. "I never said Tom couldn't have the Somerset ring. Tom, I—"

Ari turned to Tom, who had gone pale. *Why hasn't he given Sasha that ring?* she wondered.

But Sasha didn't seem to care. "I'm sure Tom had his reasons. Besides, diamonds are worth more than sapphires. And Ari's right. It is a pretty token of his love."

"Yes," Ari agreed, squeezing Reine's hand within her own. "Yes, it is."

She turned away, biting on her lip hard. It was the only way to stop the tears that were building from beginning to fall.

He gave Sasha a ring, she thought again, hurt building within her.

The only token he'd ever given her was a worthless piece of card.

CHAPTER 14: SPARK

Ari was here, but it was all wrong.

Tom took a deep, gasping breath, rubbing at his forehead anxiously. His mother pressed a glass of whisky into his hand, and he looked down at it dumbly, the scent of peat and malt suddenly strong in the air. Tom winced, for the smell of whisky was as familiar to him as the smell of roses, freshly cut grass, and — once upon a time — Ari's skin. This was his father's whisky. He took a sip, only to immediately begin coughing on the hard, smoky burn in his mouth and throat.

Doug always made drinking this whisky look easy. He made everything look easy.

His father, dead these seven years, but living on in his son, in the memories brought forth by an amber liquid in a crystal tumbler, and now also in the small girl being put to bed by her mother upstairs.

Doug's granddaughter, Tom realised. *My daughter,* his mind then added.

Abruptly, Tom's hand began to shake, the whisky sloshing precariously within his glass. Within a second, it was plucked from his hand, and Sebastian was staring at him hard.

"So," Sebastian began lightly, sipping Doug's whisky slowly, and for a moment Tom wondered at the sheer *audacity*

184

of this man to drink his father's whisky with such ease. "You're Tom Miller."

"No—" Tom began to argue, before his shoulders slumped. "Yeah."

"Tom Miller is fiction," Marnie protested, pouring a large measure of whisky out for herself. "Just a character invented by a confused twenty-five-year-old. He wasn't real."

At that Sebastian shook his head. "He was real to Ari."

Tom felt a dart of pain. "I know. I never meant to hurt her," he offered weakly, "I loved her."

"Truth be told, I don't know if I believe that," Sebastian replied, sinking into a nearby armchair. He stared at Tom again, his eyes drifting over his face, shoulders and body, and Tom shifted nervously.

"What?"

Sebastian shrugged. "I'm just looking. Trying to find her in you."

"Reine," Marnie said, and Tom noted how his mother sounded a little breathless when she spoke the girl's name. "She's beautiful."

"Yes," Sebastian's voice was warm, "yes, she is." He stared at Tom again, his eyes searching over him, and he emitted a bitter kind of huff that sat sourly in the air. "She has your eyes."

There was disappointment in his voice that made Tom shift again, and he looked over to his mother desperately. Marnie however sat bone-still, staring back at him.

She wasn't going to help him out of this. She was going to make him clean up his own mess.

"What did you think of her?" Sebastian pressed him, and Tom closed his eyes.

"Ari's as beautiful as she ever was," he answered honestly, and once again, that dart of pain ran through him.

"I didn't mean Ari," Sebastian spat. "I meant Reine. What did you think of her? Of your *daughter*?"

But at that, Tom's mind went blank.

"What did you think of her?" Sebastian asked again, his voice darkening. For a man who spent most of his day talking in a light, flippant and merry tone, Sebastian had quite the threatening timbre, Tom thought. He shifted again.

"She . . . she's just a kid," he replied honestly. "What am I supposed to think of her?"

It was clearly the wrong thing to say. "Well, fuck you, Tom Somerset," Sebastian said tightly. "And fuck you too, Tom Miller."

In a flash, Tom was on his feet.

"*What* exactly do you want me to say here?" he exploded, frustration running through him. "That I saw her and immediately thought, 'yes, that's my child'? That I saw her and loved her? That I saw her and wanted to be a father to her?"

"Yes, that was the general idea," Sebastian snapped back.

"Well, I'm sorry to disappoint you," Tom replied, running a hand through his hair. "The truth is that I looked at her and saw a kid. A kid. That's all. I didn't look at her and feel an instant swelling of love. I didn't look at her and feel a paternal pride. I hardly looked at her at all, in fact, because she's just a kid and a kid I don't know and at that point I only wanted to look at her mother."

"A kid you don't know?" Sebastian downed the whisky in one go, before slamming the tumbler onto a nearby table. "A kid you don't know? You helped *make* her."

"A fact I've only just learned in the last twenty-four hours."

"And a fact that means nothing to you, clearly."

"I didn't say that," Tom snapped. "Don't put words in my mouth. I didn't say that Reine being my daughter means nothing to me."

"You're acting like it doesn't," Sebastian returned. Tom watched as he turned to Marnie, who was sipping at her own drink, her fingers clutched tight around the glass.

"What do you think of all this?" Sebastian asked her, an accusing note to his voice. "You obviously know everything."

Marnie gave a shrug. "Not everything. I still have questions."

"But you know a lot," Sebastian replied, and Tom watched as his mother shrugged again.

"I started putting it together when Ari talked about Tom Miller. I'd known Tom had gone by that name for a few years . . . and the dates all made sense. But I don't know everything."

Sebastian gave Marnie a look. "That was at lunch yesterday. You've known for over twenty-four hours, have spoken to Ari in that time, and never said a word."

Marnie sighed. "I couldn't say anything to her. I didn't have the full story."

Sebastian crossed his arms over his chest like a petulant child. "None of us have the full story."

"Exactly," Marnie said softly. She glanced over at Tom, resting her eyes upon him sternly. "The only people who have the full story are Tom and Ari. And so we're going to let them tell it."

"Ari might be ages putting Reine to bed yet and Luis—"

"Oh no," Marnie interjected quickly, her eyes never leaving Tom's. "We aren't going to make them tell the story to us. They're going to talk to each other."

"Mom," Tom said, his voice hoarse, "I don't know that I can. I don't know if I can."

Marnie stood, coming across the room to stand next to Tom. She laid a hand on his shoulder comfortingly. "You owe that girl the truth, Tom. You owe her that, at the very least. You need to talk with her."

"She'll hate me," Tom whispered brokenly.

"She probably already does," Marnie answered honestly, "And she has good reason to. At this point, you've got nothing to lose."

Sebastian, on the other side of the room, threw up his hands. "What? We're just supposed to . . . let them talk? While we, what? Have dinner and make small talk with *Sasha*?"

"No," Marnie said firmly. "Sasha is Tom's fiancée, and he owes her the truth too. He also promised her the pleasure of his company at dinner. He's going to show her the respect she's due. I may not like that woman, but I won't have her treated with callousness. There's been enough of that in this family already."

Tom winced. *Callous*. He'd treated Ari callously. Once again, he ran a hand over his face, hearing the truth and sense in his mother's words, even while he shuddered at the thought of them.

"Sasha will want to talk about the wedding," Tom muttered, "she'll want to talk about the wedding over the dinner table with . . ." he swallowed hard ". . . with Ari right there."

"Yes," Marnie agreed, "most likely. And you're going to listen and nod and smile and then, afterwards, put it right with both of the women in your life. Your fiancée . . . and the mother of your child."

"Your child," Sebastian repeated loudly. "Your *child*. The fruit of your loins. Of your cheating, lying, no-good loins."

"Stop saying loins," Tom snapped. "I get it. I know I need to think about . . . about *her* as well—"

"Not her," Sebastian snapped back. "*Reine*. She has a name, and Luis and I worked damn hard to give it to her, so can you use it please?"

"Wait a minute . . . you named Reine?" Marnie cut in. "I thought it was Ari."

At that, Sebastian rolled his eyes. "No woman full of hormones and heartbreak should be entrusted with naming a child. Ever. I kid you not, Ari wanted to name Reine 'Millie' when she was born. *Millie*. Like Vanilli," his eyes narrowed, "or like her absent, cheating, lying and no-good father's fake surname. Well, thank God, we got her to dodge that bullet. We had to sit her down and explain that if her mysterious Tom ever did return for her — and make no mistake, Tom, she truly believed you would — her baby would end up with the name Millie Miller. Millie Miller." Sebastian shuddered. "Reine was the much better choice."

"Reine is a beautiful name," Marnie nodded approvingly. "A beautiful name for a beautiful girl."

"Damn right, and it's time your son started using it." He gave Tom a long, piercing stare. "If in my presence I hear you refer to Reine as *her* or *she* or, heaven help you, *it*, I will personally have you taken out by the nearest available assassin."

"Are assassins easy to come by in your world?" Marnie asked wryly, and Sebastian turned to her.

"My dear, I work the *wedding circuit*," he replied easily. "After hair and make-up, they're next on my contact list."

"I would never call her . . ." Tom paused ". . . I would never call Reine *it*. Never. Fuck, do you think if I'd known about her I would have stayed away? Do you think if that day when I saw her as a baby I'd thought she was mine, I wouldn't have done anything to be in her life? Of course I would, of course I would have done everything in my power—"

"Hold the phone, Somerset, there's a good chap," Sebastian interrupted, holding out his empty tumbler to Marnie, who diligently poured another measure into it. "What did you mean just then, when you said '*that day when I saw her as a baby*'?"

Tom paused. There was a loaded silence in the room, and Tom had to take a deep breath before speaking.

"I saw her . . . I mean, Reine. I saw her. As a baby," he confessed, "but I . . . I didn't think she . . . I didn't believe Reine could be mine."

"When did you see Reine? Where?" Sebastian asked icily, and Tom shifted in his seat. He was reminded suddenly of the time he'd cheated on an assignment at elementary school and been dragged before the irate assistant principal to explain himself. He'd wondered at the time where the actual principal was, before deciding that the level of fraud committed on the grade five Westward Expansion topic was so great the principal no longer bothered with reprimanding the many youngsters who did it. Still, even as the assistant principal railed at him, the threat of being taken to stern Miss Abbott — with her lined face, thin lips and wire-framed glasses — was enough to make him sweat the entire time.

It was the same feeling today. Sebastian was going to rail at him about Reine, Tom knew. But he also knew he had to face Ari too. And that was the meeting he was really worried about.

189

"At Ari's apartment," Tom said, clearing his throat. "I came to see her."

Sebastian inhaled sharply. "You went to her flat? When?"

"A little over two years after I'd left her in Germany."

For a moment, Sebastian stared at him. Tom stared back, waiting for Sebastian's inevitable anger, waiting for the rage to start so he could snap back. Talking about Ari and that hideous day when he'd gone to her door — expecting to find the love of his life and instead coming face to face with what he'd assumed were her husband and baby — always put him in a bad mood. If this man wanted a fight, Tom was ready to give it to him.

But Sebastian surprised him.

Tom watched as the blond-haired man nodded slowly, taking a deep drink of Doug's whisky.

"So," he said lightly, "you actually went back for her."

"Yeah, I did," Tom replied tightly, trying to keep the bitter tone from his voice. "Of course I did. I *loved* her. I still—" He stopped, biting on his lip hard. He saw Sebastian's eyes flash, and abruptly shook his head, standing up. "I loved her, I promised I would go back for her, promised I would find her, and I did. *I did.*"

Sebastian nodded slowly again, before holding a finger up to him. "Hold that thought, Somerset."

Tom watched as Sebastian turned to Marnie, pointing to his glass of whisky. "I say, Marnie, this stuff is fucking fabulous. Like liquid cigarettes. I love it."

"It was my husband's favourite," Marnie admitted, "I can't stand it myself, but he loved it and, for whatever reason, I can't stop buying it."

"Bless you, that's hard," Sebastian said, and the tone of his voice made Tom wonder if this man ever missed the parents who'd thrown him out. Maybe that was why he'd taken so well to the little family he'd created with Luis, Ari and Reine. Maybe there was comfort to be found in the parenting of a small child.

Tom swallowed heavily again. Parenting. He would never know now, would he?

"Losing Doug was one of the hardest things I've ever been through," Marnie replied softly.

"When did he pass?"

"Eight years ago, nearly. Just after Tom came back from Europe."

At that, Sebastian turned back to Tom. "So, that was true? You really did abandon Ari in Germany because your father was sick?"

"Not sick," Tom corrected him, "dying."

"And then you went back for her? Two years later? That's quite a gap, Somerset."

Tom sighed. "I needed time after my father died. I can't explain it . . . I needed time to grieve and to think and to be ready—"

"Ready?" Sebastian cut in, and the snap was back in his voice. "Ari was in London, pregnant and then raising your baby all alone, while you waited to be *ready*? Ready for what, may I ask? A written fucking invitation from the King?"

"Ready to face the truth," Tom at once snapped back. "Ready to face the truth of who I was, what I'd done and to beg Ari's forgiveness. I don't expect you to understand. I don't even care if you do, to be honest. All I care about is her. All I've ever cared about in my life has been her. And I've lost her. I've lost her. The one bright light in my small, pitiful existence has been lost to me, and I'll have to live with it for the rest of my small, pitiful existence." Tom ran a hand over his face. "If you want to hate me, then fine, hate me. It doesn't matter. No one will ever hate me more than I hate myself."

Tom heard his mother give a sad sigh, but Sebastian only rolled his eyes.

"You know, normally the brides are the dramatic ones," he reflected, throwing back the rest of Doug's whisky, "and Marnie, you really must write down the name of this stuff for me, by the way. It's Scottish, yes?"

"Actually, no," Marnie told him. "Japanese."

"Japanese?" Sebastian raised an eyebrow. "Impressive. You know, when Luis and I take Reine to Tokyo for the next BarbieCon, I might take a day to myself and visit the distillery. Get away from all the pink and plastic, as well as the slightly creepy doll collectors — and I do include my husband in that — fighting over a mint in the box 1983 Fabulous Fur Barbie. I could pick up a barrel or five of this marvellous stuff."

"You have to be a special client of the distillery owner to buy barrels," Marnie replied.

"And I'm going to guess by your tone that you are one of those special clients?"

At that, Marnie smiled. "No. Actually, I'm the owner. I had the Somerset estate buy up the place after Doug passed."

"Excellent. Maybe you can give me a special rate then."

"Even with a special rate, it's still very expensive."

Sebastian shrugged. "Well, luckily for me I just got paid an extraordinary sum of money from a client to plan her son's wedding."

Marnie grimaced. "Well, that client sounds like a damn fool."

"She's not. The son, on the other hand . . ."

"All right, all right, quit it," Tom finally snapped. "I get it, I'm a fool. I shouldn't have lied, shouldn't have abandoned Ari in Germany and shouldn't have assumed Reine wasn't mine when I saw her."

"Ah yes, *that*." Sebastian turned back to Tom casually. "You came to Ari's flat in London, saw Reine, and didn't immediately put two and two together?"

"He did, but made five instead of four," Marnie chimed in. "He thought Reine was your husband's child."

"*Luis*," Sebastian spluttered. "You thought Reine was Luis's? Jesus, Somerset, did you even look at Reine? Any fool can see that she's yours."

"I just . . . she was so little and Ari and I . . . the timings . . ."

"The timings? You had unprotected sex with her and then the next time you pop by her London flat there's a new small girl about the place and you didn't stop to think about it? What, did you suddenly start believing Ari was some kind of . . . I don't know, self-fertilising starfish?"

Tom shook his head in exasperation. "I know Ari isn't a fucking starfish!"

"Besides, starfish aren't self-fertilising," Marnie put forward. "They're broadcast spawners."

Tom's mouth dropped open as he turned to his mother. "How do you even know that?"

"I told you, didn't I?" Marnie replied blithely. "I read the internet. There was this blog by this man who was an assistant to a marine biologist out in . . . oh, somewhere in the Pacific. It was very entertaining. I was quite addicted at the time."

"Oh, I should read that," Sebastian's interest was piqued. "Do send me the link. As for you," he turned back to Tom, "you're not just a fool, you're a fucking idiot. If you'd stayed for thirty seconds and spoken to Luis, you'd have realised in an instant he wasn't Reine's father."

Tom dropped back into his chair, his shoulders slumping in defeat. "He just . . . he was so handsome . . . so easy-going with Reine . . . and she had this stuffed rabbit. This pink stuffed rabbit." Tom closed his eyes as a painful memory struck him. "Every time it wobbled in her little hands, your husband just . . . fixed it for her. Without even watching what she was doing. It was like he just knew. That's why I walked away. Because of a fucking pink rabbit."

Behind him, Tom heard Sebastian give a sigh. "The pink rabbit? Luis gave it to her when she was born. Honestly, Somerset, if you'd just spoken to him . . . I love him, but he has no boundaries, my Luis. I'd call him an open book but that would be wrong, because in his world there is *no* book. Instead, there's just pages and pages of text, which he'll tell you about without being asked or invited. If you'd just said to him, 'cute kid' he'd have straightaway replied with something like 'oh thanks, she is cute, she's my sister's and hey what a great accent you have, why, you must be an American. Speaking of Americans, do you know a guy named Tom

Miller by the way because we're searching for him?' and then you'd have known."

Tom felt something constrict tightly inside his chest. There was a sheen of sweat developing on his skin, and he felt sick, nausea building within him. All of a sudden, the world felt like too much. The room felt like too much and the two people beside him — his mother and this man to whom he was now forever linked because of a small girl — felt like too much. Tom stood, running his hand through his hair.

"I have to get out of here," he muttered, lurching towards the door.

"No Tom," his mother snapped, "you promised Sasha you'd be there for dinner!"

"You also promised Ari you'd be there for life!" Sebastian called after him.

But Tom didn't care. He fled through the open doors, tearing away from the house, tears stinging his eyes.

He needed to get away. From them all.

* * *

There's no reproach from Doug when Tom walks through the door and back into his life. Doug simply seems glad to see him, reaching for Tom's hand over the cotton blankets and squeezing it once.

"Hey," Tom says, and it strikes him painfully that it's such a simple word to use in the circumstances. Just three letters long and spoken in one short exhalation of breath. He's been gone for years, absent and silent and angry and lost, and now he's back with just one word to offer in greeting. It doesn't feel like enough.

But Doug gives him that same lopsided smile as always.

"Hey, Tom," he mutters, his voice raspier than Tom last remembers it. "You're a sight for sore eyes."

Guilt builds in Tom's stomach. "I know I've been gone a while,"he says softly.

Doug shakes his head. "Doesn't matter. You're here now. That's what counts. And you're a good kid."

194

Tom winces. "I don't know about that." He can't help it. He thinks of Ari, and of the look on her face when he said goodbye to her.

"You are a good kid," Doug persists, before giving him a grin. "So good that I know you'll go and get my whisky from the cabinet downstairs and bring it up to me."

"Mom won't?" Tom asks wryly, sinking into the chair next to his father's sick bed.

"Nah," Doug scowls briefly. "She's got me on this bullshit organic, gluten-free diet. She reads too much online. Thinks she's gonna cure my cancer by cutting out free radicals and carbohydrates. The damage is done though."

"You could have asked Corentin," Tom suggests, but Doug shrugs. Now that he's sitting, Tom can see the effort each movement is taking his father. He can clearly see the small flickers of pain that cross his face, the slight shake to his hand and the paper-thin quality of his skin. He sounds like his father, but he looks like a broken, dying man. Tom feels a deep stab of pain, which he does his best to keep hidden.

"I could," Doug replies, "but we all know how that would have gone. Always in cahoots with your mom, that kid."

"I'll get your whisky," Tom promises. "Might even have a glass myself."

"You don't drink whisky. Especially not my whisky."

"I don't know. It feels like a good time to start," Tom replies, trying to keep his voice light, but his father peers at him, looking concerned.

"What's going on, kid?"

"Nothing," Tom lies. "There's nothing going on."

"Yeah, right," Doug says bluntly, "you're just back from your mysterious years-long European vacation, you're sitting by the side of a dying old man, and you've got heartbreak written all over your face."

"Heartbreak? Of course my heart is broken. My father is the dying old man in your story," Tom reminds him, but Doug sees through his words almost at once.

"Who was she?"

Tom's stomach drops. "I don't know what you—"

"Cut the crap, kid. Of course you do. Corentin said you'd been travelling with a woman in Europe."

195

Tom presses his lips together. He'd only made it through his transatlantic flight, and then his journey home, by blocking Ari from his mind. It hurt deep inside him whenever he thought about her. He'd heard people talk about aching for someone, and always scoffed at the idea. How could you ache for someone? How could your body physically respond to an emotional event? How was that possible?

He'd learned quickly just how possible it was. From the moment he'd turned his back on Ari, from the moment he'd given her that final kiss, his body had begun to ache. It was worse than the most awful stomach ache and worse than the most awful headache. He couldn't eat and couldn't sleep. He was functioning on auto-pilot, hardly aware of his course or surroundings. He was a shell of a man. He ached everywhere, and every pain was for Ari.

"There was a woman," Tom replies softly. "There is a woman," he corrects himself. "I love her."

"Ah." Doug nods, and Tom sees recognition in his eyes. His father was young once, Tom reminds himself. "What about that girlfriend of yours . . . What was her name? The one from school?"

"Sasha," Tom says, but the name feels wrong on his lips. "She's not my girlfriend. Not anymore. I ended it with her before I left for Europe."

Doug sighs. "Sasha. That's it. Pretty thing. But she's not the woman you're in love with, right? There's someone else?"

"Yeah. There's someone else."

"Good," Doug replies, and the grin is back. "Sasha's pretty, but she's missing a spark. You need the spark, Tom. Always go for the girl with the spark. I've been in love twice in my whole damn life, and both times, the girls had spark."

"Two times?" Tom asks, raising an eyebrow. "Does Mom know?"

Doug grins again. "Yeah. She knows everything about everyone, especially me."

"Who was the first girl?"

Tom watches as his father shifts his head on his pillow. He looks almost wistful as he relives his youth. "Girl named Yvonne. Childhood sweetheart of mine . . . a bit like you and that Sasha girl. But she had a bit of spark. She had a bit of fire. She had a zest for life and living and we had a hell of a time together."

Surprisingly, Tom feels a dart of betrayal for his mother.

"Why didn't you end up with this Yvonne then?" he asks, his voice a little sharp, and he hears his father give a laugh.

"Because I met your mom. Just one look at her and I knew she was the right woman for me. You know your mom and I have had our problems, but she's always the one. Always has been, always will be."

Something inside of Tom softens, and he squeezes his father's hand once more.

"Tell me about this woman of yours. The one in Europe," his father asks, and Tom gives a bitter smile.

"You'd like her," he says, and it's the truth, he realises. His father wouldn't just like Ari. No, he would love her.

"Yeah?"

"Yeah. She's quick and curious and sharp as a tack. She eats anything and everything and finds adventure where you wouldn't even think adventure could be found," Tom says, and he warms at the thought of her. "She paints. Paints the most beautiful things you've ever seen. I have a pile of her paintings in storage in the city. Every time she painted something she didn't think was good enough to keep, I took it and shipped it home. There's this one painting, the one she did in Norway and—" Tom stops, colour flooding his cheeks. "I'm talking too much."

Doug, to Tom's surprise, has that wistful look on his face again. "You need to go back and get this woman and bring her here, Tom."

Tom slumps. "I can't do that. Not yet."

"Why the hell not?"

"I need time."

"Time to do what?"

Tom licks his lips. "Time to work out how I'm going to explain."

Doug looks at him warily. "Explain what?"

"About why I lied to her. About why I deceived her."

"Why would you do that?"

Tom shrugs. "I didn't mean for it to happen. I really didn't. I just . . ." he pauses, clenching his fists. The physical exertion distracts from his mental anguish, and it feels good when he releases and flexes his hand. "I was in an airport, and I saw this . . . this woman. She was striking. She was beautiful. I could tell she had . . ." he gives his father a small smile, ". . . spark. I didn't mean to talk to her. I really didn't. But we kept exchanging glances and then I . . . I couldn't help myself. I had to talk to her. It snowballed from there. I lied to her, again and again, because I kept meaning to walk away. I told myself it was just one conversation. And then it was just one kiss. And then just one night. And then, before I knew it, it had been just six months. By the time I realised I wanted it to be forever, it was too late. The damage was done." Tom sits back in his chair, looking up to meet his father's gaze. Doug's eyes are soft, regarding him with compassion.

"You're an idiot, Tom, you know that? You love this woman. Love her. That's not a small thing. You have to go back for her. Explain everything, just as you did to me. She'll either forgive you or—"

"Exactly," Tom cuts in, almost angry. He's not angry at Doug though. He's angry at himself. "Or. It's the or that frightens me. I love her, and I had it good with her, and the stupid, hurtful lies I told might cost me that. I want to be with her . . . but once she knows the truth, how will she ever want to be with me?"

"I don't know the answer to that question," Doug replies. "I don't. But you have to go back and try. You'll never forgive yourself if you don't."

"I know. I really love her. I want to be with her. But what happens if she turns me down? What if she moves on? I don't know how I could handle that. I don't know how I can live life without her now."

Doug suddenly looks weary, and Tom realises that this conversation is costing his father energy he doesn't have to give.

"Tom," Doug says softly, "if that happens, you'll move on. Take it from an old man who knows. I had Yvonne, and then I met your mother. There might be another woman—"

"Not for me," Tom cuts in firmly. "She's the only one for me. You said you saw Mom and knew. I saw Ari and I knew."

"Okay. But I don't want you to end up a lonely, bitter man. I want you to be happy. I'm your father. I need to know you'll be okay, once I'm . . . once I'm not around anymore."

At that, Tom feels tears begin to sting his eyes. "Dad."

"It's okay, Tom," Doug replies. "It's okay. Things will be okay, I promise. So long as you face up to your troubles and stop running from them, things will always work out. Go back to Europe, Tom. Find this woman. Make things right. If it's the last thing you ever do for your dad, do this."

Tom nods, still clinging to his father's hand.
And after he nods, his face crumples, and then he begins to cry.

* * *

He found himself in his father's old work shed. Doug had been a pilot — with a hangar full of light aircraft and a small runway on one side of the estate — but he'd also been a racer, and kept a shed full of old cars and parts he'd tinkered with. Marnie hadn't had the heart to get rid of any of it, and so it still sat to this day, dusty and neglected and worn. *Just like my heart,* Tom thought with a scowl. He sat by the side of an old Chevy, his long legs touching the nearby wall, playing with an old wrench and spark plug.

He found solace in keeping his hands busy, being both furious and disgusted with himself.

He'd run away. Again.

It was an old habit he found hard to break, running from his feelings and his troubles. And tonight, with Ari once again in his life, he'd been assaulted by both.

Ari. *Ari.*

The wrench fell from his hands, and once again, Tom felt that old ache build within him. He'd told himself for years that he no longer loved her. He'd told himself for years that this ache — this constant, fucking awful ache for her — was just a residual feeling of old. That it wasn't love he still felt for her, but merely nostalgia.

But that had been a lie, not just to himself but also to Sasha. He still loved Ari. He'd always loved Ari. He was always *going* to love Ari, and both she and Sasha needed to know that.

Tom took a deep breath, feeling the calm of his father's presence wash over him. Whenever he felt trouble at his mother's house, he did one of two things: went up into the sky in one of his dad's beat-up old planes, or came in here to mess around with one of his dad's beat-up old cars. He needed his dad. Needed his memory. Needed his father, even when his father was gone.

He picked the wrench back up as resolve ran through him.

He couldn't marry Sasha. He just couldn't. Not while he was still in love with Ari.

And Ari . . . he needed her to know how he felt. Needed her to know the truth. Needed her to know how sorry he was, how sorry he would always be.

He stood, intending on returning to the house, when a nearby rustle caught his attention.

Someone else was here, he realised. Someone else had followed him.

Ari, he immediately thought — or maybe hoped. *Ari's here.*

"You can come out," he said softly. "I'm here."

The wrench dropped from Tom's hand again, the noise bouncing around the old shed, because it wasn't Ari.

It was Reine.

She was dressed in a pair of pyjamas, a robe around her shoulders, her hair dressed in braids down her back. She was clutching the old, battered pink bunny Tom remembered from years ago, and was staring up at Tom with wide, almost fearful eyes.

"Reine," Tom said, stepping back and looking desperately from side to side. "What are you doing here? Does your mom know you're here? Does mine?"

But Reine continued to stare up at him, clutching her bunny. She chewed on her lip in a way that reminded Tom instantly of Ari, and he could see the small child was working up courage. But courage for what?

"I know who you are," the child said, her voice barely above a whisper but full of bravery. "I know who you are."

Tom felt his mouth go dry. "Do you?"

"Yes." The child nodded, and Tom could see that her hands were gripping the bunny with a tightness that must have been hurting her fingers. "Yes, I know."

"Who am I?" Tom asked, terrified already of her response.

The child stood taller. "You're my father."

200

CHAPTER 15: THIRTY-SEVEN

There were very few men who Marnie liked and even fewer who she respected. Perhaps it was her upbringing — that sheltered youth as the prodigal daughter of a deeply talented but also deeply disturbed man. Perhaps it was the plethora of men who seemed to constantly surround him, dark-suited and tall, who glanced at her childish presence with annoyance and then later, when she developed into a rebellious teenager with resentment and attitude, a deep and unsettling suspicion.

She hadn't understood Doug either, if she was entirely honest with herself. Doug had been sexy and exciting, and she'd been seduced more by the idea of him than anything else. To discover that beneath that alluring exterior had been a kind man with a compassionate heart had been a surprise — discovering that she liked that kindness had been a seismic shift that had rocked her to her very foundations. Doug's kindness had been both a gift and a curse. Deeply attractive on the outside and unable to withstand causing hurt within, Doug had been easily led and easily swayed. Married — perhaps unsuitably — to a woman with a core of steel who was always working, Doug's affairs had been many, and he'd adopted a devil-may-care lifestyle that Marnie could never fathom but likewise never condemned. The women, the gambling, the airplanes . . . even now, Marnie was taken aback that not only had their shotgun marriage worked, it had lasted until Doug's death. Marnie had loved her husband, but she hadn't always *respected* him.

And her boys.

Corentin and Tom had been the brown-eyed babies of her dreams. When they'd first placed her tiny infants in her arms, which curved naturally around them, she'd looked down at her little sons and wondered where they'd been all her life. For they were so much a part of her in that moment that she couldn't remember a time when they'd ever been away from her. In her boys, Marnie found a reason to justify her not-always-happy marriage, her decisions and life choices. In them, she found a renewed sense of purpose. She had to make a good world for her sons. She had to leave the world a better place than she'd found it. Her error, Marnie knew now, was misplacing that sense of purpose into working more and working harder, and not spending her time with her precious babies, who did not remain babies for long, but became wide-eyed toddlers and then, with alarming speed, quiet and pensive boys. Before she knew it, Corentin and Tom were grown. Corentin, as calm and placid and self-aware as he'd been as an infant, was happy enough, his choices and decisions his own. Tom though . . . It hit Marnie hard that where her beautiful boy once stood, a sullen and resentful man had taken his place, and she'd been struck with the first pangs of regret at her absence from his life.

She loved both her sons, but she didn't always *know* them.

As for other men . . . well, Marnie could only shrug. Her father, husband and sons had been the only men in her life to really count. The rest had been mere background, an echoing chamber of complaints and disapproval, and she hadn't liked any of them.

So, ten minutes into dinner with Luis De León, Marnie was heartily surprised to find that not only could she tolerate him, but that she was actually beginning to *like* him too. He was witty and verbose, pleasant and winningly attractive, and Marnie's heart had fluttered when he'd leaned over the table to fill her wine glass and winked at her.

"Sheesh, I bet you were a stunning bride, once upon a time," he told her, filling her glass nearly to the brim. "I can see where she gets her good looks from now."

"Oh, Marnie's not my mom," Sasha cut in breezily. *Of course*, Marnie thought with a scowl, *that vapid woman would imagine this conversation was about her.* Sasha was sitting at the table with a white wine spritzer in her hand, an empty plate shining before her. Marnie didn't know what she hated more: that Sasha had turned down the sumptuous Thai-infused scallops that had been painstakingly prepared alongside a quail egg salad, or that she'd cut into an exquisite Edmond Vatan Sancerre Clos la Neore with club soda.

"That's right," Ari broke in softly, and Marnie's eyes immediately flicked to her. "Sasha's mother has sadly passed, Luis. Marnie is our . . . our groom's mother."

Hearing Ari's voice break on the word 'groom', Marnie felt a deep stab of pity, and another deep stab of frustration with her son.

"Oh," Luis replied quickly, "I'm sorry. I didn't know."

Marnie turned to him, hearing the lie in his voice. In that moment he looked decidedly awkward, chewing on his lip uncomfortably. *I can see where she gets her good looks from now* . . . Luis had been talking about Reine, obviously. He knew it and Ari knew it and Sebastian knew it and Marnie knew it, but not one of them could say it out loud because of Sasha, who still knew nothing. Thinking quickly, Marnie realised that somewhere between the airport and here, Luis had been briefed on the situation. He knew that Tom was Reine's father, and also the mysterious Tom Somerset who had broken Ari's heart.

Surprisingly, Marnie didn't feel angry with Luis. No. She felt almost grateful to him.

I can see where she gets her good looks from. He was the first one of them all to acknowledge her as Reine's grandmother. The first one to acknowledge that biological link, which Marnie still fervently hoped would soon transfer into an emotional one.

Yes, she realised. She liked Luis De León. Unlike his husband, he was genuine, and she sensed in him an ally of sorts. An ally she hoped to use to her advantage.

So Marnie decided to rescue him, and with him this horribly awkward situation.

"When did you first start designing wedding gowns?" she asked lightly, piercing a scallop with her fork.

Luis grinned back. "You know something? I've been designing them all my life. I was the kid in class who drew princesses in ball gowns rather than dinosaurs or dragons. I was the kid who sat on his abuela's knee learning to crochet so I could dress my sister's Barbie doll for her wedding to Ken."

"Ken and Barbie," Sebastian chimed in drily, "it'll never last. Ken's always clearly on the rebound from GI Joe."

"Obviously," Luis returned, with another grin that made Marnie's stomach flutter. "Anyway, I've been designing all my life, in one way or another."

"When did you turn professional?" Marnie was astonished to find she was actually interested in his reply.

"I moved to New York for design school. I was lucky, growing up in El Salvador can be tough for a man like me. I won a scholarship though, went through on a free ride, which meant I could really concentrate on my specialty. After I graduated, I transferred to London to work under Stephanie Allin. Wedding design is a tough industry, especially if you specialise in it like me, and don't produce other collections. But I got lucky. An old girlfriend of mine was up and coming in the wedding business herself and referred me to a minor member of the British aristocracy. I designed my first gown under my own name. Word spread, and soon I was inundated with design requests. I opened my Kensington boutique not long after, and I've been there ever since."

"An old girlfriend?" Sasha asked, and Marnie could see the confusion on her face. "But I thought you were . . ."

"Gay?" asked Luis, and when Sasha nodded, he gave a shrug. "I don't like to define myself, but I believe in love being love, and I've always fallen in love with personalities rather than genders."

"Personalities?" Marnie asked, inadvertently raising an eyebrow towards Sebastian. "You fall in love with personalities?"

"Yeah," Luis grinned. "I do. And my Sebbie here has enough personality to get me through three lifetimes. Keeps me on my toes." He reached over to stroke his husband's arm lovingly, which Sebastian permitted with an affectionate roll of his eyes.

"Oh, that's so sweet," Sasha gushed. "That's what I want Tom and I to be like. Just so, you know, in love and everything."

"How did you meet?" Luis asked, taking hold of his wine glass and drinking heartily. "Ari hasn't brought me up to speed with that yet."

Ari. Marnie's eyes flicked once more to the woman at the corner of the table, her plate of food untouched, her eyes soft and sad. Marnie felt pity threaten to overwhelm her. This conversation, this dinner, this whole day . . . it must have been killing her.

"We were childhood sweethearts," Sasha replied dreamily, fingering the edge of her wine glass as she spoke. "We met at summer camp one year. It was meant to be. We were meant to be. Tom, the son of Marnie Somerset, and me, the prettiest and wealthiest girl at camp . . ." Sasha trailed off with a happy sigh.

"Pretty *and* wealthy?" Sebastian asked, with an exaggerated shock that Marnie wasn't sure how to read, although she suspected it wasn't meant kindly.

Sasha nodded. "And I was runner-up Miss Teen Rhode Island."

"Noooo," Luis replied in mock disbelief, "Runner-up Miss Teen Rhode Island? You don't say?"

"It's one of the reasons I decided on Tom," Sasha nodded seriously. "You know he's descended from French royalty? Well, nearly. Close enough, anyway. And I had a crown — well, I *nearly* had a crown — of my own. Tom and I just . . . made sense, you know? The perfect match."

Marnie looked once again at Ari. She'd gone white, her hand clenched around her napkin, her eyes downcast. Heartbreak was etched onto every line of her slumped being, and Marnie decided enough was enough. She cleared her throat.

"Maybe we should talk about something else—" she began, but Luis was too quick, already leaning towards Sasha.

"And you've been together ever since that summer camp?" he asked, refilling Sasha's glass.

"Mm-hmm." Sasha nodded, before she scowled. "Well, there was this period of a few years where Tom went . . . Well, he was travelling and then his father died and then . . . Well, it doesn't even matter. We took a little break though."

"A little break?" Luis asked, but Marnie could see his eyes resting on Ari.

"Yes," Sasha said, and there was an edge to her voice. "Just a little break. We both needed to decide on what we really wanted out of life. I had options other than Tom, you know. Other men wanted to marry me."

"Well, of course they did, darling," Sebastian replied. "You were runner-up Miss Teen Rhode Island."

"I know, right?" Sasha said emphatically. "But I still went back to Tom, in the end."

"You went back to him?" Luis pressed her, his eyes still on Ari.

"Yes," Sasha nodded. "He came back to me . . . oh, a few years after his father died? Not that it matters. We ran into each other at a polo match upstate. Such a dull sport." Sasha rolled her eyes. "Who likes horses, anyway?"

"Clearly your fiancé does," Sebastian said blankly, "if he was at a polo match."

"No." Sasha picked at a cuticle. "No, he wasn't there for the horses. He was there to buy this painting from some guy. I remember, because he told me all about it afterwards at dinner."

"A painting?" Ari suddenly broke in, and both Marnie and Luis glanced up at her in surprise. She was staring at Sasha with interest, though her voice was still soft and broken. "He was there to buy a painting?"

"Yeah." Sasha nodded boredly. "Tom got really into some undiscovered artist while he was in Europe. He's been buying up their pieces for years. And this guy — the one at the polo match — well, he'd picked up one of their paintings for pennies at some market in London. A painting Tom had been searching for *for ever*. Tom bought it from him for five figures. It makes no sense to me, but I figure, at least he's spending money on art and not on other women. All men have to have their hobbies, I guess, and art is decidedly less dangerous than flying planes. It was a really ugly painting though, when it was delivered. I didn't care for it at all. It was of . . . I guess it was a little girl? A little girl with—"

"Broken earth beneath her feet?" Sebastian interrupted her, and Sasha gave him a surprised glance.

"Yes, that's exactly it! How did you know?"

"Let's just say I've seen it before," Sebastian replied, and Marnie watched as a look passed between him and Luis. A look they finished by glancing at Ari.

"Tom has it hanging in his study in our New York apartment," Sasha said, and there was pride in her voice now, Marnie noted. "There're quite a few paintings by the same artist there. He hasn't bought a new one for a while though. I guess the artist stopped painting or something like that."

"Something like that," Ari mused quietly.

"Well," Marnie cut in, "perhaps we should talk about the wedding gown now? Luis, you must have some ideas—"

But Luis, annoyingly, was still staring curiously at Sasha. "You said you met again at this polo match?"

"Yes." Sasha nodded. "Once he'd bought the painting, he came to talk with me. Not that the talking lasted long though. He . . ." Sasha inexplicably giggled ". . . well, we went back to his place and. . . I think you can imagine what happened next."

Abruptly, Ari stood, her chair scratching the floor as she came to a stand. "Please excuse me," she said coldly. "I'm just going to check on Reine."

"Ari—" Marnie called after her, but she'd already gone, her arms wrapped around her stomach, her back stooped.

* * *

"What do you think then?" Tom asks, and Marnie scrunches up her nose.

"It's an interesting choice, I suppose."

Tom gives a half-smile. "You mean you hate it."

"No, I don't hate it . . . I just . . ." Marnie looks around once more at Tom's new apartment. Everything is shiny and new. The carpets are cream, the wood fresh, and there is the lingering smell of fresh paint in the air. "I just don't know if it's you."

Tom looks around too, taking it in, as if for the first time, the home he has chosen for himself.

"I don't know if it's me either," he agrees, running a hand through his hair. "But I have to try something new. I need a change, Mom."

"Yes," Marnie agrees softly. "Yes. We all do."

"Dad's gone, and I can't stay with you in that big pile upstate anymore," Tom explains. "Just as I can't live in that rented house over in Brooklyn anymore. I'm trying to be a grown-up now, Mom. I have a job—"

"—which you hate." Marnie can't help herself from breaking in, but Tom ignores her, carrying on as if she hasn't spoken at all.

"—and I have Sasha to think of now too."

Who I hate, *Marnie thinks, though she bites her tongue on that one.*

"Will Sasha live with you?" she asks instead, running a hand along a white chaise longue. Suddenly, this room makes more sense. Tom, she realises with a start, hasn't chosen a damn thing in this room, or this entire apartment. No. This whole apartment with its cream and white theme and gold-edged frames reeks of Sasha and her grasping, new-moneyed hands.

"Eventually," Tom replies, but Marnie hears the hesitation in his voice.

"Tom—" she begins, but he suddenly looks anguished, holding up a hand to stop her.

"Don't, Mom, please don't."

"I just want you to be happy, Tom."

"So do I," he agrees, but he still looks wounded. Not for the first time, Marnie sees the lines around Tom's eyes, the tiredness in his face, the sheer brokenness of her son's body. He looks and sounds beaten by life, and she longs to reach out and take that sadness away from him.

"I want to be happy, Mom," he carries on, sinking into a nearby chair. "I'm tired of grieving. I'm tired of this half-life, of waiting for someone to walk through my door who I know will never—" abruptly, Tom stops. He shakes his head, running a hand tiredly over his forehead. "I need to live again. I want to be happy. Dad told me to be happy. He wanted me to be happy."

"Yes, but with Sasha? I just—"

"Mom," Tom implores again. "I have no other choice."

"Of course you do!" Marnie argues. "You're attractive and clever and kind and . . . and of course you have other choices, Tom!"

Tom shakes his head at her sadly. "No, Mom. I guess what I mean is . . . I've made my choice."

Marnie exhales heavily, trying to keep the annoyed huff from leaving her lips. Standing taller, she spins on her heels — although it's nearly impossible on this high, velvet pile carpet, which creeps around her ankles like a fucking nylon jungle — and heads away from the main living area, following a narrow hall towards the bathroom. With a scowl, she passes the bedroom, which is decadent and plush and looks very much like a nineteenth-century whore's boudoir, before she sees a darker, smaller room and pauses.

Pushing on the door, Marnie takes a closer look. This room is different from the others, with hardwood floors and light blue walls. There's a desk by the window, covered in paperwork, though Marnie notes, with a flush of pleasure, a well-made model of a De Havilland Comet by the lamp. She feels a touch of Doug in this room, and knows, with absolute certainty, that this room is Tom's through and through. There's no Sasha in this room. There's just her son.

Looking up, she suddenly finds herself taking in the artwork on the walls. There are three paintings, all of a similar size and kept secure in simple wooden frames. Acrylic paint, Marnie decides, on oil canvas. Traditional and tasteful but also eye-catching. The first is of a mountain village at night, stars speckled above it. The second is of a pebbly beach at sunset, all oranges and pinks and light. The third, however, is much darker. It's of a small child with dark hair, holding the hand of an unseen figure, staring out at a shattered landscape, with broken earth beneath her feet. Still staring at the image, she hears Tom enter the room behind her, and whistles under her breath.

"Sasha didn't choose this," she says matter-of-factly, and feels, rather than sees, Tom nod behind her.

"No."

"You chose this," Marnie adds. "It's beautiful."

"Yes."

Marnie finally turns, indicating to all three paintings. "They're all by the same artist?"

Tom swallows heavily, his eyes scanning over the paintings he's clearly chosen, framed and hung. "Yeah . . . I, uh . . . I bought one of the artist's paintings while in Europe." He leans against the wall. "I guess it became a bit of an obsession."

"You've been collecting their work?" Marnie asks, not displeased. An appreciation of art has always been strong in her family, and she's happy to find Tom following suit.

"Yeah, I have. This one," he indicates to the image of the small girl, "this is the last one they released. Took me a while to find it."

"How do you know it's the last one?"

"They haven't released anything since."

"Oh. Do you follow the artist online or something like that?" Marnie asks with interest.

"Just their art," Tom replies, and he swallows again, full of discomfort.

"You should get in touch with them," Marnie says, trying to show an interest in her son's interests. "Ask if they'll take a commission, ask them to—"

"No," Tom replies flatly. "No."

"But Tom—"

"No," he says again. "Come on. Let's go out for lunch."

But Marnie continues to stare at the paintings, feeling a prickle run down her back, a sudden awareness making the hair stand up on her skin.

"I have a feeling I've seen this artist's work before," she comments, and hears Tom clear his throat.

"One of the paintings I sent from Europe," he explains, and there is a tightness in his words. "It's hanging in the hall at your place."

"*The Ends of the Earth,*" Marnie suddenly says, as memory strikes her. "Yes, you're right. Well, why don't I send it to you? You obviously love the artist—"

"Mom, stop," Tom whispers, and she turns at the torment in his voice.

"Tom?"

"Just leave the painting where it is, okay? I don't . . . I don't want that painting here. It's where it belongs."

Marnie pauses, the prickle down her back running stronger. "Tom, who is the artist?"

"Just some artist," Tom replies, looking down, evading her eyes.

The prickle runs stronger again, turning into an odd feeling in her stomach. There's something more going on here, Marnie is nearly sure of it.

"Okay," she nods. "Tom, how many paintings has this artist produced?"

At that, Tom looks up. "Thirty-seven."

Marnie takes a deep breath. "And how many do you own?"

Tom sighs. "Thirty-seven."

"You bought them all?"

"Yeah," Tom mutters. "I bought them all."

"Why?" Marnie asks, almost scared to hear his reply.

At that, Tom gives an unexpected but bitter smile. "I just wanted the scraps," he says tiredly, though Marnie can make no sense of his words. "I couldn't have what I wanted, Mom, so I bought what was left to me."

"Tom—"

"I bought what was left to me," he says again, and his voice is blank. "I bought what was left."

* * *

211

You're my father.

Tom's heart beat fast within his chest, and he felt a clammy sort of cold strike his skin. The little girl who looked up at him, still clutching her bunny, appeared suddenly fierce, a determination in her stance that reminded him overwhelmingly of his mother.

"What makes you say that?" he asked her, trying to hide the sudden tremble to his fingers.

Reine pulled her bunny to her face, ducking her chin into the soft pink plush. "Because Mummy told me about you," she declared.

"She . . . she did?"

"Yes," Reine replied. "We had to draw our family tree at school. I asked Mummy to describe you, and she said my daddy was tall, dark-haired and American." Reine looked up at him, and Tom felt his hands shake again. "You're tall. Your hair is brown. And you're American."

"Lots of men are tall, brown-haired and American," Tom stuttered. "Why . . . why would you think I was—"

The words died in his throat as Reine reached out a small hand, placing her cool fingers within his own. Instantly, his hand curled protectively around hers, and he stared down at their intertwined fingers.

"Look," Reine said, and she tugged on his hand, pulling him across the old and dirty room. Reine's feet were bare, and Tom was suddenly struck with a desire to lift her into his arms. God knew when this hangar had last been cleaned, and there might be shards of glass, or broken metal, or slippery engine oil embedded on the floor.

"Careful," he said, the word coming out in a broken cry, and Reine glanced down, looking carefully as she picked her way across the hangar.

She stopped in front of Doug's old truck, rusty but reliable, which Tom knew Marnie had kept out of an unusual sense of nostalgia. Before the truck was a filthy and partially cracked mirror, which Doug had used for reflective engine work. If he closed his eyes, Tom could still picture Doug on the floor, his legs sticking out from the body of the truck, a mirror on his hand, asking Tom to diagnose the issue from the reflection before him.

Now, Reine pulled him to the mirror, pointing at the reflection, asking him to do much the same.

"Look," she said again, and so Tom did.

The girl in the mirror had hair the colour of dark honey — different to his own, he reasoned. The girl in the mirror had tanned skin, as though she had recently seen the sun, he reasoned likewise. The girl in the mirror was nothing like him. The girl in the mirror was like her mother. The girl in the mirror was all Ari.

But then his eyes met Reine's in their reflection, and he inhaled sharply.

The girl in the mirror had his eyes, he saw again. The girl in the mirror had his cheekbones. The girl in the mirror had his lips and smile and height. The girl in the mirror was Ari, but she was also him. The likeness was obvious, and Reine had recognised herself in him, just as he'd recognised himself in her. But there was more than that. When Tom looked at Reine, he wasn't just reminded of himself, or of her mother. He was reminded of his study back at home in New York. He was reminded of a painting that hung on his wall, of a small girl clutching an unknown man's hand, staring out at a cracked landscape.

He wasn't seeing Reine for the first time, he realised with a profound sense of relief and gratitude. He'd seen her before. He had been looking at her every day for years now. In a way, she'd been with him every day.

"See?" Reine asked, and he looked down at her, taking in her presence with a renewed sense of wonder. The little girl looked almost proud, as if she had worked out a great secret, or solved a troubling puzzle.

"You're my father."

Tom took another deep breath, staring at their reflection, his hand still clutched tightly within Reine's own.

"Yeah," he agreed, and he squeezed her hand, watching their reflections. "Yeah, I am."

CHAPTER 16: CHEESE

Ari got as far as the door to her room before she had to stop and take one long, shuddering deep breath. Her lungs felt tight and her stomach queasy, and she laid one hand against both, trying to ease the discomfort in vain. *This*, she thought to herself miserably, *must be what dying feels like.*

But she wasn't dying. Her heart still beat steadily, and her lungs still drew air, despite having taken what felt like a mortal wound to her soul. Ari sank unhappily to the floor, clutching her knees to her chest and trying to hold back the tears that threatened to spill down her cheeks.

Childhood sweethearts. Meant to be. You can imagine what happened next.

The same words swirled around and around Ari's fevered mind, hurting her horribly and conjuring up images she had never hoped to have. It was all too easy in that moment to imagine Sasha — pretty, delicate and confident Sasha — wrapped tenderly in Tom's arms, the place she had belonged since their shared youth, the place she belonged now, and the place she would belong forever more. A place only briefly inhabited by Ari, during Tom's long but ultimately temporary sojourn to Europe. He'd been lost when Ari had known him — she could see that now. Lost and aimless and

214

searching, his eyes always soft and sad. She'd tried to help him, by loving him and making love to him and holding him together in any way she could. It had been a futile task though, and no wonder. He'd never wanted her love, Ari realised. Not when he had Sasha to come home to.

Ari swallowed hard. Thinking back to those halcyon days in Europe, she could see now — with an almost blinding clarity — that she had offered Tom everything she'd wanted for herself, loving and needing Tom in a way she so desperately wanted to be loved and needed. Perhaps that need had overwhelmed him. Perhaps her love hadn't been enough. She'd fixed Tom just enough for him to return home to Sasha's arms, and his true persona of Tom Somerset, and Ari had been left in the wake. Their love, their relationship . . . It had all been for nothing. He'd used her for a purpose, and once that purpose had been served, she'd been easily discarded and forgotten.

For a moment Ari sat, staring sadly into the distance. This house was so large and impersonal, with shining walls and cold stone floors. Tom had grown up here, she reflected. He'd been a boy in these rambling halls — become a man in these endless rooms. This was his home, his world, and she felt so out of place in it. There was nothing for her here other than the man who'd abandoned her and his waspish fiancée. Abruptly, she longed to be in London, back at home in her little house. It was nothing compared to this mansion, just a typical London two-up, two-down, but it was hers. She'd worked hard for the money for the deposit, sacrificing her youth and nights out and — most cuttingly of all — any and all hopes of achieving her artistic ambitions. She worked harder still to afford her monthly mortgage, giving up weekends and holidays and precious time with Reine. Luis and Sebastian were still indignant about it, she knew. When she'd first told them she was looking for a house, they'd been casual almost to the point of ambivalence.

* * *

"A house?" Luis asks, scratching his head. "Why would you want your own house?"

"Yes," Sebastian adds, gesturing to the living room of the flat she rented from them, "you live here."

"I can't stay here forever," Ari tells them. "We all knew this was a temporary measure. Just until Reine and I were on our feet. Well, we're on them now and it's time for us to have a home of our own."

"But you live here," Sebastian says again, looking puzzled. "This is a zone one flat that you rent for a pittance. There's a Le Pain Quotidien down the street and a Majestic Wine Warehouse on the corner. Why on earth would you ever want to leave?"

Ari sighs, watching Reine pull herself up into Luis's lap. She sees him smile as the small toddler snuggles into his arms, burrowing her chubby arms into his cashmere cardigan, and she feels a pang of guilt for Tom.

That should be him, she reminds herself. Tom should be the one getting Reine's cuddles and kisses.

"Well, a garden for Reine, for one thing," Ari says easily, brushing off her sadness and walking into the kitchen to make tea. "She needs fresh air."

"So we'll take her to the park more," Luis protests.

"Or there's that new brasserie at the top of the Fenchurch Building," Sebastian adds. "That's thirty-four floors up. Way above the pollution. The air's plenty fresh up there, I bet, and I hear the pastries are to die for. We'll let Reine wobble around while we do brunch."

Ari stares at him as the kettle boils. "That's not fresh air."

"It's fresher than you're going to get anywhere else north of the river," Sebastian sniffs.

"Exactly," Ari replies quietly, and both Sebastian and Luis freeze.

"No," breathes out Sebastian, while Luis holds up a hand.

"Ari, honey, we love you. We cannot — I repeat, we cannot — let you move south of the river."

"That's all I can afford," Ari argues, pouring tea into three mugs. "And you'll like South London, there are museums and parks and shops and—"

"And knife crime, lower life expectancy and a subpar transport infrastructure," Sebastian finishes for her, his voice aghast. "How are we supposed to visit?" He shudders. "On the bus?"

"Yes," *Ari says simply. "Or the DLR. Or you could get the train."*

"You mean National Rail?" *Luis asks, horror-struck.*

"I've seen this place in Greenwich," Ari continues, ignoring them both. "You'll love it. It's small, but it has a little garden and it's near the DLR. And oh, my goodness, it's a ten-minute walk to this cute little ice cream place, you're going to love it—"

"We can get ice cream here, Ari," *Luis says.*

"Selfridges deliver now," *Sebastian adds helpfully.*

"You can't go, Ari," *Luis insists. "You haven't thought this through."*

"I have, I really have—"

"Well, what about Tom?" *he cuts in.*

Ari freezes at Tom's name, midway through holding out a scalding cup of tea to Sebastian, who plucks it gently from her hand.

"What do you mean?" *she finally asks, her voice quiet.*

"I mean what about Tom?" Luis repeats. "Part of the reason you rented from us here was because you didn't want to put down too many roots. You know, just in case Tom Miller drifted back into your life to waltz you and Reine off into the sunset. I don't know about you, but buying a house sounds an awful lot like putting down roots to me, Ari."

Ari pauses, chewing on a nail thoughtfully. "Reine needs a home," she answers carefully. She looks at her little girl, now fast asleep in Luis's arms. "Tom said he would come back for me, and he will, he really will . . . but he's taking his time, and I . . ." She trails off helplessly. "I don't want Reine being like me."

"Why not?" *asks Sebastian, indignant. "You're okay. Well, I mean, you're mousy and perpetually bedraggled and you have the confidence levels of an endangered sloth, but still, you're okay."*

Ari swallows. "I want her to have roots. I want her to have stability."

"We give her that," *Luis protests, hugging the little girl in his arms tightly. "She has stability here."*

Too much stability, *Ari thinks.* I'm doing this for Tom.

"You need to let me do this," she tells them both. "You've taken such good care of me for so long now . . . it's time to let me take care of myself and my daughter. I need to do this. I really do."

217

Ari watches as Luis and Sebastian exchange a look.

"It would give me back this place for my dolls," Luis mulls. "Mattel just released a new line of inspiring women Barbies, and it would be a shame to take Emmeline Pankhurst out of her box and put her straight into storage."

"But Greenwich," Sebastian intones, shaking his head.

"We could get the boat from the Embankment," Luis offers, and Ari shoots him a grateful glance. "Stop off at the Southbank. Buy cheese at Borough Market. You like cheese. I like cheese. Ari likes cheese."

"Ari likes anything with calories," Sebastian replies with a roll of his eyes.

"This is good cheese though. Artisan cheese. Expensive cheese."

Sebastian seems to consider Luis's words. "Like that cheese we bought in France. You remember, on our first trip together, where you got steamingly pissed on Bergerac red wine."

Luis instantly bristles. "I wasn't drunk. I was pleasantly tipsy."

"You fell into the Dordogne."

"An evening swim. What of it?"

"Your arms were still full of the cheese we'd bought."

Luis crosses his arms over his chest. "You told me that the water gave the cheese a salty expression."

"I was being nice. I was trying to woo you, after all," Sebastian replies with a shrug. "I wanted you, even after you ruined three hundred euros worth of Rocamadour."

"Oh, you're never going to let me live down that Rocamadour, are you?" Luis explodes. "We can always buy more cheese, Sebastian! Ari's moving to Greenwich. We can get cheese every damn time we visit her by calling at the market!"

"Will you both please stop talking about cheese," Ari seethes, gesturing to Reine, who startled awake at the rise in Luis's voice.

Luis glances down, smiling at Reine warmly and brushing her hair away from her face. He plants a kiss on the girl's head, before taking a deep breath. "We'll all make this work," he says, more forcefully now. "This move. We'll make it work for Reine."

* * *

218

They had made it work, Ari reflected. She'd bought the little house and filled it with things and found Reine a place at a good state school. And for all Luis and Sebastian's initial complaints, she was certain they were happier with the new arrangement. They had busy lives of their own outside of work and her and Reine, and they were more attentive for the distance. She couldn't stop them from making Reine a little bedroom of her own in their flat, however.

* * *

"It's just common sense," Luis says, as he hangs pink cotton bunting above a little white bed. "You work so much, Ari. She'll need to stay here with me while you and Sebastian are off at weddings."

Ari frowns, even though she hears the sense in his words. Her workload is always a cause of concern for her, and she frets about the hours it sucks away from her time with Reine. But what else can she do? She's a single mother who has a mortgage and bills to pay and a child to raise. Her hands are tied. She has to work, to give Reine the childhood she deserves.

A childhood so different from her own.

* * *

Taking a deep breath, Ari stood, keeping her hand on her stomach to steady herself. She had to think of Reine. She had to cast aside the broken heart Tom had inflicted upon her, just as she had to cast aside the hurt from Sasha's careless words. She had to be a grown-up, and put her child and career above the considerations of her heart.

Tom was just a man, she told herself, standing taller. There would be other men. There would be other relationships. It was time to admit defeat and move on. Ari took another deep breath, biting hard on her lip. She'd been on occasional dates in the past few years but hadn't allowed anyone to get too close to her fractured heart. She'd always thought staying single was best for Reine, and she'd been so busy with her work. But now it was time to stop making excuses. The truth — the stark, unwavering truth — was that she'd stayed single out of loyalty and love for Tom. Tom, who'd proven himself undesiring of her affection and fidelity. Tom Miller, who was really Tom Somerset, who was about to marry Sasha.

She had to let go of him, and the memory of him. She'd been wrong, earlier, when she'd thought their relationship had been for nothing. It hadn't been.

She had Reine.

With another deep breath, Ari moved quietly into her room, cutting through into the room where Reine slept. She'd left the window open to air out the smell of fresh paint, and the curtains ruffled in the breeze. Quietly, Ari tiptoed towards the bed, seeing the mound of blankets, thinking Reine must have moved in her sleep.

She stared at the empty bed, suddenly filled with horror.

Her heart hammered hard, and she inhaled sharply, flicking all the lights on and searching frantically around the room.

"Reine!" she called out. "Reine, where are you?"

But Reine was nowhere to be seen, and Ari, frightened beyond belief, tore out of the room and fled back down the stairs.

At the dining room table, Luis, Sebastian, Marnie and Sasha were still drinking wine. They looked up when Ari stumbled into the room, tears trickling down her cheeks.

"Reine," she said frantically, "she's gone. She's gone."

* * *

"Does your bunny have a name?" Tom asked as his daughter stared up at him, her eyes wide and bright.

They were sitting on a worn blanket on the floor of Doug's old shed. There was a nip in the air, so Tom had draped his jacket over Reine's shoulders. The garment swamped her, but she didn't seem to mind, and it was keeping her warm. More than that, Tom couldn't deny the flash of pleasure it gave him to see his child wearing his clothes. If he'd helped to raise her, he would have already draped her in his jackets and sweaters, his scarves and hats. Even Doug's old vest, which Tom kept in a closet at home, would have been pulled over Reine's head. Tom could picture it now, his daughter as a small toddler, stumbling around while Doug's vest dragged on the ground, his mother taking endless photographs of Reine in Grandpa's clothes. He and Ari would be laughing in the background, Ari's arm wrapped around his waist and the sweet smell of her hair in his nose. Tom sighed, an ache suddenly building within him. He'd missed out on so much.

But there wasn't time to think about the ifs and buts and onlys. Reine was here, and so was he, and he needed to make up for the years he had missed.

"Or is she just called Bunny?" he added gently, reaching out to pull on one of the pink rabbit's ears.

"Margaret Thutcher," Reine replied seriously, hugging her bunny close.

"Margaret Thutcher?" Tom asked, raising an eyebrow, and Reine nodded.

"Uncle Sebastian named her. He says girls need a role model to look up to."

"So . . . Margaret Thutcher," Tom repeated, still sceptical, and watched as his daughter nodded. He gave her a smile. "Okay. Margaret Thutcher. I like it."

"Do you like bunnies?" Reine asked him, and he paused for a moment, pondering her question seriously.

"I don't know," he finally answered. "I've never had one. I like your bunny though. Margaret Thutcher."

"I like ponies too," Reine told him. "My Little Pony is my favourite."

"I've heard of that," Tom said. One of his colleagues at work once told him that he had a daughter who talked non-stop about My Little Pony. She was always asking for the newest toy or T-shirt. Tom made a mental note to ask his colleague where he could get the same. He'd buy Reine the entire range.

221

"I think I've seen them advertised."

"I like Pinkie Pie the best," Reine said. "Or maybe Fluttershy."

"Okay," Tom nodded, although he had no idea what she was talking about now. "What else do you like?"

"What do you mean?" Reine asked, wrinkling her nose in confusion. She looked so much like Ari for a moment that Tom had to stop and take a breath.

"I mean . . . what's your favourite food?"

"Chocolate biscuits," Reine answered, without missing a beat. "But my mummy doesn't let me eat them. I'm not normally allowed treats. When she's around, that is."

Tom frowned. "What do you mean, when she's around?"

For a moment Reine's face clouded. "Mummy works a lot."

Tom felt his stomach sink.

"She works?" he asked, keeping his voice light.

"All the time," Reine complained. "She and Uncle Sebastian are always away at weddings, or away planning weddings. I have to stay with my Tío Luis then. I don't mind, we have lots of fun and he takes care of me," Reine added loyally, though her words made Tom hate Luis De León intensely at that moment, "I just wish Mummy was around more. I like it when there are no weddings, and she can be a normal mummy. Not working Mummy."

Tom sat back, deflated. "I'm sorry your mom has to work, sweetheart."

Reine looked up at him, her eyes suddenly brighter. "At least I'll have you now as well," she said. "That's what daddies do, right? They help?"

Her words were a question that tore at Tom's heart. All of a sudden, he felt an almost violent protective instinct roar through him.

"That's right," he told her, keeping his voice light. "I'll be there from now on. I'm going to help."

He meant every word. He would ask his work for a transfer to the London office. He would pick Reine up from school. He would spend time with her on weekends. He would financially contribute to lift the burden from Ari's shoulders. *Fuck Uncle Sebastian and Tío Luis*, he thought angrily. He would be the father in Reine's life from now on.

Reine nodded, sitting back and clutching Margaret Thutcher to her small body. "Good. Mummy will like that."

Tom doubted it, but chose not to say anything. Reine didn't need to know about his and Ari's complicated relationship. She didn't need to know that her father was a pitiful excuse for a parent and a partner, who had been absent from her life for too long.

"We should get you to the house," he said, "you must be tired and it's cold out and if your mom knew you were missing—"

"She knows," said an icy voice, one that made Tom's sphincter tighten and stomach clench. He turned towards it.

"Hello Stella," he said coolly, nodding towards the immaculately put-together woman who stood languidly in the doorway.

She ignored him — her gaze settled on Reine. "Hello, Small," she said, and her voice was missing the frostiness she usually inflicted on Tom. "Are you all right?"

Reine nodded. "Hi Stellie."

Stellie, thought Tom in shock. His daughter called the great Stella Snow *Stellie*? He was certain if he'd dared to address her as *Stellie* she would have his balls on a plate for supper. If she could find them, that was. Whenever Stella Snow was around, they retracted so far back into his pelvis a good surgeon would struggle to get to them.

"Your mother is frantic about you," Stella carried on lightly. "It was very naughty of you to sneak out of bed like that."

"I needed to talk with my father," Reine replied sagely, and Tom watched as Stella nodded, seemingly completely unsurprised.

"Well, everyone is looking for you. Come on. I have a pack of chocolate Leibniz in my bag. You can have one on the way to the house."

"How did you find her here?" Tom asked, and Stella glanced over at him, her face falling into a sneer.

"Well, I just followed the scent of gormless desperation and the tracks of a man whose structurally unsound face weighs him down," she replied. "You should have brought her back to the house the second she turned up here. Her mother is a wreck."

Guilt flooded through him. "I know. But I just . . . I've never had the chance to . . ." he trailed off miserably. He gave a long sigh. "I didn't know, Stella. I really didn't."

"Well, Jawline, that much was evident," Stella said with a shrug. "You've had five minutes of parenting though, and the woman who has had nearly eight years more is in a state because she thinks her daughter is missing. Take her back to the house," she gave him a keener, more searching look. "Sort out your mess."

"I will," he promised, coming to a stand and pulling Reine up into his arms. "Come on, Reine. Your mom is missing you."

Reine reached over to Stella, who was holding out a biscuit in her hand. "Don't tell your mother," Stella warned. "You know she's not keen on you having chocolate."

Reine grinned at her, crunching the chocolate-covered cookie into her mouth, and Tom looked at Stella with interest as they started to walk.

"How did you meet Reine?" he asked her. "You seem to know her well."

"The small and I get along splendidly," Stella replied bluntly. "Whenever Luis De León works on a wedding dress for a ceremony where I'm the photographer, the small is invariably with him. We have a lot in common, the small and I."

"Like what?" Tom asked in disbelief, shifting Reine in his arms. How could his young, innocent daughter have anything in common with the icy Stella Snow?

"My mum was a single, working mother too," Stella said with a shrug. "She was overworked, overtired and overwrought, just like Ari. I don't like children as a general rule, but the small and I, well . . . I know just what she's going through."

Tom felt guilt hit him again. "I should've been there for Ari. I should've been there for both of them."

"You'll be there now," Reine offered, and Tom felt his heart skip a beat.

His daughter was beautiful, clever *and* kind. She was the best of them both. He hugged her tightly to him.

"Yeah," he said, "I'll be there now. All the time."

But on hearing his words, Stella turned to him sharply. "Don't make promises you don't intend to keep, Jawline."

"I intend to though," Tom argued.

Stella looked at him long and hard. "Maybe you feel that way now, but then maybe things will change. My own father was a malingering and steaming pile of garbage. He said things like that. Children remember when you break a promise. Don't be *that* father, whatever you do."

"I'm going to be there," Tom said again, firmly. "I'm going to be there."

"Fine." Stella nodded. "But I'll wait and see."

"Speaking of being there, why are you here?" Tom asked, shifting Reine's weight again as the house came into view.

"Oh, I have a sixth sense for when things are about to get interesting. I'm a connoisseur of human emotions, Somerset, and I know when something big is coming. Don't worry, I've had Brandon pack my soft lenses. They'll be kinder on your misshapen jawline."

"Thanks," Tom said roughly, opening the door to the house and depositing Reine down.

"Ari?" he called out, still marvelling at the sound of her name on his lips. "Ari, where are you?"

A thundering of footsteps came through the hall, and Tom watched as Ari, her face tear-stained and blotchy, snatched Reine into her arms.

"Thank God," she whispered, holding their daughter close. "Thank God. Reine, where have you been? I was so worried."

Another thundering of footsteps followed, and Tom watched as Sebastian, Luis and his mother tumbled into the room.

"I was about to call the police," Marnie snapped when she saw Tom in the doorway. "I was about to call a private investigator. I was about to call *Corentin*," she added, and Tom winced.

"There's no need for that," he told his mother. "I found her — she's safe."

Sebastian and Luis had crowded around Ari, and Tom could see Sebastian checking Reine's arms for marks or bruises.

"She's fine, she's fine," Luis was saying, "and Margaret Thutcher is okay too. Sunshine, *nos asustaste de muerte. No puedes salir corriendo así. Te queremos tanto . . . nos asustaste. Qué haríamos sin ti?*"

He ran his hand protectively over Reine's head, and Tom felt a streak of anger. *He* was Reine's father, not this man. He needed to talk to Ari. He needed to make right his wrongs.

"Ari," Tom said, looking down at her. "Ari, we need to talk."

She looked up at him, and there was betrayal written in her eyes. Tom winced once more, knowing he was the cause of her hurt.

"Please," he begged her. "Please, talk to me."

"I need to be with Reine right now," she replied, and her voice was cold. "I thought I'd lost her."

Tom felt his stomach sink and heart grow heavy. She would never forgive him, he realised. He would never earn back her trust.

Or her love.

"Ari—"

"I wasn't lost," a small voice broke in, and all the adults fell silent as Reine spoke.

"*Qué quieres decir*, Reine?" Luis asked, running his hand over her hair again.

226

"I mean I wasn't lost. I was talking with my father."

Instantly, Ari looked up at Tom with sparks of anger in her eyes.

"You told her?" she asked him furiously. "You told her? You told her that—"

"Wait. She was talking with *who*?" another voice asked, and Tom whirled around, coming face to face with Sasha.

"Oh, this is going to be good," Tom heard Stella whisper over the thumping beat of his heart. "Brandon, get my Leica ready. The one with the soft lens," she added, winking at Tom.

"Sasha—" he began, but his fiancée was staring at him, her arms crossed over her chest.

"*You're* that girl's father?" she asked incredulously. "You?"

Tom swallowed heavily, turning back to Ari. He needed to talk to her. He needed to make things right. He needed to put her and their child first. He would deal with Sasha later.

He was a moment too late though, for the space beside him was empty. Ari had already gone, and she'd taken Reine with her.

CHAPTER 17: BANANA BREAD

Under normal circumstances, Ari was a meticulous packer. Years of living in government-funded shitholes had seen to that. You never knew when you might have to leave, never knew what you might need to take or have. Her suitcases had become an art-form of organised preparation, with sections for clothes, make-up, toiletries and what Sebastian sneeringly called her 'end of the world prep'. It was a zipped and water-proof red bag that contained painkillers, antihistamines, disinfectant and antiseptics, as well as bandages and extra travel bottles of soap, shampoo and washing-up liquid, and Ari never went anywhere without it.

"Honestly, it's a wedding," he would say whenever he saw the red pack being tucked carefully into Ari's suitcase. "Valium and pep pills. That's all you need."

Ari remained firm, however. Her teenage years living alone had served her well. You never knew when you might need to disinfect a new room, play parent to yourself and treat an injury, or wash your socks in a sink. She found comfort in being prepared for all circumstances — it felt easier when she had basic necessities with her at all times.

She thought Luis understood. He never rolled his eyes at her emergency supplies or laughed at her water purification tablets. Instead, he would pat her on the back and shake his head in amazement at her packing skills.

"You can never find Reine's violin when she needs it, still don't know what day your recycling men come and have kitchen cupboards so messy they make me want to cry, and yet your suitcases are always works of art," he told her. "You're an enigma sometimes, Ari. You really are."

Tonight, there was nothing enigmatic about Ari's packing. She walked hurriedly from room to room, throwing things into the open cases on her bed and frantically searching out items in the cupboards and drawers.

She needed to get out of this place, out of this family and out of this damned wedding. She would have Sebastian refund Marnie's cheque and tear up their contract — actually, no, Ari thought, stopping to take a deep breath. She would do that herself. There would be a malicious satisfaction in ripping Tom and Sasha's names into oblivion — a painful kind of release in throwing the business of their wedding back in their privileged and self-satisfied faces. She would go back to London and pretend this whole farce had never happened. She would move on. She would thrive. She would forget.

She had to forget.

"Have you got Margaret Thutcher?" she asked Reine absently, still flinging clothes into her case. "Thank God I didn't unpack your bag. Go and get it, Reine. Quick as you can."

"No."

"Make sure you get your toothbrush from the bathroom, and your book from the bedside table too."

"No."

"And when you've done that, I'll get you dressed in some clothes . . . we'll drive to the airport. Get the first flight out we can and—" Ari stopped, turning to Reine slowly. "What do you mean, 'no'?"

Ari's daughter was standing with her arms crossed, her bunny clutched to her chest. Her face was set into determined

229

lines, her eyes dark and full of challenge. Ari stared at Reine, suddenly struck by the fact that in that moment, she looked almost entirely like Marnie. It was disconcerting and almost terrifying.

"I mean no," Reine said again, and she stamped her foot for effect. "I'm not going anywhere, Mummy."

Ari's mouth dropped open. In seven years, Reine had never once spoken back to her.

"Right now, I cannot deal with this." Ari stopped, taking a deep breath. "Young lady, you need to go and get your things. Right now."

"No." Reine stamped her foot again. "I'm not leaving."

"Yes, you are," Ari argued. "I am your mother, and I know what's best for us. And right now, there are people downstairs who are *not* the best for us."

"Like who?" Reine challenged. "You mean my father?"

Ari inhaled sharply, dropping to the bed. She stared at Reine, deciding to be honest.

"Yes," she told her. "Your father. He's not good for us, baby."

Reine stared back at her. "You mean he's not good for you," she retorted. "But he might be good for me."

At that, all the breath seemed to leave Ari's body, and her eyes filled with tears. "Reine—"

"Reine, go with Uncle Sebbie." Luis's voice sounded through the room, and Ari watched as Reine looked towards him.

"I'm not leaving, Tío Luis," she said. "I want more time with him."

"We're not going to make you leave, Reine," Luis replied good-naturedly. He walked towards her, picking the girl up and cuddling her to him. "But we think that, just for tonight, you should sleep in our room. That way we can keep an eye on you and Margaret Thutcher," he winked at the girl, "make sure the two of you don't go on anymore midnight walks."

"Yes, come on, Reine," Sebastian stepped forward, taking her from Luis's arms. "I snaffled a bottle of port from the stash downstairs and downloaded a few episodes of *Great British Bake Off* onto my iPad. Let's go and make a night of it."

"You can't watch *Bake Off* without me!" Luis said indignantly.

"Oh relax, I'll screenshot the bits where Paul Hollywood's flashing his baby blues and giving that dismissive-sexy look," Sebastian snapped back. "And you know how watching someone fall apart over a botched crème patissière relaxes Reine."

"Fine," Luis replied, "but don't you dare watch bread week without me. You know I need all the tips I can get for my banana bread."

"Oh, you and your banana bread," Sebastian rolled his eyes. "Every time I suggest a bit of light baking, you bring up your banana bread. It isn't *that* special. Every man and his dog can make banana bread, Luis."

"Not with my passionfruit and cream cheese frosting," Luis said indignantly.

"You mean the gloop that turns a perfectly serviceable bread into a sickly cake? Hate to break it to you, but yes, they can."

"Sickly?" Luis looked affronted. "My banana cake isn't sickly!"

"Look, all I'm saying is that if you're going to make a fruit cake—"

"Banana cake isn't fruit cake."

"Oh, I'm sorry, I mustn't have got that memo from the Worldwide Food Organisation announcing banana's transition from fruit to protein. Silly me."

"Sebastian, Luis—" Ari began, rubbing her eyes.

"You're just being pedantic," Luis said, crossing his arms. "Banana cake is not a fruit cake."

"Luis—" Ari tried again.

"My God, Luis," Sebastian stood taller, shifting Reine in his arms. "How many times do we have to have this conversation? I've told you for years, *all banana cakes are fruit cakes but not all fruit cakes are banana cakes*. It's so simple, so—"

"Sebastian—" Ari said, her patience dissipating.

"I don't think banana cake is a fruit cake," Reine piped up, and at that, Ari's patience finally snapped.

"Can you two quit it!" she snapped. "Now you've got Reine talking about flipping banana cake!"

Sebastian and Luis, to their credit, instantly fell silent.

"Look, honey, just don't watch bread week," Luis said eventually, looking placatingly at Sebastian. "That's all I'm asking."

Sebastian sighed. "You know I wouldn't. I know bread week is your favourite."

Luis nodded. "Thanks. I'll only be a minute or two with Ari here anyway."

"Fine, fine, fine," Sebastian shrugged. He put Reine down. "Go and say goodnight to your mum, love."

Ari gazed miserably at the little figure of Reine through her tear-misted eyes. The little girl must have sensed her sadness, because she suddenly flung her arms around Ari's neck, hugging her tightly.

"We need to get out of here," Ari tried again, holding back her tears as she held her daughter tight. "We can't stay here."

"Ari," came Sebastian's voice, light with warning, before he pulled Reine from her arms. "Come on, miss. Let's get you settled. And have a little talk about fruit cake."

Ari watched as Sebastian carried Reine away, feeling panic begin to build within her once more. Her chest felt tight and her pulse raced, while her skin felt clammy with cool sweat.

"Luis," she said brokenly, "Luis, we can't stay here, we can't, we have to get out of here—"

"Ari," Luis said calmly, sitting on the bed next to her, taking her hand. "Take a deep breath, honey."

"I can't, I just can't."

"Ari." Luis shifted so that Ari was facing him. He squeezed her hand lightly. "If you walk away tonight, and take that little girl—who is full of perfectly valid questions right now, by the way—with you, you're only delaying the inevitable."

Ari sniffed, nodding miserably and wiping her eyes. "I know. I just . . . I just don't want to—" she looked at Luis with helpless eyes "—it wasn't meant to be like this, Luis. It wasn't meant to be like this at all."

Luis nodded sadly. "I know, honey."

"I wanted to be the one to tell him. I wanted to be the one to tell *her*."

"I know that too."

"What do I do?" she asked him. "I don't know. I've taken care of myself for years now, and this is the first time I've ever not known what to do."

Luis paused. Ari stared at him.

"What?" she whispered. "What do you think?"

"You aren't going to like it."

"So what?" She gave a bitter laugh. "I don't like anything about anything right now. At least I trust you. You can tell me something I don't like, and I still know that you only want what's best for me and Reine. Please, tell me what you think. And be honest." She sighed. "I've had enough lies to last me a lifetime."

Luis took a deep breath.

"Well," he began, clearing his throat, "for one thing, you can't run away. Oh, I get why you want to, and we're tempted to come with you. Honestly, not five minutes ago Sebastian was on the phone to British Airways to see if we could all check into the red-eye home."

"But I bet they were fully booked, right?" Ari asked.

"Yes. Well, *mostly*."

Ari stared at him.

"They only had seats left in economy," Luis admitted. "And while I'm happy to turn right on any flight, you know Sebastian won't eat his plane food off of anything but fine bone china. And what would we do at the airport if we can't get into the first-class lounge? Duty-free only entertains for so long, Ari."

233

"I used to like airports," Ari replied absently, thinking of a warm pair of eyes gazing at her from across a cold terminal floor. "I used to like them a lot." She stopped, shaking her head. "Okay, so we fly tomorrow?"

"Sure," Luis nodded. "I'll get us booked on the first flight home with first-class availability."

"Reine and I can fly economy."

"The hell you can." Luis almost looked affronted. "You stay with us."

"You both love Reine so much." Ari sniffled again as tears threatened to run down her cheeks. "You love her more than she even knows."

"We love you too, you know. Which is why I'm gonna say this. You need to talk to that man."

"Luis—"

"No, Ari, listen to me. He's an absolute shit. *Culero*, I would say at home. But whatever he is and whatever he's done . . . he's still Reine's father." Luis took a deep breath. "And she knows it now too."

Ari nodded sadly. "I know."

"It's like a can of worms has been opened," Luis went on. "And look, we can fly home and try and squeeze the lid back on. Do some damage control and all that. But worms are still gonna find their way out, Ari, and Reine will want to know more about her father and he's gonna want to know more about her . . . and that mother of his." Luis gave Ari a knowing look. "She's a hard one, that Marnie. I don't think she'll give up on Reine easily."

Ari nodded.

"But look, while Sebastian and I are fully prepared to take on Marnie and Tom — Tom, whatever his name is — we aren't prepared to take on Reine about this. She has a right to know where she came from and who her people are."

"But they aren't *good* people—" Ari started to argue, and Luis nodded, understanding written across his face.

"Maybe not. But she'll still want to *know*. Honestly, Ari, do yourself a favour and save her rebellion for her teenage years. She's a little young to peak at seven."

234

Ari sighed. "All my instincts are telling me to get away from this place."

"And they're probably right. But trust me on this one. Talk to him. Give him time with Reine. Work something out."

"God," Ari exhaled, allowing her head to rest against her hands. "How did it come to this? Visitation rights for Tom and fucking *Sasha*."

"Sasha? I don't know about that," Luis said with a shrug.

"What do you mean?" Ari peeked at him from between her fingers.

"Well, let's just say I'm not having my girls start on that wedding dress anytime soon. I don't think it would be a practical use of their time."

"Luis—"

"Look, Ari, just talk to the man. Sort something out. Not for him, not for you, but for Reine, okay? She's the important one. Everything else is just . . ." Luis paused, clearly thinking something through. "Water under the bridge?"

"Not in this case. Not water under the bridge." Ari sighed. "It's magic gone wrong." Instinctively, she reached for the queen of spades in her pocket, before her fingers made contact with the hard seam of her coat and an overwhelming misery engulfed her. *That's right*, she thought sadly. *I tore her up.*

The queen was gone.

"Ari?" Luis asked curiously. "You okay?"

No, she longed to reply. *I haven't been okay in years.*

"Ari?"

"I used to like airports," Ari said again, and now a tear did run down her cheek. She looked up to Luis with hollow eyes. "I used to like them a lot."

* * *

There was too much noise and Tom couldn't think.

In one ear he had Sasha buzzing, her words sharp and demanding.

"What did she mean? That kid is yours? Tom, what the actual fuck? How could you not tell me? I can't believe how selfish you are. This is meant to be *my* special weekend. This is not meant to be about you or *her* or anything else. What the fuck, Tom?"

In the other ear he had his mother, jumpy like an excited rabbit, her eyes wide.

"You spent time with her? She knows you're her father? Oh my God, Tom, this is the best thing ever. We were so worried about her, but she was with you the entire time. You'll bond with her, and then I will, and then I'll have everything I ever dreamed of. This is wonderful, Tom."

There was other noise too. The clicking of Stella's camera as, frame by frame, she caught every uncomfortable word being thrown in his direction. Luis and Sebastian, muttering between themselves, throwing him dirty looks like he was the devil incarnate. There was a more intensive noise too, like a roaring wave in his ear, as his heart beat fast and his head buzzed with adrenaline.

"I can't do this now," he said desperately, breaking free from the circle of people around him and walking away. "I just can't do this."

"Tom!" Sasha screeched. "Don't you dare walk away from me!"

"I just need to think," he replied miserably. "I just need time and space to think."

"What, eight years wasn't enough time for you?" Sebastian asked snidely, and Tom snapped his head in his direction, regarding him warily.

"You can think what you like about me," he said to him quietly. "It's not your opinion I care about."

Sebastian's face remained sharp, dislike spread across his features. "I'm going to give you some good advice you in absolutely no way deserve. You don't have time to think. Ari is probably upstairs packing her bags right now. Time is not something you have the luxury of."

Tom stared at him.

"She doesn't want to talk to me," he said shortly. "You think I'm going to make things worse by barging upstairs and demanding she stay? I'm in no position to make any demands of her, and I'm not going to. I know this will seem unbelievable to you, but I still care about Ari." Tom swallowed hard. "More than any of you will ever know. And I care about that little girl now too."

"You care about them?! I don't believe this—" Sasha began to speak, but Luis scoffed before she could finish her sentence.

"A ten-minute conversation with Reine and you *care* about her? Please."

Tom watched as Sebastian moved closer to him, taking Luis's hand in his own. They were a unit against one soldier, Tom realised. They were displaying their unity to him and Marnie.

"You haven't been there for either of them," Sebastian carried on mercilessly, picking up where his husband left off. "You've missed every birthday. Every school run. Every wobbly tooth. Every holiday. You've missed everything."

"I know," Tom replied tightly. "And I hate that, almost as much as I hate knowing I can't change it. But you should both know this." He leaned towards them, using his height and strength to tower over the pair. They might be a unit, but they were fucking with the wrong soldier. "I intend to be there for the rest of them. Every birthday. Every holiday. Every wobbly tooth. You better get used to my face, because you're going to be seeing a lot of it."

"Don't you think you should talk to me before you start planning Chuck E. Cheese birthday parties and decking me out in a tutu to play the tooth fairy?" Sasha asked, louder now, stepping towards Tom and pulling him towards her. "Aren't you forgetting that I'm your *bride*, Tom? How are you even this kid's father? How are you even—"

Tom ran a hand over his face. "Can we please talk later?" he begged Sasha. "I can only deal with one problem at a time, and I—"

"Oh," Sasha interjected, stepping back and crossing her arms over her chest. She glared at him. "Oh, I'm a *problem* now, am I? Well, Tom, that's fine. I'm going to go upstairs, lock the door, and when you come to find me later, you'll see just how much of a *problem* I can be."

"Sasha, I just think that Tom—" Marnie began, but Sasha spun on her heels to face her.

"Oh, can it, Marnie. No one cares what you think."

Tom watched as Marnie frowned. Luis, his stern expression fading momentarily, leaned towards his mother.

"I care what you think, dona," he said kindly.

Sasha bristled. "I'm going upstairs. I'm putting on a face mask and don't want to be bothered for at least the next hour. And Tom," she turned back to him viciously, "don't you dare make any more cute little family plans until you've spoken to me, understand?"

Tom said nothing, watching as his fiancée stomped away.

Sebastian watched her go too. "Good luck with that," he told Tom bluntly, nodding after Sasha's retreating form. "And good luck with your grand plans to play Dad to Reine. Right now, you can't even bring yourself to go upstairs and talk to Ari. You think you're going to be playing happy families with Reine in the near future? Think again."

Tom inhaled sharply.

"You're one to talk about happy families," he said quietly. "Neither of you are Reine's father. And no amount of playing happy families with her is going to change that."

"Tom—" his mother warned sharply, but Tom cut her off.

"No, Reine is *my* daughter," he carried on, "and that's how I'll be treating her from this moment on."

Luis and Sebastian both gaped at him, while somewhere in the background Tom heard Stella let out an impressed breath.

"This is solid fucking gold," she murmured. "Brandon, make sure you have my extra rolls of film ready. I don't want to miss a moment of this."

Tom cleared his throat as an uneasy silence fell across the hall.

"Well," Sebastian's sharp tone cut through the frosty atmosphere like a knife, "we'll see about that. We're going to go upstairs now and check on Ari and Reine. You take all the time you need, Somerset . . . Miller . . . whoever you are. But just think about this. Tomorrow, two of us in this room will be leaving with Ari and your daughter. And let me tell you now, it won't be you or your mother."

"Hey," Marnie said, obviously affronted.

"Sorry," Sebastian nodded to her. "In case I didn't say it earlier, the salmon today really was divine."

"The chef marinated it in coconut milk," Marnie replied quietly.

"Coconut milk? How delightful."

"I'll send you the recipe."

"Please do. You have my email."

"Tom—" Marnie said, turning to him, but Tom shook his head at her. He watched as Sebastian and Luis went up the stairs, before turning and leaving as well.

He needed silence. He needed to think. He needed a plan.

* * *

Sometimes in New York, when feeling troubled, Tom liked to sit under Ari's paintings. He would lock himself in his study, taking comfort from the layers of paint he knew she'd studiously applied, feeling close to her even from a distance of years. He would stare up at her work, remembering her hands as they held a brush, remembering the splodges of paint on her fingertips, recalling the light in her eyes as she worked at the thing she loved best. He would remember Ari, and his mind would clear.

Her memory was better than any prescription drug. Her memory was better than any therapist or counsellor.

Here at his mother's house, with his study denied to him, Tom found himself in the long gallery, sitting under *The*

Ends of the Earth. He stretched his long legs out on the floor, closing his eyes and letting his head rest against the wall. He brought forth memories of Norway, remembering an orange and pink sky and how Ari's skin had glowed underneath it. He remembered a faded hotel room, and how Ari had looked and felt in his arms. He remembered happier times and felt his mind clear.

When he opened his eyes again, there was a figure at the end of the gallery.

Ari.

Tom sat up quickly, watching as she walked towards him. She looked small and wan, wrapped up in a long coat, her hands crossed protectively over her stomach. She looked at him and, even in the dark, Tom could see that her hands were shaking, and her cheeks pale.

"Ari—" he began, but she shook her head, silencing him.

"Can I . . ." she began, and her voice wavered. "Can I talk to you?"

"Yes, of course," Tom replied earnestly. "Please."

Ari shook her head again, clearing her throat. "Um, can I . . . talk to you as Tom Miller? Just for a minute?"

Tom Miller. Tom felt his stomach sink.

"I, um—"

"I just . . ." Ari shrugged sadly ". . . I just need to tell him something."

"It's still me," Tom whispered. "It's still me, Ari."

"No," she said shortly, and the word echoed down the empty hall.

"Ari—"

"Please," she begged. "Please pretend. Just for a minute."

Wordlessly, Tom nodded. He watched as Ari brushed a tear away, coming to Tom's side and settling next to him on the floor. She glanced above her head, sighing at the painting above.

"It was never my best work," she said quietly.

"You know I loved it."

"I gave it to you for a reason," Ari said. "I never thought you would stay as long as you did, you know. I always expected you to walk out the door one day and never come back. I thought this painting would be something you would remember me by. That it would sit on your wall somewhere, and that maybe one day you would tell people about this great artist you once knew." She gave a bitter sigh. "I guess I was both right and wrong, in a way. You did leave one day, and you never came back. You also hung the painting on a wall. It just wasn't your wall. And you never told anyone about me. No one at all."

"Ari, I never meant to hurt you," Tom said miserably.

"That's Tom Somerset talking, not my Tom." Ari looked at him pleadingly. "Please pretend. Please."

"Okay," Tom exhaled hard. "Okay."

Ari took a deep breath. "Tom, there's something you need to know. I got pregnant. That time at the *Hotel de la Reine* . . . when we weren't careful. I got pregnant and I had a baby."

Tom was dimly aware of his heart beating fast in his chest. Ari was doing this because she needed it, he realised. This was something she had to do, something that was giving her peace and a kind of comfort. Instinctively he reached over and took her hand. He squeezed her fingers, her skin cool against his, and he felt a tremulous rush of hope run through him when she squeezed his hand back.

"I had a baby girl," Ari said softly. "February twenty-sixth."

Tom felt something warm run through him. He knew his daughter's birthday now. He would never forget that date again, he promised himself.

"She was eight pounds and nine ounces. The midwives all laughed when she was born, asking how a small thing like me could produce such a big baby. I told them her father was big. I told them your name. They were so kind," Ari sniffled. "They didn't ask where you were. They didn't ask why you weren't there."

"I wish I'd been there," Tom said fervently. "I wish to God I'd been there."

"I had Luis with me. Sebastian stayed for as long as he could manage. At one point a doctor came in to measure my cervix and Sebbie went out for a snack and never came back. Luis found him in a Subway sandwich shop three miles away the next day." Ari smiled. "Reine was born with a shock of dark hair. She looked just like you."

Tom felt inexplicably sad. "Can I . . . have a baby picture of her? Or any picture. I know I have no rights here, but it would . . . it would be nice to see her." His voice wavered, betraying his uncertainty.

Ari paused. "My Tom wouldn't say that. That's Tom Somerset."

Tom looked down. "Sorry . . . I just . . ." He sighed. "I'm sorry."

Ari sighed too.

Tom looked at where their fingers lay entwined. He could remember holding her hand during happier times. Could remember taking her hand as they walked down European streets. Could remember gripping her hand as they lay in the snow of a French mountain, Ari's face ethereal against the soft white ice around her. Tom looked at her face now, only to find her gazing steadily at him. She held his eyes for a moment, and Tom felt a jolt of bittersweet pain run through him. The gallery was quiet, moonlight stealing in from the windows, and he took a deep breath.

"I'm glad we have a baby," he said, honesty rolling off him in waves. "You've made me so happy, Ari. So happy."

"Really?" Ari asked, and her voice broke on the word. Her eyes were glistening with unshed tears, and Tom squeezed her hand again.

"Yes. God, yes."

Ari took a shaky breath. "Thank you for saying that. You don't know what it means to me."

Tom winced. "Don't thank me. Don't thank me. Please don't."

Ari continued to gaze at him. "You wear your hair shorter now." She reached her free hand up, as if to touch his cheek, before she thought better of it, letting it drop back to the floor. Tom longed for her to touch him, to caress him and tell him everything would be okay, but he knew it was a useless hope.

"When Reine was about six weeks old," Ari continued, her eyes now down, "all her dark hair fell out and came back in this honey blonde shade. I was devastated. I cried over her. It felt like another part of you being taken away."

"Corentin has hair like Reine," Tom explained gently. "And my grandfather had the same."

"Oh," Ari breathed. "I didn't know that. I wouldn't though, would I?"

"I'm sorry," Tom said again. "I'm so sorry."

Ari's eyes travelled up to Tom's face, lingering on his eyes. "Why didn't you come for me?" The tears finally fell down her face. "Why didn't you find me?"

Tom felt his heart break into small pieces. Useless now to tell her he *had* found her. Useless now to tell her he'd made a terrible mistake. Useless now to tell her anything at all, other than that he was sorry. Sorry for everything he'd done, and sorry for everything he'd missed.

"I don't know how I can ever make this up to you," he whispered.

"I don't want Tom Somerset now," Ari said, wiping her cheeks with the back of a hand. "Please be Tom Miller. Just for one more minute."

He nodded. "I'm sorry."

"I'm tired of hearing that word," Ari said softly. "I'm tired all the time, actually. I work so hard, Tom. I have to put a roof over Reine's head. Feed her and keep her healthy. I have to worry about her schooling and make sure she gets to all her activities and clubs. I have to pay bills. I have to keep a house clean. I have to exercise, and I have to work, all the damn time. Wedding after wedding after wedding, an endless parade of white satin and salmon en croute. It's exhausting. I feel like I'm spinning plates in the air, and there's always one on the precipice of breaking. Luis and Sebastian do what they can . . . But I'm on my own. I wish you'd come for me." Ari wiped her cheek again. "I wish you had."

Tom took a deep breath, squeezing her fingers.

"I'm here now," he promised. "I'm here now for you both."

"But I don't want Tom Somerset," Ari replied, crying openly now. "I want my Tom. And it breaks my heart to learn that he doesn't exist. That he never existed. That it was all a lie."

"It's still me," Tom whispered miserably. "Ari, it was always me."

"No," Ari said bluntly. "That's not true. Because I loved him, and I think I hate you."

Tom sat back, jolting away from Ari as though she'd struck him. Her words were like salt rubbed into a festering wound, and he felt tears prick at his own eyes.

She would never forgive him, he realised. She never would.

Closing his eyes, he inhaled slowly. There was a ball of pain inside him, sharp and jagged. It ached with every breath he took. It would never go away. That pain, and the knowledge he had only himself to blame, would live with him until his dying day.

But it wasn't about him anymore. It was about Ari and Reine. So he took from Ari's words what he could.

"I loved you too," he said, reaching towards her, cupping her face in his hands. "I loved you too."

She looked at him with wet, wide eyes.

"I loved you so much, and I still love you," he uttered fervently. "I'll never not love you, Ari."

"I love you too," she replied, and she brought her hands up to his, stroking his long fingers. "I'll never not love you, Tom."

He couldn't help himself. He leaned towards her, pressing his lips to hers. Her kiss tasted like the salt of her tears — or maybe it was the salt of his tears, Tom couldn't be sure. All the same, it was sweet and loving and tender, and his heart broke a little again when he realised it was a kiss of farewell. The last kiss Tom Miller would ever give Ari, and the last kiss Tom Somerset would ever give her too.

When they pulled apart, Ari sighed, dropping her hands back into her lap. She chewed on her lip for a moment, looking at him.

"You can be Tom Somerset now," she told him softly. "You can stop pretending."

"I meant it," he said. "I meant every word. I'll always love you. That was never pretend. That was real."

Ari shook her head. "It doesn't matter now. We need to think about Reine. It isn't about us anymore. It's about her."

She stood, dusting her hands on her coat and looking down at him.

"I'm glad you kept it," she said, nodding to her painting. "When I first got here, and I thought you'd sold it . . ." She shook her head. "Anyway, I'm glad you didn't."

"I'll give it to Reine, if you like."

"One day you can," Ari said. She swallowed hard. "I . . . I want you to get to know her. You should know her. I won't . . . I won't stop you from seeing her, in case you were worried. We can work something out."

"Yes." Tom nodded, his throat constricted with pain. "Thank you."

"Don't thank me for being a good mother. Don't thank me for putting my child first." Her tone was unnaturally sharp, and Tom realised the brief moment of openness she'd shared with him was closing up. Her shell to him was hardening, closing him out of her heart forever.

"We'll talk in the morning," Ari announced. "I'm too tired to think about you now. Go back to your fiancée, Tom."

"Sasha and I—"

"I don't want to know," Ari cut him off bluntly. "I'll speak to you tomorrow. Before Reine and I fly home. She starts school again in a few days . . . and I need space from you. We'll work something out before I go."

"Ari—" Tom tried again, but she turned and walked away. Tom watched as she disappeared down the gallery, her head bowed, her shoulders slumped.

He slept right there on the gallery floor, exhaustion winning over the tumultuous turning of his mind.

When he woke in the early morning, he padded upstairs to his room, opening the door to find Sasha surprisingly still there, fast asleep in their bed. His foot stood on something soft as he quietly entered the room, and he looked down, surprised.

A glossy piece of paper was under his shoe. Tom bent down to retrieve it, examining it carefully in his hand.

His heart constricted in his chest when he realised it was a photograph of a baby.

This baby could only have been a few hours old when this picture was taken. Their hair was dark, while their skin still had that pinky-red tone of a newly born infant. The child was wrapped in a pink blanket, a pink hat on her head, and she was fast asleep, with dark lashes against her cheeks.

This was *his* baby, Tom realised, and for a moment he clutched the image to his chest.

Ari had given him a photo. She had given him a baby photo of Reine.

Head bowed and heart low, Tom quietly started to cry.

CHAPTER 18: ANGER

Ari was no stranger to anger. Not at all. Over her lifetime, she'd experienced many things that she had every right to feel angry about. Her emotionally devoid parents for one, who'd kicked Sebastian out for being gay, and her out for supporting him. Then there was the British welfare system, which struggled to house and support her once her parents had sent her packing. There was also her mortgage company, who continually questioned her ability to finance her own home without a husband, and also her daughter's headmistress, the terrifying Miss Bates, who continually questioned Reine's well-being.

"You must understand our concern," Miss Bates had intoned, looking down on Ari loftily. "Given your . . . shall we say, odd family circumstances?"

"Odd family circumstances?" Luis had seethed later, indignation written hotly over his face. "I'll show her odd family circumstances. I'm going into that school first thing tomorrow to speak with this Miss Bates, and *esta vez le voy a decir por dónde sale el sol.*"

"Luis—" Ari had begun to argue, but Sebastian had held up his hand.

"Let him go in and fight your corner, Ari. He'll feel better, you'll feel better, we'll all feel better. It's his turn to drop

Reine at school anyway, so you and I can start on the final run to the Dobson wedding next Saturday. If Luis wants to speak with Miss Bates, let him. I know that man. He'll go in like a lion and come out like a kitten."

"Sebastian—"

But Sebastian patted Ari reassuringly. "Trust me on this one."

The next morning, Ari watched as Luis stalked towards the school, Reine's hand held tightly in his own. Reine's My Little Pony lunchbox was strapped across his chest, his face set into hard and determined lines. She then watched later when, at lunch, he walked quietly into Ari and Sebastian's Mayfair office, his hands in his pockets.

"How did it go?" Ari asked, and Luis had clicked his tongue, looking doggedly at the floor.

"Well, I don't think she'll be questioning our *family circumstances* again any time soon," Luis said.

Sebastian stepped forwards, a knowing look on his face. "And?"

Sheepishly, Luis looked up. "And I'm now secretary of the PTA."

"And?" Sebastian continued, looking at Luis with bemusement.

"And I'm designing the costumes for the school production of Charles Dickens's *A Christmas Carol*."

"*Luis*." Ari shook her head, but Luis merely looked indignant.

"What did you want me to do, Ari? She was going to dress Victorian orphans in taffeta. *Taffeta*. Victorian orphans don't wear taffeta."

"What are you going to dress them in then?" Sebastian had asked, raising an eyebrow. "What do you think poor Victorian orphans wore?"

"High quality Egyptian muslin in various shades of brown, of course," Luis replied, as Ari and Sebastian had exchanged a look. "That's right, isn't it?"

No. Ari was no stranger to anger.

Odd then how it seemed to desert her after seeing Tom. Odd how all her rage and fury seem to have been swept aside, leaving nothing but a ball of hurt within. She felt weary and worn out, disappointed and empty, but the fire of her anger was gone, leaving nothing but ashes of sadness.

The next morning, flanked by Sebastian and Luis, she stared at Tom across the table. His mother was by his side, looking as cool and collected as ever, with reams of paper in front of her that she passed back and forth with another man. Ari hadn't been expecting this to be a formal meeting. She thought she and Tom would simply talk over a coffee, coming to some sort of informal arrangement that suited them both. Clearly, she'd been wrong.

"My lawyer, Andrew A. Andrews." Marnie gestured to the man by her side, and Sebastian's mouth dropped open.

"Don't say a word," Ari hissed under her breath, clamping a hand on Sebastian's arm, willing him to be quiet.

"The man is called *Andrew A. Andrews*," Sebastian hissed back. "And you don't want me to ask him about that?"

"No, *Sebastian Aloysius St John Lightowler*, I don't," Ari snapped. "I'm more concerned," she raised her voice for Marnie and Tom's benefit, "about why there is the need for a lawyer at all."

At that, Marnie glanced up, looking at Ari keenly. "I'm sorry, I should have explained sooner. Mr Andrews—"

"Andrew A. Andrews," Sebastian interrupted.

Marnie glanced at him. "Yes . . . Anyway, Mr Andrews is here to go over the financial paperwork."

Ari sat back. "What financial paperwork?"

Marnie smiled at her. "I believe my son owes you eight years of child support. We'd like to settle that today."

Ari glanced at Tom. He was staring at her, his eyes wide and sad, an aura of defeat around him. His shoulders were slumped, his skin pale, and the shadow of a beard grew across his chin, exacerbating the dark shadows under his eyes.

"Did you know about this?" Ari asked him, and he nodded slowly.

"After we talked, I didn't get much sleep," he replied softly. "I asked my mother to get Mr Andrews—"

"Andrew A. Andrews," Sebastian interrupted, still staring at the elderly lawyer, and Tom glanced at him.

"Yes . . . I asked my mother to get Mr Andrews here, as soon as possible, so that I can financially settle with you."

"Why the rush?" Ari asked, thoroughly confused. "I thought we would work something out . . . I thought this was about Reine—"

"It is about Reine," Tom replied gently. "I want to make things right, Ari, and this is how I start."

"By throwing fistfuls of money at me?" Ari snapped. "By paying me for *services rendered*?"

Tom winced. "No, not like that—"

"That's exactly how it feels," Ari cut him off, but there was no anger in her words. Just that echoing emptiness — a hollow feeling of sadness.

She shook her head, sighing softly. "Fine. Whatever."

"Ari—"

"Just leave it," Ari snapped. "I will say, though, that I feel at a distinct disadvantage without my own lawyer here to advise me."

It was part lie, part truth. She didn't have a lawyer, well, not one on retainer, like the staid grey-haired gentleman who sat at the table, clearly on call for the powerful Somerset family. But Tom and Marnie didn't need to know that, and so, when Luis went to open his mouth, Ari kicked him sharply under the table. Sebastian, who saw her action, immediately fell into line.

"Yes," he said slowly, still staring at Andrew A. Andrews. "We should have sent for our lawyer, Mr . . . um . . . Mr Xavier X. Xavier."

Ari groaned, momentarily closing her eyes. When she opened them, Marnie was staring at Sebastian.

"Your lawyer is called Xavier X. Xavier?" she asked. To her credit, Ari could hear how it pained her to keep the tone of disbelief from her voice.

"Yes," Sebastian lied, sitting up and straightening his shirt. "He's quite the barrister."

"No one messes with Triple X," Luis piped up, and although Ari knew he was trying to be helpful, she groaned again all the same.

"Right," Marnie replied slowly. "Okay, well, hopefully we can keep these arrangements friendly, and so *Mr Xavier's* services—"

"Triple X," Luis interjected. "They call him Triple X. If it helps, we can call Mr Andrews Triple A?"

"Like a battery," Sebastian whispered, and now Ari kicked *him* under the table.

"I think I'd prefer to be called Mr Andrews," Marnie's lawyer offered, his voice dry.

"Andrew A. Andrews," Sebastian said, staring at him.

"Okay," Marnie cut in. "So, anyway, hopefully we can keep it so that your, um, your *Mr Xavier's* services won't be required. Tom has been very generous in his financial settlement offer here, Ari, and all that we need is for you to sign a few papers so that we can discuss the next few days, and the time both Tom and I would like to spend with Reine."

"Where is Reine?" Tom asked suddenly, sitting up.

"You mean you've only just noticed she isn't here?" Ari asked, biting down on her lip to stop herself from saying something she would later regret.

"I just . . . I know the three of you share her, and—"

"We don't share her," Luis spat. "We *raise* her."

Tom took a deep breath. "I know. I know. And I don't want to get in the way . . . Actually, I do. I do want to get in the way of that. I want time with her. I want to help raise her from now on." Ari watched as he inhaled deeply. "I want joint custody."

Ari felt the blood drain from her face. Joint custody? She hadn't been expecting that. She thought he might ask for visits, maybe the odd holiday or two. But joint custody? Ari swallowed nervously, looking at Luis and Sebastian. The two men had faces like stone, their hands tightly clenched into rock-like fists. But while Sebastian's face held barely concealed anger, Luis's chiselled jawline had dropped, betraying his absolute devastation at Tom's words.

"Luis—" Ari began gently, but at the sound of her voice, Sebastian leapt to his feet.

"Absolutely fucking not," he seethed, glaring at Tom. "Honestly, we thought you'd throw money at her to get her out of the way. Pay her off and see her out. With a reprehensible track record like yours, that would almost have been the decent thing to do. At a stretch, we might have organised a few visits, but this . . . raising Reine, when you know absolutely nothing about her, have spent zero time with her and—"

At that, Tom also jumped to his feet. "You think I don't know all this? You think I don't hate myself for everything I've missed? But you know something, I can't take the past back. I can't go back in time and fix what I did wrong. But I can do better going forward. Reine is my daughter, I fully accept that. In fact, you know something? I take joy in the knowledge. Sheer, wonderful joy in knowing that she is my child. She is my daughter, and I want to get to know her. I want to spend time with her. I want to be a father to her. *A father*," Tom said firmly. "And whatever the two of you think of me, this decision is between Ari and I. Reine's *parents*."

Silence descended over the room. Ari could hear her own breathing, pained and shallow, echoing across the table. She sat, stunned, while she processed Tom's words.

He wanted to be a parent. He wanted joint custody. He wanted to help raise Reine.

"No," she said finally, coming to a stand. Her legs were shaking, and she gripped the table's edge, hoping to disguise her fear. "No," she said more firmly. "Tom, I want to talk with you. Privately. Everyone else needs to get out."

"Ari," Marnie stood too, looking at her plaintively. "Ari, this is a shock to you, I realise. But you must understand—"

"I want you all to get out." Ari's voice was hardly higher than a whisper. "Get out."

252

"Ari—" Sebastian began, but she turned on him too, slamming a hand down on the table.

"Please," she begged. "Please get out of here and let me talk to Tom."

Luis stood, clapping a hand on Sebastian's shoulder. "Come on. Let's go. Ari needs to talk to *Tom* here." Luis gave Tom a withering glance. "You can expect to hear from our lawyer."

"Yes," Sebastian nodded at Marnie and her lawyer, "we're going to hire someone so good Mr Andrew A. Andrews will need to buy another vowel — probably an A — and get ready for a fight. We won't walk away from Ari and Reine so easily as *Tom Miller* did."

Ari watched as the two men walked out of the room, hand-in-hand, their heads held high. Marnie, surprisingly, immediately followed, leaving only Ari, Tom and Mr Andrews in the room.

Mr Andrews was shuffling papers into a worn briefcase, looking at Tom and Ari with appraising eyes.

"I haven't read through all the information Marnie sent me last night, but I've seen enough this morning — more than enough — to understand that this is a complicated situation," he said, clicking his briefcase closed. "If it goes to court, it could drag on for years, both in London and the State of New York. It will be expensive, hurtful and in no way in Reine's interests. My advice to you is to settle this as adults." He gave them both a stern look.

"That means quickly and out-of-court. If I may be so bold," he turned to Ari, and she chewed on her lip nervously, "I would advise you, Ms Lightowler, to accept the very generous financial settlement my client has offered you. His offer has not only gone well beyond the state-mandated requirements for child support, it's also completely against my advice."

Mr Andrews leaned forward, pressing a cheque into Ari's hand. She unfolded it with trembling fingers, gasping audibly when she saw the numbers Tom had written in his hurried cursive. It wasn't just the sheer amount of money he'd offered that gave her shock — although it was an insane amount, and much more than she'd ever expected — it was the handwriting too.

It was Tom's handwriting. The loops and curls and messy flourishes . . . Ari had seen them all before. With a pang of pain, she remembered the small notes he used to leave on her pillow. *I'm just getting coffee, be back in ten minutes* or *Getting a run in before our day starts, don't shower without me.* Ari had always teased him for his messy handwriting.

"You write like you're always in a rush," she would say, smiling.

"They're notes to you," Tom replied, running his thumb over her cheek. "I'm always in a hurry to talk to you. You call them messy, but I call them lovingly rushed."

He'd written love notes after that, his handwriting becoming messier and messier, until it was a running joke between them. Ari paused, staring at the cheque in her hand. Whenever Reine asked for a story about the man who'd fathered her, Ari would talk about Tom's handwriting.

"He made my world a little more beautiful with his writing," Ari would say, smiling at her child. "He wrote the sweetest things to me. Wonderful things."

And now he was writing her cheques. Making a beautiful thing ugly and paying her off. Ari felt her heart harden as she folded the cheque, banishing Tom's words and her memories of Tom Miller into papery shadows.

"Eight years of child support, plus hardship expenses," Mr Andrews intoned. "I've also been instructed by Marnie that Reine is to be written immediately into her will. Likewise, with Mr Somerset here," Mr Andrews gave Tom a short glance, "he's also asked that Reine be written into his will — and, should he father more children, be treated equally among them."

Sasha, Ari at once thought. *He was thinking of the children he would have with Sasha.*

"It's really too much—" Ari began, and Mr Andrews nodded.

"Yes, it is. I estimate Tom's share of Reine's care to be sixty-nine per cent of your combined income—"

"Wait," Ari stopped, turning to Tom. "How do you know my income?"

Tom stared at her, his eyes still wearing that empty, haunted look from before. Mr Andrews cleared his throat.

"Once Marnie established that Reine was her son's child, she asked my firm to do some research. A quick check of the UK Companies House register gave me most of the information I needed, and then we found out the details of your mortgage, your rental costs prior to this and—"

"Did you know about this?" Ari's voice was hoarse as she turned to Tom. "This . . . utter invasion of my privacy? Did you know?"

"No," Tom replied firmly. "Not until this morning, at least, not until Mr Andrews arrived. I'd . . . I'd already settled on the sum I wanted to offer you, Ari. I told you, I want to step up now. I want to reimburse you for the years you've struggled on your own, help out with all reasonable costs. Reine's housing, her clothing, her schooling, her medical care—"

"I live in *London*," Ari shook her head. "We have the NHS, I don't pay for medical care. Her schooling is free. Don't kid yourself, this—" she furiously thrust the cheque into Tom's hands "—isn't about *reasonable costs*. This is guilt money. Well, I don't want it."

"Ms Lightowler—" Mr Andrews began, but Ari spun angrily on her heel to face him.

"Tell Marnie to keep her nose out of my business," she spat. "Reine and I are doing just fine, and we'll keep on doing just fine, thank you."

Mr Andrews gazed at her evenly. "Ms Lightowler, Marnie Somerset is not a woman to be trifled with, and she wants access to her grandchild—"

"And I intend on giving her that access," Ari said, "but not like this. Reine and I are not for sale."

Mr Andrews sighed. "The two of you need to settle this." He picked up his briefcase and moved to the door.

"Or, Ms Lightowler, you will be hearing from me again. I've given you fair warning."

He left the room, his shoes clicking as he marched down the hall, and Ari turned back to Tom, who was gazing at her miserably. She stared back at him, meeting his eyes and holding them. After a moment, Tom slumped back into his chair.

"What do you want me to do?" he asked her, defeated. "What, Ari?"

"What a life you live," Ari said sadly, shaking her head. "One where everything can be solved by just handing someone a cheque."

"Welcome to my world," Tom replied bitterly, his hands clenching on the table. "Welcome to my world."

Ari gazed at him, tears pricking at her eyes. "No wonder you were so lost all those years ago. No wonder you ran. No wonder you hid." She gestured to their palatial surroundings, the cold marble floors, the expensive wallpaper.

"I would have run from all this too," she added, falling into a chair beside him.

"I was lost, all those years ago. But you found me," he whispered, looking directly at her. "You found me."

For a moment, his gaze felt too intense, and Ari tore her eyes away.

"What are we going to do?" she asked. "What now, Tom?"

When she chanced a glance at him again, he was staring at her with a melancholy smile.

"What?" she asked, puzzled. "What is it?"

"It's just . . ." Tom began with a sigh. "It's just, I think that's the first time you've ever said my name this weekend without anger."

"Tom," Ari said again, and he was right, there was no anger in her tone. "It's a good name. I always thought it was a good name."

Tom gave a smile at that. "I like Reine's name," he said, and she knew he was changing the subject, veering away from any and all talk of himself. "You chose well, Ari. I can't think of a name more perfect for her."

256

She smiled back at him. "I nearly called her Millie. Millie Lightowler. Sebastian talked me out of it."

"Maybe," Tom cleared his throat. "Maybe, if you ever have more children . . ."

"No," Ari answered at once. "Reine's it for me."

Tom nodded.

"You and Sasha . . ." Tom's eyes snapped to hers ". . . you might have children. And then Reine . . . she . . . she would have siblings. She'd like that."

Tom was looking at her oddly. "Look, Ari, about Sasha . . ."

But Ari didn't want to hear it. She didn't want to hear how easily and quickly he'd replaced her in his life.

"I'm sure you'll be very happy," Ari offered, trying to be kind. "Obviously, I won't be able to plan your wedding now, but I'm sure Sebastian will do it. He's never one to turn down a well-paying contract."

"You think I should marry Sasha?" Tom asked, an odd tone to his voice. "Still? Even now?"

"Why wouldn't you?" Ari shrugged, trying to alleviate the knot of pain growing in her stomach. "Why would things have changed?"

Tom made no reply, exhaling heavily.

"She's beautiful," Ari added, through a throat that was now thick and dry. "Very beautiful. Like that old queen of diamonds card you used to have."

When she looked back at Tom, he was staring at his hands with empty eyes.

"Right," Tom said blankly. "Right."

Suddenly, Ari felt overwhelmed with sadness. She closed her eyes for a moment, trying to calibrate her racing thoughts.

"Did you mean it?" she asked.

"What?"

Ari swallowed. "About wanting joint custody?"

"Not really. I wouldn't do that to you." He sounded tired. "Reine's yours. I know that. I just . . . I just want to get to know her. I meant what I said earlier, Ari. I want to

257

be her father. But only under your terms, okay? Without lawyers and contracts and . . . and my *mother* sticking her damn nose in."

"Okay," Ari felt herself relax. "Okay."

"I'm sorry I wasn't there," Tom carried on. "I'll be sorry for that every day for the rest of my life. Even if you believe nothing else I ever say again, please believe that."

He sounded so miserable that Ari knew he was telling the truth. He *was* sorry. "Come on," she heard herself say, feeling her body stand, surprised by her own actions. "Come with me."

Tom looked up at her. "What? Where?"

She reached down and took one of his hands, which was still clenched into a tight fist. As she wrapped her palm around his strained muscles, she felt it relax, and his fingers linked with hers as easily as they had ever done. There was something in this, Ari knew, but she ignored the feeling, just as she ignored the spark that went through her at the touch of his skin.

"Just come with me," she said. "Please."

* * *

As Ari led him away from the house and towards the woods, Tom felt his heart racing happily. He didn't stop to ask where she was taking him and why. For all he knew, she could have been leading him into the forest where Luis and Sebastian were lying in wait, ready to murder him for deserting her. He probably deserved it, to be fair. He didn't dare ask her where they were going, or why. All he knew was that Ari was here and willingly holding his hand and wanting to spend time with him, and he knew better than to open his mouth and ruin the moment. Something had shifted between them, and Tom felt hope raising its head. Maybe they could move on from here, he thought to himself. Maybe there was a way forward from this.

As they entered the woods, Tom glanced up at the grey sky. It was dark and foreboding, a little like the tortured workings of his mind.

"Will it rain, do you think?" he asked. The words were so innocuous, so pathetically every day, that he winced as soon as they were spoken.

This was Ari, and he was talking about the fucking *weather*?

Ari, to his surprise, only laughed. It was a sound he hadn't heard in eight years, and his heart pulsed painfully at the noise.

"Maybe," she remarked, looking up. "I haven't had a single sunny day at this place, you know. I'm sure it's beautiful when the sun shines, but honestly, on days like this . . ." she gestured to the forbidding outline of the house behind them ". . . I don't know how you bear it."

Tom shrugged back. "I'm not normally here. I live in the city."

"Yes," Ari answered, and her tone had changed. "With Sasha."

Tom instinctively knew he needed to change the subject. Sasha, like Tom Miller, were topics that made the smile fall from Ari's lips and her voice go from honey to ice.

"I used to play in these woods when I was a kid," he offered quickly. "My mom was always working, and my dad had his cars and planes. I would play out here, waiting for them to have time for me."

At that, Ari looked at him. "That's awful."

"No," Tom shook his head. "I was a quiet kid. The trees suited me."

"Reine can be quiet," Ari admitted. "I worry about how quiet she is sometimes."

"Really?" Tom felt a dart of worry. "But she has friends, right? At school?"

"Yes." Ari nodded. "She has friends. She also has friends from her violin lessons. Oh, and her My Little Pony fan club meetings. But still, she's quiet."

"She's in a My Little Pony fan club?" Tom asked.

Ari laughed. "Yeah, Reine's a big fan. I think it broke Luis's heart a little that she never really got into Barbie dolls.

259

He had grand plans for going to Barbie conventions with her."

Tom felt a dart of jealousy shoot through him. "But Reine likes the ponies instead?"

Ari nodded. "Mm. It's okay though. Luis made his peace with it. He's now head of the My Little Pony fan club, London chapter, and don't tell anyone this, but I think — I *think* — I've seen him writing Applejack and Rarity fanfiction."

Tom nodded. "Does she go horse riding?"

Ari laughed again, stepping over a patch of mud. "No, but God, Sebastian would love that. He's forever trying to make a lady out of her. He and Luis are already planning their outfits to wear to Queen Charlotte's ball when Reine's eighteen."

"What's Queen Charlotte's ball?" Tom asked.

Ari gave an embarrassed shrug. "A debutante ball."

Tom swallowed. "If Reine ever does that, please don't tell my mother. She can get . . ." he paused ". . . overexcited sometimes."

"Really?" Ari asked, and there was a teasing tone to her voice that Tom hadn't heard in years. "You mean the woman who only had to hear once about the possibility of having a grandchild, and then redecorated an entire wing of her house to accommodate her — as well as having a custom playground built — can get overexcited?"

Tom flushed red. "Sorry about all that. My mother has had too much time on her hands, far too much time, actually, since she retired. There's nothing like a project to keep her occupied."

He felt Ari stiffen next to him. "Reine's a person, not a project."

Tom immediately stopped, pulling on Ari's hand. "I know. I'm sorry. I just meant . . ."

Ari shook her head. "No. I'm being oversensitive. Don't worry about it."

Tom felt another flash of guilt. "If you're oversensitive, it's for a reason. I'm sorry."

Ari sighed. "Look, Tom, if we're going to move on from here, and . . . *co-parent*, you need to stop apologising."

"I'll never stop being sorry," Tom replied. "I'll never stop telling you how sorry I am."

"Okay," Ari nodded. "Okay. But not with Reine, right? She doesn't need apologies now. She just needs you to be there for her, okay? That's what Reine needs."

"I can't wait to start," Tom told her, and he meant it. It was the absolute truth. He couldn't wait to start spending time with Reine.

"Well," Ari replied with a smile. "No better time than the present."

She gestured forwards, and Tom's mouth dropped open with shock. For there, in the clearing of the woods, sat *Stella Snow*, of all people. But it wasn't the Stella he knew, the one who made his sphincter clench and his blood freeze in his veins, it was a strange, alien Stella. She was sitting on a log, looking almost *relaxed*. A dirty pair of boots were on her legs, covering a pair of mud-splattered jeans, and she was pointing up into the trees, talking animatedly. Next to her stood Reine, looking equally relaxed in muddy clothing, eating a chocolate cookie and staring at whatever Stella was pointing at.

"Stella is watching Reine?" Tom spluttered. "*Stella?*"

"Yeah." Ari shrugged. "They actually get along really well."

"But she's . . . she's so—"

"She's so what?" intoned an icy, stern voice, and Tom at once snapped to attention.

"She's, um, uh . . ."

Stella rolled her eyes. "Verbose as always, I see, Somerset. My God, an odd jawline *and* a babbling brook of a mouth. How a man like you produced something so glorious as this little girl, I'll never know."

"It's nice to see you again," Tom replied through gritted teeth. "Thank you for watching Reine."

"Oh." Stella gave him an odd look, her eyes drifting down to his and Ari's linked hands. Whatever she was thinking she kept firmly to herself.

"You're playing Dad now then, are you? That's terribly interesting. Very well. I'll leave you to it."

"Mummy." Reine stepped forwards, swinging her little arms around Ari's waist. She looked up at Tom with excited eyes. Ari must have seen, for she at once let go of Tom's hand — he felt a flash of disappointment when her fingers disentangled from his own.

"Thanks for this, Stella," Ari said. "I know how busy you are."

"Oh, I cleared my calendar, don't you worry," Stella said with a shrug. "Car-wreck weddings are a delight, you know. And this one has been an almighty smash that I wouldn't miss."

"Well, that's good to hear, thank you, and—" Before Tom could finish the sentence, Stella reached into her pocket and held up her phone. At close range she snapped a photo, the flash momentarily blinding him.

"*Will you please stop doing that?*" Tom hissed, clutching a hand to his eyes, mindful of his language.

"Why?" Stella asked blankly. "I'm going to exhibit you, my darling oaf. You'll be the talk of the town when these photos hit the canvas. Honestly, it's the most exciting thing. I haven't been this inspired since my *Decaying Plant* series, only in place of rotting vegetables I now have you."

"I don't remember agreeing to that—" Tom began, but Stella put her finger over his lips.

"Hush now, Jawline, my erstwhile rotting carrot. There's no agreement needed in art. Besides, you have parenting to do now."

"Yes, but—"

"It's been a pleasure as always, Small," Stella said, ignoring him completely now, and turning to Reine. "But don't eat all my Leibniz."

"Bye, Stellie," Reine sang out cheerfully, and Tom watched as the tall woman left the clearing, her hands in her pockets, her head held high.

"Right," Ari said, and there was a nervous energy about her that Tom could feel radiating around them. "Right."

Tom suddenly felt nervous too. Even more nervous than when Stella had been with them.

"Ari, you don't have to do this right now, you know," he offered, but Ari shook her head.

"No. I really do."

Tom watched as Ari sank to her knees in front of their little girl, taking one of Reine's chocolate-covered hands.

"Reine, do you know who this man is?"

"Yes. He's Tom," answered Reine, who suddenly looked shy. "And I think . . . I think he might be my father?"

The young uncertainty in her voice made Tom wince. He looked at Ari, who nodded shortly, giving him permission.

"Yeah," he added, sinking to his knees next to Ari. "Yeah, I am. And I'm going to be around a lot more from this point on. Is that okay with you?"

Reine looked first at Ari, and Tom knew she was silently touching base with her mother. Ari nodded silently again, and with that Reine offered Tom a shy smile.

"Yes. Yes, that's okay."

They spent the afternoon in the clearing, finding sticks and leaves. Tom walked with Reine and Ari through the woods he knew so well, pointing out all the interesting turns and paths he remembered from his own childhood. He took Reine to his old den and felt a rush of gratitude when Ari sat outside, feigning tired legs. He knew she was simply giving him time with his daughter, and he relished the half hour he had alone with the little girl, who took a real interest in his old collection of childhood treasures.

When they walked back to the house, hungry and tired, Tom couldn't remember ever being so happy. Actually, he could. He'd last felt this light and free in Europe, when he'd been with Ari. She was the thing that lightened his soul best, he realised. He stopped suddenly, staring down at her in shocked recognition.

"What is it?" Ari asked in concern, but Tom shook his head, scared of frightening her with the intensity of his feelings.

"Nothing, it's just . . ." He watched as Ari brushed a strand of stray hair away from her face, looking at him curiously.

"I know it's been a long time, but with you, nothing is ever just *nothing*. What's going on?"

Tom gave her a soft smile. "You know what you were saying earlier, about the queen of diamonds card being beautiful?"

Ari nodded, her face falling a little.

At her look of hurt, Tom quickly carried on. "Well, I was just thinking that I . . . Well, let's just say that I still prefer the queen of spades. Always have, always will."

Ari blushed, a pretty pink colour dusting her cheeks.

Between them, Reine looked up. "Are you going to marry my mummy now?"

Tom glanced at her in surprise.

"Reine!" Ari said.

"Well, you know—" Tom began, but he couldn't finish his words.

"He can't marry your mother, dear," a curt voice interrupted. "You see, he's already planning on marrying me."

Tom looked up, right into the blazing eyes of Sasha.

CHAPTER 19: FISH IN A POND

Getting over Ari isn't easy.

Tom sits around his parents' house — no, his mother's house now, he painfully corrects himself — and doesn't do much of anything. His father's plane sits abandoned in the old hangar, and Tom takes her into the skies on occasion, keeping his flying hours up. His father would have liked that, Tom reminds himself. If there was one thing Doug Somerset ever took seriously it was his flying. He might have been a race-car driver by design, but he was a pilot at heart, and Tom can't bear the thought of his father's plane going to rust and ruin in Doug's eternal absence.

"You can keep her, you know," Marnie tells him one evening, and Tom looks up at her, blank-faced and confused. He couldn't keep her, he thinks. He lost her. She's moved on, married to someone else, with a baby. His mother doesn't know what she's talking about.

"The plane," Marnie clarifies, looking at him with concern.

"Oh," Tom replies. "Right." For a moment he sits quietly, mulling over her words.

"And anything else you want to keep of your father's," Marnie offers, her voice rippling with pain and loss anew. "Anything at all. All his stuff . . . all his junk . . ." There's a bittersweet smile on her face as memory strikes. "Maybe it's time to move on. Find it all a new home."

Tom shrugs. "Thanks, but there's nothing I want. Not really."

His mother frowns. "Not even the plane?"

"I don't have anywhere to keep her in Brooklyn."

"Brooklyn? Who said anything about Brooklyn? It can stay here. Besides, since when do you live in Brooklyn? You've practically moved back here since your father died. That was two years ago."

"If I'm in your way—"

"No, that's not what I meant," Marnie cuts him off. "All I'm thinking is that your place in the city is costing you a small fortune every month in rent, and you've hardly been back to the place. Why don't you give it up? Stay here with me?"

At the almost pleading tone to her voice, Tom shrinks back. His mother retired during the worst of Doug's illness to care for him, and her lack of purpose is starting to show. Suddenly, Tom realises that she's thinking of making a project out of him. If he continues to stay here, continues to mope and grieve and dwell on what could have been, he might as well give up now. He takes a deep breath and sits taller.

"I don't think that would be a good idea," he says, as gently as he can. "In fact, I've been thinking recently about going . . . Well, maybe going back to the apartment. Getting a job. Doing some travelling."

"You only just got back from London," Marnie complains. "And you want to travel again?"

Tom swallows hard, trying in vain not to think about Ari, the image of her baby in another man's arms.

"Yeah," he says softly. "I want to travel again."

"Another European jaunt?"

Tom tries not to flinch. "No. Somewhere new."

Somewhere, *he tells himself,* that doesn't remind him of Ari.

Marnie chews on her lip, and Tom can sense her displeasure. "What is it?"

His mother taps a finger on her table. "I don't think travelling is a good idea. You were a mess after your father died, and then, just when you seemed to be getting brighter and better, you took yourself off to London and went straight back to square one. You've been in a dark mood since you got back from England, you know. I've been worried about you."

"I'm fine," Tom lies, and his mother, to her credit, doesn't try to argue with him.

"If you say so. But let me say this. Travelling isn't the answer for you."

Tom sighs. "So, what is then?"

Marnie gives him a pointed look. "Staying here with me. Maybe meeting a nice woman——"

"Mom——"

"Let me finish," Marnie complains. "You could meet a nice woman. Start a family. Maybe take up that position on the board of the family business they keep offering you——"

"No," Tom says firmly. "That's not for me. It was a great role for you. But it's not for me."

"It's a family business," Marnie says again, and her finger is tapping double-time on her glass tabletop now. "It's wrong for it to be run by a bunch of strangers in suits when you're sitting right here twiddling your thumbs and spending all your time feeling — forgive me — sad."

Tom gives her a look. "Mom," he says softly. "It's just not for me."

At that, Marnie slumps back in her chair. "No," she says bitterly. "It isn't for you, just like it wasn't for your father and just like it wasn't for Corentin."

With a sigh, Tom comes to a stand. He walks over to his mother and crouches beside her.

"Mom," he says softly, "I'm sorry I'm a disappointment to you."

Marnie sighs too, reaching over to take one of Tom's hands. "You aren't a disappointment to me," she offers. "Never that."

"Corentin——" Tom begins, and Marnie gives a short laugh.

"I love your brother, but he left a decorated naval career to become a Druid. Tell me any family that wouldn't find that a little odd." She gives Tom a small smile. "Okay, I'll pin all my hopes on a grandchild one day then."

"Mom——"

"I'm just kidding," Marnie says quickly, but Tom knows his mother, and can hear the grain of truth in her tone.

"Sure you are," he says.

"I am," Marnie argues. "But you really should try and meet someone, Tom. It isn't healthy for a man of your age to be alone. I mean, there's never been anyone special in your life since you were a teenager. You should fall in love a little more." Marnie squeezes his hand, and

267

Tom knows she's thinking of Doug. Even with all their troubles, Tom knows his mother loved his father.

"Love is wonderful. Magical, even."

Magic.

Tom takes a deep breath as, once again, Ari's face and smile come to his mind. Without even thinking, he feels for the playing card he keeps in his pocket. These days, the fool is always with him, still chasing Ari's queen. Always chasing Ari's queen, Tom realises. Reassurance floods through him when he feels the familiar outline against his fingers, the edges now beginning to wear thin with his repeated caressing.

Marnie's eyes, always sharp, follow his movements.

"What's that?" she asks, nodding to Tom's hand.

"Nothing," Tom replies, trying to keep his voice calm.

"Tom," his mother begins, and he looks into her eyes. They're brown, as deep and warm as usual, though tinged with what Tom thinks might be doubt.

"Yeah?"

His mother stares at where the card had sat in his hand. "There hasn't been anyone special in your life recently, has there?"

"What makes you ask that?" Tom replies, trying to sound neutral. Trying to sound as though there's no guilt in his soul or heart.

Marnie's gaze moves from his hand to his eyes. "I don't know. Just a feeling I'm getting."

Tom's mouth runs dry. "Your feeling is wrong. There's no one. There's been no one."

It's not a lie. She's no one to his mother. But, in his heart, Ari will never be 'no one'. Not to him.

Marnie nods. Whether she believes him or not she doesn't say. Of all her many brilliant qualities, Marnie's uncanny ability to know when to speak and when to stay quiet always did shine the brightest. Whatever she's thinking, whatever cards she's holding, she chooses to keep close to her chest.

"Okay," Marnie simply nods, and Tom stands.

"Maybe you should sell Dad's plane," he offers. "Maybe it's time for all of us to move on."

"Sell his baby?" Marnie scoffs. "What a ridiculous idea. She's yours, and she'll be here whenever you need her."

Something inside of him eases at that thought. "Thanks, Mom."

"Tom?" Marnie reaches over, taking his hand once more.

"Yeah?"

"I meant what I said. Maybe instead of finding playing cards in books you could find a nice woman. I want you to be happy, Tom. I really do."

"Thanks," he says again, "so do I."

It's only later, as he's falling into bed, that he realises he meant it. Of their whole conversation, that was the most honest thing he said.

He does want to be happy. He just doesn't know how to be happy without Ari.

* * *

He goes back to his apartment in Brooklyn, though 'back' isn't really the right word when it's the first time he's ever actually lived in it. He rented it on an impulse during Doug's final illness, bought furniture for it and registered all his mail to be delivered there, but never got round to moving in. His first night there is strange, with the noise of the city keeping him awake, the shadows and lights playing on his wall unfamiliar and distracting. He figures he's grown too used to his mother's house, too used to the quiet countryside and dark skies. He knows it will take time to adjust to the change, and time is something he has plenty of.

The apartment comes with big built-in bookcases — probably why he rented it in the first place, Tom reflects, having always been a reader — which he fills liberally with literature. Among the contemporary thrillers and great American novels, Tom starts quite the collection of self-help books. Books on grief and moving forward. One particularly catches him, and he stays up an entire night reading it. It talks about the human body and how it repairs itself. Wounds and disease wreak havoc, but the body can heal, creating new tissue. Tom wonders if heartbreak works the same — can't help but wonder if the shattered pieces of his soul will ever reform, just as he wonders if the ache inside him will ever ease. He knows wounds leave scars, and maybe that's what will happen in his case. Maybe Ari will be the scar on his heart he'll carry forever. In a way, he almost hopes so. There's a cold kind of comfort in knowing that he'll carry part of her with him until he dies, a cold kind of comfort *in knowing the flame of his love will burn for ever, even if that flame leaves ashes of grief within.*

But he has to move on. He wants to be happy. His father told him to be happy.

He finds work easily. The family name and his mother's reputation still carry a lot of weight in the world of finance, and he picks up work as a trader for a private banking firm. The salary isn't outrageous, but the bonuses are, and Tom throws himself into the role with gusto, trying not to admit to himself that he doesn't really have much else to do these days. He develops a routine, which is strangely comforting in its unending familiarity, and he sticks to it rigorously. He regularly puts in twelve to fourteen-hour days, but he makes a point of travelling to his mom's house at least one day a week. There, he has lunch with Marnie before taking his dad's plane into the sky. He loops and swirls in the air for an hour or two, emptying his mind and still-troubled soul, before returning to the ground and giving her a maintenance check.

"She's still the same old beauty, Dad," he always whispers when he closes the log book, before making the slow walk back to the house. He takes tea with Marnie in the evening, and most days he'll end the meal by offering his mother a kiss before hopping into his car. But one night she stops him.

"Before you leave, you should see something," she tells him, and leads him down to the gallery, her heels clicking lightly on the marble floor. "That painting you bought? In Europe? It's finally ready. The framer took his sweet time with it, I have to say. He said he wanted to use Norwegian Fir to make the frame, keeping with the theme of the painting, or some such nonsense. Well, I'm no artist, and obviously Peterson's been framing my pictures for years, so I won't judge his choices . . . But I think American Oak would have worked just as well, don't you?"

She switches on a light at the end of the long hall, and there in front of them is The Ends of the Earth, *just the same as the last time Tom saw it. He inhales sharply, the painting momentarily flooring him, and he has to take a moment to steady the sudden rise in tempo of his heart.*

"You put it where I asked," Tom whispers gratefully. "You put it where it belongs."

The orange is still as vibrant as he recalls — the greys and whites just as beautifully blended. Tom tucks his hands in his pockets, the ghost of a smile crossing his face as he remembers how delicately Ari would hold a paintbrush in her hands, nibbling on the end while she considered how to translate her thoughts and feelings onto canvas. He remembers how her tongue always poked out when she painted — how her brow furrowed in concentration. Momentarily, Tom closes his eyes and allows himself the luxury of remembering. Allows himself to remember her hands, and how paint would stay under her fingernails and in the slight creases of her skin. Remembers how they always smelled of flowers and turpentine, an odd but addictive mix. Remembers how her fingers felt running down his cheeks.

When he opens his eyes again, he gives his mother a warm smile. "Thank you," he says, honestly and gratefully, and Marnie smiles back.

"It's not a bad piece, you know. I couldn't make out the signature though. Who'd you say it was by again?"

"I didn't," Tom replies tightly. "I got it in Norway."

"Well, if you ever see any more of their work, I wouldn't mind having another."

"More of their work?" Tom parrots back, a thought suddenly striking him. More work. Ari might have painted more work.

"Mm. Yes. You know I like things in sets. A companion piece to this one might be nice."

"I'll look into it," Tom replies, keeping his voice even. "I'll look into it."

* * *

It becomes a hobby over which Tom has little control. Ari, he learns, has an online shop where she sells a few of the canvases she's created. He buys one before he thinks the better of it, before buying another just a few days after that. Within a month, he's emptied her shop. He then waits for her site to update, waits for her to sell the pieces she must currently be working on. But the site seems neglected, and a worrying thought builds in Tom's mind, that maybe — just maybe — Ari's given the whole thing up. Maybe the baby takes up all her time, Tom thinks with a painful swallow. Or maybe her good-looking, well-built husband does, his mind adds bitterly.

271

So, he starts to seek out her earlier work. He finds a few pieces from a seller who operates out of Greenwich market, and another few from a small gallery in Brighton. Soon his collection of her work spirals from three to twenty-two, and then swells again to thirty-one. He has them framed, catalogued and hung, keeping his favourites in his Brooklyn apartment and loaning the rest to small, independent galleries in New York. A few buyers contact him, looking to buy some of Ari's work, offering him double, even triple what he originally paid for each. But he always turns them down.

He let Ari go. He lost her. But he won't lose her work. He won't lose all he has left of her.

He learns from an art contact that one of Ari's paintings sold to an American stockbroker, and Tom makes a point of traipsing to a polo match to buy it from him. The guy's an absolute shit, cocky and smarmy, and through gritted teeth Tom negotiates a buying price. The guy seems to realise Tom's determination to own the piece, and as such haggles like a fucking pro. Tom ends up offering a five figure sum, just to shut the guy up, and he stands in the sun afterwards, holding an ice-cold glass of water to his head, wondering just what sort of madness has infected him.

He has to admit that if this is his attempt at letting Ari go, he's not doing a very good job of it.

It's then, while a headache builds behind his temple, that he hears a voice he recognises. He turns when it calls his name, and comes face to face with Sasha.

"Hello stranger," she practically purrs. "I haven't seen you in years."

* * *

Sasha looked as immaculate as always, examining her perfectly manicured nails with a remarkably detached expression, given her anger the day before. Tom paced around her, his mind racing, with what felt like a hundred thoughts striking him at once. He turned them over and over in his head, trying to decide which one to tackle first. Ari, Reine, Sasha, his mother . . . Tom collapsed onto the sofa in the room he was sharing with Sasha, running a hand tiredly over his face.

Above everything, he knew it was time to do what he'd been putting off for days. No, weeks.

No, he thought again, as realisation hit him. Something he'd been putting off for *years*.

"Sasha," he began, his voice low but firm. "Look—"

"Oh, for fuck's sake," Sasha cut him off, leaning back on her hands and staring at him with an irritated expression. "Don't say what I think you're about to, Tom. Don't be that stupid, okay?"

Tom stared at her. "What do you think I'm about to say?"

Sasha rolled her eyes. "I'm getting the feeling that you're about to try and call off our wedding."

"Sasha—"

Sasha held up a hand to stop him. "But you must know how utterly ridiculous that would be, don't you?"

Her words made him pause. "Ridiculous?"

Sasha gave him a pointed look. "Utterly and completely ridiculous. I mean, I know you've always had idiotic tendencies, despite being a mostly intelligent and well-thought-of person, but to cancel our wedding would be beyond stupid."

Tom shook his head, trying to stay calm. "Sasha, for you and me to still get married — now, with everything that's going on, everything that's *still* going on . . . *that* would be the stupid thing to do. Not calling it off."

"Everything that's going on?" Sasha raised an eyebrow. "Let me just clarify the situation for you, Tom. We're at *your* mother's house. We have *my* wedding dress designer here. We have *my* wedding photographer here. We have *my* dream wedding planners here. Now, just because you happen to have slept with one of those wedding planners a million-who-cares-years ago, does not mean anything between us has to change."

Tom stared at her. "I have a child with that wedding planner, Sasha. That changes things."

Again, Sasha rolled her eyes. "This is just another one of your idiotic tendencies showing, Tom. You don't even know

273

for a fact that the kid is yours. You're just taking the mother's word for it. For all you know, the kid belongs to someone else, and Ari just saw this place and the money you have and decided she wants a piece of it. I don't blame her. I'd do the same, if I were in her shoes."

Deep inside Tom, something hot and ugly erupted. *She's awful*, a voice in his head suddenly said. *Sasha is a truly awful woman.*

"Don't talk that way about Ari," he said, his tone sharp. "Reine is mine."

"Okay, so let's say she is," Sasha shrugged, as if it were no matter. "You and your mother have enough money to buy Ari off. We ship those two back to merry olde England and you and I can get on with our lives. Simple."

Tom's hands clenched, and he felt his jaw tighten. "I want to be a father to Reine. I don't want to buy anyone off."

Sasha sighed. "Fine. So, you'll fly across to London once a month, give the kid a few gifts and take her out for lunch or something, and then come back. We still don't have to change in this situation, Tom."

Tom swallowed down a rising lump of bile. "Okay." He leaned back in his chair. "So, say we get married, and one day have children of our own? I'll want Reine to know her siblings. I'll want Reine to spend time with us as a family."

"Sure, fine." Sasha stood, going to the mirror and running her fingers through her hair. "She can babysit for us. She'll be old enough by that point anyway."

At that, Tom closed his eyes. *She's horrible*, his mind said again. *What have you been doing? What were you thinking?* "Sasha," he said slowly, opening his eyes. "I don't want to marry you."

"Well, I don't particularly want to marry you either, but that's my own idiotic tendency I'm willing to work through."

"You don't want to marry me?" Tom asked her in disbelief. "If you don't want to marry me, why the fuck are you still here? Why the fuck are we having this conversation?"

Sasha sighed again, spinning on her heel to stare at him. "Please get real here, Tom. You and I have hardly been couple of the year, have we? We're very different people with very different needs. But you know something, in many ways we work. We're of a similar background and we look fabulous together in photographs. We aren't meant for one another, but we work together. We make sense."

"But if you don't love me, and I don't love you—"

"Love." Sasha rolled her eyes, opening her make-up case and pulling out a lipstick. "Please. You think I'm here because I *love* you? Of course I don't love you, Tom, and I've known for a long time that you don't love me."

Tom stood, looking down at Sasha angrily. "If you don't love me, then why are you here?"

Sasha applied her lipstick without even looking back at him, the scarlet shade making her mouth look sweet and appealing.

How can something so beautiful spew such ugliness? Tom thought. *How can something so lovely be so ugly inside?*

"Well," Sasha replied evenly, blotting her lips on a tissue, "I'm here because you were a catch, Tom. With your money, looks and background, you're the prize fish in the pond, believe it or not. So, I caught you." Abruptly she turned to him, giving him a long and appraising look. "But just because I caught the fish doesn't mean I want to eat it, Tom. It was never about the fish for me. It was about *catching* the fish, which I did. Now, how does this shade look on me? Good, right?"

Tom stared at her in disbelief. "I don't want to marry you, Sasha."

Sasha pressed her lips together, a touch of anger seeming to strike her. "Oh, for fuck's sake — look, Tom, please get real here. If this is about Ari—"

"Don't bring her into this," Tom interrupted. "This isn't about Ari, not right now at least. This is about you and I being completely unsuited for one another."

"Of course this is about Ari," Sasha spat, walking over to the cupboard and pulling out a dress. "Admit it, if she hadn't walked through the door this weekend with her little brat you would've married me and never thought the better of it—"

275

"I would have thought the better of it one day," Tom said violently. "I would've woken up from my stupor eventually."

"Fine, if you say so, like I care anyway. But let me tell you this." Sasha stepped closer to him, jabbing a finger in his chest. "If you think Ari's going to take you back just because you've ditched me, you've got another thing coming. She doesn't love you anymore, Tom. She never loved you, in fact. Just the man you pretended to be. She hates you, Tom. Really and truly."

Tom felt all the air pulled from his lungs as he exhaled hard at Sasha's words. Her cruelty was like a punch to his stomach, and he recoiled away from her, stumbling back towards the wall.

Abruptly, Sasha's face changed. "You're going to end up a lonely man if you break up with me, Tom," she said, suddenly sweet. "And you know how you hate to be lonely."

"Sasha, don't—"

"I'll keep you company," Sasha promised, stepping towards him, running one of her long nails down his cheek. "With me, you'll never be alone."

"Don't, stop—"

Sasha stepped even closer. "You know you can't cope when you're alone, Tom," she carried on relentlessly. "You know you don't make good decisions when you're lonely."

"Yeah," Tom croaked, shaking his head. "That's how I ended up with you in the first place."

He collapsed into the chair again, where he suddenly began to laugh. He laughed and laughed and laughed, until Sasha began to look at him with concern.

"What's so funny?" she asked, her tone sharp. "Why are you laughing?"

"I'm funny," he told her, "I'm the reason I'm laughing."

"Tom—"

Tom wiped his eyes. "I don't want to marry you, Sasha. I really don't. You know something? You're only ever nice to me when you want something. That's how you've always been, and I'm just seeing it now. I guess before all this, I was willing to . . . not overlook it, that's not right, but, I guess,

276

be *blind* to it. But now that I know, to be completely honest, I'd rather be lonely than with you."

Sasha's painted mouth dropped open as she gaped at him.

"I'm sorry we got to this point," Tom added, and the laughter and smiles disappeared. "I'm sorry I let us get this far. If it means anything to you, I'm sorry I used you. Because I did use you, Sasha. You're right, I don't like being alone. That fish in the pond, the one you wanted to catch? I think it wanted to be caught, and it didn't matter who held the rod."

"Tom," Sasha spluttered.

"I don't want to marry you, Sasha," Tom said again, for the final time.

"But . . . but . . . but Ari doesn't want you—"

"I told you, this isn't about Ari. Not really. This is about me now. And it's about you too, in a way. I don't want you to be unhappy, Sasha. I really don't. Life's too short to be unhappy. And you'd have been unhappy with me, eventually."

Something in Tom's chest loosened, and he took a deep breath. His lungs felt cleaner, less tight, and he smiled up at Sasha. It was a bittersweet smile, one he hoped she understood.

"Thank you," he said honestly. "Thank you for getting me through the last few years. Thank you for being with me."

For a moment, Sasha stared at him. Her mouth still hung open, and her beautiful face was set into a porcelain mask of shock.

"Sasha?" Tom asked in concern.

At his words, she snapped back into action. "*Thank you for being with me?* Thank you? You are fucking kidding me, right? Years of you moping around and all I get is a fucking thank you?"

"That's all I have to offer right now."

"Well, you can keep it," Sasha snapped. "Fuck you, Tom. Fuck you."

And with that, she stalked out of their room, slamming the door behind her.

* * *

277

Ari was sitting in the garden with Reine, shivering in her coat while the little girl played. She felt cold and tired, weary right down to her bones. She wrapped her arms around her legs, burrowing closer into herself. Reine had a little collection of dolls out, ones Marnie had pressed into her hands earlier.

"They were mine, once upon a time," Marnie had said. "It would be so lovely if Reine could take them. It would make me very happy."

Ari hadn't had the heart to refuse Marnie. The older woman was trying hard, Ari reflected. She was treading carefully, clearly desperate to be in Reine's life while giving Ari the space she thought she needed.

Ari rested her head across her folded knees, watching Reine move the dolls around the garden, talking to them, or making them talk to one another. She was still her usual vibrantly intelligent self, and Ari felt a flicker of relief. Despite the upheaval of this weekend, Reine was okay — happier, even, for the time she'd been spending with the man she now knew to be her father.

Ari blinked. She couldn't help but wonder what was happening with Tom and Sasha. Couldn't help but wonder what they were doing, saying or thinking. After Sasha had come upon them earlier, Tom had whisked her away into the house, leaving Ari and Reine with apologies and a promise to find them later.

Ari didn't know what to think or how to feel. This afternoon, Tom had tried so hard with them both. He'd really made an effort where Reine was concerned, and Ari couldn't help the flush of pleasure that had rushed through her when she'd seen her child playing with her father. It was something she'd long worried she would never see, something she'd hoped against hope Reine would experience. Reine had Sebastian and Luis, it was true, but seeing her with Tom had been a long-held and deeply cherished dream for Ari.

The sound of a car pulling into the gravel driveway made Ari look up, and she peered across the grass, watching as a man stepped out of a beaten-up old Sedan. He stretched, looking up at the house, before turning back to the car and pulling out a case — just as beaten up and old as his car — from the back seat.

Another visitor? Ari thought. *How many more people does this house need right now?* She went to call out to Reine, always wary of her child when a stranger was present, when the man suddenly seemed to clock her, peering at her curiously.

"Hello," she called out, raising a hand. "Are you looking for Marnie? Or Tom? I think they're all inside."

The man peered at her more closely, then put his case down and walked in her direction.

Bollocks, thought Ari. She wasn't really in the mood for a conversation with anyone. Not when her mind was still thinking about what was happening between Tom and Sasha.

"I know you," the man said, nodding as he walked closer. "You're just some woman."

Ari blinked twice. "Um . . ."

"Forgive me, that was abrupt. I mean, I've heard about you," the man corrected himself. "I spoke with Tom about you, years ago. You were just some woman then, although clearly not, since he was mad about you. And obviously Mom spoke with me about all this."

Ari blinked again. "I'm sorry, I don't understand, I've never . . ."

"Oh, of course. I'm Corentin. Tom's brother."

"Oh." Ari nodded, trying to give the impression of knowledge. "Right."

"You're Ari."

"Yes, well—"

"So, you've been in this place a whole weekend? Good for you. Can't stand the place myself. Too much goes on here."

Ari nodded, keeping one eye on Reine. "Yes."

"Prefer things a little quieter myself. Keeps me closer to the old ones."

Old ones? thought Ari. *Does he mean Marnie? Marnie's not ancient.*

"Okay, well, I think Marnie is inside and—"

279

Ari was cut off by the sound of a door slamming, and both she and Corentin looked up to see Sasha stumbling in her heels across the gravel drive. She swore loudly when she lost her balance, then recovered and moved towards her car. She stepped into the vehicle with another profanity, slamming the door closed before starting the engine loudly, tearing down the drive and away from the house.

Ari's stomach turned when she pondered what Sasha's sudden departure might mean.

She looked from where the car had been to the front door of the house, where Tom stood. He wasn't watching Sasha's car depart. His eyes were only for her, and Ari felt a tingle run through her when she met his gaze and held his eyes.

"Ah," said Corentin from next to her, his voice knowledgeable and rich. "Looks like I've arrived just in time."

CHAPTER 20: SALMON

"So, you're saying you broke up with Sasha, and the wedding is off?"

Marnie was staring at Tom, her eyes hard, her hands tightly clenched upon the polished mahogany of her desk. Standing over her shoulder, one hand stroking the gnarled ends of his tatty beard, stood Corentin. He was staring at Tom just as intently as his mother, but his eyes were softer, more like a worn shale to the steady diamonds of Marnie's gaze.

"Yeah, that's what I'm saying," Tom replied, feeling distinctly uneasy. He'd always hated standing up to his mother, but when you added Corentin into the mix the situation felt a thousand times worse. It was as though all the vibrant energy Marnie exuded was magnified by two — although with Corentin there was an added dimension of disapproval and regretfully felt disappointment in Tom's life choices. Not that he ever said anything to Tom. No, Corentin's feelings manifested themselves entirely through sorrowful eyes and woebegone smiles and shared looks with their mother. Thank God Marnie only ever called for his brother in the rare moments when she felt out of her depth or out of control, finding in his presence a reassuring and calming sort of backup. Corentin wasn't so much her son as much as a living and breathing emotional support blanket, Tom often thought.

"And Ari—"

"It wasn't about her." Tom immediately cut down that seedling of thought in Marnie's brain before it sprouted roots and branches. "Not really."

"Not really," Marnie replied thoughtfully, sitting back and looking up to her brother. "Did you hear that, Corentin? Not really."

"I heard him, Mom," Corentin intoned, still gazing at Tom thoughtfully.

"Sasha's gone back to the city," Tom carried on, ignoring the weight of his brother's eyes and staring at his mother. "Clearly we can't live together anymore. So, I'm going to pack up my half of the apartment this week, although I'm going to pay the entire rent for the next eighteen months."

"Well, I hardly think there's any call for that—"

"I didn't treat Sasha very well, Mom," Tom said firmly. "Whatever you think of her, I proposed to her for all the wrong reasons. There's no need for her to be financially impacted by my poor life choices. I won't hear any argument on this. I'm paying her rent."

A glimmer of something seemed to pass through Marnie's eyes, magnified again as it spread to Corentin's. Tom watched his mother and brother exchange a look, before Corentin cleared his throat.

"I'm sure you've made the right choice here, Tom."

Tom stopped, taking a moment to process his thoughts, because Corentin's words had almost sounded like *praise*.

"Hmm." Marnie leaned forward now, tapping her fingers on her desk. "Well then, you'll be moving your things back here I take it?"

Tom swallowed, suddenly feeling nervous. "Actually, I — probably not, Mom."

"What do you mean, 'probably not'? If you're not going to be living with Sasha, then of course you'll come back here."

Marnie sounded indignant, if not downright offended. "You have nowhere else to go, Tom."

Tom felt his mouth go dry, his pulse hammering in his head. "Actually, Mom, I thought I might go . . . to, uh, London."

At that, a heavy silence fell over the room.

"I'm sorry, what did you say?" Marnie asked.

Tom cleared his throat, standing taller. "I'm going to London."

Another weighted silence fell, followed by another exchange of looks between Marnie and Corentin.

"Tom, have you spoken to Ari about this?" Corentin asked quietly.

"No, I haven't. Not yet."

Abruptly, Marnie stood, walking over to Tom and taking his hand. "Look, Tom . . . I know you're keen to be a father to Reine, and I'm just as keen for you to have that place in her life. But London is . . . well, it's Ari's city. You can't just move there out of the blue and expect her to be okay with that."

"I can't just stay here and do nothing though," Tom replied miserably. "I have eight years to make up for, Mom. *Eight whole years.* Ari needs support, and Reine needs a father."

Corentin, with a sigh, sank into the chair Marnie had just occupied. "I think what Mom's saying, Tom, is that maybe you should discuss this with Ari before you make any real plans. Give her a chance to be okay with it. Give her a chance to contribute to the thought process."

Tom took a deep breath, working beyond the initial stab of annoyance he felt, eventually finding the sense in Corentin's words. There was truth to them, he realised. London was Ari's city, where she kept her home and where she worked, and he needed to be respectful of that.

"Yeah," he muttered. "Okay. I'll talk to Ari before I make any decisions."

"Try to talk to her alone," Marnie suddenly piped up. "Without Luis and Sebastian there, I mean. Don't misunderstand me, I like Luis — I like him quite a lot, actually — but he and his husband . . . Well, they've got an agenda where Ari and Reine are concerned. They'll do what they can to protect that, I imagine. Not that I blame them, but still . . ."

"Yeah." Tom nodded slowly. "You're right. I'll try and talk to Ari alone."

"After dinner," Corentin suddenly broke in, and Tom looked up to find his brother staring absently out of the window. "The skies are clearing, do you see? It would be a nice evening for a walk. It's quiet and peaceful out there now."

Tom blinked in surprise. Corentin was right. After days of grey clouds and cold rain, the sun was suddenly breaking through from above. In the distance, the dark blanket of clouds rolling slowly across the sky seemed to be splitting open, revealing sharp yellow rays that hit the earth in a bright display of hope and colour.

"Ides weather has passed," Corentin announced, and Tom was suddenly acutely reminded of Doug. Doug, who loved the sky more than anything else.

"Yeah," he agreed, feeling a wave of calm wash over him. "You're right. It has."

His father wanted him to be happy. His father wanted him to make the right choices. Even from the beyond, he felt Doug's presence there with him in that room. Everything, Tom abruptly thought, was going to be okay.

"You know," Corentin began, in a tone of voice Tom recognised — it was knowing and rich, and Tom knew it meant Corentin was about to impart desperately important wisdom of some kind, "traditionally, the Ides celebrated the new moon and the festival of—"

"Jupiter, yeah, I know," Tom broke in, impatient as always where his brother's painfully slow teachings were concerned. "Mom made me read *Julius Caesar* back in school too, you know."

"Actually," Corentin carried on calmly, "the Ides were first associated with Mother Earth. A day of celebration, where people brought offerings to the Goddess. *Anna Perenna,* the Romans called her, although she has different names in other cultures. The Ides were celebrated joyfully, where the first new moon of the year meant casting off the old and celebrating the new." Corentin glanced at Tom knowingly. "A bit like you, hmm? Casting off the old. Celebrating the new."

"Corentin—"

"Just something to think about, Tom," Corentin replied calmly, coming to stand beside his mother. "It's just something to think about. Take Ari for that walk after dinner."

"Yes," Marnie said, before adding, with a plea to her voice, "although Tom? Try not to fuck it up this time, okay? I really like Ari, Tom. I want her and Reine to be part of our lives."

"Yes," Corentin nodded sagely. "Also, as an aside, I know Mom's fortune may seem vast, but we can only afford to pay the rent for so many ex-fiancées and ex-lovers a year. Keeping Ari on side might save us a penny or two."

"Not that I'm complaining about settling Reine's costs," Marnie cut in quickly. "I mean, she's your daughter and my grandchild, and it's entirely right we take on our responsibility to her. But think of the salmon."

"Salmon?" Tom asked, feeling thoroughly confused. "What does salmon have to do with Ari and Reine?"

Marnie shook her head. "It doesn't have anything to do with them, but I've already paid for five hundred and eighty salmon fillets to be delivered for your now cancelled wedding in six weeks. It wasn't cheap and it's too late to cancel. What am I going to do with five hundred and eighty salmon fillets, Tom? Open a sushi restaurant?"

"I can pay you back for the salmon—"

"I'm not asking you to do that." Marnie shook her head. "I just . . . I just want you to sort things out with Ari, okay? Sort it out. Please."

"Mom," Tom replied softly, "I'm going to try my best, okay? That's all I can promise right now. I'll try my best. I want this to work with her . . . I still love her, Mom."

"I know," Marnie replied with a sigh. "I know you do."

"I've always loved her," Tom said, the weight of truth heavy on his tongue.

"So, she's not just some woman then?" Corentin asked wryly, and Tom turned to him, shaking his head.

"Not just some woman," he replied. "My Ari. And I want to win her back."

* * *

"You know, I've been thinking . . ." Sebastian remarked, looking at Ari and Luis with a serious expression.

"Dare I ask?" Ari replied, popping two paracetamols into her mouth and chugging them back with a mouthful of water.

"It's just, now that Reine has that incredibly awkward blank space on her birth certificate filled, she should really move schools."

Ari stared at him, affronted. "There's nothing wrong with being a single mum. Besides, Reine loves her school, and *I* love her school. Why would I move her?"

"Also," Luis cut in, "you forget that I'm the secretary of the PTA. If Reine leaves the school, they'll ask me to leave too." His face darkened. "And I just know that cow Barbara Canning has her eye on my role."

"So? Let her have it. You complain about the PTA all the time," Sebastian replied flippantly.

"Yeah, but it's still mine." Luis crossed his arms over his chest. "Until that scheming witch Barbara Canning gets her way, that is."

"Forget Barbara Canning," Sebastian replied.

"I try, but she's insidious. Sometimes I dream about her at night, you know."

"Don't remind me." Sebastian groaned. "Nothing like being woken in the middle of the night by your leg kicking my stomach while you shout 'Barbara, get away from that cake stand!' or 'Barbara, you bitch, that's my patch to sell raffle tickets! Stick to the back gate where you belong!' or—"

"Guys, I have a massive headache building right behind my temple," Ari cut in, rubbing her forehead, "and I'm already maxed out on painkillers. Sebastian, get to the point and tell me why I need to move my child from the school she loves to — that's a point, where do you even think I should move her?"

"Why, a good British public school, of course," Sebastian replied confidently.

Ari groaned. "Not this again. She's not going to St Paul's Girls School, okay? I don't care how good their synchronised swim team is."

Sebastian gave a frustrated sigh. "Things have changed since you last said no, Ari. Reine's a Somerset now. Think of her marriage prospects."

"Her marriage prospects!" Ari rolled her eyes. "Oh, for the love of God, is this about Prince George again? If I've told you once, I've told you a thousand times — stop trying to marry my child into the royal family."

"I was only half-serious before," Sebastian carried on without blinking. "But Ari, honey, think about it. With Reine's looks and background, plus all that French royal blood and money now, she could go *all the way*."

"You're being ridiculous, Sebastian," Luis chimed in. "Reine isn't going to marry a prince."

"You don't know that," Sebastian returned easily. "And just think, if she did, you could design her wedding dress."

At that, Luis sat up, a flicker of interest in his eyes. "I'd be like the Emanuels."

"Think of the miles of taffeta you could use," Sebastian smiled at him. "The yards and yards of silk and satin."

"Don't persuade Luis into this, Sebbie," Ari said with a frown. "Reine is going to make her own choices in life. I'm not going to encourage her to spend her life chasing after a prince who may or may not even be interested in her."

"What, you mean just like you did?" Sebastian quipped, before he clapped a hand over his mouth. "God, Ari, I'm so sorry—"

Ari shook her head. "Just don't," she said quietly, wringing her hands together. "Just . . . just don't, okay? I'm not ready for jokes about it yet, and I don't know if I ever will be, to be honest."

"If it means anything to you, Tom's not *really* a prince," Luis chipped in, patting Ari's shoulder consolingly. "Men who treat women the way he treated you don't deserve an accolade like *prince*."

"Accolade?" Sebastian raised an eyebrow. "My, my, aren't we using fancy words today?"

"It's the company I keep." Luis nudged Sebastian with his elbow. "Rubs off on me occasionally."

"We should really go down for dinner." Ari rested her head on Luis's shoulder, closing her eyes. "Reine's in bed. The poor kid was wiped . . . jet lag, late evenings, meeting her father, and then what happened with Sasha today—" Abruptly she stopped, opening her eyes to find Luis staring down at her.

"What about Sasha today?" Sebastian asked, his voice sharp.

"I let Tom have some time with Reine," she admitted, trying to ignore the look of pain that crossed Luis's eyes. "When we were headed back to the house, Sasha came upon us. Reine asked . . ." Ari paused. "Reine asked Tom if he was going to marry me now, that sweet little girl, and Sasha, well . . ." Ari trailed off. "Sasha told Reine he couldn't, because he was going to marry her."

"That utter c—" Sebastian began, but Ari cut him off, holding her hand over his mouth.

"Watch your language." She nodded towards Luis. "Remember you're rubbing off on your husband here."

"He'd be the first to agree with me."

"Yeah, at home we'd call her a *zorra*, even though you all know I don't like to swear," Luis admitted. "What happened then?"

"Tom made his apologies and dragged Sasha up to the house. Half an hour later she came flying out the door, hopped into her car and hasn't been back since."

Sebastian and Luis's mouths both dropped open.

"Has he . . . broken up with Sasha?" Luis asked, his eyes wide.

"Maybe. Or perhaps she just needs some space. This weekend has been intense, and it hasn't really gone the way Sasha planned, has it?" Ari paused, reflecting sadly. "It hasn't gone the way any of us had planned."

"I don't think that would matter to a woman like Sasha," Sebastian said thoughtfully. "I've seen too many like her. The eyes-on-the-prize kind of bride. Trust me, they don't let their grooms go easily. Maybe she's just gone to recalibrate. Sharpen her claws and restyle her hair to cover her horns . . . I just can't see her letting Tom Somerset escape her clutches."

"But he did," a chipper voice interrupted them, and Ari looked up to see Stella standing in the doorway of the room, a camera in her hand. "They've definitely broken up."

"How . . . how do you know that?" Ari asked her shakily.

Stella shrugged. "I was taking some candid shots. Overheard him tell her—with a bluntness I didn't think he had in him, to be honest—that he didn't want to marry her. That he never wanted to marry her, in fact."

Ari's heart fluttered, and she bit hard on her lip to stop her body from reacting treacherously. *It shouldn't mean anything to you*, she reminded herself. *Don't let it mean anything to you.*

"Good for him," Luis said, surprisingly warm-voiced.

"But not for us," Sebastian moaned. "I really wanted to plan that wedding."

"Really?" Ari asked. "You mean the wedding of my child's father? The wedding of my ex-lover Tom Somerset, who I've been waiting for all these years? You really wanted to plan *that* wedding?"

"Well, not *that* wedding," Sebastian clarified. "It was just—this was going to be our big US break, you know? Now I'll have to return Marnie's money, cancel the press release and work off all the calories I've consumed this weekend from eating nothing but salmon with rich sauces. Honestly, what is it with Marnie and salmon? She had me order a fuckload of it for the wedding, and I don't think we can cancel it at this point—"

"Sebastian," Luis said under his breath, before he shot Ari a look. "You okay, honey?"

"Fine. Why wouldn't I be?" Ari tried to keep her tone smooth.

"Well, your child's father, and the ex-lover you've been waiting for all these years, just dumped his fiancée two days after you waltzed unexpectedly back into his life. That's gotta mean something to you, right?"

"No," Ari replied.

"Ari's not so easily swayed by Jawline's sad eyes and awkward posture." Stella nodded with approval. "Besides, after all this time, you should really make him work for it. You and the small deserve so much more than what he's offered."

Ari, Sebastian and Luis all turned to Stella in surprise, who at once responded by clicking her camera in their direction, the flash making Ari blink.

"This show just gets better and better," Stella muttered. "See you all at dinner, chaps."

For a moment Ari, Sebastian and Luis sat in silence.

"Well, she seems brighter than usual, doesn't she?" Luis finally said.

"Yes, but the wedding's off," Ari murmured, "The wedding's off, and yet the wedding planners, dress designer and the photographer are all still here and about to have dinner. That's weird, right?"

"Maybe there's something in the water. Or the food." Sebastian turned to Ari with wide eyes. "Maybe it's the salmon."

Ari took a deep breath. "We should get down for dinner. Wait for Marnie to break the news that there's no wedding, work out an exit clause and get the hell out of here."

"Exit clause?" Luis shook his head. "Tom Somerset is the father of your child, Ari. You don't get an exit clause here. You're gonna have to be a grown-up and work out a plan."

"You told me this already," Ari replied.

290

"Yeah, and I guess today you made inroads, letting Reine's . . ." Luis paused, and Ari once again saw that flicker of sharp pain go through him ". . . Reine's *father* take some time with her. But you need a solid plan now, honey. A visitation schedule. Informal at first . . . but something you can solidify in law later if needed."

"Solidify?" Ari repeated wryly. "You really are talking fancy today, aren't you?"

"I told you, it's the company I'm keeping."

"It's the salmon," Sebastian interjected firmly. "Marnie's lacing it with something. Though while Sasha was here, it was probably poison."

"Okay." Ari nodded, ignoring Sebastian and coming to a stand, rubbing at her aching temple. "I'll speak to Tom tonight. Work something out with him."

"Good girl." Luis stood too. "Come on, let's go downstairs. Apparently Tom's brother is joining us for dinner tonight."

"I hope he likes salmon." Sebastian laughed, and Ari watched as Luis jokingly ruffled his husband's blond hair. Sebastian shooed him away, smiling all the while, and something in Ari's chest began to ache. Abruptly she stopped, wrapping her arms around the two men, hiding her face against Luis's warm shirt.

"In case I haven't said it, or forget to say it later," she said, unexpectedly feeling on the verge of tears, "thank you. Thank you for . . . well, everything."

She felt Luis squeeze her back, just as she momentarily felt Sebastian falter against her. When she looked at him, he was taking a deep breath, clearly in the act of getting himself together.

"Bollocks, even *I'm* feeling watery and emotional at the moment," Sebastian bemoaned. "Maybe there really *is* something in the food."

Ari stared at him. "It's okay. You can say it."

Sebastian gave a sigh of relief. "That fucking salmon."

* * *

"So, you really gave up a decorated naval career for the priest-hood?" Stella was saying, staring at Corentin with what Tom worryingly considered adoring eyes. His brother was sitting back in his chair, nodding at the elegant dark-haired woman easily.

"I did," he said. "But I don't like to think of it as 'giving up'. I like to think of it more as a natural sidestep. I'm still very proud of my naval career, but my heart was no longer in it. Esoteric Druidry called me, and I answered that call."

Tom took a sip of wine, resisting the urge to roll his eyes.

"I understand entirely," Stella replied. "I was a Royal Navy girl myself, once upon a time."

Tom nearly choked on his wine.

"Were you now?" Corentin asked, looking at Stella with new interest. "Where were you based?"

"HMS *Raleigh* originally, before I was moved to HMS *Tyne*. I was a natural with the camera though, so they moved me to the photographic unit, and that's where I really honed my skills and talents."

"You were in the navy?" Tom spat out, and the adoring eyes Stella had for Corentin turned into small stones when she glanced at him.

"The Royal Navy, I thank you," Stella replied sharply. "And yes, I was. I like rules and regulations, you see. The Royal Navy suited me."

"And you went from the navy to wedding photography?" Luis asked, scratching his head. "How did I not know this?"

"The navy, weddings . . ." Stella shrugged, taking a sip of wine. "White uniforms all look the same once you've seen them through the lens."

"A wedding dress is not a uniform," Luis replied emphatically.

"It's the expected dress code for an event or place in a particular shade stocked by select retailers," Stella replied easily. "That's a uniform."

"Actually, she has a point, Luis," Sebastian said. "Did you know Ari and I once planned a wedding at the Bulgari

Hotel in Knightsbridge, and, I kid you not, if the bride wasn't in a particular designer, they wouldn't host the wedding. Maggie Sottero fans were not getting through that door, let me tell you."

"Was I on their list? I mean, was De León Designs?" Luis quickly asked, and Sebastian paused.

"Let's not make this awkward, hmm? Besides, I want to hear more about esoteric Druidry. That's where you wear robes, right?"

Corentin nodded. "Some of us do, when the occasion calls for it. I guess they're just another type of white uniform though, eh?" He gave Stella a playful wink, which made Tom shudder.

"Oh, I don't know about that," Stella replied, and Tom stared at her, because was she *flirting with his brother*? "I always thought robes were rather dashing and sexy."

Dear God, she *was* flirting with him. Tom clutched at his wine glass, desperately trying to catch Ari's eye from across the table, only to find her with her head firmly down, her hand wrapped around the stem of her own glass.

He'd been trying to catch Ari's eye all evening. From the moment they'd sat at this wretched table, waiting for the Oscietra caviar to be served, he'd been waiting for Ari to look up, to notice him, to give him even the smallest flicker of hope that his breaking up with Sasha meant something to her. But not once had she even glanced in his direction, sitting quietly sandwiched between Sebastian and Luis, who were watching Stella and Corentin interact with interest, Tom realised.

"Robes? Dashing and sexy?" Sebastian wrinkled his nose. "You mean capes, right? Not robes. Robes aren't sexy."

"Robes can be sexy," Stella returned, and Tom watched her give Corentin a playful wink back, making his stomach turn.

"Robes?" Sebastian asked again. "I mean, robes are what wizards wear, and I can't think of a sexy happy medium between Gandalf the Grey and Harry Potter, can you? But capes? I can absolutely think of a few men who have been sexy in capes."

"Your father once wore a cape," Marnie suddenly cut in. "It was a Halloween party, and he was dressed as Dracula, but he was still dashing and sexy."

"*Mother*," Tom groaned, to which Marnie shrugged.

"What? He was sexy and dashing. So sue me for finding your father attractive, why don't you?"

"I remember that Halloween party," Corentin mused. "You're right, Dad was sexy and dashing. Maybe I should switch to capes." Then he grinned, and Stella gave a high laugh, tapping Corentin on the shoulder playfully.

This cannot be happening, Tom thought. *How can I be sitting across the table from the absolute love of my life, not communicating at all, while my priestly brother scores with my former wedding photographer?*

"I'm sure you'd look dashing and sexy in capes too," Stella replied. "I have to admit, I own a cape or two myself." She gave Sebastian a sideways glance. "In tweed. They're an autumn staple when you're about town."

"Indeed." Sebastian nodded knowingly, and at that, unable to bear a second more, Tom stood.

"You know, I'm really not very hungry," he announced.

Five pairs of eyes immediately shot to him, although the sixth pair, the pair Tom really cared about, kept resolutely down.

"Are you all right?" Marnie asked in concern.

"Yes, I'm fine. Just not in the mood for any dinner."

"Because of Sasha?" Stella asked, her voice once again cool.

"Sasha? No, I—"

"Because we all know she's gone, Jawline," Stella added, her words echoing across the room in the sudden silence that followed.

Tom sighed, shoving his hands into his pockets. "Oh, you do?" Though his words were addressed to the table, they were really meant for Ari. Ari, whose eyes remained down, her face still and expressionless.

"Yes. Marvellous decision, actually. Top form of you." Stella nodded her approval. "Though I'm aware heartbreak can affect the stomach. I've never experienced it myself, but if you weren't hungry because you were, I don't know," Stella waved a hand, "*missing* her or some such thing, well, we would all understand."

"Yes, I can concur with that," Sebastian broke in, buttering a bread roll. "When my favourite woollen vest was put through a cottons cycle and shrank—"

"*Dios mío, otra vez el chaleco.*" Luis groaned. "You never let me forget that vest."

"It was Pierre Cardin," Sebastian shot Luis a sharp look. "And you washed it with your cotton slacks like it was *TK Maxx.*"

"I like TK Maxx—" Ari broke in, and Tom's eyes shot to her once more. Her tone was placatory, almost calming, and it occurred to him that she must have been playing peacemaker between these mismatched men for years.

She was always fixing things, Tom realised. Cars, engines, her art, her brother's marriage. She'd even tried to fix him, once upon a time, although neither of them had realised it. Tom swallowed as he looked at her, an ache building within him. It was his turn to fix things now, he decided. His turn to make things better.

"Everyone likes TK Maxx for their cut-price candles, but that's not my point," Sebastian interrupted. "I sobbed over that ruined vest for weeks."

"He's not lying," Luis said ruefully.

"I couldn't eat for days afterwards."

"Let me get this straight," Marnie sat up. "You were heartbroken over . . . a vest?"

"A *Pierre Cardin* vest," Sebastian corrected her. "I don't think you quite understand what that means."

"No, I have no idea. But surely you can't compare the loss of a fiancée to a vest?"

"Loss of a fiancée?" Sebastian scoffed. "She walked out, she's not dead. Unlike my vest, which is never coming back."

Tom shook his head, standing taller. "Speaking of walking out, I'm going. I need some air."

"I'll come with you," a small voice offered, and Tom jolted with surprise. He looked across the table to find Ari finally looking at him, her face uncertain, chewing on her lip with nerves.

"Yeah, sure," he answered. And, damn it, there was a wobble to his own voice he hadn't intended. He was giving away his own nerves.

There was quiet in the room as Marnie, Sebastian, Luis, Stella and Corentin watched Ari stand and walk across the room. The silence was awkward and thick, and Tom suddenly found himself wishing Sebastian would start talking about vests again.

"Right, so, um, we're going to, uh . . ." he spluttered into the quiet.

"Of course," Marnie replied smoothly, and Tom could see that she was trying to hide her delight.

"It's a lovely evening for a walk," Corentin added, and Tom watched as Stella turned to him with a soft smile.

"Why, aren't you just a romantic," she gushed.

At that, Tom turned away.

"Come on," he said to Ari softly, "let's get out of here."

"Okay." She nodded. "Okay."

* * *

The ground was wet beneath her feet, the forest floor sodden and sticky with mud and fallen leaves. An earthy smell of damp was in the air, moist and rich with decay. It was a clear evening, a pink and orange sky breaking through clouds the colour of slate, and Ari looked up through the overhanging canopy of leaves to look at the light. Leaning back against an old birch tree, Ari took a deep breath, trying to gather her thoughts.

Tom leaned against another tree, and she could feel his eyes upon her, heavy and intense. She'd forgotten how intense his gaze could be — forgotten how one look from him could render her legs to jelly and make her heart beat hard within her chest. She'd forgotten so much . . . all the while forgetting absolutely nothing at all.

"It would have been a nice venue," she offered quietly, breaking the silence of the forest around them.

"For the wedding?" Tom asked, looking around. "Yeah, maybe. A good venue, but it wouldn't have been a good wedding."

"I'm good at my job," Ari stated. "I would've made this work."

Tom nodded, looking back at her with those intent eyes. "You would. But I wouldn't — not with the wrong bride."

Silence fell again as Ari took his words in.

"You really . . . you really broke things off with Sasha?" she asked, hating how timid she sounded.

"Yeah, I did," Tom confirmed. "I just . . . it would never have worked out, long-term. I didn't love her, Ari. I never loved her. The only woman I've ever loved in my whole, entire, stupid life has been—"

"Please don't—"

"—*you*."

Ari took a deep breath, pressing herself more firmly against the tree.

"I really did love you," Tom carried on, stepping towards her. "I was crazy about you. Everything about you. There was nothing about you I didn't like or want."

"Then why didn't you come for me?" Ari asked, her voice breaking. Her stomach hurt with unexpected longing, her head hurt with building tears and she felt an angry sadness wash through her. "Why didn't you come for me?"

"I—" Tom began, before he shook his head, stopping and taking a step back. Ari watched as he ran a hand through his hair, scowling at the ground. "I'm an idiot," he said. "I was a mess after my father died. I was a mess *before* my father died too. You were the only bright spot. The only time where I ever thought I was getting things right."

"By lying to me, and pretending to be someone else."

Tom sighed. "I don't expect you to forgive me for that. I'll never forgive myself for it, so why should you? When I first started using the name Tom Miller, I was running from myself and the family background I thought was strangling me. The weight of expectation on my shoulders, from my mother, father, brother . . . even from myself . . . It was too much. Running away felt so easy," Tom reflected sadly. "A fake name felt like a chance to get away from it all."

"You never said what you were doing before you met me," Ari said, sliding to the ground and wrapping her arms around her knees. "I knew so little about you. I *still* know so little about you."

"There's time to learn," Tom said softly. "I'm not going away again, Ari."

"I know," Ari agreed. She gave a long sigh. "You have Reine now. What are we going to do about her, Tom? I meant what I said. I'm not going to keep her from you. I want you to spend time with her."

"I'll come to London."

Ari chewed on her lip. The thought of Tom being in London, all the time, made her feel somewhat nervous, though she couldn't articulate why.

"You'd move to London? For Reine?"

Tom paused. "Not just for Reine."

Ari hugged her knees harder, looking away from the intensity of Tom's gaze. The ground was still damp beneath her, and she was certain her dress was muddied and wet, but she didn't care. The sensation of the wet leaves against her legs distracted her from the sudden rush of troubling thoughts that ran through her mind — thoughts that made her fingers tremble and lungs feel tight.

"Tom . . ." she started.

"Please, let me say something," Tom begged, falling to his knees beside her. "Ari, you must know how I feel about you. How I've *always* felt about you. I still love you, Ari. I will always love you."

She turned to face him, resting her cheek on her knees. Tom looked different somehow, with dark shadows under his eyes, his face tense and strained. He looked pained, almost wretched. Ari sighed again, licking her lips, which felt dry and tight.

"I don't know that," she said tremulously. "I used to think that, when I knew you as Tom Miller, when I thought you would come for me and Reine. But now . . ."

"It's still me," Tom said painfully, reaching over to caress one of Ari's hands. He only just brushed his fingertips over her knuckles, but at his touch Ari jumped.

"No," she said sadly. "You aren't the man I knew. You aren't the man I loved. I'm . . . I'm sorry, Tom. I know how you want this conversation to go, but I can't. I just can't, and I don't—"

"Ari, look."

Ari watched as he reached into his pocket, pulling from it a shape she knew well. It was the fool to her queen of spades, she realised. *He kept it,* she thought in sudden anguish. *He kept it.*

"Before you say I can't, before you say I don't, please look at this. I've had this, carried it every day, for years," Tom told her softly, handing her the card. Its weight was familiar in her hand, her fingers curling naturally around its edges.

"I'm still a fool for you," he whispered. "I'll always be a fool for you."

Ari closed her eyes, hoping to stop the tears that were building.

"Did you keep yours?" Tom asked quietly, and Ari opened her eyes again. He looked so hopeful, with his eyes so soft and loving that she could hardly stand it. "Your queen? Did you keep it?"

For a moment, Ari struggled to breathe. It would be so easy to tell him the truth. So easy to say that she'd held onto that damned queen of spades card for years, both a token of hope and talisman against heartbreak, tucked quietly in her pocket. So easy to tell him how much she'd missed him. So easy to give in.

"No," she said, and the word was harsh-sounding, ugly, even to her. "I tore her up."

Tom's face fell, his eyes clouding over. He opened his mouth to reply before clearly thinking the better of it. He gave Ari a long look, before sinking against the tree next to her, his hand still warm against hers.

"Okay," he said. "Okay."

"What we had," Ari carried on, feeling her heart break a little within her, "I mean, what we once had . . . it was beautiful, you know? And I don't regret it. I really don't. You gave me Reine, and the most beautiful memories of my life. But I can't . . . we can't go back to those days. There's too much between us. Too many lies. Too much betrayal."

Ari watched as Tom grew pale. His head slumped back against the tree in defeat, and he exhaled long and hard.

"I didn't want to go back to those days," he said, his voice broken. "I wanted to move forward. To new days. You, me and Reine."

"No," Ari said. "I can't. But you . . . you can move forward with Reine in your life. As much time as you want with her."

Tom nodded. "Thank you. I know I've done nothing to deserve your trust where Reine is concerned . . . but thank you."

For a few moments they sat in silence, their fingers now entwined. Above them, a slight wind whistled through the trees, and somewhere in the distance a bird called. Ari closed her eyes, trying in vain to block them all out. She just wanted quiet now. Somewhere calm where she could lick her wounds and heal.

"You should paint again," Tom suddenly said, and Ari startled.

"What?"

"You should paint again," he said again, and when Ari looked at him, his face was serious. "You don't know how good you are."

"Sasha told me you'd bought one of my paintings for a small fortune," Ari replied with a bitter smile. "Wish I'd seen some of that money."

Tom squeezed her hand. "Your work is a habit I can't quite give up. I've tried."

Ari stared at him. "You mean you bought more than one?"

Tom swallowed, giving Ari a small shrug.

"I bought them all."

Ari's mouth dropped open. "All? You mean you . . . How many of my paintings do you own, Tom?"

He looked away from her to the trees. "All of them."

"All of them?"

"Thirty-seven, at my last count."

"Tom . . ." Ari began, before trailing off. There was nothing she could say, no words she could muster.

"I really do love you, Ari," Tom said softly. "I really do."

Ari felt her heart splinter once more.

"I know," she whispered back. "I know. But Tom . . . there's nowhere for us to go from here."

"That's not true," Tom replied, and he sounded small and sad. "There's still our ending."

He reached over, tracing a finger down Ari's face. Ari couldn't help herself, pressing her cheek into the large palm of his hand.

And when he moved forward to kiss her, she met his lips willingly.

CHAPTER 21: RETINOL

One Year Later

With a dramatic sigh, Sebastian walked into the office and mock-collapsed onto Ari's desk.

"You will not *believe* what that bloody bridezilla wants now," he groaned. Ari leaned back in her chair, crossing her arms over her chest and looking at him evenly.

"Language, Sebbie," she chided. "I could've had a client in here. Reine could've been here."

Sebastian at once stood, straightening his tie. "Is there a client here?"

"Well, no—"

"Is Reine here?"

"No, she's at school."

With another dramatic sigh, Sebastian collapsed once more over Ari's desk. "You will not *believe* what that bloody bridezilla wants now."

Ari leaned forwards on her elbows, tilting her head so that her gaze met his.

"No, I probably won't," she replied. "What is it this time?"

Sebastian groaned again. "Her bouquet," he muttered. "She wants it made from *Cosmos atrosanguineus*."

"Okay then." Ari gave a small shrug. "So, a particular type of flower. That's not the end of the world, Sebastian. An easy request, in fact, compared with some of her others."

"Easy?" Sebastian stood, shaking his head at Ari in disbelief. "*Easy?* I don't know how much you know about rare plants, Ari, but for your information the *Cosmos atrosanguineus* is only grown in Mexico. *Mexico.*"

Ari paused. "Mexico?"

"Mexico," Sebastian emphasised again, sinking into his own office chair and swinging it around so that he faced Ari. "We only have *four days* until this wedding, Ari, and I can't go to Mexico. I'm covered in so much anti-ageing Retinoid product these days that if I step out into the sun, I'm pretty sure I'll burst into flames."

Ari rolled her eyes. "You don't need all that retinol."

"I'm old. Of course I need it."

"Sebbie, you only just turned forty. Don't be so overdramatic."

Sebastian waved a hand at her dismissively. "When you get here, you'll know," he warned, before running a hand over his eyes. "So, what do we do about this flower then?"

Ari tapped her pencil on her desk. "Give it to her, naturally. If that's what she wants, that's what she'll get. She's a bride, after all." Ari thought for a moment. "I'm sure one of our suppliers in Holland will have some. One of the exotic flower specialists maybe. I'll send a message to them all straight away. Did she say why she wanted this particular flower or . . .?"

"Apparently it smells like chocolate," Sebastian replied, sniffing. "Her and chocolate. You know what she's like."

Ari smiled. "Yeah, I do. Okay, so we ship one over, whatever it takes, whatever it costs. You remember what they said — money is no object."

Sebastian nodded, sighing once more. "Sometimes I miss the old days, you know. When I first set this business up, I planned weddings free-of-charge to hard-up brides who just wanted their special day to be special. Women and their families who'd scrimped and saved for years to buy a designer dress or a fancy cake." He gave Ari a woebegone smile. "I once had a couple who'd saved for years to rent an entire Premier Inn by the side of the M25 so their friends could party with them the whole night. I remember getting there and seeing the laminate floors and worn carpets and hearing the screech of traffic outside and secretly hating it."

"Well, no one likes the M25," Ari offered, reaching out to pat Sebastian's hand.

"I don't know," Sebastian replied. "When I compare couples like Mr and Mrs M25 to our current 'money-is-no-object' twosome I kind of miss it."

Ari stared at him. "You need to lay off the retinol, because that doesn't sound at all like the brother I know and love."

Sebastian stood, collapsing into his own office chair. "I just need a—"

"No more cigarettes," Ari cut him off instantly. "It took Luis six months to break you from your last nicotine addiction. None of us want to go through that again with you."

"I wore so many patches I was like a fucking quilt," Sebastian breathed out, before he shook his head. "Actually, I was going to say I need a *holiday*."

"After the wedding," Ari promised. "Just a few more days and you and Luis will be lying in the sun."

"Lying in the sun? I think not. Luis might, but not me," Sebastian corrected her, gesturing to his skin. "Retinol."

"Lest I forget." Ari smiled.

"Are you still okay for Luis and me to take Reine for a couple of weeks?" Sebastian asked, and suddenly there was a hesitant tone to his voice. "We don't see her as often as we used to. We miss her."

Ari paused, instantly closing her laptop. "Sebbie—"

"Oh, I know, it's all for the best, and don't get me wrong, Luis and I are loving having our weekends back and our social lives and all, but . . . but we miss her. We didn't know how much time we had with her until suddenly it was cut in half, you know?"

"Yes, I know. I know."

She really did. Tom had been good to his word, slotting himself into Ari and Reine's life and keeping his promise to be the father to Reine that she deserved. Twice a month he flew over to London from the States, picking up Reine from school on a Thursday and keeping her until Monday. He'd taken a small flat near Ari's little house, and both he and Marnie had become regular fixtures in Reine's life, never missing any event, no matter how small.

Ari still remembered the look on Miss Bates's face when she, Tom, Marnie, Luis, Sebastian, Corentin and Stella turned up at the school nativity to see Reine play Sheep Number Three, her costume lovingly hand-stitched by Luis in the finest Merino wool. She wished she'd taken a picture of the headmistress's disapproving face, although, looking back, she was fairly sure Stella did. It was hard to miss Stella's flashes. Miss Bates was probably still temporarily blind.

It had been odd, those first few months with Tom sharing parental responsibility. Ari, unused to having a co-parent to rely on, had been given her first free weekend in years. She'd sat listlessly at home until Sebastian and Luis persuaded her to come to their flat for a Christmas party they were hosting, and it had been an eye-opening experience for her. She'd walked into their flat to find it full of fabulously dressed people, all friends and acquaintances of Luis and Sebastian that Ari hadn't even known existed. One woman, taking in Ari's off-the-rack jacket and flat ballet shoes, had looked at her with sceptical eyes until Luis had rushed over for an embrace and to take her coat.

"Oh," the woman said, loudly, "that must be Sebastian's sister. You know," her voice dropped to a whisper, "the *single mother*."

Ari had never realised quite how much she'd leaned on Luis and Sebastian until she suddenly didn't need to. With Tom on the scene, she hadn't needed the hours and hours of babysitting or childcare, and Luis and Sebastian had been able to step into the roles of loving uncles rather than pseudo-parents. Luis and Sebastian had a life away from Ari and Reine, and Ari was glad for it. It had been a strange transition for all of them, but a positive one, she reminded herself.

The most positive effect, Ari soon learned, was on Reine. The little girl, still quiet and thoughtful, had adapted well to suddenly having a father, and had learned to love Tom. She'd slipped into calling him 'Daddy' just recently, and although Tom hadn't made a big deal of it, Ari had seen the soft look that came into his eyes when he told her about it afterwards.

She'd seen that soft look in his eyes before. It was the look Tom wore when his heart was full. Once, Ari had liked to imagine that only she could inspire that look in his eyes. It was wonderful to know she was wrong, and that her child — *their* child — could inspire it too.

"Of course you can take Reine on holiday with you," Ari carried on, patting Sebastian's hand again. "She's looking forward to it. Did you decide where you'll be going yet?"

Sebastian shrugged. "Our 'money-is-no-issue' couple threw a spanner into the works when they scheduled their wedding for the day we were due to fly to Nice. Never mind. We'll find something else."

"Well, just let me know," Ari stopped, clearing her throat. "Um, Tom and Marnie want to take Reine away for a week too."

Sebastian looked up instantly. "Really?"

"Yes. Marnie was thinking about Spain, apparently." She paused again. "They've asked me to go with them."

For a long moment, Sebastian stared at her. "Okay. How do you feel about that?"

"I've never been to Spain. It might be nice."

"What do you mean, you've never been to Spain? Every Brit has been to Spain. Vomiting into the foam of an Ibizan nightclub is practically a rite of passage."

Ari shrugged. "I've never been."

Sebastian frowned. "You mean, you never got there when you and Tom travelled across Europe? Back when he was Tom Miller?"

Ari shook her head. "No, we meant to . . . it was on our list . . . but then . . ."

"But then Tom knocked you up and ditched you?" Sebastian asked.

"Something like that."

"Hmm. Well, you should go — wait, Marnie's paying, right?"

"She's offered."

Sebastian grinned. "You should definitely go then. I've told you before, you hit the sperm jackpot with Tom — you know, aside from the whole seven-year-long abandonment thing — oh, and all the lying. Anyway, you should definitely start riding that child-support pony."

Ari grimaced. "I don't want to ride any sort of . . . metaphorical ponies."

Sebastian gave her another grin. "So maybe go to Spain and ride Tom then? Honestly, the man clearly wants you so much that even I almost feel sad for the poor fucker and—"

"Sebastian!"

"Oh, blush all you want," Sebastian said, rolling his eyes. "But the two of you aren't fooling anyone, you know."

If anything, Ari blushed harder. "We aren't — we don't . . . look, there's no way I want to go down that path again, and—"

"You totally want to." Sebastian reached over to poke Ari in the arm. "And I can't say I blame you. The man's a total ride. Even I'd love to slather that man in retinol and take him down to town."

"What would Luis say?"

"Oh, he feels *exactly* the same. I know we didn't like Tom at first, but he does kind of grow on you. If you gave him another chance—"

"Well, I'm not giving him another chance," Ari finally snapped, coming to a stand. She stomped over to the coffee machine, setting it to make a cappuccino. "I gave him a chance years ago and he let me down. I'm not going down that path again. Never ever."

Ari watched as Sebastian sank back in his seat.

"Fine," he said eventually. "Fine. So, things can just carry on as they are, with you and Tom constantly giving each other *looks* and being all awkward and quiet and sexually frustrated. Fine."

Ari took a deep breath, waiting for the coffee machine to finish frothing her milk, staring into the depths of her black coffee, the liquid hot and dark, just like the look that came into Tom's eyes when he stared at her.

Shaking herself, she turned back to Sebastian. "We should go through the wedding plan for Mr and Mrs 'money-is-no-object' again," she suggested. "Are the flights to Iceland all confirmed?"

"Yes," Sebastian nodded, flicking through some papers on his desk. "I still think it's ridiculous, but yes. The wedding will take place in a cave next to the black sand beach under the aurora borealis, as planned."

"Good."

"And the hotel is booked, with a four-course Icelandic meal to be served after the ceremony."

Ari nodded, sipping at her cappuccino. "You made sure it was vegetarian, right? The groom was insistent."

"Of course I did—wait, salmon counts as vegetarian, right? It's not really meat. It's too coral in colour. Meat isn't out there like that."

Ari looked at Sebastian in horror. "Um, no?"

For a moment, Sebastian looked concerned. Then he gave a shrug, flicking to another sheet of paper.

"Okay, so I'll cancel the salmon. I've done a lot of that this last year. I'm an old hat at it now." He paused. "An old, wrinkly hat."

"You aren't old," Ari said again. "Stop with the retinol."

Sebastian gave her a look, before nodding to the coffee machine. "Make me a latte, will you please? I'll contact our florist, get the bridezilla's order ASAP. I'll probably head home after that—"

"You literally just got here," Ari said flatly.

"I need to pop into Waitrose, we're throwing a dinner party tonight. Luis's making duck."

"That sounds nice," Ari replied absently. "I should think about what I'm going to eat tonight. I haven't really had time to shop though . . . not with this Icelandic wedding spectacular just around the corner."

"It's Tom's turn to have Reine this weekend, right?" Sebastian asked.

"Yes, he's picking her up after school today. His flight was delayed."

"Okay, so, come to our place then? We'll make space for you. I'm sure Luis will pick up an extra duck. Or maybe three, given how much you eat."

Ari gave Sebastian a look. "Thanks, but it's okay. I'll probably just order pizza or something. Maybe watch Eastenders."

She didn't tell him that she wasn't comfortable around his friends. Sebastian and Luis had their own lives outside of her, Ari knew, and it was best to keep it that way.

Sebastian pulled a face. "Fine. Go home and eat your sad pizza and watch your sad soap opera. But don't say we don't invite you places."

"I never said that you didn't—"

"And don't say I didn't tell you to ride the loins of the man whose child you bore either," Sebastian added triumphantly. "Because my darling, if you pick any *end* tonight, try and make it his, and not the one on the telly from the east side of London."

Ari gave Sebastian another look. "You really are like a dog with a bone on this. If I've told you once I've told you a thousand times—"

Sebastian held up his mobile to cut her off, showing an incoming call. It was their current bride, Ari noticed. Mrs "money-is-no-object".

"*Phone call, sorry,*" Sebastian whispered without looking sorry at all, swiping right with an enthusiasm Ari found almost disturbing.

"It'll keep," she warned, but Sebastian merely shrugged.

"*Darling*," he said, using the tone of voice he exclusively reserved for brides.

Then his face changed. "*Darling, look—*"

Ari watched as Sebastian's face changed again, this time turning an angry and blotchy kind of red.

"*Darling*, I just think—" he tried once more, before swapping the phone to his other ear. "Look, you bossy fucking hag, if you think that you can just call us up and demand every little thing like some bitchzilla bride from hell—"

"Sebastian!" Ari snapped, snatching the phone from his hand. Holding it to her chest for a moment, she shook her head at Sebastian in reprisal, before taking a deep breath and bringing the phone to her ear.

"Hi Stella, how nice to hear from you. What can we do for you and Corentin today?"

* * *

Tom looked tired when he walked into Ari's house later that day. There were dark circles under his eyes and his skin looked waxy and pale. He gratefully sat when Ari asked him to, gulping at the coffee she pushed his way.

"You can't keep doing this, you know," Ari said kindly, pouring herself a glass of water. "All this travel. What time even is it for you right now?"

Tom sat back in his seat. "What time is it now? Half two? I guess it's half nine in the morning for me then. I tried to sleep on the plane, but just . . . Anyway, I got half an hour here and there. I'll be fine."

Ari looked at him with concern. "Go and take a nap upstairs. I'll pick up Reine from school."

"I think I'm a little big for Reine's bed, don't you?"

Ari felt herself blushing. "Oh, well, yes, um, I guess you could, uh, take my bed, maybe, and then—"

Tom gave her a soft smile. "I'm fine, Ari. I want to pick her up. Besides, it's probably for the best that I keep going until tonight. Beat the jetlag tomorrow."

Ari nodded, though she frowned just the same.

"All this travel though, Tom. You can't keep doing it. We need to work out something new, something different. Something easier on you."

Tom sighed. "Look Ari, you did the hard work for nearly eight years. Eight years without me. It's my turn. Let me do this."

She sank into the seat next to his, sighing in return. "You don't have to keep punishing yourself, you know."

"I'm not punishing myself."

"You are. I know you too well. I know how you think and feel. You are punishing yourself and that's not what I want."

She glanced to the side, meeting Tom's eyes. He was staring at her with an odd expression — a thoughtfulness to his eyes.

"What is it?" she asked.

"Nothing — well, it's just . . . that's the first time I've heard you say that in years."

Ari frowned, puzzled. "To stop punishing yourself?"

"No." She watched as Tom swallowed. "That you know me too well."

She paused, chewing her lip awkwardly. "Oh. Right."

Next to her, she felt Tom inhale deeply. "I like it when you know me," he said, before Ari heard him swallow again. "I like that you know me. The *real* me."

Ari inexplicably felt her heart pick up tempo, and she gripped her glass of water hard, so Tom wouldn't see the sudden tremble to her fingers.

"Well, there's a lot to like about you, Tom."

She chanced a glance at him again, and once more found his eyes intently upon her. Abruptly she stood, moving to the kitchen sink and dumping the remains of her water into it. She heard rather than saw Tom sink deeper into his chair.

"Have you heard from the happy couple recently?" he asked, with tension in his voice.

Ari turned back to him, giving a crooked smile. "Actually, I spoke to them both this afternoon. They wanted to change

311

Reine's flower girl dress *again*. Luis's going to pitch a fit when he finds out. Do you know how hard he worked on the first three versions? His fingers bled and he nearly went blind sewing Egyptian gold thread into the white satin."

"Well, Corentin was always changeable," Tom replied gruffly, and Ari shrugged.

"Surprisingly, he's being quite laid-back about the wedding. Stella is the one in charge there. Poor Corentin will need all the blessings from his goddess he can get if he's going to successfully navigate marriage to Stella long-term."

Tom shook his head. "No, Corentin will be fine. He grew up with my mother. Trust me, he's had all the prep he needs for marriage to a strong woman."

"Do you still find it weird?" Ari asked him curiously.

"What, you mean my brother marrying the woman who terrifies me more than any other? The woman who told me just last week about her birth control implant so that she doesn't pass on my 'unfortunate' jawline to an unsuspecting child? Yes, I still find it weird."

Ari smiled. "They seem sickeningly happy."

"Yeah, I guess. Mom's flying in tomorrow for the family dinner here before we all fly to Iceland on Sunday morning. Are you coming?"

Ari went to her fridge, opening it to retrieve a cucumber from one of the shelves. "To Iceland? Yes. I'm kind of planning the wedding, Tom. My presence there is a contractual requirement."

"No, I meant the family dinner," Tom clarified. "Are you coming?"

"I'm not family," Ari replied instantly, at which Tom frowned in disapproval.

"Yes, you are. You're Reine's mother, Stella's friend and my . . . well, you should be there."

Ari picked up a knife, slowly slicing the cucumber into batons. "I'll come if I'm invited. Pass me one of the boiled eggs from that pot there, will you? I'm making Reine a snack for your place. I know you won't have had any time to shop."

"No I haven't, but eggs? Reine hates eggs."

"They're good for her," Ari said firmly, "she needs the protein."

"So, give her some sliced chicken," Tom returned. "At least she'll eat that."

"She should be eating eggs. An egg is an adventure—" Ari stopped, the knife still in her hand. For a moment, a strange kind of quiet fell over the room, and she looked over to Tom, who was smiling at her.

"We had some good times, didn't we?" he asked softly, and Ari nodded, feeling tears prick at her eyes.

"I have some falafel," she said over the lump in her throat, "I'll put that in instead."

Ari quietly packed the rest of Reine's snack box, handing it to Tom awkwardly, doing everything she could to avoid her fingers touching the long lengths of his. She had a feeling if her skin brushed any part of him that she would fall apart in his arms.

"Thanks," Tom said, his tone even, almost curt. "I better go and get Reine. I'll see you at dinner tomorrow night."

"Maybe."

"No," he said, more firmly now. "I'll see you then. You'll be my guest, even if Stella and Corentin haven't invited you."

"Okay." Ari nodded. "Give Reine a kiss from me and tell her I'll see her tomorrow."

Tom nodded, walking to Ari's little door and turning the handle. Before he stepped out into the street, he turned back, giving Ari a pained look, Reine's snack held tight in his large hands.

"We really did have some good times, right? I didn't imagine it? It wasn't just . . . all me?"

Ari felt her heart pulse painfully.

"It wasn't all you," she replied honestly. "We had some wonderful times. We really did."

Tom gave her another look of bittersweet sadness, before he nodded, and stepped out into the London afternoon.

* * *

Ari pulled out dress after dress, throwing them on her bed and frowning at all of them. Stella had called her that morning, bright and early at 5 a.m., insisting that she come to the pre-wedding 'family dinner'.

"You really must come, Ari. The small is going to be there."

"Oh, right," Ari had replied, brushing at her sleep-encrusted eyes wearily. "Yes, okay. I guess it would be nice to see Marnie again, and you know I haven't met your family yet."

"My family?" Stella gave a high and tinkly laugh. "My God, those *reprobates* aren't going to be there. Why, the very idea."

"You mean your family aren't coming to . . . the family dinner?"

"My mother is no longer with us, sadly, and I don't want my alcoholic arsehole of a father anywhere near my wedding. No, it will just be a tight little gathering. Your fellow is going to be there, too, so—"

"Tom's not my fellow," Ari instantly cut in, and she heard Stella pause.

"I know that," she said impatiently, "I meant your brother. And De León too, I suppose. Trust me, I'm well aware of the current stalemate between you and Jawline. Marnie complains about the two of you *all the time*."

Ari blushed, rolling over in her bed and burying her head under a pillow.

"That's good to know. Okay, I'll see you tonight, Stella."

"Lovely. Dress sharp, Ari. It's at Whyte's and I'm bringing my Leica. Don't worry, I've told Jawline I'll rub some Vaseline on the lens to soften him out."

Ari held another dress against her body, berating herself for allowing her wardrobe to become so work-centred and practical, her outfits all functional to the point of being unattractive. Since Reine, she'd never thought to invest in pretty or dainty things, preferring dull colours that absorbed stains easily and disguised the smell of milk, baby vomit and motherhood. With a frustrated frown, she sank onto her bed, looking with irritation at the discarded piles of clothing around her.

You need to get a grip, she lectured herself sternly. *It's a work event, really. Tom only invited you because of Reine. It's not like it's a date or anything.*

Ari took a deep breath, standing again and going back to her cupboard. She shifted through hangers and hangers, still undecided and annoyed, before closing the door sharply and heading downstairs.

She picked up her purse and her phone, then headed out into the Greenwich afternoon, walking towards the DLR.

She needed to do some shopping, she thought. She hadn't bought herself anything new in a long time, and now that Tom was sharing parental responsibility for Reine, finances weren't as tight as they used to be. Buying something new to wear to a special dinner wasn't unusual, Ari told herself, other people did it all the time.

It's not a date, Ari reminded herself. *It's not a date.*

* * *

"*Caracoles!*" Luis said in amazement when Ari stepped out of her Uber. "You look amazing, Ari."

Sebastian gaped at her, and Ari gave him a nervous smile.

"Your mouth is hanging open so wide I'm going to have to step over it to get into the restaurant," she joked, her stomach jittery.

Sebastian pulled himself together rapidly, closing his mouth, though he continued to stare at her. "It's just . . ." he began. "I've *never* seen you look like . . . Well, like *this* before." He paused. "I'm not sure I like it."

"What do you mean, 'this'?" Ari asked, going to finger the shoulder seam of her dress nervously, before remembering that this particular dress didn't have one.

She'd found it in a store in Canary Wharf, a simple white number with a halter-neck top that hugged her body to just below her knees. The halter-neck tie flowed down her back, and she'd pulled her hair up into a simple chignon to show it off. She'd spent time on her make-up, applying it carefully and making her eyes smokier than usual, and had gone to the trouble of pulling on a pair of tall heels, knowing they accentuated the curve of her calves. There was nothing wrong, Ari thought, with showing off her calves. She didn't run 10k a week just to keep them covered with long trousers and shapeless shift dresses, after all.

"You look stunning," Luis said warmly. "That's what he means."

"You look like you care," Sebastian explained. "Don't get me wrong, you've always dressed well, but not like you *care*. I don't know how else to explain it."

Ari shook her head. "No, it's okay, I think I understand." She blushed. "Thank you for being so kind."

"The question now," Sebastian carried on, "is *why* you suddenly seem to care and have dressed to the nines?"

Ari blushed deeper, watching as Sebastian and Luis exchanged a look. Inexplicably, Luis leaned towards her and kissed her on the cheek.

"He's not going to believe it when he sees you tonight," he said warmly, and Ari shifted her weight from one foot to another.

"I don't know what you're talking about—"

"Please, I think you do," Sebastian said. "Luis's right — Tom's not going to believe it when he sees you tonight. In fact, he'll probably drop dead right here outside of Whyte's. It would be a good place to go, actually. A refined place to die."

"And even with that jawline, he'd make a beautiful corpse," a sharp voice cut in. Ari jumped before she, Luis and Sebastian all turned, finding Stella standing next to them, looking at Ari with obvious approval.

"Stella, hello," Ari stammered, leaning towards the woman to kiss her cheek.

Stella, however, stepped back.

"No offence, Ari, but your lips are quite the cherry-red tonight, and I don't want that lingering on my expensive face-cream."

"*Retinol*," Sebastian mouthed at Ari, before he also turned to Stella. "You look lovely. The perfect blushing bride."

"Really? Yesterday you thought I was a *bossy fucking hag*," she remarked back.

Sebastian waved a hand. "Last-minute wedding stress, darling, gets the better of us all."

"Mm." Stella frowned at him, but said nothing, turning to Ari. "Did you order my flowers?"

Ari nodded, standing taller. "The chocolate-scented *Cosmos atrosanguineus*? I found a supplier in the Netherlands. They'll be picked and shipped to Reykjavík, where I'll deliver them personally to the florist. Your bouquet will be beautiful. Please don't worry."

"I never worry," Stella replied smoothly. "I hire people to do that for me." She gave Ari a long look. "So, tell me something? Are you trying to kill my brother-in-law-to-be tonight? Because your brother is right. Jawline *is* going to drop dead when he sees you. Honestly, if I weren't about to marry the love of my life, I might even have taken a pop at you."

Ari blushed again, looking down. "I just . . . You said to dress sharp—"

"Not sharp enough to deliver a mortal wound like this to the father of your child," Stella remarked, gesturing to Ari's dress. "Still, fair play to you. You're stunning. Well done. Show the Jawline what he's missing. Now, shall we go inside? Corentin's on his way with Marnie," she gave Ari another look, more thoughtful and contemplative. "Time for you to shine, Ari. You know, they say the best revenge is served cold, but tonight, I think hot is the way to go."

With that, Stella stalked into the restaurant, Luis holding the door open for her. He gave Ari a pointed look as she walked past him, her heels clicking against the cool tiled floor. She followed Stella into the restaurant's private room, where a waiter pulled aside a curtain to reveal an intimately set table with stunning crockery. Behind the table sat Reine, who called out happily to Ari when she saw her, but Ari's eyes were mostly on Tom.

Tom, whose eyes went wide when he saw her, at once standing like the gentleman Ari suspected he was, but who, in his haste to stand, somehow managed to upend the table-cloth from where he'd been sitting, so that the immaculately laid glassware and crockery came crashing to the floor.

CHAPTER 22: DINNER

When Ari walked into Whyte's that evening, Tom's mouth ran dry, all the fluid in his body immediately decamping into clammy hands and an inexplicably sweating back. He felt his heart speed up and a rush of adrenaline flow through him, which was ridiculous, because Ari had told him quite firmly that they had no future together, and Tom had always been respectful of that decision. Even if Ari looked amazing in her dress, which showed off the creamy tone to her skin and the ash blonde shimmer of her hair, Tom knew he had no reason to hope. He'd given up on hope over the last year, pushing it down, again and again, until the emotion was nothing more than a fine rubble under his feet.

"Wow, Mummy looks so pretty," he heard Reine exclaim next to him, and he looked down at his daughter, giving her a warm smile.

"Yeah, she does," he agreed, before giving Reine's cheek a small pinch. "Make sure you tell her that, okay?"

"You should too," Reine returned, sipping at her apple juice innocently. "She only puts on that lipstick when she knows you're going to be there, but you never say anything about it."

There it was again, that small twinge of hope. Tom gave Reine another smile, then looked back to Ari, wondering if she knew just how much information about her life their daughter inadvertently provided.

Reine, Tom quickly learned, was an exceptionally observant child who watched and listened to the adults around her. Unlike those adults, however, Reine had yet to develop any sort of social filters, and so shared the information she gleaned without a drop of restraint or awareness.

"Tío Luis bought a new Barbie doll for four thousand pounds and Uncle Sebastian was so mad he opened her box and then Tío Luis got mad and scratched Uncle Sebastian's leather satchel and then they didn't talk to each other for the whole weekend I was there," she told him once, her eyes wide with innocence. Another time, she was sitting in a restaurant with Tom and Marnie, colouring in the paper children's menu, when she noticed Marnie's wine. "When we went for dinner at Stella's house last week Uncle Corentin got out a bottle of wine for her and Mummy and Mummy said she was cutting back and then Stella said that the only person who should be cutting back is you, Grandma, because you always have a glass in your hands these days," Reine remarked easily, switching from a blue crayon to a red one. "She said you'd end up a fermented old prune if you weren't careful." She then turned to Tom, looking at him curiously while Marnie seethed beside them. "Daddy, what's a prune?"

It was the information Reine unknowingly dropped about Ari though, that Tom was really interested in. Through Reine's innocently made comments, he learned that Ari had been dating again, though none of the men had lasted more than three or four dates, for which Tom thanked all of the gods he'd ever heard of as well as Corentin's goddess, just to be on the safe side. It was through Reine he'd learned that Ari was painting again, working on a few pieces in the time she'd gained since he'd become a responsible parent, and it was through Reine that he learned Ari made an effort when he was going to be around, tidying her house, straightening her hair and putting on the perfume he had grown to love. These days, that light floral scent made him think of Ari's dewy skin and warm smile, as well as the curve of her neck and the delicate tapering of her wrists.

Now he smiled at this newest addition to his hidden treasure trove of facts about her, and went to stand when she walked across the restaurant to their private table.

It happened before he could stop it or even knew what had gone so horribly wrong. Still jet lagged and tired, he'd rushed Reine home from her violin lesson earlier that afternoon and then attempted to get her into the tulle dress Luis had packed for tonight's dinner. Tulle was a mystery to Tom, because how many fucking layers of fabric did a little girl really need? Luis clearly thought eight million, or at least that's how it seemed to Tom, as he fought to get Reine into the frothy and yet somehow completely inflexible number. Still learning about how to be a father to a young girl, he'd then spent an hour and fifteen minutes with YouTube open while negotiating Reine's seemingly unending layers of hair, unsuccessfully trying to do something called a 'waterfall' braid before taking a private moment to swear and then settling on a simple ponytail. Thinking they were late, he'd rushed Reine into an Uber to Whyte's, tucking her into her chair at the table and making sure the tablecloth was tucked firmly over her clothes, because no way in hell was he laundering all that tulle when she inevitably spilled something oily and tomato based all over herself.

So, when he stood to welcome Ari, gobsmacked as he was by her utterly glorious beauty, he'd forgotten about Reine and the tablecloth, which, pulled tight across him to cover her, got caught in the bulk of his arms and hands when he stood. The tablecloth went with him, and Tom watched in horror as all the glassware and crockery came crashing down before him, as well as the two delicate but overly long tapered dinner candles, which spilled hot wax onto the shattered remnants of what had been a beautifully set table.

"Daddy!" Reine yelped, just as Sebastian demanded, "What the hell was that?" But Tom could only stand and stare at Ari, his mouth open.

"Jawline, if that was your attempt at some sort of pre-dinner magician's trick, it's gone horribly wrong," Stella intoned drily.

"Yeah," Luis added, shaking his head at the sight. "You know you're supposed to pull the tablecloth off while everything else stays standing, right?"

"Right," Tom muttered, bending down to check on Reine, who was thankfully fine. He picked the little girl up so she was nowhere near the broken glass.

"Reine, *cómo va todo ese tul, cielo*?" Luis asked, opening his arms to take Reine from him.

Once Reine had been handed over, Tom turned to Stella.

"I'm sorry, it was an accident, I had the tablecloth over Reine and—"

He was surprised to see Stella give a shrug.

"An awkward jaw and oafish hands," she said easily. "I'm not surprised, to be honest. Never mind. It's all right. Whyte's will set us another table in the main restaurant, I'm sure." She gave him a pat on the back. "Don't worry. I'll ask them for some plastic plates for you too. I'm sure they'll have them somewhere. You clearly can't be trusted with fine china."

"I really am sorry," he said again, his cheeks red, but Stella waved him aside, turning to find a nearby waiter and walking with him into the main restaurant. Luis, with Reine in his arms and Sebastian by his side, followed, leaving just him and Ari standing in the private room. He met her gaze and sighed.

"That wasn't how I wanted that to go," he explained, and Ari nodded.

"I know."

"I'll offer to pay for all the broken glass," he added, and Ari was still looking at him, so he offered a wry smile. "If that had been a magic trick, and it had actually worked, it would have been amazing, right?"

His joke seemed to work, because Ari laughed. "I guess so, though I knew it was an accident, and not a magic trick."

"How?" Tom asked, leaning back against the wall and gazing at her. "Maybe I've been practising at home. You don't know what I do in my spare time."

Ari smiled again, moving across the room to lean against the wall next to him. He could feel her bare shoulder through the thin fabric of his shirt, and he felt a shiver run through him.

"I knew," she said gently, turning her head and gazing up at him softly, "because I've seen you do better magic tricks before."

An image came into Tom's mind of a lonely airport and a cold floor beneath him. Before him stood a young woman, her long hair falling over her shoulders, holding the queen of spades in her hands. Her eyes were warm and laughing, and Tom could still feel — even over the distance of many years — how his own smile had formed in return.

Tom took a long and deep inhalation of breath, followed by a wistful sigh. He knew Ari was thinking the same thing, knew that she felt the same way, and his eyes locked with hers. It was a shared moment over a shared memory. Momentarily losing himself in the blue depths of Ari's eyes, all his sighs and deep inhalations were gone, his breath now caught tight in his chest.

It was just for a moment though. Ari seemed to shake herself together, then she straightened, one hand going to check that her hair was still in place.

"You look beautiful," Tom told her softly, his voice more intense than he meant, and he watched as her cheeks tinged pink.

"Thank you," she returned. "Now come on, magician man, they'll be waiting for us."

* * *

Dinner was as awkward as Tom imagined it was going to be. Stella was her usual imperious and elegant self, monopolising the conversation over ice-cold aperitifs and white wine, while Corentin gazed up at her with a smitten smile, his beard trimmed and neat. Marnie, unused to anything other than Corentin's undivided attention, sat in the corner with a glass of sparkling water in her hand, her eyes narrowed, while Luis and Sebastian sat next to Reine, chatting amicably with her about the newest release of Rainbow High dolls.

Rainbow High had been a hard parenting lesson for Tom. Trying to make up for lost time, he'd rushed out when Reine had first come into his life by buying her all the *My Little Pony: Friendship Is Magic* toys he could find. Ari had told him not to, that Reine didn't need it all, but Tom had been adamant.

"I've never bought her a birthday present," he said firmly. "Let me do this."

A lot of research, some stressful eBay bidding, and a cool four-hundred and fifty pounds later, and Tom's shopping was complete. He'd invested in a full set of ponies and a stable, as well as a castle so big it didn't fit in any of his cupboards and so had to sit, pride-of-place, in the living room. He showed it all to Reine with the pride of a lion, and the little girl played with it for about two weekends before turning up the next time with a garishly bright and — in Tom's eyes — *skimpily dressed* doll clutched tight in her hands.

"This is Misty," she told him excitedly. "She's the sky blue doll."

With Misty in her life, Reine never looked at the My Little Pony toys again.

"I tried to warn you," Ari said, not unkindly, when Tom bemoaned the crates of pink and purple plastic horses he now had sitting in his London flat. "Children go through phases. For Reine, My Little Pony is out and Rainbow High in."

The only person happy about this change in Reine's affections seemed to be Luis, who'd started his own collection of Rainbow High dolls, to keep Reine company.

"I mean, they aren't Barbie," Luis remarked to Tom when he picked up Reine one afternoon. "But I like the changeable legs on them. Barbie could do with changeable legs." He'd leaned closer to Tom, as though about to admit a terrible secret. "You know, I always feel a little odd popping kitten heels onto my Florence Nightingale Inspiring Women Barbie. It feels a little wrong, if you know what I mean."

Tonight, Luis was in his element, dressed smartly in a button-down shirt and tailored slacks, talking dolls with Reine, and his good mood seemed to infect his husband, who stared at him with an adoration Tom had never seen before. Sebastian and Luis were good together, Tom thought, before his gaze drifted back to Stella and Corentin, who also seemed content and happy.

He and Ari, Tom suddenly realised, were the only people at the table who'd yet to find that kind of contentment in life.

That's a lie, Tom abruptly lectured himself, *you found it. You had it. But you let it slip away. You let her get away.*

His eyes fell back on Ari, who glanced up, meeting his gaze. For a moment they stared at one another, and Tom felt his own cheeks grow hot.

Don't kid yourself, he quickly reminded himself. *She told you herself, there's no chance for you.*

Pulling his eyes from Ari's, Tom looked down, scowling at his plate of *Lyonnaise quenelles*, the cream sauce suddenly looking congealed and sickly.

"I say, Jawline," Stella suddenly piped up, her voice grating, "do you know who I heard from recently? That old disaster of a fiancée of yours. Sasha whatever her name was."

Tom's eyes went back to Ari's, but this time she didn't meet his gaze. She was looking down, her hands clasped in her lap, her lips pressed together.

She would never forget about Sasha, Tom knew. She would never forget that betrayal, just as she would never forgive his lying to her so consistently and for such a long time. Tom Miller would always be the ghost sitting between them — the elephant in the room they both pretended not to see.

Tom sighed, sitting back in his chair and closing his eyes for a moment.

"Getting married, she told me," Stella carried on, seemingly unaware of the torment Sasha's name inflicted upon Ari. "Wanted me to take her pictures."

At those words Tom opened his eyes again, watching as Ari sat taller, her eyes at once falling upon Luis, who was shifting uncomfortably in his chair.

"Luis . . ." Ari began, her voice sharp.

Luis gave a sheepish shrug. "So . . . Miss Teen Rhode Island *might* have called me too."

"Might?"

Luis shrugged again. "Okay, so she *did* call me."

Ari gave a disbelieving shake of her head. "She wants you to design her wedding dress again, doesn't she?"

"Yeah," Luis admitted.

"I suppose," Marnie suddenly said, "Sasha had a plan she liked for her wedding with Tom. I don't care for that woman, and I never will, but credit where credit is due, her recycling skills are top notch. So, getting married, is she? Did you know about this, Tom?"

Tom looked to his mother, trying to comprehend what she was asking him and why. It was hard to care about Sasha when Ari was there and hurting.

"No," he answered shortly. "I didn't know, and I don't care."

"Did she call you?" Ari suddenly turned to Sebastian, who spluttered on his wine. "Did she want you to plan her wedding?"

Sebastian gave a shrug, though non-committal. "A couple of weeks ago I chose to decline her call. She left a message — quite a snotty one, in fact. She and her new man, *Harold*, he's called, of all the names . . . Well, they were hoping I could be persuaded to plan their wedding."

"With me?" Ari asked icily.

Sebastian laughed. "Don't be ridiculous, darling, of course not. She can't bear you. Hates your guts, in fact."

Sebastian gave Tom a look, before turning back to Ari. "Don't take it personally. Look at you. Tonight, you're blowing Rhode Island right out of the water. I mean, call the BBC and get the meteorologist on the phone, London is *hot* tonight because of you, Ari."

Ari blushed, an adorable pink from her neck to her cheeks, and something inside of Tom ached.

"I turned her down," Stella cut in, and Tom hid a grimace as he watched his brother fold an arm over her shoulders in affection. "Sasha. She's all sharp edges. Doesn't photograph well. In that respect, at least, you were perfectly matched, Jawline."

"*Stella*," Corentin said, his voice a playful warning, and Stella shrugged.

"I turned her down too," Luis added, reaching over to rub Ari's arm. "I'm too busy with this one's constant demands anyway." He gestured to Stella.

"Oh, that reminds me. Small's flower girl dress. You need to add to it again."

Luis stiffened, one hand wrapped around a fine bone china cup of coffee.

"Add to it . . . again?" he asked, utterly indignant. "Why? It's finally perfect."

"We decided the gold silk in Iceland might be a little, well, *cool*," Stella explained airily.

"And given that Stella and I will be wearing matching robes, we thought it was a good idea if Reine had one too."

"You want me to make a robe for Reine? *Te pasas*, we fly tomorrow, Stella!"

"So, plenty of time then," Stella returned easily. "I don't understand why you're looking at me like that."

"Well, for starters I don't have a design ready, or any fabric—"

"Actually, we were hoping you could use the rest of the Koigu Kersti cashmere our robes are made from," Corentin interrupted.

Tom watched as Luis's face changed, going from consternation to thoughtfulness in under a second. Across the table from him, Ari caught his eye and shook her head.

"*Wait for it*," she mouthed to him.

"Koigu Kersti cashmere, hey?" Luis sipped his coffee. "It's a beautiful fabric. Rare, too. Well, I suppose if I make it a basic shape with some sophisticated French darts and maybe some channel stitching on the pockets, it will work. I could line it with the same silk from her dress, too."

"You're going to be up all night sewing now," Sebastian complained. "Don't let them play you like this."

"For Koigu Kersti cashmere they can play me anytime they like," Luis replied. "Hell, for Koigu Kersti cashmere they can play you too, just like a violin." Luis turned to Stella and Corentin. "All right. I'll make the robe, but I'm sleeping the moment we hit the hotel in Reykjavík. No more alterations after this."

"Speaking of alterations," Marnie broke in, clearing her voice, "won't you need Reine tonight then too? So you can make this cashmere robe thing?"

"I have her measurements," Luis replied, before a worried look crossed his face. "Actually, it would be nice to have her close by, just so I can get the fit perfect before we leave tomorrow."

He turned towards Ari, who at once shook her head.

"Don't look at me," she told him. "It's Tom's weekend, not mine."

Luis turned to Tom with puppy-like eyes, and Tom sighed.

He'd developed a kind of grudging relationship with Luis and Sebastian over the past year, one born out of necessity and shared love for a small child. It wasn't strong enough to be called friendship, but nor was it merely an acquaintanceship either.

Luis and Sebastian, dedicated to Ari and Reine, and fiercely defensive of both, had watched Tom warily as he tried to build a relationship with his daughter. They'd been in the background, respectfully giving Tom the space he needed with Reine, while ready to jump in at a moment's notice to offer help and advice. This support had surprised Tom, who'd expected nothing more than criticism and hard words from them. Instead, they'd been kindness and understanding personified, particularly Luis, and it hadn't taken long for Tom to acknowledge that Sebastian and Luis were good people with good intentions.

"I know it's your weekend," Luis was saying now, "and I'm aware you've travelled a long way for it. But if Sebastian and I could just take Reine for tonight . . ."

Tom held up a hand, aware of Stella and Corentin's eyes upon his back. "Don't worry about me, I wouldn't dream of standing in the way when there's a wedding emergency. So long as Reine is okay with it, I'm okay with it."

"We should get going then," Luis replied, standing. "Reine, *mi cielo, estás bien si te quedas conmigo y el* Uncle Sebastian *esta noche? Voy a hacerte una capa tan suave y hermosa que será como usar algodón de azúcar.*"

Reine looked to her mother, and Ari nodded.

"I'm picking her up at 8 a.m. sharp," she warned Luis, leaning over to plant a kiss on Reine's head. "We need to be at the airport on time."

"Please," Sebastian broke in, waving his hand, "You know how much we love Heathrow. An hour in the lounge sipping champagne before a flight and a good rummage through Harrods always makes the travel experience less trying on my nerves."

"That's great," Ari said. "Except we're flying from City this time."

Sebastian's face fell. "You're kidding, right?"

Ari shook her head.

"But . . . but there's nothing at London City Airport. One post box, a sad little WH Smith selling wine gums and one poky overpriced bar filled with city banker types does not an airport make, Ari. What the hell were you thinking?"

"I don't know," Ari mused. "I just thought the convenience of getting to City outweighed the lounge experience at Heathrow and—"

"Urgh, stop." Sebastian rolled his eyes. "Fine. I'll see you at City. But next time I'm booking the flights. And the airport lounge."

"I'm coming with you," Marnie suddenly announced, standing quickly.

"That's fine," Sebastian replied. "The airport lounge is members only, but I'm sure I could rustle up a guest pass—"

"Not to the airport," Marnie bristled. "I meant to your house, now. I want to spend some time with Reine before the madness of the wedding begins tomorrow."

Sebastian shrugged. "Fine by me. Given that Luis's going to be up sewing all night now, I could do with some company after Reine's gone to bed. I'll make tea. We can watch *Bridgerton*."

"What's that?"

Sebastian and Luis exchanged a look.

"You don't know *Bridgerton*, Marnie?" Luis asked.

"No. Will I like it?"

"Mom—" Tom began, but Sebastian had already begun speaking.

"Tell me, Marnie, how do you feel about shirtless and attractive men?"

Tom watched as his mother grinned.

"I'd say I was on the positive side," she replied. "Honestly, if you'd seen Tom's father back in the day, in his tight trousers and V-neck shirts—"

"Mom!" Tom exploded, covering Reine's ears. "Too much information."

"Tom," Marnie replied calmly, "don't be such a prude. Women of my age have sex, you know."

"Ooh," Sebastian grinned. "You're going to love *Bridgerton*. Come on, then, let's go so Luis can get this cape started. You ready, Reine?"

"I'll have a bike drop the cashmere to you ASAP, Luis," Stella said, also standing. "See you all in Iceland."

"You're leaving too?" Ari asked, frowning. "You don't want a glass of red wine or anything?"

"Oh, I'm allergic to tannins," Stella explained, giving Ari a smile as her fiancé helped her into her coat. "So, no red wine for me."

"That's right, and I've developed an empathy allergy to them too, in support of my wife-to-be," Corentin added.

Tom saw Ari staring at his brother and Stella.

"I've never, um, heard of an empathy allergy."

"Oh, it's the newest thing," Stella explained. "I get headaches when I'm exposed to tannins, and strangely, as soon as Corentin and I moved in together, he started getting headaches too. A large coincidence, wouldn't you agree?"

"Not really," Tom muttered, and Ari give him a look.

"Okay, Stella, well—"

"See you in Iceland," Stella cut in, kissing Ari on the cheek, which Corentin did likewise. Stella then turned to Tom, winking and giving him the finger guns.

"You can go home now, Jawline," she told him. "Your familial duty is complete, and there are no more plates in here for you to break anyway. See you at the wedding."

"Right, I—"

"See you, bro," Corentin offered, and Tom gave a small wave, watching his brother disappear into the London night with Stella on his arm.

"Well," Ari cleared her throat, looking at Tom awkwardly. "I, um, maybe I should—"

"I'd like a glass of red wine," Tom interrupted her. "I'm not allergic to tannins."

Ari smiled. "You want a glass of red wine? With me?"

Tom tried to fight back a blush. "Yeah. But not here. This place is creeping me out with all of the white walls, white floors and pale food."

"I know a place across town," Ari offered. "Shall we get a black cab?"

Tom nodded. "That'd be great."

* * *

Ari took him to a small pub across the road from a large train station that Tom didn't recognise. The pub was old and set by itself on a corner, like a slab of cake sharply cut at the sides, or a triangle of cheese taken cleanly from its wheel. The inside was cosy though, and he and Ari found a table in a nook by the bar, a small corner where they had a degree of intimacy.

"This is a Victorian pub," Ari explained. "It's one of my favourites. It was built on the site of an old Dominican friary. Catherine of Aragon fled here when Henry VIII was trying to divorce her."

"Oh," Tom replied, but no other words would come. Sitting here with Ari, their thighs just inches apart, in a cosy corner of a noisy bar, he was acutely reminded of their European travel days, and he was certain she felt likewise.

For a few moments they sat in silence, sipping at their red wines, when Tom decided to throw caution to the wind.

"I didn't say earlier," he began, "but you look beautiful tonight. Absolutely stunning."

Ari blushed, her hand immediately going to the halter of her dress, adjusting it slightly.

"You, um, *did* say it earlier," she told him. "Not that you needed to."

"Oh, but I did," Tom argued. "You're beautiful, and I should tell you all the time and—"

"No," Ari smiled, putting her hand on his arm, as though to steady him. "I mean, you didn't need to say it, because I knew you were thinking it. You turned the table upside down when I walked into the room."

Now it was Tom's turn to blush. "Oh, yeah. Right."

"Did you pay the restaurant for the crockery?"

"Yeah." Tom shrugged. "Who knew plain white plates could be so expensive?"

"Sorry."

"No." Tom turned to her, moving her hand from his arm so that it was nestled within his own palm. "No. Don't ever apologise for being beautiful in my presence. Don't apologise for that at all. It's not your fault that I'm awkward around you when you look beautiful."

Ari gave him a gentle smile. "Tom, to be honest with you, you always seem a little awkward around me."

"That's because," Tom spoke softly, "you're *always* beautiful to me. You've always been beautiful to me. And so I'll always be a little awkward around you. That's my curse." He looked at her, sighing a little and longing to run his hand down her arm. "A curse I'm happy with."

Ari stared at him for a moment, her eyes as blue as the sea on a clear summer's day.

"Are you really okay with it?" she asked him.

He stared back at her. Her palm was warm and soft within his.

"Okay with what?"

"Sasha getting married."

Tom swallowed. "Of course I'm okay with it. I was never in love with Sasha, you know. Never."

Ari sat back, her eyes drifting to the glass of wine before her, though she kept her hand within his.

"I think back to last year, sometimes," she admitted. "I go over everything Sasha said about you. The things she told us about your relationship, so we could plan your wedding."

"Sasha was never anything more than a Band Aid." Tom sat back too, squeezing Ari's hand. "Not having you . . . it was like a gaping wound, like being torn in two, and Sasha was something I used to piece myself back together. That was all. I'm not proud of myself for it . . . I'm ashamed of myself for so many of the things I did."

"I don't want to talk about Tom Miller tonight." Ari squeezed his hand back. "There's nothing more to say there."

"I thought I'd lost you forever," Tom replied with a sigh. "If only I'd known . . . Well, I didn't. And I can only keep going forward from here."

"Yes," Ari agreed. "Going forward is good."

Tom licked his lips. "Reine told me you're painting again."

Ari blinked in surprise. "She did?"

"Yeah. I'm glad. I love your work. I was crushed to hear you'd stopped because of me."

"I didn't stop because of you — well, not directly. I just . . . I didn't have time. Or the inclination, perhaps. But now, with you here, and helping with Reine . . . I have both again."

"How's it going?"

"The painting? Slowly. I'm out of practice."

"Just keep going. I believe in you."

"I know," Ari replied. "You were always my biggest fan."

"I want first dibs on your newest work if you decide to sell it," Tom joked.

"What? You want to make your collection a neat thirty-eight?"

Tom felt himself go red.

Ari squeezed his hand again. "I'm glad you bought them. You inspired so many of them. It's fitting that they belong to you."

There it was again, that ocean blue in her eyes.

Tom cleared his throat, looking down quickly. "So, my mom's seen your newest work?"

"And Luis. And Sebastian. And Stella and Corentin. Oh, and Brandon too. We had coffee last month."

"Everyone but me, then."

"Not everyone. I don't think the Prime Minister has seen it yet. But then, he's a little busy trashing the economy," Ari joked.

"Can I see it?" Tom asked abruptly. "I mean, would that be okay? I know it's a work in progress, and I wouldn't want to intrude, but . . ." He trailed off, suddenly worried he'd overstepped.

Ari was looking at him thoughtfully, chewing on her bottom lip.

"Okay." She nodded slowly. "Why not?"

* * *

Tom loved Ari's house. It was small but perfect, and it smelled like her and Reine. He remembered the first time he'd visited, the house unnaturally pristine, with Ari looking both absurdly ashamed and proud of her home at the same time.

"It's just a typical two-up, two-down," she'd explained. "But it was all I could afford, and I had the kitchen re-done, and the bathroom too."

Tom hadn't seen the flaws Ari was fixated on. He didn't see the slightly worn carpets, or the faded curtains, or the crack in one of the kitchen tiles. Instead, he saw a warm, colourful and pleasant home with Reine's drawings on the fridge and boots by the door and flowers in a vase and realised, with an overwhelming feeling of pride, that Ari had accomplished it all by herself. She was amazing — Ari — and her home helped prove it.

When Ari unlocked the door and led him in, switching on the lights, she slipped her heels off by the door and motioned for him to follow her.

"Do you, um, want a cup of tea or anything?" she asked him. "Or I have wine. I have all the wine," she added, giving a self-effacing laugh. "Red, white and pink."

"Tea would be great," Tom replied, even though he hated tea, which tasted bitter, earthy and almost soap-like to him. He couldn't understand why the British were wedded to the stuff, the whole nation seemingly coming to a stop at four o'clock so they could drink the vile brown brew. He knew Ari loved tea though, and Reine likewise drank it, though hers was always served weak and milky, with a chocolate biscuit on the side.

Ari stopped, turning back to look at him.

"You hate tea," she said, her voice flat. "You used to drink coffee whenever I had my tea."

"Yeah." Tom ran his hand through his hair. "But you offered tea."

Ari smiled at him. "I was being English. Offering tea is just a way of making people feel welcome, and you *are* welcome here, Tom. I also offered you wine, you know."

Tom paused. "I didn't want to say yes, just in case that you, I don't know, thought I drank too much," he replied, somewhat sheepishly.

Ari looked at him for a long moment. "Tom," she finally said, "I know you're a good father to Reine. I'm not going to take her away from you. Please stop thinking you're on probation with me or something, okay? I'm going to have a glass of wine, and it would be lovely if you would have one with me."

Tom smiled at how easily Ari had read him, feeling his shoulders relax a little. "Okay, thanks. Another red would be lovely."

Ari nodded, pouring out two glasses and handing one to Tom.

"Come on," she told him, "I'll show you the painting. It isn't finished, obviously, so please don't judge it."

"I won't judge it, I promise," Tom replied as Ari began leading him up the stairs. "Are you happy with how it's coming along?"

Ari nodded. "I think so. You know me, sometimes I get hours into a painting and then inspiration deserts me. This time, though, I'm happy. It's good to have a brush in my hand again."

She waved him into her bedroom, and Tom swallowed. He'd never been in this room before.

He'd seen Reine's room, obviously, with its white-framed single bed, fairy lights along one wall and books covering nearly every surface. Ari's room, though, was different. It was small, not much bigger than Reine's room, with light green walls and natural wood furniture. It was neat and tidy, although clothes were strewn across the bed, and pot plants covered her windowsill, a flood of vibrant green that smelled clean and fresh. On her bedside table was a pile of books, mostly poetry and cosy mysteries, with a half-finished mug of tea balanced precariously beside them.

Being here, in Ari's personal space, was intimate and revealing, and it suddenly occurred to Tom that he'd never been in any of her bedrooms before. She was the love of his

336

life and had borne his child, but their history had taken place in sparse hotel rooms, rental cars and the occasional tent or caravan. They'd travelled across Europe together, sharing beds, bathrooms and cupboard space, but they'd never *lived* together. Not really. Tom recalled the little knick-knacks and mementos Ari had bought as they'd journeyed from country to country, each item a small hint into her mind and world. They'd only been hints though — Tom hadn't been with Ari long enough to learn that she preferred earthy colours to bright ones, that she read cosy mysteries before she slept, or that she was so frightened of small spaces her window was nearly always kept open.

He still had so much to learn about her. There was still so much he didn't know.

"What do you think then?" Ari asked, gesturing to the corner of her room. Her easel swallowed up an enormous portion of the little bedroom, and paint splatters were clear on the nearby wall. An old, large piece of fabric protected the carpet, and Tom stepped on it gingerly, not wanting to disturb the space she'd reserved for the thing that, after Reine, he knew she loved best.

"It's amazing," he breathed out, as his eyes swept across the canvas before him.

It was a woodland scene set at dusk. The trees were captured perfectly, so textured and real that Tom could nearly feel the rough bark beneath his fingertips. The scene was dark, with only a little autumnal light filtering through the heavy canopy of bronze, red and orange leaves above. The work was sweeping and painstakingly rendered, and Tom knew Ari had put her heart and soul into this piece.

"It's wonderful," he added, shaking his head in admiration for her talent. "Honestly, Ari, you've outdone yourself. It's a work of art."

Ari leaned against her bedroom door and smiled. "That was kind of the point. But thank you all the same."

"It's almost too good. I don't know if I'm going to have enough money to buy it," Tom lamented. "Maybe you can offer me a pay-by-instalment package?"

Ari shook her head. "Sorry, this one's not for sale."

"It's not?"

"No. It's a gift for someone."

"A gift?" Tom asked with a frown, instantly wondering who the recipient would be and whether they would accept an offer from him.

"Look at the painting more carefully," Ari told him. "Does it seem at all familiar?"

Tom's eyes at once snapped back to the canvas. He took in the shadowy trees, the leaf-lined forest floor, the way the orange and red hues of light ebbed through the trunks and branches. He took in the curve of the land, the way the ground seemed to tilt to one side, as though this was a clearing before a stream or pond—

"This is the forest near my mom's house," Tom suddenly announced, recognition hitting him hard. "The clearing in the woods. My mom and dad were married there, you know."

"I know," Ari replied, and Tom turned to her, acutely aware that *he'd* also meant to get married there.

To Sasha.

"This is a gift for my mom, isn't it?" he asked, swallowing down his shame.

Ari nodded. "She's been so good with Reine. And me. It's a small repayment, but . . ."

"She'll love it. She loved *The Ends of the Earth*, even before she ever knew you painted it."

"Mm," Ari made a non-committal sound of reply. "She's been great. One thing, though — I could do without all the knitted goods." She laughed. "She made me a cardigan. It was awful. She made a matching one for Reine, and it was worse."

Tom laughed too. "It's a shame Corentin went into Druidry and not Dark Age Catholicism. Mom would have made him some great horsehair shirts. I admit, I'm not looking forward to our trip home from Iceland on Wednesday. Her needles clacking all the way over the Atlantic." Tom

338

shuddered. "How they haven't been banned as a dangerous weapon on flights, I don't know."

"Knitting needles aren't a weapon," Ari chided him, but she smiled all the same.

"No? Try wearing one of Mom's homemade jumpers for more than four hours and we'll talk again."

Ari laughed, taking another sip of wine. "Thank you for being so complimentary about my painting," she said, changing the subject. "I want to get it right, and your words . . . they're encouraging. I'd forgotten how much I was encouraged by you."

By me or Tom Miller? Tom couldn't help but think, before another thought struck him. *It was me, it was always me.*

He took a deep breath. "I used to love sitting next to you while you painted," he admitted. "When we were . . . when we were together. I used to love it. You would paint and paint, and I would just sit and watch you and wonder how I'd ever gotten so lucky as to meet you. I'd been unhappy for so long, and then you were suddenly there, and my world was just . . . better. Everything was better. For years, I'd been unable to sit still. I was like a bird, ready to jump at the slightest disturbance. With you," Tom's eyes drifted lovingly over Ari's face, "I felt like I could be still. I felt like I could rest. I would sit by your side while you painted and just feel . . . easy."

Ari licked her lips, nodding slowly. "I liked painting with you next to me."

"You mean Tom Miller—"

"You," Ari cut him off, and then she blushed. "I like having you next to me. *You*," she added quickly, reaching out to take Tom's hand. "You," she said again, her eyes bright. "You, Tom."

It occurred to Tom that he should kiss Ari. It occurred to him that this was a moment, and one that he should seize. Ari was here, and she was beautiful and sweet and loving and *Ari*, and he was here, and he was in love with her and wanted her and adored her with his whole heart. Kissing her was the most natural thing in the world to him, and he was made brave by the wine in his blood and the love in his heart and the bright, blazing look in Ari's eyes that told him a kiss would be more than welcome to her in this moment. It occurred to Tom that he should pull her into his arms and run his thumbs down her cheeks. It occurred to Tom that he should smile before lowering his mouth to hers. All of this occurred to Tom, but he didn't have time to act, for Ari stepped forward, wrapping an arm around his neck and pulling his face gently towards hers. She brushed her lips softly over his own, a caress more than a kiss, like the flutter of a butterfly's wings.

"Hi," she whispered, and it was *that*, that small sound of welcome on her lips, that broke him and made him pull her to him hungrily, seizing her lips with a ferocity that surprised them both. Ari gasped a little in his arms as he kissed her, and he stopped, pulling himself back enough so he could check she was okay.

"Ari, is this—" he began, but the words were cut off by her lips on his, and now she was kissing him, and he was kissing her back, and they were stumbling and unbalanced as he pushed her up against her wall, his hands in her hair and against her face and tracing her neck and anywhere else he could put them. He moved his mouth from her lips to her cheeks, before trailing down to her neck and shoulders, and Ari was making breathy sounds that were driving him crazy, and the only way to stop them and regain control was to kiss her again, swallowing her small noises of pleasure with his lips and tongue.

Ari's hands were around his waist, but he felt them move up the curve of his back to his neck. His body tingled with the contact, and he pressed against her more firmly, wanting more of that, wanting more of this and wanting more of *her*. Just her.

Her hands continued moving though, pulling away from his body and moving to her own. Tom stopped kissing her briefly, his mind doing a double take when he realised she was slowly unknotting the tie in her halter dress, the straps falling loose and the bodice falling to her waist. Half-naked in his arms, she kissed him again, encouraging him with little words of nonsense to kiss her back, to move his hands from her waist to her breasts.

"Please," she murmured between fervent kisses, and Tom nodded, lifting her gently and moving them both towards her bed. She settled against her pillows, her hands moving up to cup his face, and he smiled at her before kissing her on both cheeks, once on the lips, and then lowering his head to mouth at her breasts and nipples.

There was a familiarity to their movements that made him want to weep with joy, a familiarity to the feel of her in his arms as he stripped her of what little clothing remained, just as there was a familiarity in the press of her hands against him as she divested him of his shirt and trousers. It was a feeling of home, a feeling of happiness, a feeling of belonging. He knew how to make her smile and make her sigh and make her body arch with pleasure. He knew how to draw forth from her lips quiet gasps, just as he knew how to make Ari bite down on her lip and quell them. Everything about this was wonderfully, achingly familiar, except for one thing. One thing felt different. One thing felt new.

"*Tom,*" Ari uttered when he slid inside of her, and it was that, Tom realised as pleasure ran through him, hot and fast like a molten wave. It was the sound of his name — his true name, without the guise of another between them — on her lips, that made this whole experience so achingly familiar and also so blindingly new. Ari was making love with him, and the ghost of Tom Miller was nowhere to be seen, nowhere to be found.

It was just him and her. As magical as it ever was — more magical than it had ever been. Him and her, together once more, without any secrets or lies between them.

Underneath the waves of pleasure, something like gratitude rose inside him, and he took a moment to stop, to slow things down and just look at her. Her eyes met his and she gave him a small, tremulous smile.

"Say it again," he asked quietly, running one hand over her hair. "Please."

"Tom," she replied, still smiling. "Tom."

He smiled back, before lowering his mouth once more to hers.

"I love you," he whispered into her. "I love you."

"Tom," she whispered back, "I love you too."

CHAPTER 23: CAME BACK FOR YOU

The sky was only just turning pink when Ari reached Victoria station. The tube had been sticky and hot, with a few early-morning travellers wearily drinking their coffee as they made their way through the underbelly of the city, but Ari had hardly noticed them. She'd been caught in her own world and thoughts, on autopilot as she made the familiar journey from train to platform, platform to street, and then by foot to Luis and Sebastian's elegant Ebury Street flat.

She pressed the buzzer once, and then — after a few seconds without any response — pressed it again. When there was still resounding silence, she pressed it again, and again, and again.

"My God," a voice finally crackled down the intercom, annoyed and sharp. "If this is another flipping early morning delivery of a special edition Barbie doll I'm going to—"

"Sebastian, it's me," Ari broke in, leaning her head against the wall. "Let me in."

For a moment, the line went quiet.

"Ari?" Sebastian crackled again. "It's . . . it's six in the morning, Ari. Reine's still asleep. She's fine. Unlike how you're about to be if you don't let me go back to bed. You said 8 a.m."

"This isn't about Reine," Ari replied. "Please let me in."

"Ari, we've had a genuinely late night here and I'd like to get in another few hours of shut-eye before we hit the airport. Besides, Luis is passed out in a ball of cashmere at the moment and I—"

"I slept with Tom," Ari admitted, her words blunt. "We had sex."

Another moment of silence pulsed before Ari heard the door unlock as Sebastian buzzed her in. She climbed the stairs two at a time, her head bowed, and when she reached the third floor she found Sebastian waiting for her on the landing.

"Well, well, well." He grinned, folding his dressing gown over his middle and looking her up and down with knowing eyes. "So, you're *finally* taking my advice."

"Stop it and give me coffee please," Ari replied, walking past him into the hall. She slipped her shoes off — because Luis was surprisingly strict about shoes on polished wooden floors — before poking her head into Reine's little bedroom. Reine was curled up on her side, her honey-blonde hair in a neat braid, clutching her bunny. Ari smiled at the sight, before turning back to Sebastian.

"Thanks for having her," she said, but Sebastian only shrugged.

"She's never a problem. Her relatives, on the other hand . . ."

"If you mean me, I'm sorry for getting here so early. I just needed to talk and—"

"Not you, you muppet," Sebastian replied, pulling on Ari's arm. He led her through to his and Luis's room, where Ari blinked in surprise.

Marnie was passed out on their bed, curled up on her side, clutching Sebastian's silk pillow.

"Dare I ask?" Ari turned back to Sebastian, who gestured for her to follow him through to the kitchen.

"We watched *Bridgerton*. We drank more wine. We thought about making an Uber order for cigarettes—"

"Sebastian!"

Her brother held up his hands. "We considered it, that's all. In the end I settled for another glass of red wine while Marnie got out her knitting. Oh God, Ari, her knitting. It was a blessing that my husband was up to his armpits in voodoo thirsty cashmere, because holy shit, he'd have had a stroke if he'd seen the sweater she's apparently knitting."

"Koigu Kersti cashmere," Ari corrected him, but she smiled. "She made Reine and I matching jumpers earlier this year."

"Burn them," Sebastian ordered as he started the coffee machine. "Burn them and then bury the ashes."

"She means well."

"Yes, I'm sure she does. Black coffee, love?"

"No. I'll take milk today. And three sugars."

Sebastian raised an eyebrow at her but started the milk frother all the same.

"Anyway, she passed out in her wool at around 2 a.m. and then Luis passed out in his Wagyu Nursie cashmere at about four, so I slept on the sofa in the living room and left them all to it."

"Koigu Kersti cashmere," Ari corrected him again, before wrapping her hand around her coffee gratefully. "Thanks."

Sebastian eyed her carefully. "You okay?" he asked.

"Yes."

"Are you sure?" he pressed, looking at her steadily.

Ari shook her head. "No."

Sebastian sighed, tying the knot in his robe again and slumping into the seat beside her. "Sorry love. Was he that bad in bed? Well, never mind. It has been a hot minute since you last shagged him. You know the old saying about women ageing like fine wine? Men aren't like that. We're like lettuce. Still kind of holding the shape but mostly limp under the leaves."

"No, I didn't mean—no, he was good, he was *really* good and . . ." Ari trailed off, blushing deeply.

Sebastian stared at her.

"Oh," he intoned, nodding. "So, this is more of an emotional thing?"

"Yes."

Sebastian nodded again. "I should probably wake Luis up for emotional things. He's good that way. Or Marnie."

Ari winced. "Please don't tell . . . my, um—"

"Lover," Sebastian supplied helpfully. "Your lover. We're grown-ups here, Ari. You can say it."

Ari blushed again. "Please don't wake Tom's *mother* so I can talk about sex with her son, okay?"

Sebastian shrugged. "Okay, well, that leaves me then. So, you had full sex with him then? It wasn't just a kiss and a cuddle before you fell chastely into the same bed?"

"We had sex."

"Did you mean to?"

Ari stared at him. "What do you mean?"

Sebastian cleared his throat. "I have limited experience with straight women — outside of all the brides, that is, and I don't think they count, since sex isn't their aim — but even I know that when a woman turns up to dinner looking like you did last night, in a dress like the one you were wearing, she means business. Tom, that poor sap, didn't know what hit him."

Ari chewed on her lip, looking into her coffee. "I didn't mean to . . . Well, it wasn't my intention to sleep with him." She paused, looking up to find Sebastian staring at her sceptically. She gave him an awkward smile. "But I guess it wasn't my intention not to sleep with him either."

Sebastian nodded, sipping his coffee. "I get it."

Ari sighed, swirling a teaspoon in her coffee restlessly. "I just . . . When I'm with him, I feel so . . . I don't know. He's easy to talk to and he makes me smile and he's trying so hard with me and Reine. When it's just us, I remember all the things I loved about him. I remember why I waited for him for so long."

Sebastian frowned. "Don't take this the wrong way, but that doesn't sound particularly promising. I mean, he's easy to talk to? He's trying hard? He makes you remember why you loved him?" Sebastian sat back in his chair, exhaling long and hard. "Ari, the guy is crazy about you. That's clear to anyone who spends more than a millisecond with him. If you aren't crazy about him too, well, then, giving him hope like this is just plain cruel."

Ari sat back, stung. "Of course I'm crazy about him," she whispered back. "How could you think I'm not?"

"Because of wishy-washy statements like 'he makes me smile'."

Ari took a deep breath. "When I'm with him, I feel like my body is on fire," she said, her voice warm. "When I'm with him, I want the moment to last forever. When I'm with him, all I can think about are his hands on my body and his mouth over mine."

"I didn't want wishy-washy but I'm still your brother. I don't need to hear things like that." Sebastian grimaced, then pointed his thumb behind him. "And Tom's mother is in the next room."

"I don't care," Ari replied. "When I'm with Tom, I feel happy. When I'm with him, I want him to be happy too. I think about him all the time, and I mean him, Tom Somerset, not Tom Miller."

"They're the same person, love."

"No and yes." Ari shook her head, clutching her coffee tightly. "They are and they aren't. Yes, Tom called himself Tom Miller once upon a time, and lived in this made-up character's persona. But they're different too. Tom Miller lied to me, and I don't think Tom Somerset is capable of that. Tom Miller had no direction, other than running from who he was. My Tom knows exactly what he wants and he's working hard to achieve it. Tom Miller never came back for me." Ari stopped, swallowing painfully, remembering once again how she'd been abandoned. "But I think . . . I think Tom Somerset would come for me. I really do."

Sebastian blinked twice, staring at her. "I don't understand."

347

"I know, it's hard to wrap your head around it," Ari said. "I think what I mean is that Tom seems quite sincere."

"No, I—" Sebastian began, but he was interrupted by Luis, who came stumbling into the room, wrapped in a blanket, his eyes bloodshot and red.

"Who said something about cashmere?" Luis blurted out, looking momentarily panicked, and Ari laughed, shaking her head.

"I said *sincere*," she told him. "Not cashmere. You need more sleep."

"I can sleep in Iceland," Luis replied. "What I need right now is coffee. What time is it?"

"Twenty past six," Sebastian replied. "Ari and I were just having a chat."

"Right." Luis nodded, picking up a croissant from the table. "It's really early for a chat though. And will you look at my fingers? Red raw from sewing all night. Honestly, if that robe had been for anyone but Reine . . ."

"Ari slept with Tom last night," Sebastian said.

Ari watched as the croissant fell from Luis's hand to the floor. He turned to her rapidly, his eyes and mouth wide open.

"You what!"

"She slept with Tom," Sebastian said again, frowning at the pastry flakes. "They had sex."

"*No me digas*," Luis breathed. "Did you really? Was it good?" He slapped a hand to his chest. "Were you *careful?*"

"Luis," Ari said, blushing red, but Sebastian shook his head.

"Actually, he has a good point. Were you careful?"

"Yes, were you?" Luis asked again. "And, if by chance you weren't, can the next one be a boy?"

"Luis! We were careful," Ari replied, staring into her coffee. "Just."

"Ooh, so it was good then?" Luis carried on, dumping the croissant on the table and smiling gratefully at Sebastian, who pushed a steaming mug of coffee towards him.

348

"Yes, it was, and yes, we were careful, and—"

"No, no, no," Sebastian interrupted. "Tell us that part later. Go back to the earlier bit. Before this one woke up."

"The earlier bit?" Ari frowned.

"Yes, the bit where you were saying you thought Tom would come back for you?"

Ari sighed. "Oh, right. Um, I was saying that Tom Miller never came for me, but I think that now, if it happened again, Tom Somerset would."

Luis frowned. "I'm confused."

"That's understandable. It's one man pretending to be two people . . . sometimes I still don't understand it myself."

"No, not about that. We've had a year to wrap our minds around the whole Tom Miller–Tom Somerset thing. I mean, I'm confused about the part where you said Tom Miller never came for you."

"Exactly," Sebastian nodded, "I lost the plot around there too."

Ari paused, looking at her two friends. "Tom never came for me," she said flatly. "We all know that."

A beat of silence went through the room, and Ari watched as Sebastian and Luis exchanged a look.

"Um," Luis said slowly, "except that, uh, we don't know that because Tom *did* come for you."

Something inside of Ari went still.

"What are you talking about?" she asked, her voice hoarse.

"He came for you, love," Sebastian said patiently. "A little late, granted, but he came for you."

"No, he never did, he never came—"

"Ari," Luis cut her off gently. "He came here. When Reine was a toddler. I saw him with my own eyes."

Ari stared at him. Inexplicably, her eyes filled with tears. "What?"

"I didn't see him," Sebastian chimed in. "But Luis told me about it later. Attractive man, kind of distracted. Turned up at the flat across the hall when you were living there."

"I was watching Reine for you while you were at a wedding," Luis added. "He asked after you, but when I said you were out, he nodded and looked . . . well, kind of sad."

"To be fair that's kind of how he looks most of the time," Sebastian rinsed his mug in the sink, putting it next to the dishwasher. "So that part you don't really know."

"No, he looked sad," Luis argued hotly. "I've had time to think about this, to remember what happened. He looked sad — gutted even — and said 'nice kid' before walking away."

"He came for me?" Ari whispered, brushing one of the tears from her cheek. "He *came* for me? You mean he kept his promise?"

"Yeah." Luis shrugged. "He came for you."

At this point, Ari stood, her cup spilling coffee over the countertop. "Well, why didn't you tell me!"

"He looked like a delivery man!" Luis replied, while Sebastian got a cloth from the sink. "You had a baby. People were always delivering toys or wipes or nappies to you. How was I supposed to know he was Tom Miller? It's not like he was wearing a name tag!"

Ari blinked, crossing her arms over her chest. "Fine, okay, well, why didn't you tell me recently then?"

"We thought you knew," Sebastian cut in, wiping up the coffee and throwing the cloth over the counter into the sink. "We figured Tom had told you."

"Well, he didn't," Ari said, exhaling hard. "He didn't say a thing."

For a moment, silence fell.

"Well, that's just odd, isn't it? Of everything that happened, out of everything he did, the one redeeming piece of Tom's story is that he came back for you, just like he said he would." Sebastian sat in his chair again, looking thoughtful. "Why didn't he tell you?"

Ari shook her head. "I don't know."

He came back for me, her mind repeated, clear and calm. *He came back for us.*

"So, he just . . . left again? Never came back?" she asked Luis.

"He thought I was your husband or something," Luis replied, looking almost proud. "He thought Reine was mine. That you'd moved on."

"Why would he think such a thing?" she asked, but it was more a question for herself. "Why?"

"Oh, because the man's hardly Albert Einstein, is he?" Sebastian rolled of his eyes. "He made some stupid choices and did some stupid things. Reine's cleverness is a testament to our parenting choices, not her genetics."

"She's had good schooling too," Luis added, though Sebastian held up his hand.

"Let's not go there. You and Barbara Canning are still at each other's throats over raffle prizes."

"He came for me," Ari whispered again. "He came for me."

"Yeah," Luis said, his voice soft. "Of course he did. He loves you, Ari. That's the one constant in his story, you know? Whether he's Tom Somerset or Tom Miller, or both, he always loves you. That part of his story never changes."

"And you love him too," Sebastian added with a shrug, and Ari blinked.

"No, I—" She stopped, closing her mouth.

Of course I'm in love with him, the voice in her head spoke up, clear and confident. *I've always loved him. He wouldn't have broken my heart so badly if I didn't. I love him, and I'm always going to love him. I told him last night that I loved him, and I meant every word.*

"Everyone knows, don't they?"

"Which part?" Sebastian searched for clarification, before shrugging again. "Actually, scrap that. Because yes. Everyone knows everything. Well, except you, who apparently didn't know that he came back for you, and Tom now, who has no idea how you feel about him but probably isn't feeling very hopeful right now."

"Why?" Ari asked.

351

"Well, love, because you're here in our kitchen instead of in bed with him. That's why."

Ari paled. "I just . . . I needed to talk. To process what happened. I didn't know," she added tearfully. "I didn't know he'd come back for me."

"Well, you do now," Luis replied, reaching forward to brush away another of Ari's tears. "So, what are you going to do about it?"

Ari stood, lightning fast. "I need to speak with him. Right now."

"Go," Luis nodded. "He might not have woken yet. Go quickly."

"Yes, I'm going," Ari replied. "I'm going. Oh, God, Reine—"

"We'll bring her to the airport. Just bring her bag and passport with you," Luis told her.

"Yes, we'll bring her." Sebastian nodded too. "We'd take her to the airport lounge, but there isn't one," he added with a pointed look in her direction.

"Fine, next time I'll book Heathrow, next time I'll—"

"Ari," Luis said firmly, "go."

* * *

She let herself into her small house just forty-five minutes later, having run from the DLR to her door, but it was already too late.

Her bed was empty, and Tom had gone.

* * *

The flight to Reykjavík went by in a blur. Ari nervously ate peanuts, tapping her fingers on her tray table while mentally trying to run through her to-do lists. *Liaise with florist, check over bridal gown, check over venue, liaise with Chef and service staff . . .*

"*Vos sí jodes mucho,*" a voice suddenly intoned, and Ari felt a hand clamp down on her fingers. Luis gave her a look, taking a deep breath.

"Please stop that tapping. You have things on your mind, I understand," he began patiently. "But I had less than two hours of sleep last night. I need to get another hour in before we arrive."

"Sorry," Ari whispered, feeling mortified.

"It's fine," Luis reassured her. "Your brother is out, at least," he added, nodding to Sebastian, who was curled up against the window, snoring lightly. "And Reine is okay."

Ari immediately looked to Reine next to her. The little girl was entirely preoccupied with her iPad, her fingers moving over the screen with a confidence and fluidity Ari almost envied.

"I was just thinking about Tom," Ari admitted, looking back to Luis.

"I know," he replied. "You didn't see him then? Or get a chance to talk to him?"

"No." Ari shook her head. "He wasn't there when I got back."

Luis sighed. "Well, speak to him in Reykjavík then. At the hotel. There's nothing you can do here, forty thousand feet above the North Sea." He paused, looking at her for a moment. "So, what are you going to say to him when you see him?"

Ari chewed on her lip. If Luis hadn't still had a tight hold of her hand, she knew her fingers would have begun nervously tapping again. Instead, she squeezed his hand, giving him a small smile.

"I don't know. I figured that when I saw him again, I would just . . . know."

Luis nodded, looking thoughtful — his eyes, though still sleep-worn and tired, were kind as they gazed upon her face. Ari chewed on her lip again.

"It's times like this I wish I still had my queen of spades card," she told him, abruptly sad. "Whenever I felt uncertain, I would get her out." She squeezed his hand again, missing the feeling of the worn card on her fingertips. "But I tore her in half. I tore her up."

353

Suddenly, Luis's eyes flashed.

"Ari—"

"It's okay. It was my decision."

"Actually, um, maybe it wasn't," Luis replied, and he shifted uncomfortably in his airline seat.

"What do you mean?"

Luis took a deep breath, before sighing. "Don't be mad, okay?"

He opened the bag by his feet, pulling something from within. "It's just, I'd seen you with this so often and that day, in the diner, when you tore it in half . . . Well, I didn't want you to regret it later, so I figured it wouldn't hurt to pick it up, and then I figured it wouldn't hurt to repair it—and let me tell you something, stitching eighteenth-century card back together was hard work, I had to use a really strong silk thread to get the effect I wanted and—"

"Luis." Ari's eyes grew wide as she took in what he held in his hand. "Luis, is that . . ." her voice broke ". . . is that my queen of spades?"

Luis nodded. "Yes. I took it from the table after you ripped it in half, brought it home with me and repaired it. Look, see," he handed Ari the card, "I did the best I could. She'll always have a scar, you'll always be able to see she was damaged at one point. But overall, I'm happy. I used linen coloured silk to match the colour of the original card, and used one of my lightest steam presses to take out the, uh, what's the word—um, crumples? Can you say that for paper as well as fabric?" He looked at Ari curiously, who nodded wordlessly. "Right, to take the crumples out. Don't worry, I put her between linen before I applied the press, so that her paint wasn't damaged. I'm a designer, not an art restorer, but even I know she's an old lady who needs some TLC. You should take better care of her, you know, she's worn away on one side where you've stroked her, and she—"

Shaking her head, Ari reached over and embraced Luis as tightly as her FAA approved seat belt would allow.

"Thank you," she whispered. "Thank you."

When she pulled away, Luis gave an embarrassed half-shrug. "It was no problem. I know you love her," he added, before giving Ari a pointed look. "Just like I know you love him."

Ari nodded mutely, still clutching the card in her hands. The queen was just as stately as Ari remembered her, even with the new line of delicate stitches holding her together. The blue of her dress and eyes were still faded, her crown still dark, and Ari remembered the first time she'd seen her, cool and crisp in her hand against the background of a darkened airport terminal. Tom had been on the floor, his long legs spread out in front of him as he'd looked up at her curiously. She'd told him then and there she was keeping this queen, and she had, for years and years afterwards, guarding her with as much jealousy and secrecy as she guarded her memories of Tom and their time together.

"I didn't know how much I missed her until now, when I've got her back," Ari said, running her finger over the familiar lines and folds.

"Like Tom," Luis suggested, but Ari shook her head.

"No. He's different. I missed him, but the Tom I have now . . ." Ari trailed off, before giving a gentle smile. "He's better."

"You need to talk to him," Luis reminded her, before he gave a yawn. "I'm tired. How long until we land?"

Ari checked her phone. "Another seventy minutes."

"I'm going to close my eyes." Luis yawned again. "Are you going to be okay?"

Ari smiled. She glanced over to Reine, then at the card in her hand. She smiled again.

"Yes," she told him. "I think now I'll be just fine."

CHAPTER 24: AURORA

There was a distinct pleasant rush to the day of a wedding she'd planned, Ari had to admit. Before she even got into the business, Sebastian would tell her about the adrenaline surge he got from an efficient wedding ceremony, followed by a flawlessly well-oiled reception afterwards. Ari hadn't understood and didn't understand until the evening of her first wedding, when — after the bride and groom had departed and the guests had dispersed into hotel rooms — she'd sat in the middle of the confetti-covered dancefloor, her blood singing and skin tingling.

Sebastian had been right. It was a rush like no other.

Stella and Corentin's wedding day, however, was somewhat different. Corentin had been adamant about being married in an Icelandic cave, and Stella, who had clearly photographed too many traditional white weddings, highly approved of his unusual choice.

"Iceland in February will be cold and unpleasant," Ari warned them, having done her research, but their minds would not be turned.

"The cave we've chosen to be wed in is perfect. It's only a fifteen-minute walk across sand dunes, so accessible to all our guests," Stella had argued. "Not that there'll be many of those. We want it to be intimate."

"Intimate but also close to the bowels of Mother Earth," Corentin had added.

Ari had glanced at Sebastian, who simply shrugged.

"I'm sure we will manage it," Sebastian had replied. "We've done trickier venues. But, just FYI, it's best not to use the word 'bowels' on a wedding invitation. I'm sure you understand."

Stella and Corentin wanted their wedding to take place in a little town called Vík, in a cave near the black sand beach. By the time their flight landed, and they'd made the three-hour car journey to the small Icelandic town, Ari was wrecked. She'd hoped to hand Reine over to Tom for the night, so she could start work first thing in the morning, but he hadn't been in his hotel room when she'd knocked on the door. Instead, Marnie had taken Reine's hand.

"Where's Tom?" Ari asked, immediately concerned, but also acutely disappointed. She'd wanted to see him and speak with him herself.

"He went for a walk," Marnie replied easily, smiling at Reine. "Needed to clear his head, he said. He was in a bad mood all the way over here. I asked him why, and he said he didn't get much sleep last night."

Ari blushed bright red, but Marnie, whose eyes were only for Reine — and the little bag of make-up the child had brought — thankfully didn't see.

"Well, when you see him, let him know that I—" Ari began, before chewing on her lip, falling into silence. *Let him know what?* she wondered. *Let him know that I know he came back for me? Let him know that last night meant something to me too?*

"Ari?" Marnie was suddenly all eyes and ears. Ari blushed again. She needed to talk to Tom, but not like this. Not through his mother, however well-meaning Marnie was.

Ari gave her a smile. "Let him know that, uh, I'll be around to see Reine tomorrow."

This wasn't a big town, Ari reflected. If Tom was out walking, she would find him. She bent to give her daughter a kiss and a cuddle, before straightening and smiling once more at Marnie.

She took two steps towards her room, knowing she would need her winter coat to withstand the icy air outside, when Sebastian grabbed her arm.

"Where are you going?" he hissed, and Ari glanced up at him.

"To find Tom, to talk with him—"

"Not right now, we have a code red."

Ari paused. "I don't know what that means."

Sebastian took a deep breath. "Name for me the three worst things that can happen the night before a wedding."

"Groom takes off," Ari replied, before she frowned, "but Corentin's here. So, next is venue cancellation, but we're here. So that only leaves . . ." Ari went pale. "No," she whispered.

"Yes," Sebastian nodded. "The airline lost Stella's wedding dress."

* * *

She would make the three-hour drive back to Keflavík with Corentin by her side. They decided not to tell Stella about her missing dress, but Corentin, who was sharing a connecting room with Tom, Reine and Marnie, overheard Ari's whispered conversation with his mother about why she suddenly had to go back to the airport, and why she probably wouldn't be back until the next day.

"I'm going to speak with Icelandair, see what they can do," Ari had said hurriedly. "If worse comes to worst I'll pick up an off-the-rack dress in Reykjavík tomorrow. Luis will do what he can with it."

"If only he hadn't blunted his fingers sewing last-minute fucking capes," Sebastian had added, with a shake of his head. "I'll be staying here to keep this end moving. Make sure the venue is ready for the dinner tomorrow night and that the cave is dressed for the ceremony."

"Okay," Marnie had nodded. "You're going alone, Ari?"

"Yes, it'll be fine," Ari replied. "I've been here before."

I met Tom here, she'd suddenly thought. *Keflavík Airport was where we first met. The first place we kissed. Where we first fell in love.*

She took a deep breath. "I'll be fine."

From the back of Marnie's room, she saw Corentin push forward. "I'm coming with you," he'd said.

"No, that won't be necessary," Ari argued.

"Ari's right. You need your rest for the ceremony tomorrow," Sebastian had added. "And you should enjoy your last night of freedom. From marriage." He paused. "And Stella."

Corentin was already pulling on his coat though. "I'm coming. Ari shouldn't go alone."

Ari nodded, suddenly exhausted, and in no mood for an argument. "Okay," she'd agreed. "Let's go."

The sky was already aflame with the aurora when Ari and Corentin piled into her rental car. For a moment Ari paused, looking up in wonder.

"Ever seen the Northern Lights before?" Corentin asked her, and she shook her head.

"No. I came here once before to see them . . . but it didn't work out." Reminding herself of the task at hand, she took off her coat and started the engine. Next to her, Corentin nodded.

"I came once before too. Not to see the lights though. To find Tom."

Ari made no reply, choosing instead to concentrate on navigating the unfamiliar vehicle away from the hotel and onto the main road.

"He'd already been and gone by the time I made it here," Corentin continued. "Mom was frantic about him. Iceland was the first confirmed sighting we'd had of him in about a year. And with our dad as sick as he was . . . Anyway. I was too late. He'd headed off into mainland Europe by that point."

"With me," Ari filled in the blanks. "He was with me."

"With you." Corentin nodded. "I'm glad he was with you. You made him really happy."

Ari squeezed the steering wheel beneath her hands. "I hope so."

"You know, I didn't catch Tom in time because of a volcano," Corentin reminisced. "I would've been here to find him earlier, but my flight was delayed into Reykjavík because of an eruption."

Ari nodded. "That's why I didn't see the lights when I was here, because of that volcano. The sky was thick with ash and dust. The volcano also grounded all the flights out of Iceland. I was stuck in the airport for two days."

"Is that how you met Tom?" Corentin asked curiously.

"Yeah," she nodded, "at the airport."

They fell into silence for a few moments.

"Talk about the universe sending out a sign. If I'd managed to fly in, and you managed to fly out, well, both of our lives would be very different." Corentin sounded thoughtful. "If that volcano hadn't erupted when it did, you wouldn't have met Tom, and then I would never have met Stella, and we wouldn't be back here, where it all began, to get married."

"You'd have still met Stella," Ari replied. "Tom would still have been with Sasha."

At that, Corentin snorted. "Sasha? No, that's not true. He would never have gone back to Sasha if he hadn't been so broken-hearted over you. I know Tom, and that's the truth."

Ari made no reply, keeping her eyes on the road ahead. She heard Corentin sigh. "You know, I'm glad Stella and I decided to get married here. Mom wanted us to get married in the woods at home."

"She wanted Tom and Sasha to get married there too." Ari's words came out sharper than she intended.

"Yeah," Corentin mused, completely unbothered by her tone. "The woods are special to Mom. She married Dad there. I think getting married under this though," he gestured to the sky above them, "is pretty special too. It's going to be a wonderful handfasting. Normally I'm the one performing the ritual . . . it'll be different being on the other side tomorrow night."

. Ari smiled. "I would never have put you and Stella together. I hope you don't mind me saying that."

She glanced over at Corentin briefly, who was grinning. "No? That's funny. She suits me, I think."

"You seem happy together," Ari remarked. "Really happy."

"We are happy." He paused, and she could feel his eyes upon her. "You know, I would put you and Tom together. You complement each other. No wonder the volcano erupted. The old ones wanted you together."

Ari glanced at him again. "You believe that?"

Corentin relaxed back in his seat. "They say there are seven gifts to Druidry. You know what the last one is?"

Ari shook her head. "I'm afraid I'm not at all clued up where esoteric Druidry is concerned."

Corentin laughed. "It's magic."

For a moment, Ari felt the air still in her lungs. A memory tugged at her. For a moment, she was in Keflavík Airport, looking down at Tom.

"Give me a chance," he replies softly. "Just give me a chance, and I'll show you magic is real."

Bringing herself back to reality, Ari cleared her throat. "Magic?"

Corentin nodded. "The magic of being alive. The magic of our journey. The magic of wisdom and inspiration. The magic of healing."

Ari made no reply, keeping her eyes ahead.

Now, Corentin cleared his throat. "Stella and I . . . our handfasting tomorrow . . . the ceremony . . . you know it's all just for show, right? It'll make Mom happy, but Stella and I made our commitment to each other months ago."

"Really?"

"Yeah. We exchanged tokens."

Ari glanced at him again. "Tokens?"

She felt rather than saw Corentin smile. "When we moved in together, she gave me a pendant that belonged to her mother. I gave her a brooch that belonged to Mom. We carry them with us everywhere."

"Like wedding rings?"

"Yes, I suppose so. But these items were chosen by Stella and me. They mean something to us, and in our minds, we're already . . . I guess married is the word you'd use. You know something? Before you say I do, the love and commitment should be there."

"That's sweet," Ari replied.

"Isn't it? You know something else? My brother, every day for the past nine years, has carried something of yours in his pocket."

Ari felt herself go red. "Corentin—"

"A card," Corentin continued. "Tom calls it the fool, but the Rouen card maker who painted him would've called him the page. Who is this page in service to, I've always wondered."

"Look, I don't think—"

"A queen, if I had to bet," Corentin went on. "And I think you're his queen, Ari. I really do. For all his faults, Tom loves you."

Ari made no reply, and she heard Corentin sigh again.

"Don't listen to me though, if you don't want to. I'm just a fool in love who wants to spread a little magic around. Sharing my joy, if you will."

Ari took a deep breath. "There's, um, a queen of spades card. In my jacket pocket. I've . . . um . . . I've had her for a long time."

She felt Corentin shift in his seat, and when she glanced at him, he was gazing at her with warm eyes.

"An exchange of tokens," he said softly. "Well, well, well."

"You think it means something?"

"Does it matter what I think? We're all on our own journeys here, Ari. That's part of the magic. So, if you want it to mean something, it means something. Let me tell you this though." Corentin leaned forward, his words abruptly loaded. "It means something to Tom."

* * *

Icelandair were firm. There was nothing to be done until the morning.

"Our first flight from the UK arrives at 7 a.m.," the representative said. "Most likely the dress got delayed in baggage control at Heathrow and will be on the next flight. There's still a chance it may turn up in our own baggage hall here or come in on a UK cargo flight, but—"

"What time does the cargo flight land?" Ari asked fretfully.

"We have one from London landing at five past four," the representative replied.

Ari swore quietly under breath, before turning to Corentin.

"I'll wait here," she offered. "You drive my rental car back to Vík and get some sleep before the ceremony tomorrow."

"Ari—"

"I'll be fine, honestly. If the dress isn't here by 10 a.m. tomorrow, I'll get a taxi into Reykjavík and grab whatever I can off the rack."

"It's 11 p.m." Corentin frowned.

"I know." Ari shook her head. "But I need to be here for the cargo flight landing. If I drive back to the hotel now, I won't make it back in time. So, I'll stay here."

Corentin looked unconvinced. "You need to sleep too, though."

"I've slept in airports before," Ari replied, thinking once again of Tom. "Look, I'll be fine. I've got my brother and your brother on speed dial these days."

Corentin still looked sceptical, and Ari sighed.

"This is my business, Corentin," she explained. "This is what I do. We've lost dresses before, and it's awful. I've seen brides weep over lost dresses. I've seen brides have panic attacks over lost dresses. I don't want that for Stella."

Corentin frowned. "Stella's made of stronger stuff than that."

Ari shrugged. "Maybe. I don't intend to find out. I'm her wedding planner. It's my job to either find that dress or come up with a Plan B. You're the groom. It's your job to be there for your bride. Don't make me call Sebastian to come and collect you. Because he will. And then you'll have a three-hour drive back to Vík while he talks about the newest season of *Bridgerton* and the deposition he just gave his neighbour about her untrimmed bush."

Corentin frowned again, and Ari offered him a confident smile.

"Corentin. Please go."

* * *

The Icelandair desk closed at midnight, and Ari settled down in a plastic bucket seat by the window. She set her phone to low-power mode, wrapped her shoulders with a blanket — given to her by the sympathetic Icelandair representative — and tried to drowse for a couple of hours. It was hard to sleep when her mind was working overtime, and the hustle and bustle of the airport kept her alert. Outside, she could see the red and green lights of the runway blinking in the distance, as well as the bright lights of airplanes as they pulled up to the terminal. Passengers left the airport, but there were no departures until the early morning, and soon the building became quieter, more conducive to resting, if not sleeping.

The plastic bucket seat, however, did not become more comfortable. Wearily, Ari set her blanket on the floor, stretching her legs out and thinking about the last time she'd been in this airport.

Her thoughts always went back to Tom. He was ingrained in her being now, like a fingerprint on her soul. She would always think of Tom, she realised. For the rest of her life, every day, she would think of him, and not just because of Reine. Tom had given her a child, but he'd also given her memories, some tinged with love, others with heartbreak and grief.

The heartbreak and grief were fading now though. It would never completely leave her, but it was fading, and she felt — well, maybe *healed* wasn't quite the right word, but renewed. Renewed, and refreshed.

He'd come for her. He'd kept his word and come back for her. Ari hadn't known how important that promise had been until she'd learned Tom had kept it. He'd come back for her. He'd kept his promise to her. It had been real and wonderful, and he'd loved her as much as she loved him. Instinctively, she knew he hadn't come for her just to claim her. She knew Tom now — knew how he thought and felt and worked. She knew he'd also come to make things right with her. To admit the truth about Tom Miller and introduce her to the wonderful man she knew Tom Somerset to be. He'd come for her. He'd wanted her.

With a sigh, Ari leaned against the wall, still staring out at the runway. She felt rather than saw someone drop to the floor next to her, and when she turned her head, she smiled to see Tom beside her, settling against the wall, stretching his long legs out over her blanket.

"Why am I getting a feeling of déjà vu?" she asked him softly, and he rubbed a hand over his face tiredly.

"Corentin messaged me when he left the airport," Tom explained. "Couldn't have you sitting here alone all night."

"I'm fine," Ari replied, and Tom shrugged.

"Yeah, but you know me, anything to speak with a pretty woman in a near-abandoned airport."

She laughed at that, crossing her arms over her stomach. "There's still at least two hours of waiting for a cargo plane to land for this pretty woman. You think your conversation can stretch to two hours?"

"For you? I'm willing to give it a shot," Tom replied. Abruptly, his face changed. "Why did you leave this morning? I woke up, and you were gone."

Ari paused, chewing on her lip. "I was scared," she finally admitted. "Terrified, actually."

Tom's face blanched. "You were scared?"

"Not of you," Ari was quick to reassure him. "I guess I was scared of being hurt again."

"By me," Tom replied, his face darkening. "You were scared of being hurt again by me."

Ari sighed. "Yes. I suppose so."

"I don't want to hurt you, Ari. I never wanted to hurt you."

"I know."

Tom reached for her hand, and Ari let him take it. "I mean it," he said emphatically. "I really do. Hurting you . . . it was the worst thing I ever did. I'll never forgive myself for hurting someone so wonderful. So beautiful. So loving. So good."

"I know," Ari said again. "I do, Tom."

Tom sighed, and Ari watched as he glanced around the airport.

"Never thought we'd end up back here again," he reflected sadly. "If I could go back in time, and do it all over again . . ."

"What would you change?" Ari asked curiously.

Tom gave her a woebegone smile. "I'd be me. The real me."

Ari sat back, gazing at him. "But you were the real you, Tom."

"No." Tom shook his head. "I lied to you. I have to believe I'm better than that now."

Ari squeezed his hand. "And I have to believe that the man I fell in love with was real. So much of it . . ." She paused. "So much of it *was* you. Tom Miller was just a name. Your thoughts, feelings . . . how you loved me . . . that was real. That was you."

Tom nodded, but he still looked unconvinced. "You told me you hated me," he said. "You said you hated me but loved him. You have no idea how much that tortured me. How much it still tortures me."

Ari winced. "I was angry."

366

"You had every right to be."

"Mostly I think I was angry because I thought you'd . . . I thought you'd abandoned me. Me, and Reine."

Tom looked up, and there was real anguish in his eyes. "If I'd known for a minute that Reine was mine . . ."

Ari smiled. "I know. We've had this conversation. I know."

"I never meant to abandon you. I really didn't."

"You said you would come for me," Ari reminded him, squeezing his hand once more.

"Yeah, well." Tom shifted, looking uncomfortable.

Ari gripped his hand harder. "And you *did* come for me, didn't you Tom?"

The hand held in hers became like stone, and Tom turned to face her. "I . . . um . . ."

Ari smiled at him. It was warm and genuine. "Sebastian and Luis told me. Luis said that you came when Reine was about eighteen months old. You thought she was his."

Abruptly, Tom looked flustered. He opened his mouth to speak before closing it again, looking out at the runway once more.

"Why didn't you tell me?" she asked. "Why didn't you say anything?"

Tom sighed. "I nearly did. But then, each time I went to tell you, I thought to myself 'why am I doing this?' and couldn't do it."

"Why not?" Ari asked gently.

Tom gave a half-shrug. "I couldn't think of a way to phrase it that didn't make it sound like some kind of pitiful excuse. I left you in Europe, pregnant and alone—"

"You didn't know I was pregnant," Ari reminded him.

"Doesn't matter. I left you. And then, what? I come back two years later, like a fool, expecting you to just . . . take me back? Expecting you to have put your life on hold for me while I figured mine out?"

"Tom—"

"I was so selfish," Tom carried on, shaking his head in disgust. "So unbelievably selfish to have done that to you. When

367

I had to go back for . . . for my dad, I could've left you with a number that worked. An address. My *real* name. I was terrified that if I did, you'd figure everything out and walk away and then I would have lost you for good. So, I left you with nothing, or next to nothing. Just a promise to come back."

"I lived on that promise," Ari admitted. "It kept me going when things were at their bleakest."

"Bleak because of me," Tom said. "I haven't forgotten that. I'll never forget that. After my dad died, I sat at home, miserable and grieving and missing you, and by the time I was ready to find you, by the time I'd worked up the courage to face you and tell you everything, to admit the whole horrible truth, I'd half-convinced myself that you'd moved on."

"Why would you think that?" Ari asked. "You know how I loved you."

Tom looked at her, his eyes anguished. She watched as he took a deep breath. "I convinced myself that you'd probably have moved on because I was so terrified to be honest with you. So, when that door opened and there was a man with your child on the other side of it . . ." Tom trailed off. "I was ready to run."

Ari rubbed his hand gently with her own. "Oh, Tom."

"I'm sorry," Tom told her. "You'll never know how sorry I am."

"I know you are. But I've told you already, I'm tired of that word. You don't have to keep telling me how sorry you are." Ari stopped, taking a deep breath of her own. "I was so mad at you for not coming for me, you know. When I first saw you again last year, I could forgive you for Sasha, and the lies, and for leaving me in Germany. But what I couldn't forgive was your breaking that promise. I told you, I lived for that promise. I put my life on hold for that promise. Thinking that you'd broken it . . ."

"Ari," Tom pleaded. "I'm—"

"Sorry, I know," Ari carried on. "I've spent the last year thinking I could never forgive you for not coming back for me. I spent a whole year thinking we could move on as co-parents. Maybe even friends. And then yesterday, when Luis and Sebastian told me you *had* come for me. That you'd kept your word . . ." Ari trailed off. "I realised it didn't matter. Not anymore."

"Why?" Tom asked her.

She offered him a tremulous, almost hopeful smile. "Because I'd fallen in love with you all over again. I'd fallen in love with you, with Tom Somerset, and I'd forgiven you. And so it didn't matter that you'd come for me. It didn't matter, because I love you."

"Ari," Tom breathed out. "Ari, please don't . . . don't say these things if you can't . . . if you don't want to be with me . . ."

Ari stopped his words by kissing him softly. The airport was quiet, lights flashing somewhere in the distance, and Tom's lips were soft, his exhalation of surprised relief warm against her cheek. When she pulled away again, she cupped his face in her hands. She could hear Corentin's words from earlier echoing in her head.

Before you say I do, the love and commitment should be there.

"Tom, I can," she told him, smiling widely. "And I do."

Tom sat back, blinking in amazement. "Thank you," he said earnestly. "Thank you for giving me another chance."

"You're a good man," Ari replied. "I always knew it. And I love you for it."

"I love you too. I'm always going to love you. You and Reine. It's you, me and her now, right?"

"Right."

Now he kissed her.

"You know," he began when they parted, clearing his throat, "we still have a few more hours before the cargo flight lands. There's an airport hotel . . ."

"I can't leave this desk," Ari replied, laughing. "Sebastian and then Stella would kill me. We'll have to find something else to do to kill the time."

Tom grinned at her. "Do you still not believe in magic? I have a pack of cards in my pocket. I'm missing a queen, but we can make do."

Ari grinned back. "Missing a queen? Actually," she reached into her pocket, pulling out the queen of spades, "you aren't."

Something in Tom's face changed. "You kept it," he whispered. "Ari, you have no idea what this means to me."

"She's been through the wars," Ari apologised. "Luis did what he could, but she's a little worn. I carried her in my pocket every day for years."

"You did?"

"Yes," Ari blushed. "I loved you, you see. Keeping her close . . . it kept you close."

Tom kissed her again. "Give me a chance," he whispered. "Give me a chance and I'll prove to you magic is real."

Ari kissed him back. "All right, magician man. I believe you. Show me."

THE END

ACKNOWLEDGEMENTS

With thanks to my husband, for loving me even when I play Taylor Swift on repeat and cry in the kitchen over fictional characters.

Also, with thanks to Amanda Woodburn and Kirstin Guy, for crying in the kitchen with me over fictional characters while Taylor Swift is playing.

Emma Grundy Haigh and Jasmine Callaghan are also owed thanks for going ahead with this book even when I talked about Taylor Swift too much in our meeting (which thankfully did not take place while I cried in the kitchen).

I also want to thank Joffe Books for their bookish brilliance and support, which has been so good that if any of their team ever wants to cry over fictional characters while listening to Taylor Swift in my kitchen, they're more than welcome. Likewise, many thanks to all the early readers of this book — including George Bomer and Sarah Roberts — who always support me so thoroughly and will never know just how much I appreciate their kind words.

And finally, my thanks are also owed to Miss Taylor Swift, for writing music I cry to in the kitchen over fictional characters. If it wasn't for "Death by a Thousand Cuts", this book wouldn't exist.

THE CHOC LIT STORY

Established in 2009, Choc Lit is an independent, award-winning publisher dedicated to creating a delicious selection of quality women's fiction.

We have won 18 awards, including Publisher of the Year and the Romantic Novel of the Year, and have been shortlisted for countless others. In 2023, we were shortlisted for Publisher of the Year by the Romantic Novelists' Association.

All our novels are selected by genuine readers. We are proud to publish talented first-time authors, as well as established writers whose books we love introducing to a new generation of readers.

In 2023, we became a Joffe Books company. Best known for publishing a wide range of commercial fiction, Joffe Books has its roots in women's fiction. Today it is one of the largest independent publishers in the UK.

We love to hear from you, so please email us about absolutely anything bookish at choc-lit@joffebooks.com

If you want to hear about all our bargain new releases, join our mailing list: www.choc-lit.com/contact